THE VIOLIN MAKER'S SECRET

EVIE WOODS

HarperCollinsPublishers

HarperCollins*Publishers* Ltd
1 London Bridge Street
London SE1 9GF
www.harpercollins.co.uk
HarperCollins*Publishers*
Macken House, 39/40 Mayor Street Upper,
Dublin 1, D01 C9W8, Ireland

This paperback edition 2026
1
First published in Great Britain in ebook format
by HarperCollins*Publishers* 2026
Copyright © Evie Woods 2026
Evie Woods asserts the moral right to
be identified as the author of this work

A catalogue record of this book is available from the British Library

UK ISBN: 978-0-00-869660-3
US ISBN: 978-0-00-877767-8

This novel is entirely a work of fiction. The names, characters and incidents portrayed in it are the work of the author's imagination. Any resemblance to actual persons, living or dead, events or localities is entirely coincidental.
Printed and bound in the UK using 100% Renewable Electricity
by CPI Group (UK) Ltd
All rights reserved. No part of this publication may be reproduced, stored in a retrieval system, or transmitted, in any form or by any means, electronic, mechanical, photocopying, recording or otherwise, without the prior permission of the publishers.
Without limiting the exclusive rights of any author, contributor or the publisher of this publication, any unauthorised use of this publication to train generative artificial intelligence (AI) technologies is expressly prohibited. HarperCollins also exercise their rights under Article 4(3) of the Digital Single Market Directive 2019/790 and expressly reserve this publication from the text and data mining exception.

Evie Woods is the international bestselling author of *The Lost Bookshop*, which has sold over a million copies globally and has been translated into over thirty languages. Shortlisted for the 2024 British Book Awards 'Page-Turner of the Year,' it has also become a *Sunday Times*, *Wall Street Journal*, *USA Today* and *Spiegel* bestseller.

Influenced by folklore and magical realism, Evie has carved out a unique style that is all her own, charming readers around the world with her warm and uplifting narratives. Drawing inspiration from the unseen forces that shape our lives and the healing power of storytelling, novels like *The Story Collector* and *The Mysterious Bakery on Rue de Paris* invite the reader to embrace the magic that already exists in our ordinary lives. Evie's new novel, *The Violin Maker's Secret*, is perfect for those who love music, mystery and magic!

www.eviewoods.com

- x.com/evgaughan
- instagram.com/eviewoods.author
- tiktok.com/@eviewoods.author

Also by Evie Woods

The Lost Bookshop
The Story Collector
The Mysterious Bakery on Rue de Paris
The Violin Maker's Secret

'Without music, life would be a mistake.'

Friedrich Nietzsche

♪

Prelude

On any given day, there are thousands of items slowly gathering dust in the Lost and Found of Heathrow Airport. A bag stuffed with £50,000 in five-pound notes, a diamond-encrusted Rolex watch, the keys to a Porsche, and two wedding dresses, to name but a few. The more bizarre include a set of false teeth, several crutches and an artificial skull. After ninety days, if the items are not reclaimed by their owners, they are auctioned for charity.

Unbeknownst to anyone, there is one very special box that holds an item with an ancient provenance. This object can change the fortunes of those who possess it – sometimes for good, sometimes for ill, but all on the whims of a young woman, who can read the hearts of those who possess her. The object is a violin, one of rare beauty and with a strange, intoxicating power. Awakening desire in the hearts of musicians for almost two hundred years, she is built of birdsong and promises, crafted from wood and bone.

Now, as if by chance, she has fallen into the hands of three unlikely guardians, hopelessly lost and yet connected by a melody only the violin can unlock. However, just as there are four strings on a violin, there is a fourth stranger, waiting in the shadows for their chance to reclaim what once belonged to them. Bound as we all are by the same universal laws, and, just like the leaf that has fallen from the tree, there are some things you can never get back.

Chapter One

♪

London, 2025

The day had started off so well. Another busy morning at Heathrow, with the sun shining high in the bluest of skies, criss-crossed by the white trails of jetliners carving their way through the atmosphere. Devlin worked as a baggage handler in Terminal 2. He was the right build, or so the interviewer had told him, and he took that as a positive. It was around the same time he had met Melissa, who didn't always see his build as a positive. She introduced him to juicing.

When most people thought about airports, they thought about leaving. But Devlin always thought about the people coming home, reuniting with loved ones and feeling that sense of familiarity. He liked working there. It was as far away as he could get from his old life. It was steady, reliable. Like the scheduled flights that arrived and departed on time (for the most part) his days had the kind of predictable structure that he could follow with his eyes closed.

And yet a confluence of two significant events was about to change the course of Devlin's life. Namely his girlfriend's birthday and a recent arrival at the Lost and Found department. Devlin had always thought that there was something a bit lonely about the Lost and Found; a room for unclaimed treasures that washed up like flotsam from discarded lives. He could imagine the passengers setting off with their prized possessions and then for some reason, along the way, being parted from them. Were they forgotten or simply abandoned?

On his morning break with his co-worker, Karim, he spotted it. It looked rather inconspicuous in its black case, battered by age and rough handling. The shape was unmistakable however, the gentle curves betraying the contents.

'That's it, it's perfect,' he said, running his hands along the edges of the case.

'Eh, am I missing something here? You planning on a career change, Devlin?'

'Nah, mate, it's for Mel.'

'Does she … play the fiddle? She doesn't seem like the musical type.' Karim's wonderfully full eyebrows formed an apex shape, giving him a perplexed look.

'It's a violin, Karim.'

'There's a difference?'

Devlin wasn't entirely sure what the difference was, so he said nothing.

'I thought you got her some perfume from the duty-free?'

'Yeah, but this is THE gift. She mentioned it years ago; how she always wanted to play the violin but her parents couldn't afford the classes.'

Judging by the case, this one probably needed a bit of tender loving care, but if he could get it at the right price, he could take it to a repair shop. Or a music store. He really knew very little about violins.

After some lengthy negotiations with Pete, the guy in charge, who insisted that every item had to be kept for three months before it could be sold – 'In case the owner comes back', he'd explained – Devlin had bought himself a violin. And somehow, he just knew it would change everything.

♪

The evening took a turn for the worse when the paramedics arrived. After that the guests had made a hasty escape from the party and Melissa opened a bottle of champagne that Devlin could not recall having bought. In fact, he couldn't remember ever having bought an ice bucket either, but there it sat, on the kitchen counter, floral bouquets reflecting in the gleam. Now *those* he could explain. The multicoloured arrangement that resembled cuttings from an exotic forest was from James at the hair salon. The plant was from her mother, Francesca, practical as ever. The dozen red roses were his own contribution. He had planned on getting thirty, one for every year of her life, but they were all under strict orders to avoid any reference to numerology.

'Do you think we should have brought your mum to the emergency room?'

'She'll be fine, you know what she's like,' Mel answered dismissively.

He did know. Melissa's mother was often prone to heart palpitations at moments of high drama. *Fit of passion*, her father would say, with a tone of admiration for his wife's Italian roots.

Melissa sat rigidly on the bespoke window seat she and Devlin had built together the summer before. She'd watched a couple build something similar on Instagram and insisted on filming it for her socials. In the end, she had to cut most of it out, as they'd spent the entire time swearing at each other. The whole apartment was an Instagrammer's dream: white walls, clean lines, and countless framed prints of botanical drawings and motivational quotes. Devlin was surrounded by other people's words: *Let your smile change the world, but don't let the world change your smile.* At least that made more sense than the nonsensical advice of *Follow Your Karma!* Surely it was karma's job to follow you?

He liked it, though, even if nothing in it belonged to him. The last of his possessions to go was the wicker coffee table he had brought from his old bedsit, replaced by a glass table that always threatened to bruise a leg if approached from the wrong angle. He missed the way his table tended to sag in the middle, as though the wicker was forming a protective hug around whatever items he put on it, including his feet.

Plus, second-hand stuff felt like less of a commitment. *Easy come, easy go,* it seemed to say. There was no point clinging on to things. Or people. Melissa called him a drifter and saw it as her personal project to de-drift him. Or un-drift him. They lived in the flat above Melissa's hair salon, Haute Couture. It had all been part of her master plan since she got her first summer job as a hairdresser. As Francesca's catchphrase went, 'People will always need their hair cut!' Based on this sound business advice, Melissa built up her empire. He admired her vision, her determination. Everyone did. Her life worked like a well-oiled machine and Devlin understood, not for the first time, that he was the spanner causing the whole thing to malfunction.

'I've never been so embarrassed,' she said, swallowing half a glass of champagne and filling it up again.

'What do you mean?' The violin lay quietly in its case on the gleaming coffee table. She hadn't looked at it since she'd opened it in front of all of their friends and family, letting out a high-pitched shriek.

'Are you really that clueless?'

There were tears now, which she immediately wiped away roughly with the back of her hand. Devlin ran his hands through his hair, as though he might find the answers there. He couldn't understand it; he thought he had outdone himself this time. Really listened to her. He stood halfway between the kitchen and the living room. He knew this because there were different coloured rugs marking out the areas..

'What's wrong, Mel?' He tried to strike a tone somewhere between concern and mystification.

'Look around you; look at what I'm wearing.'

Devlin blinked. He was never any good at cryptic clues. Just as he raised his shoulders helplessly, she got up and waved the back of her hand in his face.

'The manicure? Surely that gives it away.'

He noticed that one of her fingernails was a slightly different colour to the rest and had some sparkly stuff on it.

'Oh, for God's sake, Devlin, I thought you were going to propose. We all did. It's my thirtieth!' Her voice cracked when she said her age, the disappointment plainly evident and the blame laid squarely at his feet.

'Mel, I … I…' The words wouldn't come. Because the truth was, he had known. Deep down. He had thought about it every year. Every Valentine's Day, Christmas Day, birthday, equinox. As time marched on, the inevitability of it was beginning to choke him. He challenged himself to come up with increasingly thoughtful gifts, overcompensating for the lack of a marriage proposal. He spoke to Karim about it at work. Younger than Devlin, he had been married for five years already. And was a father to two kids.

'Do you love her?' Karim asked during one of their shifts, taking off his protective headphones.

'Of course I love her!' Devlin responded, throwing a bulky suitcase into a luggage bin.

'Then what's the problem? Afraid she'll say no?'

That wasn't it. He'd even got as far as the jewellers on the high street once, spoken to the assistant. But his mouth started to go dry and his heart suddenly started hammering, as if he'd been running a marathon. He began feeling dizzy, and when the assistant went to get him a glass of water, he ran out of the shop. It took a good ten minutes for his breathing to return to normal. He wanted to move on with his life. He wanted to settle down; he wanted stability. He wanted kids and he knew that Mel wanted them sooner rather than later. And he wanted to be the one to give her all of that. Yet when the moment came, he bottled it.

His awareness returned to the present, where Melissa was now shouting and gesticulating. Phrases like *'mortified'*, *'marriage material'* and *'not getting any younger'* snagged on his conscience. It was all his fault. He had caused all the upset; or at least that's what she was telling him, and he had no defence. How many more times would they go through this routine before she dumped him for good and found someone who *would* marry her? Without breaking her flow, she reached down and took the violin out of its case, shoving it into Devlin's arms.

'I don't even play the bloody violin!'

He held the instrument tentatively, with arms outstretched. For reasons he couldn't quite explain, it felt like he was holding a living, breathing thing. He had only peeked at it earlier, making sure it was actually a violin he had bought and not an empty case. But now he brought it closer to him. It had the deepest amber hue that looked as though you could dive into it and lose yourself forever. It seemed both powerful and yet strangely fragile. Without thinking, he held it protectively to his chest. A peculiar feeling rose from within him, a strange sense of certainty. With this, his mind began to clear. His shoulders straightened. Suddenly, he found the words.

'Last Christmas, we had coffee in that place in Covent Garden, and there were those buskers, remember? And you said you'd always wanted to play the violin.'

Silence descended. A brief respite.

'What?' she asked, cocking her head to the side.

Just as Devlin was about to add more details to the

memory – it had been snowing, it was the day before Christmas Eve, they'd gone in to see the lights – Melissa threw her hands up and left the room. The echo of the front door banging confirmed that she had gone out.

Devlin sat down on the sofa and held the violin in front of him, turning it this way and that. It had been a long time since he'd held a musical instrument in his hands. Nine years, four months and seven days, to be precise. It was a day in his life that he couldn't permit himself to think about. Yet now, he felt oddly calm. Relaxed even. The opposite to how he should have felt, given the fact that Mel had just walked out on him.

He let his thumb pluck the first string. The sound it made was unexpectedly rich and golden. It resonated around him like a forcefield. He plucked it again and without thinking, he hummed the note. G. The vibration of sound in his throat was both familiar and strange, opening up a chasm inside of him. The before and after; two parts of him that never communicated. Until now. It felt as though, after years of travelling further and further away from himself and everything he knew to be true, he was finally back home. A place that had been inside of him all along.

Chapter Two

♪

Devlin had been on his coffee break when he spotted the headline that would change everything. Up to that point, he'd been feeling more sure of himself than he had done in years. It was as though something had unlocked within him, freeing him from an invisible cage. Or like those fairy tales that his mother used to read to him as a child, where a curse had been lifted from the land. And all since that night he had held the violin in his hands. Superstition ran through his Irish DNA as surely as the blood through his veins, but even he wasn't sure how possessing the violin could alter his very being.

Devlin had always felt jinxed. Even his family name, Devlin, translated from old Irish as 'unlucky'. He was nevertheless reluctant to use his first name, which was also the result of his mother's sense of unfairness.

'Matthew, Mark and John, they're the trendy apostles. What about poor Luke?' she oft lamented. For a brief moment at school, he'd earned himself the nickname

'Skywalker', but that all changed on the day a new kid arrived and challenged him to a fight in the yard after school. Devlin hadn't a clue how to fight and, in a sort of detached way, assumed the skills would just come to him when the moment required. They didn't. And just like that, he was cast out of the group. That's when he turned to music. Playing the guitar had been his saviour, until the day it all stopped. But he didn't like to think about that.

Yet the moment that he took the violin case in his arms, everything felt different. He couldn't explain it exactly, only that his life story, the one where he was jinxed and unlucky, didn't feel like his story anymore. The bad luck felt like the early chapters in a very long book that now held the possibility to become any kind of story he could dream of. Instead of knowing every word on every page by heart until infinity, the paper was suddenly blank and waiting to be filled. The feeling was that of pure weightlessness. And although he couldn't and wouldn't explain it, he could trace it all back to the day he bought the violin. Now all of that felt under threat.

Someone had left a newspaper in the canteen and he picked it up while the man behind the counter made a rather elaborate production of making Devlin's coffee. He stuffed the first of his two doughnuts into his mouth while waiting to pay and flicked idly through the pages, when a headline almost jumped out at him:

PRICELESS VIOLIN STOLEN

He paused mid-bite, causing the jam to squirt out and fall splat onto the article. Grabbing serviettes from the silver container, he tried to wipe rather than smear the mess, which now resembled a bloodstain. An unfortunate omen, to be sure. He threw a tenner at the man who had eventually returned with his coffee and found a table in the corner. He scanned the canteen, suddenly paranoid. Satisfied he couldn't detect any undercover operatives making themselves known, he returned to the newspaper.

The highly valuable violin was stolen from Christie's the evening before it was due to go up for auction. 'These were no opportunists,' said the director of Christie's South Kensington office. 'Our security systems are top calibre, and this theft was planned down to the minutiae. The violin was in our pre-sale storage facility at Park Royal. We are cooperating with the police's investigation and that is all I can say for the moment.

Devlin felt his stomach swell and clamped his hand over his mouth. He instantly broke out into a sweat that felt both hot and cold. He knew from the moment he saw the photo of the violin below the article that he was now in possession of a very valuable and stolen instrument. He read on.

Two years after Margot Clement's death, a rare violin was discovered at her 42-room apartment on Fifth Avenue. Possibly dating back to the 1700s, the violin's provenance is still something of a mystery. It was expected to fetch upwards of £10 million at auction.

Miss Clement was the daughter of mining magnate, William Andrew Clement, one of America's richest men. She died aged 104, leaving a $300 million fortune.

Devlin looked up and tried to ground himself back into reality. He watched other people sitting at the tables opposite, pouring milk into their tea, buttering scones, chatting on their phones. None of it seemed real, as though he were watching a film. Or maybe it was him – *he* didn't feel real anymore. His mouth was so dry he almost scalded his tongue when he downed his cup of coffee. He pushed back his chair with force and it screeched loudly. A few people looked up, then returned to whatever they were doing. Devlin suddenly realised that he had two choices – return the violin and risk getting caught up in a police investigation, or go on the run and hope that whoever stole the violin in the first place would never find him. The obvious choice was the former. It was the right thing to do. Yet, somewhere deep inside, he knew that meant losing the violin and he wasn't ready to give it back. Not just yet.

Chapter Three

♪

Walter had already filled his Micra with petrol when he realised that he had left his wallet at home. Only a few months into his retirement and the lack of routine had already caused his mind to wander off, like a dog without a leash. Just last week when he was tucking into a late lunch of cheese and pickle on rye, he realised that he still hadn't brushed his teeth. His real ones. The plate with his four extra teeth was still sitting in a cup on the sink. These uncharacteristic lapses worried him.

He tried explaining to the young woman behind the counter with the blue hair, but she said she'd heard it all before. Said she'd have to call the police if he didn't pay.

'But I've been coming here for the last twenty-five years. I was here last week, for heaven's sake. You *know* me!'

'Just because I know you doesn't mean you're not trying to get some free petrol. It happens more than you think. And it's always the well-off ones.'

'I'm not well-off.'

A standoff ensued. Hayley stared at her nails, which were a garish orange colour, and showed no signs of softening her stance on petrol pilferers.

'Right, well, I can't take the petrol back out now, can I? You'll have to let me go home and get my wallet.' Walter felt sure that rationale would win the argument. Hayley did not share his belief.

'You'll have to leave the car here, Mr Pickering.'

'But it's after midnight! I'm not walking home at this hour.' Walter was finding it harder and harder to get to sleep at night, and so delayed his bedtime with umpteen chores and distractions that might wear him out.

'Isn't there someone you could call?'

The question taunted him like a schoolyard bully. All his life, Walter had been on his own. But now, at the age of sixty-six, he suddenly felt lonely.

He said nothing further to Hayley. He simply left his keys on the counter and walked out into the night. She called after him, of course, wondering if perhaps she could call him a taxi, but he pretended he didn't hear her. Besides, it felt good to hear his own footsteps echoing back to him in the quietness of the suburban streets. It was Sunday night, not much going on apart from the odd jogger and the occasional car passing by. The footpath was an odd hue of yellow from the streetlights. There was never really any true darkness in the city, everything was kept artificially bright. He remembered reading an article in *The Guardian* about how man had forever obscured his view of the heavens. You could see London from space, but you couldn't see space from London. Trading in the stars for sodium light, humanity could no longer see whence it came, nor whither it was bound.

Walter felt similarly out of touch. There had been some solace in his job as a history teacher in St Michael's Comprehensive. Back then, his day revolved around extolling the virtues of history. He could live in the past and get paid for it. When the school bell rang, he would return to his little flat in the evenings, play his classical records on his trusty turntable that he bought for his twenty-first birthday, and spend a pleasant evening marking papers and listening to Mahler. It felt like his life had a purpose.

Walter grew up as an only child and had always been accustomed to going places on his own; the cinema, dances, walks. He never minded. Never knew any different. So he didn't realise he was lonely, because he didn't know what he was lonely for. He had no luck with women. He asked them out and they turned him down flat. He knew he wasn't a looker. As a teacher, he met people every day, but what was more, he had a purpose. These days, there seemed to be far too much time to reflect on his current lack of purpose. Did it really matter if he watered the geraniums in the window box? Would anyone even notice? The last time he spoke to one of his neighbours, a couple of years previously, was when they had lost their cat. He thought it might be the start of something, a connection. So he scoured the neighbourhood looking for the little tabby with the white socks in the photocopied picture they'd given him. A few days later, he knocked on their door to tell them that he'd had no luck as yet, but that maybe it was time to start calling the local animal shelters. They'd already replaced the cat and looked at him like he was a stranger.

He had become accustomed to the seasons being structured by exams, parent–teacher meetings, excursions, more exams. The only pivotal moment of his week now was on a Thursday when he collected his pension from the post office. Even that was under threat, as they wanted to pay him electronically into his bank account. There was hardly a reason for him to leave the house at all.

So he invented jobs for himself. He spent a lot of time at the library reading all of the newspapers, and ate a hearty ploughman's with a pint of ale every lunchtime at the local. It almost felt like living. Almost. Without registering it, Walter had walked all the way back to his road and found himself outside his apartment building. Maybe he didn't need a car after all? The exercise would certainly do him good and the time spent walking everywhere would certainly use up more hours in the day. He gulped, noisily. Had it really come down to this? Wishing the hours away until his time was up?

He took the stairs up to his fourth-floor apartment, his footsteps echoing loudly in his ears, almost mocking him. YOU'RE ALONE. All alone. Once inside, he performed his tasks with a calm that was almost bewitching. It was as if he were under a spell and he chose not to fight it. He poured himself a glass of brandy and lifted the arm of the record player, letting the needle drop onto the Adagietto of Gustav Mahler's 5th Symphony. Scored only for strings and harp, the fourth movement was tender and slow. Mahler wrote it for his wife, Alma. Instead of a love letter, he sent her this music in manuscript form.

Imagine: loving someone so completely, so essentially, that your very existence depended upon their light.

Walter's mother had been the planet around which he had orbited for many years until her death, but now he was just a floating satellite. Who would lament his absence? This thought hardened his resolve and as the strings rushed to their crescendo, Walter opened a bottle of painkillers the doctor had given him. He held the entire contents in one hand and his glass of brandy in the other. He took a deep breath … and the doorbell rang.

Chapter Four

♪

'Mr Pickering! Brilliant, you still live here. I wasn't sure if you'd moved. It's good to see you!' Devlin was pumping Walter's arm as though he expected water to gush from a spout.

'I'm sorry, do I know you?' Walter felt as though his consciousness was being pulled back to a reality he had already decided to leave, and he felt quite inconvenienced by this late-night caller. 'I'm really quite busy…'

'It's me, Luke Devlin. I was a student of yours at St Michael's.'

Walter stared at Devlin's face as though it were a broken clock.

Devlin had made an assumption that now felt ridiculous. He thought his old history teacher would still (how embarrassing was this) *care* about him. But now he'd left him standing on the threshold, like a stranger. He scanned up and down the hallway, looking guilty as sin. Improbable as it seemed, Mr Pickering was the only one he thought might be able to help. He hadn't even thought about him all that much in the intervening years. Not consciously, anyway. But, holding the violin, his memories came out of the mist with crystal clarity. As a young teenage boy, there was always pressure to prove himself. That was how he'd survived. By proving he was tough when he really wasn't. By proving he didn't care about things when he really did. But in Mr Pickering's class, everything was different. For those precious forty-five minutes, it was as if normal time ceased to exist. He saw past all of Devlin's bravado and was somehow able to speak to the man he might become, if he stopped worrying about how he was perceived all the time. If he dropped the act and just let himself get curious about the world. And it wasn't like Pickering was strict either. He was a bit of a pushover, truth be told. But no one hassled him the way they did other teachers if they saw a sign of weakness. He was just so likeable and, for reasons Devlin still couldn't understand, Mr Pickering seemed to like them, too. He just had a way about him that made everyone want to listen and, to the boys' amazement, actually learn. Devlin's year all got good marks in his class. But more than that, Mr Pickering's history class, a double period on a Friday afternoon, was the one place Devlin felt like he could be himself. He felt seen and, rarer still, he felt as though someone actually believed in him.

He took a step closer and revealed the violin case he had been hiding behind his back.

'I need your help,' he said, tapping the case with his fingertips.

'I suppose you'd best come in then.'

♪

When you've been on the verge of taking your own life, entertaining guests becomes a bewildering task.

'Um, I suppose you'll be wanting, eh … no, that's not right,' Walter mumbled to himself, opening and closing the washing machine door.

Devlin registered the bottle of brandy and had just asked Walter for a glass of the same when he noticed the open bottle of pills.

'Everything all right, Mr Pickering?'

Walter handed Devlin a teacup of brandy, filled to the brim and sitting jauntily on its saucer.

'Oh yes, yes. Perfectly.'

Walter sat down in his armchair, the pills scattered before him on the coffee table. Devlin hesitated before sitting in the chair opposite. Other than the pills, everything else in the apartment was immaculately ordered and precise. Melissa would have loved it. Once she had whitewashed the entire thing. The walls were not of plaster but books, from floor to ceiling. It must have felt like living in a library.

'You still at St Michael's then?' Devlin asked, putting the violin down by his feet and taking a generous mouthful of brandy from his teacup.

'Hmm? Oh yes. No, no. Retired in January.'

'Ah, that's great. Must give you lots of time to, eh…' Devlin let the sentence trail off as both men stared at the reality of having too much time on your hands.

After a while, Walter started to emerge from the fog and slowly began to take account of his guest.

'Why are you carrying a violin case?'

Devlin paused for a moment before answering. Perhaps coming to Mr Pickering had been a mistake. He had remembered a jolly man, full of enthusiasm for teaching and bringing the Renaissance and World War I to life in the classroom. He was the most intelligent man Devlin knew. But now, everything about him was grey. His hair, his clothes, his skin. He even seemed a bit senile.

'I seem to recall you were more of a guitar man,' Walter continued.

'Hah! You *do* remember me.'

'Of course I remember you, Luke.' The colour was returning to his eyes, at least, which glistened a deep blue when he smiled. 'You got a B minus. You were capable of the A if only you'd—'

'Applied myself, I know.' Devlin had heard every version of this back-handed compliment, which always left him with a worrying sense that people expected more of him than he was actually capable of. Melissa was forever hounding him to 'move up the ladder, take more of an interest, try harder'. It was like having his own personal life coach offering unsolicited advice.

A gentle silence fell over them and they sat companionably for a time, sipping their drinks.

'You used to write poetry?'

'Lyrics,' Devlin corrected him. 'Song lyrics.'

'They were quite good, from what I remember.'

'I don't really write anymore,' Devlin said, an unbidden sense of regret tightening the muscles in his jaw. He took another mouthful of brandy before looking up and realising that Mr Pickering was looking at him just as he used to do all those years ago in class. As though he could see right through him.

'Tell you what, why don't I make us both a sandwich,' said Walter, getting up and searching the fridge for some ham. 'Then you can tell me all about this violin.'

Chapter Five

♪

On a quiet Sunday morning in the flat above her shop, Gabrielle Wilding found the page in the dusty old book she'd been looking for. She'd been tempted to throw out all of her father's books after his final betrayal. He had left her with little more than the roof over her head and the family name. Wilding's had a modest but reliable reputation as fine instrument appraisers, specialising in violins. When they had been on the verge of losing it all, her father sacrificed himself to save the business, and now this little shop on Crawford Place was her dubious inheritance. But the turnover was barely enough to pay the bills. Given the circumstances, Gabrielle should have been spending her time trying to find ways to enhance Wilding's' cachet. But as the golden morning sun glinted off the cafetière on the table, Gabrielle was indulging in her secret passion of searching for lost music and completely ignoring the pile of bills on the table.

It was only a brief mention, but enough to prove her hunch correct.

—as solo violinist to the court of Elisa Bonaparte, Napoleon's sister. Paganini had many, many affairs…

Gabrielle rolled her eyes. Women wanted to fall in love; men, on the other hand, wanted many, many affairs. She reached for her coffee cup and took a sobering mouthful of dark bitterness before continuing.

…but it is said he fell deeply in love with a courtesan, who became his muse during his time at Court Lucca. He composed a passionate romanza for her, the draft of which was reportedly found by musicologist William Lambert. The piece, entitled 'Bellezza Nascosta', or 'Hidden Beauty', has never been seen by anyone other than Lambert himself, so we can only assume that this early piece of music is lost forever.

Gabrielle sat back in her chair and gazed into the middle distance, absentmindedly twirling her hair into a coil over her shoulder. She tried to imagine the kind of man in today's world that would compose a romanza for the woman he loved. Her thoughts strained to conjure up the sort of attributes this man would possess, the emotional courage to bare his soul, the passion, the romance… Nope, impossible. Romance, to her cynical and mortally wounded soul, was dead. There was an ever-growing part of her that felt sure she was born in the wrong time. And perhaps that was why she was spending a Sunday morning researching obscure, dark tales about a long-dead violinist, rather than waking up in the arms of a Saturday-night conquest.

Gabrielle preferred to live in her imagination. That was the one place where you couldn't get hurt. Once (or twice, if truth be told), when loneliness or boredom had driven her to dating apps, she hadn't matched with anyone. Not one single, solitary man. Eventually, a man going by the name of Pete1995 must have taken pity on her and sent a nonchalant 'Hey'. She replied rather coolly with a 'Hey yourself'. She couldn't help it – this habit of coming across as the most aloof person on the planet. It made forming new connections … tricky. Still, Pete1995 must've interpreted her response as an invitation to tell her exactly where she was going wrong.

> Your profile is … interesting.

> Thanks.

> That wasn't a compliment. lol.

> Oh?

> It's like a CV. Who cares what you studied in uni. You're not looking for a job. lol.

Pete1995 was quite prone to lolling.

> Well, what would you have me write, Pete?

> I dunno. Guys like girls who don't take themselves too seriously.

Gabrielle lol'd.

> Girls like guys who write them poetry and then die in a war.

> ???

She deleted the app.

Shaking the memory from her head, Gabrielle rolled her shoulders before letting her gaze fall back to the page. There were all kinds of twisted rumours about Paganini: that he had made a deal with the devil, that he was the devil himself and even that he had killed a woman. People went so far as to say that you could hear a woman's voice when he played his violin. But there was something so captivating about him. Her father used to joke that he was the Elvis of his day, women fainting at the mere sight of him. She thought this was ridiculous, until, on a school trip, she saw David Garrett play a solo concert in an outdoor amphitheatre in Sicily. His striking blonde hair tied in a top knot; his dark, smouldering eyes that made you feel as though you were the only one he was playing for... Yes, she'd developed a full-on crush.

But it was Paganini's compositions that Gabrielle adored playing. When she used to play. And so she couldn't bear to think that any of his compositions were lost forever. Who knew how many musical pieces had been misplaced, destroyed or simply abandoned over the years. Their loss haunted her, like ghosts from the past. Perhaps if she could rescue them, she could rescue some parts of herself. Lambert's final words caught her eye.

The piece eats a piece of your soul every time you play it.

Gabrielle felt her whole body stiffen. Was that what had

happened to her? From the moment Max Daunt, her violin tutor, had walked into her life as a young soloist, she thought that she was gaining something invaluable. But all these years later, living alone above her father's old shop, nothing seemed further from the truth. Her wrist began to throb; the old injury acting up. She adjusted the support strap, tightening it a little, before emitting a frustrated sigh. 'No wallowing,' she reminded herself sharply.

She got up and took her cup and saucer to the sink, washed them thoroughly and set them on the draining board. She wiped the countertop that was already gleaming and straightened the little cactus plants on the shelf above the sink. There. All in order. For a moment, the pressure eased and even though she knew it wouldn't last, it was the only way she knew how to stay in control. She wondered if it was the same for everyone else. Did they too have a dividing line in their lives, clearly marking the before and after? The person they were before and the person they'd had to become to survive the aftermath? And if you couldn't love this new version, how could you expect anyone else to?

In her less guarded moments, Gabrielle couldn't help wishing for something exciting to happen. A chaos to challenge her order. Anything. A letter from a mysterious benefactor. A random meeting with a handsome stranger as they both reached for the last avocado in the corner shop. The kind of things that happen to people at the beginning of a novel… What did they call it? An inciting event.

Satie jumped onto her lap, right on cue, purring noisily for his lunch. Perhaps routine wasn't so bad, she thought, burying her head in his fur and pretending not to notice the sinking feeling inside. She'd had her shot at an extraordinary life and blown it. It was a disconcerting feeling – knowing that your one chance at achieving something great was already over.

That was when the phone rang.

Chapter Six

♪

'So, you were the first person I thought of,' Devlin said, having given Walter the particulars of the story so far.

'Let me get this right,' Walter began, putting his empty glass down on the table and, once again, choosing not to address the pills. 'You bought a violin from the Lost and Found at Heathrow Airport and now you think the criminals who originally stole it are going to come after you.'

'Yeah, that's pretty much it in a nutshell,' Devlin said, nodding.

'And I'm the first person you thought of?'

'Well, yeah.'

'Your old history teacher?'

Devlin half-shrugged and finished off his ham sandwich. He felt a wave of relief having shared the story with someone else. It had been killing him trying to keep it to himself.

'You didn't think to call the police?' Walter pressed on, as if talking to a child.

'Course not, what would I do that for? I'm in possession of stolen goods. What's worse, Pete sold it to me without waiting for the obligatory three months, so I'll be getting him in trouble, too. I could lose my job, go to prison.'

'So, you're just going to take your chances with a criminal gang instead, eh?'

'It's a rock and a hard place, Mr Pickering.'

'Mmm, I see. So, what do you plan to do?'

'I was kind of hoping you might...' Devlin gave Walter the pleading eyes of a homeless dog with three legs and no place else to go.

'I suppose we could try and get it back to the original owner, try and come to some sort of an arrangement?'

'See? I knew you'd know what to do,' Devlin said, beaming as though Walter had offered him a bed for the night and a nice juicy bone.

Walter, in turn, felt himself warming to the unusual situation he found himself in. What he had been about to do, before, suddenly felt a bit premature. Maybe he hadn't really thought it through properly. It was typical of life to do that, to reel you back in just when you thought you were on your way out.

'Hang on, there's just one problem though. The previous owner is dead.'

'Well, she must have left her fortune to someone,' Walter said, wondering who his flat would have gone to had he swallowed those pills. The government probably, as he hadn't made a will. He really hadn't thought that through at all. He'd rather leave it to a cats' home. Or Dogs Trust.

'Time to do some digging. I'll just clear up here,' Walter said, swiping the crumbs and the pills into his hand and carrying them over to the bin.

♪

Devlin spent an uncomfortable night on a camp bed in Walter Pickering's living room. He didn't feel right leaving the man on his own, not after the scene he had walked in on earlier. But mostly, he was too scared to tell Melissa about the violin. She'd hit the roof. Although, if he was being entirely honest with himself, which was a foreign country at this stage, he was worried about the criminal gang who had stolen the violin in the first place. Surely, they were looking for it?

He texted Mel and told her where he was staying. He'd expected a little more than just the *Fine, whatever* reply that came back.

The following morning, he woke to the smell of toast and scrambled eggs.

'You're looking better,' Devlin said, tumbling out of the camp bed.

'You're looking worse! Here, a good bit of nosh will sort you out.'

Walter had been up with the birds. While Devlin snored at volume on the couch, he took the opportunity to spend a quiet moment examining the violin himself. Taking it carefully out of its case, he was struck by its shape. Of course he'd seen a violin before, but he'd never held one, up close. The neck, the body, its very presence made it seem as though the instrument had human qualities. Female qualities. And her voice was coaxing him out of his shell. Perhaps he was guilty of anthropomorphism, but the thoughts that came into his head hardly seemed his own. He rubbed the wood where the colour had naturally altered on the back. How many shoulders had held this violin, he wondered?

'Not to worry,' he whispered to her. 'We'll take care of you.' He'd looked around to check that Devlin was still asleep. He'd think Walter had lost what few marbles he had left. And yet he couldn't help but feel as though her arrival in his life meant something. She seemed to be saying that life wasn't through with him yet.

♪

As they washed down their meal with treacle-dark tea from the pot, Walter produced a little notebook and pencil.

'Right, the way I see it, the first thing we need to do is have the violin appraised. You've seen a newspaper article and made the assumption that the stolen violin and your instrument from the Lost and Found are one and the same.'

Devlin suddenly felt the sublime weightlessness of someone else sorting out his problems.

'You're right! Maybe I've been worrying about nothing. Where will we find an appraiser?'

Walter got up and took another notebook from the drawer underneath the telephone. Devlin wondered if he was the only man alive to still have a landline. Flicking through the pages, he landed on the name he was searching for.

'Ah yes, here we are, Mr Wilding.' He said the name as though Devlin should have been familiar with it.

'He taught at Cambridge for a time and used to come to St Michael's every now and again, donating some instrument or other. But his real passion was dealing in rare and vintage instruments. He used to have a place just off the Edgware Road.'

Walter rang the number, but the call diverted to an answering machine with a young woman's voice.

'Well, it's still Wilding's, perhaps they'll be open later.'

'Okay, but what if it *is* the stolen violin, what then?' asked Devlin.

'Yes, well, I've been giving that some thought. Now, you must understand that I'm no expert on the legal implications, but I think your best bet is to get it back to the deceased heiress's next of kin. They must have put it up for auction – whoever inherited her estate. If we can persuade them to take the violin back, maybe we can make some sort of an arrangement with the auction house.'

'Brilliant, Mr Pickering! Then the criminal gang won't be my problem anymore!'

Walter sighed.

'That's the trouble with your generation, only looking out for yourselves. But I suppose you're right.'

They set out for Wilding's on the Tube. It was a bright June day that held all the promise of long summer picnics with juicy strawberries and salty dips in the sea. Devlin and Walter were, by stark contrast, sombre and lost in their own thoughts. The joviality they'd felt in the apartment had diluted into a watery sense of cluelessness among the throngs of passengers. Tourists, carefully studying maps and milling about like confused sheep, created something of an obstacle course for native Londoners. For his part, Devlin was beginning to feel a bit daft about the whole thing. The article in the paper had caused him to panic. He couldn't really explain why, but the thought of handing the violin over to someone else filled him with a kind of dread. As the carriage rocked back and forth, he held it close to his chest and began thinking of excuses to get out of this silly arrangement. Besides, Mr Pickering wasn't exactly firing on all cylinders; maybe he wasn't the best person to take advice from.

Walter, on the other hand, felt as though he had been thrown a lifebuoy. Albeit from the most unlikely of saviours. But the elation he had felt last night at being pulled back from the brink had given way to a harsh reality; somehow, he needed to find a reason to live. Or at the very least, something to combat the feelings of loneliness that had somehow found their way into his being. Like dry rot, it must have been setting in when he wasn't looking, nesting in places and thoughts he tended not to frequent. But today he had a purpose. The only trouble was, what if the purpose reached a dead end? He needed this, like one last grand adventure. Perhaps he was growing maudlin in his old age, but looking at the battered old violin case in Devlin's arms, he just knew that she had a greater story to tell, and Wilding could unlock the mystery.

Chapter Seven

♪

It took a bit of navigating, but Walter and Devlin eventually found the building, 21 Crawford Place, a three-storey Georgian terraced house with a retail space on the ground floor. The exterior was a little worse for wear, but when the sunlight hit the multicoloured bricks, it almost seemed golden. The front window was dusty and ambiguous; reluctant to give many clues as to what lay inside. A plaque beside the door read:

G. Wilding BA, MA (Music) PhD (Music History)
Appraisal, Repair and Restoration

Walter turned the handle and the door gave way, triggering an old brass bell that immediately transported them back to another age. There was a soft carpet to muffle their footsteps and a worn leather Chesterfield in an inviting toffee colour, set against the side wall. Opposite was a mahogany counter, displaying nothing but an incongruously seventies landline phone. Violins of every shape and size were displayed on the walls, like a museum.

'Do you think he's in?' Devlin asked, as Walter inspected the place like someone trying to see familiarities in a long-lost friend.

Before Walter had a chance to respond, a woman appeared from a hitherto unseen doorway and shook their hands with a very brief introduction.

'Gabrielle Wilding, how can I help you?'

Walter introduced himself and explained that he was an old friend of Mr Wilding, whilst Devlin found himself momentarily dumbstruck. In a conservative uniform of black trousers and a crisp white shirt with a black tie, knotted loosely at the neck, she was like no one he'd ever seen. Her hair was dark and rich, like a black cherry, the waves tied in a low ponytail that snaked over her shoulder. Her skin, pale and bare, gave her a striking look and her eyes, well, they burned like ice. In short, she was mesmerising and intimidating in equal measure. And now she was looking straight at him. Had she been speaking?

'Sorry?'

'The violin, may I see it?' said Gabrielle, efficiently and to the point.

Flustered, Devlin said the one thing that was sure to make the situation worse.

'I thought we were supposed to be meeting Mr Wilding?'

The temperature in the room dropped considerably and after a beat, Gabrielle folded her arms and turned to look at him square-on.

'My father is dead and I am the appraiser. Do you want me to have a look at your violin or not?'

'Oh, I ... I didn't mean...'

Walter took the violin from Devlin and handed it over with an apologetic look on his face.

'I had no idea, my dear, please accept my deepest sympathies for your loss.'

Gabrielle nodded curtly and seemed understandably eager to move on.

'I'll have a look at it – open it up and see if we can find any labels,' she said, placing the violin behind the counter without opening the case.

'Sorry, um, how do you mean, "open it up"?' Devlin asked, despite his better judgement.

'I'll have to take it apart in order to appraise it,' she replied, matter-of-factly.

'It just sounds a bit invasive, doesn't it?' Devlin wanted to stop this whole thing, tell them both he'd changed his mind.

'Thank you, Miss Wilding, you have our confidence and our gratitude,' Walter effused, either ignoring Devlin or trying to distance himself from his ignorance in such matters.

Devlin wasn't sure she cared one jot whether she had either. It didn't help matters that he was standing there in his work clothes with his high-visibility jacket on. He felt like a complete Luddite.

'Your father was a dear friend and a meticulous professional; I can see the apple hasn't fallen far from the tree,' Walter continued, entirely unaware that he had touched on a raw nerve. 'Do you play yourself?' he continued, despite her cold, hard stare.

'My father says I could play the violin before I could speak, although I'm not sure how true that is,' she replied, robotically, as though this was a line she often used with clients. She imperceptibly flexed the fingers of her left hand and that was when Devlin noticed the black bandage on her wrist. She caught him looking and, embarrassed, he blurted out their reason for being there.

'We just want to know if it's a Stradivarius,' he said, taking back control of the conversation.

It looked as though it was taking all Gabrielle had not to laugh in their faces. She looked from one to the other and then sobered as though she'd only just realised that they were actually serious.

'It's highly unlikely.'

'But you'd be able to find out?' he asked again, like a child asking if Santa Claus was real.

His tone appeared to catch her off guard. They seemed quite genuine and she needed the money.

'I have your contact details, I'll be in touch.'

And that was their cue to leave.

♪

In The Duke of York pub, the two men discussed Miss Wilding, the violin and the finer points of pub grub versus gastro pub.

'Give me a steak and kidney any day of the week,' Devlin was saying, mostly debating with himself.

'What was going on with you back there?'

'What do you mean? Nothing was going on,' Devlin replied, rather defensively.

'I think she was a little insulted.'

'That wasn't my fault! You were the one who said we were going to see a Mr Wilding.'

'Ah, so you do know what I was referring to. And besides, I wasn't to know the poor man had died!'

Both men stared at each other – the future of their violin adventure hanging in the balance, until Walter's lips curled into a smile.

'What?'

'Well, I'm no expert, but the last time I made a complete imbecile of myself in front of a woman, I was hopelessly attracted to her.'

Devlin took several large gulps of his pint, then took up his knife and fork and resumed eating, as though nothing had happened. He speared several chips with his fork, then pointed them at Walter.

'Are you sure we can trust her?'

'Are you sure you can trust me?' Walter replied evenly.

'I don't suppose I have much choice.'

Chapter Eight

♪

As soon as the two men were a satisfactory distance down the road, Gabrielle reached for the violin case and took it over to the coffee table, sitting herself down on the edge of the Chesterfield. It had taken all of her restraint not to open it while they were there, but it was always better to feign indifference with clients like that. There were always people popping by with worthless heirlooms or 'antiques' they'd found shoved up in their granny's attic, which were, more often than not, completely worthless. But she had a feeling about this one. Even the case stood out in a way she couldn't quite put her finger on. Yet the years had taught her to keep her expectations in check.

They were a strange pair, that much was clear. Not her usual type of clients. The older man seemed sweet. Devlin, on the other hand … she wasn't sure what to make of him. Although he did seem genuinely concerned about the violin, which was rather touching. And he did have quite nice eyes. But that was beside the point. Freaking out that they might have found a Stradivarius was almost laughable. Still, the world of antique violins was steeped in tales of lost, stolen and even disguised masterpieces. The criminals who stole them were never capable of selling them on – they were priceless in that regard because each one was accounted for and no dealer with a crumb of morality would touch those. Gabrielle thought back to the infamous theft of Min Kym's Strad from a Pret café at Euston Station. They ended up returning it. Still, one never knew.

She lifted the clasps with her thumb and the case opened with something of a gasp. The familiar scent of warm wood and pine sap from the rosin filled the air. With wide eyes and a racing heart, she rushed to take it all in. Tucked snugly into sapphire-blue velvet lay one of the most striking violins she had ever seen. A masterpiece of craftsmanship, exuding a sense of timeless elegance. Her fingers itched to touch it. Ever so slowly, she let them trace across the wood. The violin's frame bore the marks of countless lives – each scar and scratch telling some forgotten story of its past. Tentatively, she eased it out of the case and the moment she held it in her hands, all rational thought abandoned her. Memories of her final performance, when the pain had struck and ended her career, simply fell away. Once again, she was a little girl, holding a violin for the first time. The wonder of it, the unusual shape and curious-looking swirls and hollows. Before the darkness came and stole her voice.

Gabrielle's mother had played violin with the London Symphony Orchestra, and, like most little girls, she wanted to emulate her mother. She practised at home and when she played, the violin became her voice and she could say so much more than she ever could with words. Her entire body soared and fell with the notes, in a kind of self-expression that came naturally to her. When her mother became ill, Gabrielle played by her bedside, believing that the music would heal her mother's sick heart. When it did not, she convinced herself that if her playing had been more accomplished, it would have worked. And so she begged her father for more lessons and threw herself into her playing. Max Daunt was the most revered tutor in the UK and when he had agreed to take her on, she could see her whole life ahead of her, her dreams coming true. How quickly it turned into a nightmare.

A single tear rolled slowly down her cheek and she did not wipe it away. There was a strange sense of foreboding, that this violin could be trouble. The irresistible kind.

She turned it over in her hands, drinking in every detail. To the average person, all violins looked the same, but to Gabrielle it was like looking at a beautiful face with all of the lines, shapes and curves unique to that person. The violin had acquired a warm patina with age, sealed as it was in dozens of layers of varnish. The colour of the wood was difficult to define as it almost shimmered in the light, but she finally decided on autumnal orange. The top of the violin appeared to be made of spruce with a broad grain. There was some slight crackling along the ribs, but the belly seemed sufficiently strong to stand modern stringing.

'Who are you?' she whispered, wondering if the violin had been silent for some time, too.

She searched in the hollow heart of the violin for a label. Luthiers always left their stamp, but there was nothing on this one. The strings stretched elegantly over the slender bridge, connecting the ebony fingerboard to the tailpiece.

She ached to take it in her arms, to feel again the sensation of wood and string resonating in her bones and muscles. But that's the thing about heartache, it makes you hesitant, watchful and unsure of yourself. The muscles in her wrist spasmed, reminding her of what she could no longer do. Those days were packed up along with all of her boxes from university. Chapter closed. Since she had taken over her father's business as an appraiser, her love of playing had been relegated to a distant past, as though those longings in fact belonged to someone else. Someone she didn't know anymore. Gabby. The person she had to become to survive did not have the luxury of emotions. Even her love affairs were just brief encounters. No one would ever get close to her heart again. She made sure of it.

But this violin was calling to her, she could hear it. Coaxing and charming her with whispers of the past. Who knew what fingers had caressed the neck, what virtuosos had tucked the violin under their chin and let the instrument become their voice? She was fooling herself by thinking that she hadn't already made the decision the minute she opened the case. Wondering if she dared to cross the threshold, when her heart had already leapt without her permission. She took the rosin and rubbed it twice across the hairs on the bow. One minute it was in her hands, the next minute it was sitting snug between her shoulder and her neck, the horsehair bow glistening in the dying evening sun before she placed it against the strings and – oh, how sweet and powerful the sound. She turned the pegs until the instrument was in perfect tune and she began to play again. A polyphony of sound that seemed to travel through time, through place and people. As she played the first few bars, the notes soared higher and higher until she felt as though she were walking a tightrope, miles into the endless sky. *Don't let me fall*, she said, and the violin answered with the kind of strength she'd searched for all these years but felt incapable of feeling. She was bonding with it, against every survival instinct that she'd built up over the years – all too late, of course, because the damage had already happened.

'Danse Macabre' by Saint-Saëns. The strange melody had always appealed to her. She hadn't played this piece since the night of her final performance, or *the episode* as her father referred to it. When that searing pain gripped her wrist like a vice. It had come from nowhere and all of the subsequent X-rays and scans revealed nothing structurally wrong. The next few years of Gabrielle's life were spent attending physio appointments, trying acupuncture and reflexology and researching chronic pain on the internet into the small hours. But nothing worked. The pain persisted and her career ended. Max dropped her almost immediately and her dreams for the future had nowhere to go. They didn't belong to her anymore.

And yet, in this moment, her wrist hardly hurts at all. As she played the final notes, she recalled the meaning of the music. Death, represented by a solo violin, awoke the skeletons from their graves to dance on Allhallows Eve. As her entire body swooped and swayed with the notes, a mesmerising thought occurred to her… Perhaps this violin was dancing her back to life.

Chapter Nine

♪

Walter went back to pick up his car at the petrol station, only to find that it had been towed away.

'Well, we couldn't just leave an abandoned car on the forecourt, could we?' said the manager, with all the empathy of a stray dog relieving itself on your shoe. 'Not my problem, mate.'

'Ah yes, the battle-cry of a generation,' Walter replied, reaching for his mobile phone. 'Where's the sense of community?' he mumbled to himself. This was the selfie generation, where selflessness was a foreign concept. He paused mid-thought; if he wasn't careful, he'd end up feeling the same way he did the last time he left the petrol station.

'Right. No matter, do you have the number?'

'What number?' the manager replied, making a show of how, yet again, he had to put down the box of M&Ms he was trying to open with a pen.

'For the car pound, of course.'

'Why would I have that?'

Walter opened his mouth to speak and then closed it. He couldn't pinpoint the exact moment when everyday conversations had become such hard work, but it was difficult to remember a time when the exchange had resulted in something fruitful. Although it took all of his effort, Walter left without saying a word and feeling a horrible sense of déjà vu.

Standing on the high street, he looked in the direction of home and, had he been in a car, would have shifted into reverse. A bus pulled up at a stop he hadn't realised he was standing beside, and before he knew it, he was heading back into central London.

He alighted at St Pancras, where the British Library rose up in front of him like a beacon. You knew where you were with a library, he always told his students. The comfort of all that collective knowledge, wrapping you in its sure and steady embrace. A cathedral of learning, he used to assure the boys at school. It was at that point their eyes tended to glaze over. Anything that couldn't be downloaded via an app was considered prehistoric. Although there were the odd few, he could tell, whose faces would illuminate in the light of learning. He recalled the utter astonishment of his students during a class tour to the library on realising that they could take a book home, read it, return it and not pay a penny for the privilege. He missed that; having the chance to influence young minds, even if most of his students referred to history as 'boring' or 'extinct'. Or both.

Yet, he must have had some impact. Look at Devlin, he mused, while taking his place in the queue. After all these years, he's the one he came to for help. Not Mr Catchpole, the child prodigy (his own words) maths genius, or Mrs Davies, the Spanish teacher. She was a fine woman. Always made those Spanish cakes for the Christmas party. He was pulled from his reverie about her unrestrained laughter, and the way it made her breasts tremble, by a strong arm nudging him in the back.

'You're next,' came the baritone voice from behind him.

Fishing the newspaper clipping from his pocket, he showed it to the librarian – an efficient-looking young man, tall and willowy, with a stride that made it a struggle to keep up as he headed for the staircase. He led him to biographies of the rich and famous, where Walter began searching Margot Clement's family tree. Within the hour, he had found two possible heirs to the fortune – one in New York and one, rather fortunately, in Somerset. His blood pulsed with excitement. Maybe he didn't know a lot about violins, but perhaps he could help Devlin, after all. If the violin was really the priceless instrument belonging to the heiress, this could be the best way to restore it to its proper owner with the least amount of fuss. Looking up from the page, he quoted his favourite detective under his breath… 'The game is afoot!'

♪

Gabrielle didn't often make impromptu trips to crowded places, but the one exception was the British Library. And the reading room there was the one place, other than the shop, where she felt at home. No one was rushing; the air had a stillness that, although not devoid of sound, contained an air of deep thought. People thinking, learning, reading ... it gave a particular quality to the air, a certain vibration like the after-effect of a plucked string. It calmed her nerves to be amongst these soundwaves, like brown noise, whatever that was. People could be very, well, people-y. In normal situations. They talked too much or laughed a little too loudly. Gabrielle didn't exactly want to live a life apart from other humans. She liked being around people but only when their egos and their masks were checked at the door with their coats.

Everyone looks the same in the library. If you watch someone reading a book, you can't really tell a thing about them. When a person is unselfconscious, they're just being. So there's no expectation to perform a certain way or impose an agenda. Gabrielle felt that libraries were some of the last remaining free places on the planet. In every sense of the word.

♪

Still on the hunt for Paganini's elusive 'Bellezza Nascosta', she had spent the morning checking the archives and came across an article in the *New York Times*, dated 3rd November 1903.

> ROME, Nov. 2.—*A discovery has just been made in Genoa which will delight all music lovers. It is a well-known fact that very little remains of the musical compositions of Niccolò Paganini, the sensational violin player, for the reason that what his contemporaries deemed his most original and charming creations were often the inspiration of time and place, and often, too, their transcription was impossible. And now in Genoa,*

fourteen of his compositions have come to light, all written in the maestro's own hand.

There was no mention of 'Hidden Beauty'. Gabrielle scoured the article to find where the discovery had been made, but no more detail was forthcoming. Found in Genoa, but where exactly and by whom? She was no closer to finding out where the romanza was. It had to be out there somewhere. She chewed on the tip of her pen before marking down the details in her notebook. She'd always been drawn to these kinds of musical puzzles. As a young girl, she'd become obsessed with solving the mystery of the *Enigma Variations*. The composer, Edward Elgar, was a keen cryptographer and teased the public with the clue that Enigma was a counterpoint to a well-known piece of music. For years, people were trying to figure it out. Elgar had once said of it: 'The Enigma I will not explain – its "dark saying" must be left unguessed.'

Yet Gabrielle had always believed that if she thought hard enough and long enough, she could work it out. Understand it. Uncover the hidden meaning. Recognise the pattern to it all. She wanted to believe that there was an order behind everything, and that random chaos could somehow be overcome with logic. Well, that was the idea, at least.

♪

On her way out, something very unexpected and unfamiliar happened. In London, at least. She bumped into someone she knew.

'Miss Wilding?'

'Oh, hello, Mr Pickering, isn't it?'

'Walter, please,' he said, shaking her hand warmly.

Gabrielle didn't normally like meeting clients out in the wild. Business was conducted during business hours, that was her rule. But to her surprise, she was actually pleased to see Walter.

'I'm glad I ran into you,' he said, 'I've been doing some research—'

'Do you want to grab a coffee?' she asked, cutting him off. *Where had that come from?* she wondered. Did she want to have a coffee with Walter? What the hell had she said that for? Gabrielle didn't have a spontaneous bone in her body. Or so she thought.

'Um, yes, why not. That would be delightful.'

♪

Once they were seated at a small café that specialised in Portuguese pastries, Walter observed the little ritual opposite him. Gabrielle moved the handle of her coffee cup so it was parallel to her, then nudged the plate holding her pastel de nata forward until it aligned with her napkin and spoon. She looked up and caught him watching her.

'Habit,' she said, dismissing it.

Walter smiled warmly. If you took the time to observe people, they betrayed all of their best-kept secrets. The detached, frosty countenance she displayed at the shop hid a world of pain.

'I just wanted to say again that I was very sorry to learn

of your father's passing,' he said, pouring milk into his coffee. 'I'm sure it's been a difficult time.'

'Oh, yes, well…'

Her tone sounded more irritated than sad, but Walter didn't want to pry. Still, he felt a tug on his heart as he watched her carefully cut her pastry in half, then quarters, before licking her finger and pressing any rogue crumbs on the plate and lifting them to her mouth.

'He always spoke with such fondness about your playing. Do you still perform?'

'I … no. Not for some time.'

'Oh, right.' Walter began to falter. What did he know about helping other people? He could hardly help himself. It was easier with Devlin: he was, well, a man. Walter had never been very good with women. He taught at an all-boys school – delicacy was hardly the *mode du jour*.

'I played *your* violin,' she said, before reaching for her cup and gulping down the coffee so fast that she started a coughing fit. *What did you tell him that for?* she scolded herself. Normally she was so reserved, so vigilant. She'd had no intention of telling him anything. She wasn't sure what had come over her.

Walter handed her a napkin.

'Did you enjoy it? The playing?' he asked simply.

The question caught her completely off guard and she didn't trust herself to speak. She nodded and an unbidden smile escaped, reaching all the way up to her green eyes. He hadn't asked how it had sounded, if she thought it was worth a lot of money. Only if she'd enjoyed it.

Walter smiled in return. It was as though an outer layer had peeled away.

'Maybe it's like riding a bike,' he said. 'The muscle memory, it just kicks in, doesn't it?'

Gabrielle rotated her wrist under the table. The pain was coming and going now – she couldn't trust it. She remembered something her mother had once told her. Before she knew it, she was telling Walter.

'Like birds singing in their sleep,' she said.

'Oh, what a beautiful thought!'

'They did a study at a university in Argentina, where they found that birds were silently singing in their sleep. I don't know why they were studying something so random like that, but for whatever reason, they realised that the bird's voice box moved during sleep. One rather whimsical scientist – a contradiction if ever there was one – said that they were dreaming of their birdsong, practising their notes.'

The words had tumbled out of her – like a child rushing to tell some fantastical tale. She felt slightly horrified at this breach of protocol, just speaking her thoughts out loud without careful filtering. But strangely, it felt quite nice. And Walter seemed like someone who didn't mind if you talked about birds practising songs in their sleep.

'Nature has such an exquisite way of reminding us how beautiful life can be, doesn't she? If only we could remember to value the simple things. They are the true miracles.'

Gabrielle had often comforted herself with this memory, that even if she couldn't play the violin while she was awake, perhaps her fingers were playing the notes while she slept.

Chapter Ten

♪

Vieux Port, Montréal

Meanwhile, thousands of miles away in an old antique store, several clocks ticked away the seconds, each tick and tock echoing into infinity. The place was unrecognisable since Verity had taken over from her father. She stocked nothing but high-worth items and only the well-heeled of Montréal and its surroundings could afford to shop there.

The two men stood like an odd pair of candlesticks in the shop, dressed in their uniform of leathers. She should never have hired them for a job like this, yet despite all of her contacts, when the time came, they were the only ones available. They were part of a biker gang from Quebec City and the most she could say about them was that they didn't ask too many questions. This job had required finesse and intelligence, but all they really offered was brawn. Still, they had managed to get the violin from the auction warehouse and Verity's heart almost burst when she received their message confirming it – *PACKAGE RECEIVED*.

Yet when they showed up at the shop, there was no violin.

'Where is it? Have you stored it somewhere?'

Watching two grown men shuffle their feet and stare accusingly at each other, as though caught smoking at school, made her impatient.

'Where is my violin? You told me you had it. No violin, no money!'

That was when they spat out the bare facts. While waiting for their flight home from Heathrow, they sat in the airport bar and began celebrating their success. The violin, hidden in a sports bag, sat between their legs on the floor. Yet somehow, when they got up to leave, they picked up the wrong bag. It was only when they arrived home that they realised their mistake and discovered a sports bag full of hockey equipment.

Verity felt her whole body shake.

'No. No! It's not possible.'

The larger one threw the bag down on the floor in front of her.

She leaned back against her Louis XIV desk, her legs threatening to snap underneath her.

'How could you not have noticed?'

'Well, we had a few beers.'

'You – you had a few beers? Do you think I offered you fifty thousand dollars to have a few beers? I thought I was hiring professionals.'

'We are professionals,' said the stocky one with the short dark hair.

'Oh yes, well, I can see that,' she said, mocking them. Though she was half their size her anger outweighed both of them. 'So, who has it now?' she yelled, to which they simply shrugged.

'Idiots!!'

'We have a plan,' he continued.

'What makes you think I'd give you another chance?'

'Because now it's personal,' said the one with the long hair, smacking his fist into his palm.

'Well, it's always been personal for me,' she said, throwing the newspaper at them with the article about the stolen violin. 'I'm going to London myself, which is probably what I should've done in the first place.'

'Look, we did the job at Christie's, you owe us for that.'

'You did half of the job, which counts for nothing.'

'If we come with you and finish it this time, then you give us what you owe us.'

Verity thought about this. She could have hired somebody local, but the time it would take to do that was time away from the search. She had to find the violin and fast. She couldn't let it slip through her fingers again. Too many years she had waited for her opportunity – ever since that Middle Eastern prince had swindled her father, who was too drunk to notice. She had no idea who was in possession of it now and if things became ... difficult, these two, though utterly dim-witted, could bring an element of brute force that might turn the situation in her favour.

She bent down and examined the sports bag. There was a baggage label, a plastic cover with a phone number written on a card tucked inside. Picking up the phone, she dialled the number printed on the tag of the sports bag her two henchmen had brought back to Canada.

'Hello?' came a sweet voice.

'Am I speaking to Leslie?'

'Yes, this is she.'

Verity paused before practising her most dulcet of tones.

'Oh, hello, Leslie, my name is Barbara and I think I have your bag. It seems our luggage got mixed up at the airport.' With any luck, she would have all of this taken care of in a matter of minutes. Then she could cut these two idiots loose.

'Oh, thank God! I thought I'd never see my stuff again,' the young woman effused. 'Where are you?'

'I'm in Montréal, Quebec. This is wonderful, we can arrange a swap,' she said, trying to keep her tone even. She didn't want this 'Leslie' to get a hint of how valuable the violin was, otherwise she might not be inclined to return it. 'Smart move, writing your phone number on the label. Where are you based?'

'I'm in Vermont, so not too far. I'll arrange a courier to come pick it up, and don't worry, I'll cover the costs,' Leslie replied.

'Not at all, it's a straight swap, after all. I'll give you my address so you can return my bag—'

'Oh no,' Leslie interrupted, 'sorry, I don't have your bag.'

Verity's heart stopped beating for a moment.

'I'm sorry, could you repeat that?'

'I don't have your bag. I got on the plane and it was somewhere over the Atlantic that I realised I'd left my carry-on bag at the airport bar! You know how it is. I'm a nervous flyer, so I was downing a few mojitos—'

Verity had stopped listening.

'So you didn't pick up my bag, by mistake?'

'Sorry, Barbara, no. But I'm sure if you give the airport a call they'll have it at the Lost and Found.'

Verity perked up.

'Mmm, what an excellent idea.'

'So I'll give you my address—'

Verity had already hung up the call.

'We leave tomorrow. You pay for your own flights.'

Chapter Eleven

♪

London

'Say that again?' Devlin shouted into the phone, trying to cover his other ear from the noise of the conveyor belt.

'The police are here, I'll have to go,' replied a frantic Melissa.

Devlin froze. Suitcases of every size and shape kept moving past him on the conveyor belt, giving him the strange sensation that he was moving backwards.

'Hello? Can you hear me?'

He tried to answer, but his mouth was so dry that nothing would come out.

'Devlin, just please come home. I need you here.'

With that, the line went dead. Devlin felt sick. The police must have found out about the violin and he was going to be arrested for handling stolen goods. But he was innocent, wasn't he? With that, he shook the feeling of dread from his skin and went to find his supervisor.

♪

'Oh, thank heavens you're here,' Melissa cried, throwing herself against him. He had rarely seen her so vulnerable and though it hardly seemed the time to think such thoughts, it felt nice to be needed.

'What's happened?' he asked, doing his best impression of a completely innocent person. He had passed a police officer on his way up and when he hadn't immediately been arrested, he had grown in confidence.

'We've been burgled!' Melissa sobbed, lamenting the state of the flat, which – now Devlin allowed himself a moment to look around – gave the impression of having been turned upside down. Drawers were on the floor, dishes smashed all over the table and worktops. He felt his shoulders drop with relief. This wasn't about the violin at all. They'd just been burgled, that was all. Your regular, run-of-the-mill West London break-in.

'It's okay,' he cooed, regaining his composure. 'The most important thing is that no one has been hurt,' he went on, kissing the top of Mel's head. 'Things can be replaced.'

'Nothing has been taken, Mr…?' An older woman in uniform was standing in the living room with a notebook open in her palm.

'Devlin.'

'Mr Devlin,' continued the police officer, who seemed to be in charge. 'Do you know of anyone who might have a reason to target you in this manner?'

'Eh ... what? No. No one. Maybe they couldn't find anything worth taking.'

The woman cast her eyes around the flat, taking in the wide-screen TV, the iPad and the stereo system, all untouched.

'My jewellery!' Melissa shrieked. 'Let me just check my bedroom,' she said, running off into the hallway.

'Does that message mean anything to you, Mr Devlin?' the officer continued.

'What message?' Devlin asked, wondering why he felt as though he was the one in the wrong.

'On the kitchen wall?' she said, pointing to what was once a pristine white wall filled with inspirational wall art. It was now the canvas for a terrifying message, scrawled in black paint.

WE KNOW YOU HAVE IT

'Jesus!' Devlin walked over to the kitchen, as if getting closer to the graffiti might make it less true. Another officer was taking photos of it. It was like a bad dream.

'False alarm!' Melissa shouted, coming back into the living room. 'All of my stuff is there, but they smashed up my make-up. All my Charlotte Tilbury lipstick is ruined,' she sulked, clearly recovering from the initial shock and reverting to her normal self. She didn't need Devlin's arms around her anymore, but neither did she realise that he very much needed her arms around him. Just when he thought he was safe, he realised that the violin thieves were after him. They knew where he lived, and they wanted it back. He suddenly wished the police would arrest him; at least he'd be safe in prison.

'Mr Devlin?' the officer repeated. 'Do you know why anyone would have written this?'

Devlin couldn't open his mouth in case some vomit came out. It was already at the back of his throat. Mercifully, Melissa stepped in.

'Don't be ridiculous, of course he doesn't. Neither of us do. It's obviously kids looking for cash and when they didn't find any, they trashed the place.'

Devlin gave her a side glance. Despite their problems, she was adamantly defending his innocence. It was such a touching gesture that his mind began to replay all of the good times they'd shared, like a video montage with a sentimental soundtrack—

'With all due respect, we'll do the investigating, Mrs Devlin.'

Devlin snapped back to reality, wincing at the assumption that they were married. Perhaps Melissa hadn't heard.

'We're not … um…' he began.

Melissa exhaled the world's longest sigh.

♪

'I picked us up some fish and chips,' he called out as he climbed the stairs. He'd gone down to the hardware shop to get a brass door chain until they could get the locks changed. They had spent hours cleaning up the flat, but with hardly a word spoken between them. When he got upstairs, he noticed a sports bag and a small suitcase beside the sofa. In the kitchen, Melissa was cleaning out the fridge with chaotic energy. The sink was full of frozen food and the floor was littered with salad bags, yoghurt pots and countless jars of who knew what. This was not good.

'Everything feels tainted,' she said.

He wasn't sure if she meant the flat or their relationship.

'I see you've already packed my stuff,' he said.

She didn't turn around. All of her attention was on spraying the antibacterial cleaner and scrubbing the inside of the fridge, as though she was planning on doing a surgical procedure in there later.

'I'm sorry.'

'Yes, well, we're all sorry, Devlin,' she said in staccato as she hacked the ice in the freezer with a knife.

'Um, maybe that's not the safest option,' Devlin said, walking over and trying to take the knife from her ice-cold hand. 'I kind of prefer you when you're not electrocuted,' he added with a smile.

She let him take the knife and her whole body softened.

'I don't want to argue anymore,' she said.

'Neither do I, Mel. I never meant to hurt you, but I can see now that I have.'

She grabbed the kitchen roll from the counter and blew her nose.

'I don't know what I'm more upset about: breaking up now, or the fact that we didn't break up sooner. You've just wasted my time.'

'Well, it wasn't all a waste, was it?'

She looked up at him, as though truly seeing him for the first time.

'No offence, but yes, it was! If it was never leading anywhere, then what was the point?'

He wanted to say something about life being about the journey, or the people we met along the way, but he suddenly realised that this conversation wasn't about who was right or wrong. It was about honesty.

'No offence taken,' he said, although that felt like a lie. It hurt to think he was *that guy*. The type that wasted a girl's time. He hadn't set out to become that person. If only he could have told her about the past. But he couldn't. That time in his life was locked in a vault, never to be spoken about again.

'Just leave your keys on the counter.'

It was the last thing Melissa said to him. And that was it. The end. Although they both knew it had been over long before, it felt strange to actually admit it.

♪

After a long shift at Heathrow, Devlin unlocked the doors of Helga, his old German ex-ambulance campervan. He drove over to Karim's to collect his bags – all his worldly possessions. Somehow, his entire life had become about baggage. Karim had offered him a bed, but Devlin couldn't hack the idea of staying in a happy family home whilst his own life was coming apart. And all because of that violin. Ever since it had left his hands, it had taken all the good luck with it.

It had been a while since he'd spent the night in the converted van, but when he was busking around Europe, Helga had been his home. He'd spent months stripping out the inside and refitting her with a comfy bed and a small kitchenette. Now she was going to become his home again, he drove to his favourite spot in London with free parking – Gladstone Park. Close enough to Willesden Green tube station so that he could still commute to work. Besides, it would only be temporary, he assured himself.

He had to be practical. But where exactly had that gotten him? For so long, he'd told himself that the reason everything had gone so wrong in his life was because he was too carefree with his mindset. His life as a musician was one of trust in providence – the universe will provide. He didn't worry about the future, pension plans or climbing some corporate ladder. Devlin had the soul of a poet and the only thing that made sense to him was connecting to the world through self-expression, creativity and, yes, love. It had all been so easy back then. He would sling his guitar over his shoulder, throw an extra T-shirt and a pair of jeans into a backpack and drive Helga to some new city, busking in sunlit squares to different faces every day.

But after that day in Dublin, it was like his whole world tilted and there was nothing for him to hold onto. If he was being honest with himself, which no one ever really wanted to be, he'd been hiding inside his relationship with Melissa. Her life was so solid, so sure, he just wanted a part of that – to feel the ground beneath his feet again. The job did that, too. It was predictable, safe, secure. You move one thing here and move another thing there. Simple. No risks. It was as though his life had edges again, sides he could lean against. But the question that swam in the deep, murky waters of his subconscious, the one that kept him awake at night and chipped away at the new Luke Devlin he'd been attempting to build from the rubble, now faced him like the neon sign of the chippy across the street. *Am I happy?* He'd run away so hard and so fast from the devastation of the past, thinking he could outrun his feelings. But all he'd done was put them on hold. He suddenly realised that he'd never moved on at all and what he'd thought was a good life was the most hollow performance he'd ever played.

♪

Devlin woke to the sound of his mobile phone. He almost forgot where he was, the sound of traffic outside the campervan confusing him momentarily. He squinted his eyes at the screen but saw only a blur. God, did he need glasses?

'Yep?'

'Devlin, it's Walter. I've just been burgled.'

Devlin sat bolt upright, dislodging a whisky hangover that now threatened to sever his brain in two.

'What?'

'I've just—'

'No, I heard you,' he said, holding his forehead in place with the palm of his hand, 'I just can't believe they found you, too.'

'What do you mean, "too"?'

Devlin smacked his forehead, inducing more pain, which he rightfully deserved. He should have called Walter. As soon as he saw that graffiti he should have warned him that the violin thieves were onto him. But he didn't; he just got drunk in his campervan, listening to old demos he'd recorded. How was he supposed to explain that?

'I'm sorry Walter… I—'

'Don't tell me they broke into your place as well?' Walter asked, his empathy choking Devlin.

'Yesterday. Mel's place now. We … we broke up. I'm sorry, Walter, I should have rung you.'

'Well, it would have been the courteous thing to do, but if I'm honest, I'm not sure I could have done a thing to prevent them. At least now they know that neither of us has the violin.'

'True. But I doubt they're just going to give up.'

Devlin pulled the blanket over his head and lay back on the pillow.

'Maybe I should just give it to them. Try and make contact with them and hand over the violin.'

'And reward their criminality? Not on my watch!'

Devlin wasn't sure anymore. When he had the violin in his possession, he was gripped by a certainty that he could not let it go. Handing it over to Gabrielle, despite her obvious expertise, was the hardest thing he had to do. But since it was out of his possession, his need to hang on to it was leaving him. The memory of how good he felt, how confident, when he had it around, was dissipating. Maybe it was all in his imagination.

'Well, then, what do you suggest? I'm putting us all in danger and now the police are suspicious.' Devlin explained the message on the wall and how the officer had spoken to him.

'Good job I didn't call the police about my break-in then,' Walter said triumphantly.

'Did they do much damage?'

'Enough, but mercifully they left my vinyl intact. Listen, I have an idea, but I'll need to talk to Miss Wilding first.'

'Do you need me to come over and give you a hand?' Devlin was hoping the answer would be no – that the offer alone would be some proof of his goodwill.

'It's all right, I've been through worse.'

Chapter Twelve

♪

THE VIOLIN

Waterford, 1812

Every story has a beginning and mine began, not when my sister's jealousy sealed my fate by drowning me in the water that day, but when a young carpenter heard me singing in the woods.

Ursula, my elder sister, came into the world as she meant to go on, kicking and screaming. Her bright blonde hair cradled a wrinkled face with puckered ruby lips, crying for attention. Mother said that when I was born, she simply hiccupped and out I came. My eyes were wide with wonder and the palest shade of blue, like a robin's egg. I was born with dark auburn hair like my mother's, which always seemed something of an insult to Ursula. Our sisterhood was marked by a rivalry that I naively hoped would fade and yet, with each passing year, her envy grew like a tangled weed around her heart.

I was gifted with a melodious singing voice and from an early age, it was said that I could charm the birds from the trees with my singing. Tutors were sent for, and I practised incessantly. Ursula, on the other hand, grew to be one of the fairest young ladies in the county. Beautiful dresses were bought from the finest shops in London. It was said she could have her pick of husbands, and in her eighteenth year, the search began in earnest. She insisted that Father banish me from the house when suitors came to call.

'She'll ruin everything with her wailing and screeching, she always does,' Ursula insisted. She hated my voice and my father tended to agree with everything my sister said. My mother and I learned quite quickly that we did not have a say in our household. It was easier to simply agree. To acquiesce. To accommodate.

And so I took to walking in the woods. The further I wandered away from the house and its gardens, the looser my limbs became and the lighter my step. All I knew was that I loved to sing. Everything that was tamed in me as a young girl, by my governess and my stern father, found wild liberation in my singing. My lungs took in the air of the forests and fields that surrounded my home and breathed out every shade of my heart in the form of notes. I knew very little of life then and what might be expected of me when I came of age, but I soon found out.

Far into the meadows, with their foxgloves and buttercups, all under the canopy of the great oaks, I found sanctuary. Birdsong welcomed me into a little grove by a stream and there, with no one to hear me, I took a deep breath and sang for hours at a time. For I was alone, wasn't I?

One day, I ventured further into the woods and came across an old cabin I had never seen before. From without, I could hear the sound of wood rasping. I walked towards the open door and saw a man inside. A carpenter. The scent of cut wood filled my nose and on the floor all about him were curls of thinly planed wood.

'Good day to you,' I called out.

The young man looked up, his bright eye acknowledging me through a mop of dark hair. He was unlike the men I was accustomed to meeting. He was poorly dressed, for a start. His shirt was worn and discoloured with age. His shoes were two sizes too big for him. And his skin was slick with sweat from his efforts. All in all, he was very intriguing to me, and despite the fact that he did not reply to my greeting, I did not want to leave. I hovered in the doorway, looking for some excuse to speak again.

'Is it carpentry that you, um, work at?'

He stopped planing the wood on the bench and stood to his full height. I hadn't realised how tall he was, as he was stooped over the bench. I also now realised that his shirt was open and I hardly knew where to look.

'Can I help you, Miss?' he asked, in a tone that was not mocking but held an amused quality.

'I ... me...' I had to clear my throat and regain my composure. 'Not at all, I was simply passing—'

'Well then, you can carry on your way, Miss.'

My jaw hung loose at his impertinence. Given my social standing, he should have, at the very least, tugged his forelock. But he took very little notice of me and returned to his work.

'You are behaving in quite a rude manner, Mr—?'

Again, he responded with something of a smile, but his words challenged me.

'You interrupt my work and it is *I* who is rude? That's some strange conclusion you've arrived at, Miss—?'

'Ormond. Miss Clara Ormond. You'll know my family?' I was being a precocious brat. I knew that. But in that moment, it was the only armour I had. The only thing I felt I possessed that might command his respect. How foolish I was.

'Oh, I know your family, Miss Ormond. I expect they would not like you to fraternise with the likes of myself.' He stood back from the bench and reached into his shirt pocket. He took out a packet of tobacco and began to roll up a cigarette. I watched him as he slowly rolled the paper and licked the edges, before lighting it and breathing out the smoke. It felt titillating to be standing in the middle of the woods, unchaperoned, watching a man with an open shirt and a curious attitude smoking a cigarette. *I should return home*, I thought to myself, *Father will be worried...* And yet my feet were rooted to the spot.

'What is it you are making?' I said, crossing the threshold as if it were merely a game of hopscotch, when deep in my heart I knew the transgression my feet were committing.

He watched as I touched the objects on his bench like a spoiled child seeking distraction.

'What do you think I'm making?'

'Do you always answer questions with a question?'

He smiled and looked at the floor, trying to hide his

amusement. But when he met my gaze again, his hair falling into his eyes, I could not help but return his smile.

I returned my attention to his workbench.

'These look like boxes, but of a very unusual shape.'

'You're half right,' he said, taking a step closer to me.

'How can anyone be *half* right?'

'Well, 'tis true that they are boxes. But they are magical boxes.'

'How so?'

'No. I cannot tell you,' he said, folding his arms.

'Whyever not?'

'You'll laugh.'

'I promise I won't.'

'A promise from a beautiful young maiden,' he said. 'The sun is shining kindly on me this day.'

I blushed at the compliment.

'Are you going to tell me or not?' I demanded impatiently.

'They are instruments,' he said, turning one over in his hand. 'Well, they're supposed to be.'

'What kind of instruments?'

'The kind that rival birdsong for their sweetness,' he said, his voice softening. 'This isn't the right type of wood. It's a block of willow. All I can afford,' he explained self-consciously. I took the chance to study his face as he focused on the strange piece of wood. There was something so *real* about him. So unguarded. He had no airs or graces, no schooled manner of interacting. His honesty was dangerously alluring. Distracting myself, I looked at the shelf behind him.

'Oh dear, is that a dead bird?'

There was a sparrow lying lifeless, its poor head tilted at a strange angle. I went to gather it up, when William stood in my way.

'Don't touch that!'

But he was too late. I saw that the bird's chest was crushed and some of the bones broken and missing.

I looked at him for an explanation.

'The bird was already dead,' he said. I could sense a note of regret in his voice. 'I thought perhaps I could capture its voice.'

'Why, that's a preposterous idea!'

He looked wounded and ashamed. He took the bird ever so gently into his hands.

'I didn't mean no harm. I thought that maybe I could make her immortal.'

I regarded him anew. There was a strangeness about him, there was no denying that. But there was no malice. I couldn't make up my mind about him. Just then, I heard the church bells ringing in the distance.

'Six o'clock, saints preserve us!' I cried, and rushed out of the cabin, without turning to see if he was looking after me. And yet, somehow, I knew he was.

♪

As ever more suitors came to woo Ursula, she remained impervious to their charms and loudly proclaimed her superiority to each, turning them down one by one. I was once again banished from the house and escaped to the woods. Even though I told myself I was not going to the carpenter's cabin, that is exactly where my footsteps led me. Every afternoon I would go there and watch him work. Sometimes I brought apples from our orchard. He would pick flowers from the riverbank and tuck them into my braided hair.

'Will you not sing for me?' he asked, late one afternoon.

'How do you know I can sing?'

He smiled that playful smile that made my insides melt.

'Ah, I see. I was not alone.'

'Your voice carries clear through the woods, like a bell. If I may say, it's the most beautiful voice I've ever heard.'

'Go away with you,' I said, bursting with joy.

'I have another question,' he said, the smile fading slightly.

'What is it?'

William went down on one knee.

'Will you marry me, Clara?'

'But you hardly know me,' I replied, flustered.

'I know that you are the only girl in the world for me.'

My heart flapped about like a butterfly against a windowpane.

'But, for all you know, I could be a tyrant!'

He smiled and dropped his glance to my feet before looking back up.

'I think we both know that's not true. And even if it were, I'm not sure I'd care. I'm in love with you, Clara. And I mean to make myself worthy of you.'

'Whatever do you mean?'

He stood up and took both of my hands in his.

'I shall go to Dublin City and complete my apprenticeship there. I have found a master luthier who is willing to train me. Then when I return, I'll have a trade you can be proud of.'

I shook my head.

'William, it's not a question of pride—' I began.

'But it is for your father. And for me. Will you wait for me, Clara, until I return?'

Of course I would wait. That was not why my heart sank.

'How long shall we be apart?'

'Seven years.'

It seemed an awfully long time to wait for marriage. But I had to be mature about it. This was how things were done in the adult world. My father would respect William more for waiting, and besides, I wasn't sure if Ursula would ever marry, and I would not be permitted to marry before her.

'I'll be an old maid!' I wailed, immediately abandoning my plan to behave like a grown-up.

'You'll be twenty-four! And I'll be twenty-six.'

He could see my bottom lip trembling.

'My love, I am a skilled carpenter. It has been known that qualified woodworkers can complete the training in five years. Does that sound more agreeable?'

I nodded.

'Five years. Not a day longer.'

'Not a day longer,' he agreed. 'Is that a yes?'

I nodded. *Yes. YES!*

'Shall we seal it with a kiss?'

'I ... I've never kissed anyone before. I'm not sure I know how,' I confessed.

'Oh, well, you just…' He thought for a moment. 'Place your lips very close to mine and then—'

'And then?' I asked, moving my face towards his face. My breath raced. Our mouths were so close, I could feel his breath in my mouth. We were breathing each other's air. I'd never been so close to anyone.

'And then, it just … sort of happens,' he said, tenderly.

'What happens?' I whispered, my lips almost touching his.

'Magic.'

♪

1817

The years passed and finally my sister found a suitor. I'm not even sure that she loved him; what did any of us know about love then? Safe in the knowledge that his eldest daughter was to be wed, my father no longer banished my singing. One day, as I picked apples in the walled garden, Ursula's betrothed heard my song. As though under a spell, the following morning he approached Father and asked for my hand instead. Ursula overheard the discussion and something in her countenance cracked. A darkness seeped out and, along with it, a plan.

As we walked homeward, along the stream where the willow tree bows its branches in graceful arches toward its own reflection in the water, without a word, she pushed me in. Knowing that I could not swim, she stood there and watched as I struggled, screamed and choked on river water. Her eyes looked hard and black like two little stones. They were the last thing I saw.

♪

That very day, William journeyed home from Dublin. After five long years, he was now a fully trained luthier. He took the road straight to the Ormond household to ask for Clara's hand in marriage. Walking by the stream, he whistled a happy tune, listening to the birds answering his call. He shook his head when he remembered how naive he'd been, thinking he could capture that birdsong from the corpse of a lifeless bird. For during the intervening years, he had learned more than how to construct a violin with measurements, scrapers and glue. He had learned the secret of capturing a voice. Where once he had used the sparrow's bones in his magical box, as a luthier he learned that it is the air that makes the instrument sing. Invisible particles that enter through the f-holes in turn vibrate the wood in patterned waves. When a musician drew his bow across the strings, the air inside the violin would resonate in waves and it was those waves that entered the ear of the listener, vibrating the mechanism of the inner ear, and suddenly they would *feel*. And all of this from air … moving.

When he came to the flour mill, where the stream joined the fast-flowing brown water of the river, he noticed that the birdsong overhead grew quieter. The mill wheel had stopped turning. Something in the water caught his eye. White material. A dress. He dropped his bag and ran to the bank. It was a woman.

♪

I was caught somewhere in the air, between the earth and the sky. My body was leaving the earth without me, without my soul. That part of us that we never see; that is what clung to this earth, to William. To the life I was supposed to have. Floating in the water, my hair trailing after me like flaxen seaweed, my skirts bloated like a balloon. He pulled me from the water and dragged my body onto the grassy bank, all the while calling my name.

'Clara! Clara! Can you hear me, my love? Wake up!'

His voice sounded very far away. I tried to open my eyelids. It was so very bright that it hurt my eyes. On the other side of the river stood a group of people. I couldn't make their faces out at first, but as the mist cleared, I could see my grandparents and my cousins. Then I saw my mother, who had left us the previous year. They were waiting for me.

'Clara! I'm come home, my love. Please wake up!' William called again. I tried to answer, but my lungs were filled with river water. He rolled my lifeless body on its side. He pounded on my back. He did everything he could. Until all became silent. I was just another sparrow in the wood, cradled in his hands. And yet my soul remained within me until the very last. Slowly, a final breath left my body and as I exhaled a long, shuddering breath, my William reached into his breast pocket for a handkerchief and caught it. He held onto it tightly, before opening a case that held the violin he had made as a wedding gift for me. When the clasps shut, all was darkness.

♪

William carried my body home. The rumours flew and questions were asked. How did it happen? Ursula, for the first time in her life, remained silent. As the mourners stood in the churchyard and my earthly body was lowered into the ground, William opened the violin case. He was not much of a musician, but with me in his arms, he didn't need to be. As he lowered his cheek against the wood, I could *feel* him. I wasn't sure how, but somehow, I was a part of the wood now. The strings, the ebony of the fingerboard and baseboard running along the length of the spine. I had left one body and entered another. He lifted the bow and touched it lightly on the strings. When I sang, my voice had a resonance that I never thought possible. Everyone turned to look at William. I wanted to urge him to keep playing, but I didn't know how. And yet, as soon as I had the thought, I could feel the muscles in his shoulder tensing. He had listened to my thoughts. He began to play again and I sang out the truth. My voice accused Ursula of my murder and I condemned her for her jealousy, her spitefulness, her black heart. Of course, no one understood this in words, but their minds began to question the events.

It was enough to set things in motion and, in the end, justice was done. William had given me the power to put things right. Nevertheless, after the funeral, he swore he would never play me again. All of those years, learning how to capture something he loved, he had never stopped to question the cost. We could no longer be together. Not in the way we had wanted. And so he kept me always by his side, but silent. He wanted to get away from the pain and so he packed up what belongings he had and moved to the continent. But no matter how fast or how far he ran, there was nowhere to run away from the love he had lost or the grief that ate away at him. He could not be with me and yet he could not be parted from me. Until one fateful night, when he met the greatest maestro that had ever lived.

Chapter Thirteen

♪

Devlin's phone vibrated with a message.

> Meet me outside Kilburn Station at 11 a.m. W

What was the old man up to, he wondered? This detective thing had gone straight to his head. And signing with an initial, like he was in some Agatha Christie novel! Still, Walter was the only person willing to help him and there was no one else he could confide in. Who else would understand? They'd tell him to ditch it, or hand it in to the police. But Walter seemed to get it. The violin was worth more than that. Maybe he'd felt it, too, that intangible magic.

♪

At 11.05, outside Kilburn Station, an old silver Volvo 240 pulled up in front of Devlin, inviting him to take a step back in automotive history. Gabrielle was behind the wheel, looking even more beautiful than he remembered and just as unreachable. Walter pointed to the back door with a certain amount of urgency.

'Get in, get in,' he whisper-shouted through a crack in the window, which Devlin noticed he had to roll down manually.

'I didn't know they made these anymore,' he said, closing the door after him.

'They don't,' came the short reply from Gabrielle before signalling to rejoin the traffic. 'It's my father's old car.'

'Oh, cool.' Devlin racked his brain for something intelligent to say. *Say anything!* screamed a tiny voice in his head.

'Not great for the environment though, these old engines. I don't drive, myself. I mean, I *can* drive, but I choose not to. You know if more people used public transport, we could cut emissions by, um—'

'Devlin, you're rambling,' Walter interjected.

A silence descended while Gabrielle made her way onto the M4.

'So, are either of you going to tell me where we're going?'

'Gabrielle has kindly offered to take the violin to a colleague of hers in Bristol.'

'A dendrochronologist,' she clarified, although this clarified nothing for Devlin. Seeing his blank expression in the rear-view mirror, she elucidated. 'I'm hoping he can give us a more definitive answer on the age of your violin.'

'Oh, wow, that's a brilliant idea,' Devlin said, his shoulders relaxing slightly. Maybe he could put the worries of the break-in behind him. 'Where is the violin, by the way?'

'In the boot,' Walter answered, turning his head and winking.

Devlin squinted, but the non-verbal message wasn't getting through.

'Well, this is all great, but why am I here? I have to be in work for twelve.'

'Oh dear, you might have to chuck a sickie, then. We're going to visit an old contact of mine. By some stroke of luck, he's based just outside Bath, so I thought we'd get a lift with Gabrielle.' Walter leaned closer to Gabrielle and continued, sotto voce, 'My car's in the pound – it's a long story.'

'I hope they didn't cause too much damage when they broke in,' Devlin said, leaning forward between their two seats.

'You had a break-in?' Gabrielle asked, her eyebrow arching.

'Oh *that*, it was silly really,' he said, brushing the topic aside. 'I left my wallet on the passenger seat and they broke the window. An unforgivable mistake on my part. Old age,' he assured her. Walter was speaking as though he were rehearsing for a part in a pantomime and took to winking at Devlin when Gabrielle wasn't looking.

Finally, the penny dropped. Walter didn't want her to know about the break-in. It was a risky move, but he supposed there was no point alarming her. The criminal gang had his address and must have followed him that night to Walter's place, but seeing as they took the tube to

Gabrielle's, perhaps they'd lost them. Walter gave him a knowing smile in the rear-view mirror. That explained the note that morning too – it was safer to meet somewhere neutral in case they were surveilling the flat.

Devlin instinctively looked out the back window, searching for who knew what. How could you tell if you were being followed, when you hadn't the first clue what your assailants looked like? They had an advantage in that respect. He would have to be more vigilant from here on and think more like Walter, which was an odd prospect.

Speeding out of London on the A4, Devlin texted work and used the break-in as an excuse to take the day off. As the cityscape transformed into industrial parks and finally countryside, the unlikely trio were lulled along by some piano music that Devlin wasn't familiar with.

'What are we listening to?' he asked eventually, braving another sharp retort from the driver.

'Philip Glass.'

'Man's a genius,' added Walter, earning himself a rare smile from Gabrielle.

Devlin knew very little about classical music; he had managed to avoid it for most of his life. But he knew what he liked and there was no harm in saying so.

'I like it; it sounds like the notes are crashing into each other.'

'Exactly!' she enthused. It was the most animated she had been since they met. 'It's called "Mad Rush". There's something simultaneously contemplative and urgent about the piece; perfect for driving.'

Who even spoke like that? Devlin was so moved by her

passion, yet found himself dumbstruck by the way she expressed herself.

'Young Devlin here is something of a troubadour,' Walter said, taking on the role of the embarrassing uncle.

'Oh, really?' she asked.

'Once, maybe,' Devlin said, aiming for a tone somewhere between elusive and uber-talented.

'Professionally?'

'Does it make a difference?' What he'd meant to say was, making music was all about heart and soul and instinct – it was the record labels who wanted to put people into boxes. If you didn't have a record out, you were just a hobbyist. He'd known this kind of snobbery throughout his career, and it still irked him. That was what he'd meant to say. But all he'd managed to do was end the conversation. After he'd mumbled something about music being its own reward, she decided to put all of her concentration into the driving. They were facing into a two-hour journey of uncomfortable silence. Devlin figured it was probably for the best.

He must have nodded off, for when he woke up, Walter and Gabrielle were talking animatedly.

'Your violin is really quite interesting. The pattern and measurements are entirely distinct from any that have come under my observation.'

'You know, I had a feeling about it,' Devlin remarked. His hopes and fears were dancing a tango in his head. He wanted the violin to be special; he also wanted to not be chased by a criminal gang.

Gabrielle watched him for any sign of recognition, anything that would suggest he knew more about the violin than he was letting on. But it was awkward while trying to keep her eyes on the road.

'When I took it apart, there was no name. Ordinarily, the luthier would label it with his name. However, there was a serial number, so that could be an important clue.'

Devlin gulped. This was not his area of expertise, but the thought of opening up an instrument seemed like sacrilege.

'Gosh, it's all rather fascinating, isn't it? So how does it work, then?' Walter asked.

'Dendrochronology is a good way of trying to date the wood.'

Devlin watched Gabrielle's expression change as she took her eyes from the road for worryingly long periods, chatting enthusiastically about her trade.

'It's similar to dating a tree; you know how we use the rings to figure out its age? Every year a tree produces a ring. The dimensions vary from year to year, according to the environment in which they find themselves. Ring growth from the spring is wider and lighter, while the darker, late summer growth narrows before stopping, forming a sharp boundary. They are also affected by temperature and precipitation. All of this creates a pattern, like a barcode, and by comparing the pattern from a particular tree with already established chronologies, dendrochronologists can date the time at which the rings were formed to an exact year.'

'Isn't it wonderful what modern technology can do,' Walter said, before another silence engulfed them and Devlin could feel his eyelids growing heavy.

'Are you sure I'm not boring you?' she said, looking pointedly at Devlin in the rear-view mirror.

'Not in the slightest. I'm very interested in dedo—dendocosmology.'

She smirked a little too smugly for his liking.

'We often use dendrochronology to help support existing attributions for our high-value lots and these reports are then made available to buyers, as supporting documentation.'

'Proof of its vintage, as it were?' said Walter.

'Exactly. If we can date the wood, then we have another clue. After that it's a matter of putting all of the clues together and hopefully ascertaining who the maker was. Roger, my colleague, is also a restorer. He's the best in the business.'

Devlin began to wonder how they were going to pay for all of this high-tech testing, when Walter announced, 'We're almost there.'

'Where?'

'Larkfield Hall.'

♪

Gabrielle brought the old Volvo to a halt at what appeared to be a layby on a quiet country road, just outside a small village that Devlin had already forgotten the name of.

'Are you sure this is it?' she asked doubtfully.

There were two stone pillars, lacking the iron gates that must have joined them at one point in history.

'It does look a little … unprepossessing. Nevertheless, it does say Larkfield on the post box, so this must be the place.'

'I can drive up if you like—'

'No! No need at all, my dear, you've been far too accommodating as it is.'

Yet again, Devlin was forced to observe the conversation as a bystander.

'Well, if you're sure. I'll probably stay in Bristol tonight, so you'll have to make your own way back, I'm afraid.'

'With the violin?' Devlin asked, earning himself a hard stare from Walter and what could only be described as a look of impatience from Gabrielle.

'Thank you, Gabrielle,' said Walter, extricating himself from the passenger seat.

'I'll be in touch when I get back to London, see where we go from there,' she said, before blasting away a good portion of the ozone layer with a coughing exhaust pipe.

As she drove away, the two men appraised the long and winding avenue that lay ahead of them, lined with a forest of shrubs and trees on either side. Devlin was suddenly struck by how much his life had been turned upside down since getting his hands on the violin. Regardless of how peculiarly good it made him feel at the start, all it had done since was cause trouble. Although now that he thought of it, things only seemed to go downhill when he gave it to Gabrielle. And now *she* seemed to be in remarkably good humour. Everything was going her way and not his.

'How much are we paying Gabrielle for all this anyway? I'm not sure I can afford a dendo-whatyoumacallit,' Devlin said, shoving his hands in his pockets.

'That's not important right now.'

Walter began walking up the drive, but stopped when he realised that Devlin wasn't following.

'What's wrong?'

'What are we doing? It's obvious that it's the stolen violin. Before the break-ins, at least we could kid ourselves into thinking that it mightn't be, but now…'

Walter walked back towards him.

'Why aren't you running a mile from this, from me? For all we know, those guys could be dangerous. Like, really dangerous. And shouldn't we keep Gabrielle out of it?'

'Devlin – take a breath. Just breathe in and out, like this.' Walter pushed out his chest and sucked in a good amount of fresh Somerset air, encouraging Devlin to do likewise. 'Now, listen to me. I said I would help you and that's what I'm doing. I did some research at the library and this,' he said, pointing to the dense foliage behind him, 'is the home of Margot Clement's only living heir, Lord Ravenshaw.'

Devlin's eyes opened wide in understanding, but he kept breathing.

'Now, if we can convince him that this has all been one big—' he searched for a word '—misunderstanding, then maybe he will take the violin back and smooth things over with the authorities. No harm done.'

'Mr Pickering, I *am* impressed.'

'As for Gabrielle, it's best we keep her in the dark for now. Perhaps we shouldn't have involved her at all in the first place, but then again, there's still a chance – however slight – that this might not be the stolen violin. It could be a mix-up. I mean, how did the violin end up in the Lost and Found? What kind of criminal masterminds would steal a violin from a highly guarded auction house and then lose it in an airport?'

'When you put it like that, it does seem implausible.'

'Exactly. So we just have to keep our heads, work through our options methodically, and all will be well.'

Pep-talk over, the two men followed the path, which veered slightly to the right and downhill towards a picture-postcard view.

Walter paused. 'Last night I dreamt I went to Manderley again,' he said. Before them lay the most magnificent house, a vision of creamy Bath stone, all towers and balustrades, set in a lush, rambling garden that led down to a sparkling lake.

'Are you sure this isn't some kind of hotel?' Devlin asked, taking in the impossibly beautiful surroundings.

Neither man wanted to move in case they spoiled the beauty of the moment. However, the reverent silence was shattered by a gunshot, causing Devlin to grab Walter's arm.

'What the fuck was that?'

'Steady yourself, man. We're on an estate, there's only one thing it could be. Clay-pigeon shooting.'

Devlin began his deep breathing again, as Walter led them to the rear of the property, where they spotted a middle-aged man dressed unseasonably in tweed, ordering a tall young man to pull. Another shot tore through the air and yet another clay pigeon met a similar fate to the ones before. As though he sensed their presence, Lord Ravenshaw turned to see Walter and Devlin coming towards him, hands raised in greeting or perhaps surrender.

'I knew you lot would find me eventually.'

'Us lot, sir?' Devlin wasn't sure why he was addressing him as 'sir', but it seemed to fit the occasion.

'Reporters.'

Walter and Devlin looked at each other and silently agreed to play along.

'Yes, we're with the … um…'

'The *Evening … Times*,' Devlin offered.

Lord Ravenshaw had the physique of someone who enjoyed life to the fullest. A red bulbous nose, no doubt from a daily diet of wine, sherry and brandy. His waistline boasted of calorific dinners and his skinny legs were weary with keeping the whole show on the road.

'PULL!' he shouted yet again, as his assistant sent a clay pigeon flying into the air.

'Right, keep it brief, lads, it's almost lunchtime. I suppose you'll be wanting to know about this blasted violin, then.'

Devlin couldn't believe it. Walter was right. Lord Ravenshaw was the heir. Could it really be that simple?

'You must have been terribly upset?' Walter said, retrieving a notepad and pen from his rucksack.

'It was certainly something of a shock. But, as Lady Ravenshaw pointed out, thank heavens we decided not to auction the pink diamond!' The man guffawed to himself, finding his own class of silver lining. 'I shan't be using their services again, mind you. Poor show.'

'Indeed, a poor show,' Devlin echoed. 'Did you have a sentimental attachment to the violin? It was your great-aunt who bequeathed it, I believe?'

'Hah! This one's a ticket,' Ravenshaw said, looking at Walter. 'Poor old girl, I very much doubt she had the first clue what she owned. I believe it was a suitor who bought it for her. God knows why, she hadn't a note in her head. I imagine it was a case of what to buy a woman who has everything. Some wealthy Middle Eastern prince trying to impress her with a rare violin – the very idea. Why she couldn't find herself a nice English chap, I'll never know. Always had something for foreigners. PULL!'

Devlin and Walter gave each other a look that explained everything and yet clarified nothing. Was this really the person they wanted to return the violin to?

'So, if the police were to recover the violin…' Walter said suggestively.

'Nothing to do with me now. PULL!'

As another piece of clay fell victim to Lord Ravenshaw's impeccable aim, Devlin stepped closer.

'How do you mean, exactly? Sir.'

'Well, it belongs to Christie's now. I've already accepted the insurance payout. Can't beat cold hard cash, can you, eh? These estate houses don't keep themselves, you know,' he said, pointing back to Larkfield. 'Now, you'll be wanting a photo, I suppose.'

Walter and Devlin stood dumbstruck, trying to digest the information. The easy way out of handing the violin back to the owner was no longer an option. They were now faced with an international auction house, the police or a bunch of violent thugs – none of whom would be very understanding.

'Er, yes, of course,' Devlin said eventually, taking out his phone.

'No photographer, then? Good lord, journalism really has gone to the dogs. No money in it, I suppose. Ah well.'

And then he posed expertly, turning to the side and looping his thumb through a buttonhole in his waistcoat.

'Perfect. Thank you, sir,' Devlin said, as they turned to make the long journey home.

Chapter Fourteen

♪

Gabrielle parked on a side street and retrieved the violin from the boot. Roger's workshop backed onto a small courtyard with an old wooden door, which he had left off the latch for her. She had texted the night before but, even though she needed his help, she wasn't sure how she'd feel seeing him again. He'd been the closest thing she'd had to a best friend when they both started out at London's Guildhall. Once Max Daunt took her on as a pupil, things began to change. It can often happen to musicians – you suddenly become competitors and the friendship suffers. But there was more to it than that. There was an unspoken tension between them and, after everything came to a head all those years ago, too many unspoken words. She hesitated before crossing the threshold and silently prayed that this wasn't a bad idea.

'You're here!' he said, as she walked into the back of the shop.

'Gosh, it's so good to see you,' she said, giving him a

warm hug. It was as though all of the years just fell away and he was her old friend again. Maybe she'd been worrying for nothing.

'I couldn't believe it when I saw your message,' he said, standing back and observing the delicate changes that happen between adolescence and adulthood. 'How are you?' Before she had a chance to respond he added, 'I was so sorry to hear about your father.'

'Ah, yes. Thank you, Roger. I prefer not to talk about it, if that's okay.'

'Of course, naturally,' he said.

'You're busy,' she remarked, looking at all of the violins in various stages of repair lining the walls. He was one of only a handful of dendrochronology experts in the UK, and his expertise was in high demand.

'Thankfully,' he said. 'Cuppa?'

Gabrielle nodded and made a slow tour of his workshop, letting the timeless scent of wood and oil fill her senses. Violin restorers had been carrying out the same slow and methodical work for centuries and Roger was continuing that tradition in much the same way. There was a calm atmosphere and Gabrielle could feel the sinews around her neck and shoulders relax. Roger's tabby cat glided along the workbench in search of affection.

'Who's this?'

'Ah, that is Schubert,' Roger said, fetching a carton of milk from a mini fridge under the counter.

'Hello, Schubert,' she said, letting their noses touch.

'Here. Milk, no sugar?'

'You remembered,' she said, with a momentary pang of regret. Why had she cut him out of her life so completely?

He hadn't done anything wrong. *Yes, but the point was that he didn't do anything at all, wasn't it?* A voice came from the depths of her. She shook it off.

'I see you became a proper grown-up and got married,' she said, grasping the nettle. He'd sent her an invite, but she never replied. Thanks to Facebook, she got to see the magical day, frame by agonising frame, like some pathetic voyeur. At the time, all she could think was, well, isn't that nice? He got to have his happy ever after. The picture-perfect life.

'Oh, I didn't just get married. We went the whole hog and had a kid,' he said.

'Yikes,' she half-joked.

'I know. Not for the faint-hearted. How about you?'

'Oh.' Gabrielle waved the question away. No matter how many times it came up in conversation, she never seemed prepared for it. At this age, she should have a stock answer prepared. Something like *God no, lucky escape! I'm married to my work! Marriage is indentured servitude!*

'How's the wrist?' he asked, spotting the black support sleeve.

'I can predict oncoming rain, so it's become a kind of superpower, I suppose,' she said, instinctively rubbing it. The joke wasn't funny and neither of them laughed.

'Do you ever hear from—' Roger paused before saying his name '—Max?'

Gabrielle squirmed in her seat. She had hoped he would have the tact not to mention his name.

'Sorry, I shouldn't have—'

'No.' There was something in his tone that triggered memories from the past. He had a way of making her feel like there was something broken in her. All she ever wanted was to be normal, like Roger. But things were so far from normal, it took all of her energy to pretend that everything was fine and keep the façade on show.

'Forget I said anything. Let's see what you've brought me this time,' said Roger, diverting the conversation to one where they both felt at ease.

'I'm not sure,' she replied, opening the violin case. 'A retired teacher brought it to me. Apparently, he was an old acquaintance of Dad's. Along with a friend of his, Devlin,' she said. For some reason, this caused her to blush. She didn't want Roger to make any assumptions. But what assumptions would he make? It was just a client. She had to stop over-thinking things. 'Bit of an odd couple really,' she continued, watching him examine it. 'I assumed it was some worthless old thing they'd found in the attic, but then I played it.' She paused for dramatic effect.

'You played?'

She nodded enthusiastically. If there was anyone in this world who knew what that meant, it was Roger. They had both studied at the Guildhall Junior Department on a local authority scholarship, which at once made them outsiders as well as natural allies. He had always said that she was the more gifted musician and he seemed content to leave the playing behind when this alternative career beckoned. But underneath, Gabrielle had sensed an element of jealousy in the remark. She had always felt a bit bad for thinking that, but regardless of how effusive he was about her talent, there was a slight edge there. Though after everything that happened, she, too, had abandoned her career as a soloist.

'What do you think?'

He turned it around and around in his hands, inspecting it from every angle. Then he took out the bow and drew it across the strings, emitting the most heart-achingly beautiful sound.

'You hear it, too!' she said, seeing the look on his face.

'It's ... unusual, that's for sure. Let's see if we can find out a little more about it, shall we?' he said, losing no time in getting to work.

Gabrielle loved watching the process. It took a certain type of person to do it, as every measurement needed to be taken by hand. It was painstakingly precise.

'I used to use a microscope linked up to a computer, but now I almost always work from high-resolution images of the instrument and take the measurements on screen,' he said, placing the violin in something akin to a light box and adjusting the lens of his camera. 'I'll take measurements several times and compare the results, to ensure I get it right.'

Gabrielle squinted at the screen.

'I'm not sure I'd have the patience for this, or the eyesight.'

'Tracy says I should get my eyes insured,' he joked.

Gabrielle felt ashamed that she'd never met Tracy, but kept her feelings hidden.

'The most important thing is not to confuse cracks in the wood with growth rings. That's why I compare multiple sets to make it more accurate.'

Once he took the measurements, he began comparing them with other violins in his database.

'How long do you think it will take?' Gabrielle asked,

stroking Schubert on her lap and turning her head from side to side. She felt stiff after all the driving and fancied a bit of a walk.

'How long is a piece of string? It can take anything from ten minutes to hours. It's funny, I find that if I can't identify it quickly, then it won't happen at all. It depends on the era of the wood. Why don't you leave me to it? A watched kettle never boils and all that. Are you driving back to London?'

'No, I thought I'd book into a B&B down here, I'd like to bring the violin back with me.'

'Nonsense, you'll stay here with us. Tracy and Matthew will be home soon, they'll be delighted to see you.'

'Right, well, in that case I'll pick up some stuff for dinner,' she said, grabbing her bag.

'If you make lasagne, Matthew will be your friend for life!' he called after her.

♪

After a warm and wholesome evening with Roger's family, Gabrielle thought she would fall into sleep like a stone into water. Yet she lay in the boxroom, looking out at the moon, unable to switch her mind off. It was all so strange, the way Mr Pickering and Devlin had arrived at her shop. They weren't her usual clientele. As far as she could tell, neither of them could play or had any real interest in music. Although Devlin did seem to suffer an odd sort of separation anxiety every time he was parted from the violin. She had assumed it was of little value, yet when she drew the bow across the strings, she knew it was no ordinary violin. But the lack of markings left her clueless.

Giving up on sleep, she tiptoed down to the kitchen in search of camomile tea or hot chocolate. While the kettle boiled, she noticed a light coming from Roger's workshop.

'What are you doing up at this hour?' she asked.

'I could ask the same of you. Is the bed okay? I told Tracy we should get a memory foam—'

'No, not at all, it's perfect. I think I'm just over-tired or something. Tea?'

Roger shook his head, pointing to two half-full cups on the worktop. He was still examining the high-resolution images on the computer screen with the violin by his side.

'Have you discovered anything?'

'It's the damnedest thing,' he began, biting his lip and shaking his head. 'The dates are pointing to the early eighteen-hundreds, so we know it's old. But the spruce just doesn't match up to any of the forests in central Europe that would have been typically used in the last two centuries. And certainly not from *Il Bosco Che Suona*,' he added with a rueful grin.

'The Musical Woods,' Gabrielle translated. It was the nickname given to the forest in the Alps where Stradivari sourced the best trees that would eventually become priceless violins.

'So, what are you thinking, that it was made outside of Europe?'

'Not necessarily. The best violin makers tended to use wood from the same forest region. There are cases where I've been able to identify the exact tree that was used.

But this one just doesn't match with anything I have on the database.'

'Oh, that's disappointing.'

'Hmm. It's a bit of a mystery, your violin,' he said, taking it up and playing several notes. 'And a thing of pure beauty; clear as a bell and strong, too.'

'You don't think—' Gabrielle hesitated. If she said it out loud, it would give the idea weight and it really was a foolish idea.

'What is it?'

Taking her phone out of her pocket, she sat beside him and pulled up an article she had read the day before. It was the piece about the stolen violin from Christie's. She handed it to Roger and let him scroll down the page.

'You don't seriously think—'

'No, not really. I mean it couldn't be. You should see the two blokes that brought it in – a retired teacher and some guy in overalls. They're hardly a pair of criminal masterminds.'

Roger was looking at the image of the stolen violin.

'Do you see something?' she asked.

He turned to his computer screen and within seconds, he had a full image of the violin on the screen.

'It's closely related in style,' he said, 'and with an identical body length.' He was leaning so far forward that he looked as though he might fall into the screen. 'The scroll displays that small extra turn into the eye, see?' he said.

Gabrielle was holding her breath.

'But the hue – see here? It's much darker in colour. Besides, the dates don't add up. Obviously, it's difficult to tell from a photo, but a Strad? I don't think so.'

Gabrielle exhaled a mixture of relief and disappointment. Identifying a violin of that value could have made her name – her career. But the thought of getting mixed up in one of the greatest violin thefts this century made her understandably nervous.

'It was a silly idea,' she said, putting her phone back in her pocket. 'It was just the timing that made me curious. And there's no way they could have pulled off a theft that sophisticated.'

'Not that silly. In our business, we have to go with our gut so much of the time. Like I said, there are similarities. It could be that this violin was made by an apprentice, mimicking the style of the master luthier. You might be onto something. The amount of times I've been approached with a possible Stradivarius, and a quick dating of the wood shows it was made several years after his death. It's the difference between tens of millions at auction.'

'So, where to next?' she asked.

'Well, depending on how much time and money your clients are willing to devote to finding its provenance…' He trailed off.

'They may be time-rich, but cash-poor.'

'So often the case. But if it were me, I'd be booking a flight to Italy.'

Chapter Fifteen

♪

Walter and Devlin's return journey was funereal in its ambience. They hardly spoke on the walk back into the village to get the bus to Bath and eventually the train back to London.

'Well, we've yet to hear back from Gabrielle. That will clear things up one way or the other,' Walter said. He was opening several packets of sugar and emptying the contents into his tea.

'I still don't know what to do. Lord Clay-Pigeon-Shooter doesn't even want it back and if the auction house finds out I have it, I'll be arrested for handling stolen goods.'

'Unless the people who originally stole it find you first.'

'Yes, thank you for bringing that up, Mr Pickering. I'd almost forgotten that I was being targeted by a criminal gang!'

'You're going to have to start calling me Walter if we're going to continue on this … journey. I'm not your teacher anymore.'

'What journey? I have to get rid of it. Or try to arrange a drop-off.' Devlin didn't belong in this kind of world. It wasn't like scoring some hash as a teenager and feeling like the hard man. This was properly dangerous.

'Just be patient – wait until we have all the facts.'

'All I wanted was a birthday present for my girlfriend. I should've just got her an engagement ring. Who knew that marriage would have been the easier option?'

Walter studied his young friend. The stress of being pursued by an international crime ring, the police and a big insurance company was hiding something much deeper.

'You're thinking of getting married, then?'

'Not anymore.'

'Oh, I am sorry.'

'I … well – we've lived together for years, and it seemed like the obvious next step, but I just … couldn't.'

'I used to live with my mother.'

'You know what I mean.'

Walter couldn't say that he did. To his old, sentimental ears, it sounded like the most unromantic reason in the world to make such important vows.

'Why don't you tell me about—'

'Melissa.'

'We've got time.'

Devlin felt slightly reluctant to tell an ex-teacher who was on the verge of suicide just a few days ago all about his relationship status. Then he figured, what harm would it do? Speaking to Karim at work wasn't the same. Married friends always wanted you to get married, too, so you could all be stuck together. But maybe Mr Pickering – Walter – would be different.

'I thought we were in love.'

Walter nodded with the briefest of smiles.

'But I'm not sure I even know what love is anymore.'

Walter pursed his lips thoughtfully. Sometimes the best way to help someone was to resist the urge to give advice and just listen. Eventually, they'd come up with their own solutions or, at the very least, discover why they were so unhappy. The sorry truth was that Walter didn't have any relationship advice to offer.

Just when the silence was becoming too much, Devlin spoke.

'There was someone else, you see, a long time ago…' he trailed off. Just thinking about her made his chest feel tight. Devlin had concluded that once your world comes crashing down, you have two choices: talk about it or never speak about it again. Leave the past buried. He looked up at Walter and saw the soft wrinkles around his concerned eyes. *Maybe it would be good to talk it out?* Frowning slightly, he changed his mind. There was such a thing as too much honesty.

'The thing is, I don't even think she loved me. I mean, she cared about me, but I always had the feeling that I was the wrong guy for her. And when I think about it, that came from her. I thought it was just typical relationship stuff at first; when you try and change little things about each other – like knocking off the jagged edges so you rub along better together. But now, I think she just wanted me to be somebody else.'

He exhaled heavily and leaned his head against the window.

'So maybe the violin was the right option after all...' Walter said, looking out at the speeding countryside.

Devlin smiled, then threw his eyes up to heaven, and they passed the rest of the journey in companionable silence.

Chapter Sixteen

♪

Verity stood in the apartment above Wilding's. It felt like kismet – that the violin had led her here, of all places. It was relatively easy to hack into Heathrow Lost and Found to retrieve Devlin's address. Or rather, it was relatively easy to find a hacker on the dark web. Then it was a small matter of spying on his comings and goings, which led to the old man, and once she followed him to the Portuguese café, the young woman fell easily into the mix. Verity followed her home and, once she saw the name above the shop, knew instinctively that her journey had finally come full circle. The only problem was, the violin was nowhere to be found. She turned on her heel and heard the sound of shattered glass cracking under her step.

'Keep an eye on her. They must be hiding it somewhere,' she said.

'Where are you going?' asked Jack, the beefier of the two.

Verity cast a final glance around the apartment before speaking, as though some clue might lead her to the violin.

'I have business to attend to.'

An hour's train ride out of London and Verity had arrived in Oxford. Despite the fact that she was carrying a portfolio case with a priceless artwork inside, she decided to walk to the university. The spires reaching skyward led the way and before long, she was walking down a cobbled lane, lined with bicycles and shaded by overhanging trees as ancient as time. A brown wooden door with a mediaeval arch led discreetly to the office she sought out. A gold-plated sign on the door told her she was in the right place.

Professor Sofia Alves – History of Art

Verity smiled to herself. She knocked on the door once before entering.

'*Dios mío!*'

The woman behind the mahogany desk, with bright red curls piled on top of her head, jumped up as soon as she saw Verity enter.

'Hello, my old friend,' Verity said, kissing Sofia on both cheeks. The room was poorly lit by the daylight that strained to shine through the diamond leaded windows. A green lamp on the desk shone a warm glow on a stack of papers with red markings in the margins.

'So, you are a bona fide professor now? You've gone straight!'

Sofia gave a throaty laugh, inviting Verity to take a seat.

'I am a respectable, law-abiding woman now,' she said, mock-serious, before opening a drawer under her desk and taking out a bottle of brandy. She poured two generous glasses and handed one to her guest. 'To old times,' she said, clinking her glass against Verity's.

'And a married woman,' Verity said, before swallowing a mouthful of brandy.

'Ah, yes.' Sofia looked down at her left hand where a simple gold band shone. 'It was time to settle down,' she said. 'And you?'

Verity was looking around the room, the wood-panelled walls, the antique tomes, the overwhelming air of stuffiness and tradition. She ignored the question.

'You've done very well for yourself,' Verity said, but it didn't sound like a compliment.

'Thank you. It's a surprise to see you,' Sofia said, which didn't sound much like a compliment either.

Verity drained her glass and put it back on the desk. A student wheeled their bicycle past the window and the clock on the wall ticked nervously.

'I've brought a painting,' Verity said, reaching for her portfolio case.

'Oh.' Sofia took a sip of brandy. 'I don't really do that kind of thing anymore.'

Verity cocked her head to the side.

'What do you mean?' she scoffed.

'I mean that I like not being in prison.'

Sofia had taught Verity everything she knew about the art world. What to buy, when to buy and, most importantly, who to sell to. They had first met at Sofia's gallery in Barcelona. She was an art dealer with an impeccable eye and a moveable moral compass. Verity decided very early on that selling antiques would not earn her the kind of money she would need to get her violin back. She needed to become a part of the art world, where the risks were great and the profits greater. With no formal training, Verity formed a small network of contacts around the world who could educate her. Sofia introduced her to her lover at the time, an art forger. With a little creative revisionism, such as providing long-lost letters between dealers and buyers, they faked the provenance of artworks by Chagall, Ernst and even Warhol. They made millions together. They drank champagne and felt no remorse. In their eyes, they were cheating those who made a fortune cheating others.

'He was released after ten years, wasn't he?' Verity casually swept aside the fact that Sofia's lover had ended up in jail.

'Why do you think I moved here? I had to start my life over. I suggest you do the same.' Sofia stood up and took the glasses and bottle away, leaving them on the shelf behind her.

'I don't need you to do anything illegal,' Verity said. 'I just need you to find a buyer for this.'

She placed a frameless canvas on the desk, pushing aside the student papers that Sofia was grading.

'It's a Lowry.'

'Is it, though?'

Verity smiled but did not answer.

'I can't help you.'

'I need the money, Sofia.'

A moment passed before she replied.

'Like I said, I can't help you. Even if I wanted to, I don't have the contacts anymore. I left that life behind.' She folded her arms and looked out of the window to the alleyway where fallen leaves danced in the wind. 'Besides, last time I checked, you were not short of money.'

'Let's just say I've had some rather large expenses of late.'

Sofia stared her down.

Verity hadn't been able to tell a soul up to that point. But her ego rushed to inform her old friend of her latest exploits.

'Did you hear about the break-in at Christie's warehouse?'

Sofia's curls jolted on her head with the shock.

'That was you?!'

A warm feeling of pride bloomed in Verity's chest.

'And it wasn't cheap.'

'No. I don't imagine it was.' Sofia grabbed the bottle and the glasses and sat back down at the desk. She poured them both another glass. 'So, you're still after that cursed violin, eh?'

'And I would have it now if it weren't for…' Verity bit her tongue. She'd been stupid to hire two separate teams for the job. The Christie's theft had required flair, expertise and precision. It had cost her almost every centime she had. And so she'd hired Denis and Val to do the easy bit – transporting it from London to Montréal. *Imbeciles!*

'Verity, when will you give up this obsession?'

Verity inhaled sharply. Sofia never understood and never would.

'Will you find me a buyer for this painting?'

'I told you, I don't have the contacts anymore.' Sofia drank wearily from her glass. It felt like a ghost from her past had come back to haunt her.

'Might I suggest you find new ones? It would be a shame for your employers here to find out your real name, wouldn't it, Maria Sanchez?'

'You wouldn't—'

'I'm a desperate woman, Maria. Who knows what I'll do?'

With that, Verity stood and pushed the painting towards her old friend.

'Same terms as usual. You'll get a nice cut. I'll be back next week to collect.'

She knocked back the brandy and walked out without saying another word.

Chapter Seventeen

♪

'I think you owe me an explanation,' Gabrielle said, holding a broken lock in her hand.

Walter and Devlin stood mute on the threshold of the shop on Crawford Place.

'This is my fault—' Walter began.

'You broke in, did you?' she asked, turning the atmosphere from frosty to glacial.

'No,' Devlin stepped forward and into the shop, not wanting to have this conversation on the street. 'This is all on me, Gabrielle. It's not Mr Pickering's fault.'

'Well, it *was* my idea not to say anything…' Walter confessed.

'Look, this is all very touching to watch, but it doesn't change the fact that my home has been turned upside down.'

Devlin stepped forward. 'I'm sorry, truly. Please, let us help you tidy up,' he said, righting the coffee table that had been turned over.

'NO!' Gabrielle shouted, startling them all by her outburst. 'No, thank you. I'd rather do it myself,' she continued, looking more agitated than Devlin had ever seen her.

'Are you sure? It's no trouble—'

'No, no,' she repeated, now wringing her hands. 'You won't know where everything goes—'

'You could just tell us—'

'Please,' she said, laying a firm hand on his forearm. He saw a look in her eyes that made him pause. 'It's just better if I do it myself,' she said.

He nodded. 'Of course,' he said, stepping back. It felt like he'd stepped on a landmine. Gabrielle, like Walter, was not all she appeared to be. However, it only took a moment for her to regain her composure.

'Thankfully I was still in Bristol when it happened. God knows what they would have done if I was here.'

'So you still have the violin?' Devlin asked, wincing at how uncaring that sounded.

'Yes, Devlin, I still have the violin,' she assured him, and did not seem to take it personally. 'Whoever broke in here wants your violin, which leads me to believe there's something you're not telling me.'

Walter and Devlin gave each other a meaningful look. It was time to come clean.

'I didn't steal it, if that's what you are thinking,' Devlin pointed out. 'It's all been a big misunderstanding.' He felt like a broken record.

'What he actually means is, we're sorry. We should have told you everything from the start, it's just we couldn't be sure that this was, well, THE violin.' Walter whispered the last bit.

'THE violin?' Gabrielle arched an eyebrow.

'The one they stole from Christie's.'

Devlin had to sit down on the Chesterfield to try and regain his composure. What had he gotten himself into? And now he was dragging all of these innocent people along with him. The sense of dread carved out a hollow in the pit of his stomach and filled it with blackness.

'Hang on, where did you get this violin?' she asked, trying to shut the door to the shop and failing, as the lock had been busted. In the end, she dragged a chair from behind the counter and propped it up against it.

Devlin had his elbows on his knees and his head in his hands. His voice came out muffled.

'Lost and Found.'

'What?' Gabrielle said, a tone of disbelief twinned with curiosity.

'At Heathrow. I was looking for a birthday present for … someone. We always have a root around there, all the staff. They're supposed to wait three months, in case the owner comes back to claim it and then they get shipped off to Germany for a big auction. People bid on suitcases and bags – without even knowing what's in them. It's like some kind of travel lucky dip.'

'But your violin wasn't in a suitcase?'

'No. They said a passenger dropped off a sports bag when she realised it wasn't hers. She must have mixed it up with someone else's before boarding. Anyway, she had already opened it and, well, I saw the violin case and thought it would be perfect.'

Silence descended as they were all lost in their own thoughts.

'And what makes you think this is THE stolen violin? It could belong to anyone who was passing through Heathrow that day.' Gabrielle leaned on the counter, willing Devlin to look at her.

'Well, it's obvious, isn't it?' Walter replied. 'Whoever broke in here broke into our flats, too. They must be on to us. I don't know, maybe they found CCTV of Devlin taking the violin. I mean, who else could it be?'

'Wait,' Devlin said. 'What did your friend say, the dendo … the dendacraniologist?'

'The dendrochronologist. Roger. Well, that's just it – his tests were inconclusive. But trust me; if anyone in the world could spot a Stradivari, it's him. He's one of the top experts in his field.'

'So what does this mean? The robbers stole the wrong violin? Or what we thought all along, this violin is just a worthless antique and they've got the wrong man?'

'Oh, this violin isn't worthless, I can tell you that,' Gabrielle said, her eyes lighting up with the possibilities. 'But I don't know why they are chasing you.'

'Well, they're chasing all of us now, aren't they?' Devlin reminded her.

'So, what now?' Walter asked.

'We need to find out the true provenance of this violin,' Gabrielle said, 'and fast.'

Devlin got to his feet.

'Eh, I'm sorry, have you just missed the part where we're being chased by a criminal gang for something that isn't even what they think it is?' Devlin's mangled words echoed throughout the room. A poet he was not.

'Perhaps, by proving that the violin maker was someone other than Stradivarius, we can get them off our backs?' Walter said, looking from one to the other.

'Exactly,' Gabrielle agreed.

Devlin just shook his head, quietly declaring them both mad. 'I need to get to work,' he announced, reaching for the violin case, which had been sitting on the counter all along. Gabrielle put her hand on it and their eyes locked.

'Where are you taking it?' she asked.

'Last time I checked, the violin belonged to me,' he said, challenging her.

'And last time I checked, people called the police when their home was burgled. Shall I call them now? Perhaps you'd like to explain everything to them?'

They both still had their hands on the violin. Gabrielle found it difficult to control her temper around him and she wasn't entirely sure why.

She took her hand away and decided to play the long game. He would eventually realise that he had no choice. She was the only one who could help them.

'Look, we all need time to calm down,' Walter began, opening his wallet. 'Miss Wilding, you've been very kind and I can only apologise again that we were not more forthcoming from the start. It was never my intention to involve you in something … unsavoury.'

Gabrielle tapped the counter with her fingernails and bit her lip in contemplation. 'You're right,' she said eventually. 'I'm still in a bit of shock, to be honest. I have to get a locksmith and tidy upstairs. Of course it's up to you to decide what you want to do with the violin.' She directed this at Devlin, who was moving the chair from in front of the door. 'Just don't take too long. These people, they don't exactly seem to be the patient type.'

Devlin nodded and ducked out into the rain-slicked streets, a very sorry-looking figure. Walter followed, equally downcast.

♪

Gabrielle climbed the stairs back up to her flat. It wasn't the welcome home she had been expecting – the place was completely turned over. It would take forever to get everything clean and arranged exactly how she needed it to be.

'Satie?' she called out, walking through the living room and tiptoeing past the broken glass on the floor. 'It's okay, you can come out now,' she assured him. Several plaintive meows came from the tiny attic space, where Satie often retreated through a small gap in the ceiling above the kitchen cupboards. He pounced down and landed in her arms in the most dramatic fashion.

'There you are, you clever boy,' she said, running her fingers through his coat. 'I don't suppose you can give me an e-fit of the perpetrators by any chance?' She smiled, kissing the top of his head. His steady purrs gave her a sense of calm amid the chaos.

Neither Devlin nor Walter had asked her how she knew the break-in was connected with the violin – they had simply assumed – which was rather fortunate because it meant that she didn't have to tell them about the email that had landed in her inbox from user V514@yahoo.com that began with the line: *You are in possession of an item that rightfully belongs to me.*

Chapter Eighteen

♪

THE VIOLIN

London, 1820

If I knew little of life, as a young Irish girl with very little worldly experience, I knew even less of death. I said my prayers and hoped that I would see heaven, but now I was neither above nor below. I was trapped in a limbo crafted by a human hand. William had taken me to London, where he found work with a French émigré who had a shop on Prince's Street. To demonstrate his skill to his new employer, William opened my case, picked up the bow and attempted to play. He was full of doubt – about himself, about what he'd done – and my sound resonated with it. He put me down and a solitary tear ran down his cheek. It is only when a violin is played aloud that what the luthier has created is finally revealed to him. And whatever he had created, it was not something he could control.

'You have some skill,' said the man, 'but the tone on this

violin is quite hollow.' When he made to pick me up, William almost growled at him.

'She's not for playing,' he said, gruffly.

'Very well,' said the man. 'Your references are good. If only the same could be said for your manner. I'll give you a month's trial.'

Of course, William proved the man's decision to be a good one and he worked every waking hour, as though chiselling and rasping could somehow put distance between himself and his broken heart. But how could it, when he kept me always by his side, a constant reminder? I was sewn into the fabric of his life, for better or worse. Until one day, when he was delivering a violin to a customer in Leicester Square. He always carried me with him and refused to leave me in his workshop with his other violins. In the lobby of the Hotel Sablonière et Provence, there was quite a furore. As it turned out, the great Niccolò Paganini had arrived in London, and he had taken rooms at that very hotel. There was a crowd of people gathered around him as he remonstrated to the concierge in colourful bursts of Italian and French, peppered with the odd English phrase.

'But Sir, we have given you our premiere suite with views to the garden,' the concierge said in a placating tone.

'*Monsieur*, the windows are so covered with soot, it's impossible to see *il giardino*!' replied Paganini.

William had to agree; London, with its squalor, was indeed a shock to new arrivals.

'And as for the rats, they have made free to nibble the strings of my violin!'

'Monsieur Paganini, please accept our sincere apol—'

'*Basta*!' he cried, storming through the foyer, only to halt directly in front of William, having spotted the violin case tucked under his arm.

'Buongiorno,' he greeted him. 'It is a pleasure to acquaint a fellow violinist.'

I could sense William's excitement but also his awe in the presence of such a famed and celebrated musician. He was an intimidating sight to behold, tall and lean, his body all angles, like a crooked old man. Long, flowing black hair floated down the back and sides of his head, and his eyes were so vivid that it seemed as though he could see into one's very soul.

'No violinist, sir. Just a luthier.'

'*Just* a luthier? Never say such a thing!' Paganini said, reaching out to shake William's hand. 'You are the craftsman of magic,' he said with a wink. 'And what is this?' he asked, his gaze falling on me.

'Oh, she's … mine.'

Paganini regarded him with a deep curiosity.

'May I?' he asked, making to open the case.

'No!' William replied firmly, which only aroused the maestro's curiosity further. What could he do? Here he was, by some strange twist of fate, standing in a foyer with the most gifted violinist that had ever walked the earth. Holding this secret had kept him isolated from the world and now he had a chance to share it with the one person who might be open-minded enough to understand. William had heard the rumours. Everyone had. That he had made a pact with the devil: his soul for success. He had such a strange look about him, even in my strange, disembodied state, I found him unnerving, and so it was easy to believe that his talent was more than human. It was supernatural, devilish and spellbinding. The audience swooned before him. His eerily long fingers lent him a dexterity that was unparalleled.

They went to his rooms, where the Italian poured them both a generous glass of brandy before sitting on a chintz chaise longue by the aforementioned sooty window.

'Play,' he demanded.

William's hands shook and he fumbled with the clasp. I had no idea where this meeting would lead and my strings were taught with tension. William lifted me carefully and tucked me lovingly under his chin. I knew he must have been terribly nervous to play. He struck a chord, but his fingers grasped my neck so tightly that the sound split the air. Paganini winced.

'Allow me,' he said, getting up from his seat.

It was as though time itself froze. William could not let me go. I was afraid to leave him. And yet there was something about the entire thing that felt like déjà vu. It felt as though it were supposed to happen because it had already happened. I felt myself slacken and, in turn, so did William. As though under some kind of spell, he lifted his head, reached out his arms and just like that, my fate was sealed.

The moment Niccolò drew the bow across my strings, I felt my breastbone soar with the notes he played. I filled the room with my voice; it was as though my singing voice was amplified a hundred thousand times. I finally found my *raison d'être*. William observed us with tears in his eyes. I didn't belong in a dark case, hidden away from the world, he knew that. He knew that in Paganini's possession my voice could touch the souls of countless people around the world.

When he finished playing, the maestro came to him and bent his head forward, so they were eye to eye. With his long fingers, he wiped the tears from William's eyes and spoke the words that only he could.

'Surely you did not create such a wondrous instrument to keep it locked away?'

William shook his head.

'My dear luthier, I have played many, many violins. But this one, she is ... like the soul of a prima donna.' He held me in his hands and inspected the finer details. 'And yet you have not stamped your name anywhere.'

It was some time before William spoke.

'I made this violin as a wedding gift.' The deep lines that formed on William's face were haunted with ghosts of a love that could never be. 'She was murdered.'

'I see,' said the maestro. He had felt my presence when he played. Renowned for his playing, it was his ear that made him so incredibly gifted. 'There is a touch of the dark arts about this violin,' he said, not as a question.

'Not dark,' said William. 'Never that.'

Paganini poured them both another brandy.

'I will tell you the story, but by God, you will hardly believe it.'

A smile formed on Paganini's lips.

'*Vedremo*. We shall see...'

As the hours passed and the candles burned down to the wick, William told our story. Moved by the luthier's tale, Paganini took a blank sheet of paper and began to jot down staves with musical notes in pencil.

'You have heard of the Bach motif?' he asked.

William shook his head.

'He used musical nomenclature to spell out his name in his scores. A trifle conceited, but then many of us composers are.'

'I'm not sure I understand your meaning, sir.'

'*Precisamente!* It is a cypher, a cryptogram, hidden in the music.'

'But, sir, I cannot read music,' William explained, but the maestro was not listening. He continued to hum and scribe for another quarter hour.

'There,' he said, handing William the piece of paper. 'Your names were never joined in life, but now they will live on forever in these notes.'

William looked at the page, filled with black circles and lines, crotchets and quavers.

'I have given this piece the title "*Bellezza Nascosta*" – "Hidden Beauty". The riposte spells out the letters of your names: C-L-A-R-A and W-I-L-L-I-A-M. Clever, isn't it?' he asked, in a self-congratulatory tone.

For the first time since Clara's death, William felt a smile spread across his face.

'Thank ye, I thank ye very much indeed. How much do I owe you for such a thing?'

Paganini paused for a moment.

'Will you entrust your beautiful violin to me? Let us perform in front of the grandest audiences in the world together. You must know it is her destiny!'

He could have refused. Wanted to refuse. But he could sense the stirring in my frame. My breath quickened and the strings vibrated with motion. I wanted to go. I wanted to experience the life I had been denied. A life unlike any I could have ever imagined.

'I will pay you any price,' he added.

Finally, William spoke.

'There is no price, only a promise. You will return her to me.'

♪

We travelled to Vienna. At first, there was discord between us. I was bereft at leaving William and not a little frightened by what fate might have in store for me with this strange man.

When he played me, he complained that I dug into his collarbone too much, that my shape was not to his liking. Well, as you can imagine, this put us on an immediate wrong footing. He carried me about, locked in my case like a little coffin, and refused to take me out, preferring instead to play his Amati. But two days before his opening night in Vienna, he lost his preferred violin in a gambling debt. And so it was that we shared our debut together.

He turned the pegs to tune me, but he found that I was already perfectly in tune. I shimmered with delight as he drew the bow achingly slowly across my strings with the lightest of touches, followed by fiendishly quick pizzicato where he plucked the strings with his strangely shaped fingers. Pausing for a moment to look at his reflection in the dressing-room looking glass, he stared at us both as though determining how we would look together in front of an audience. In his long black frock coat with his gaunt features and wild black hair, he had a ghoulish air about him. I burned, all russet curves, at his side. I despised his vanity, but like so many of the women who sat in the front row, I was drawn to his electrifying passion. There are very few people in this world, in any given lifetime, that surpass the perceived limitations of human endeavour, and when you find yourself in the presence of one such person, you abandon clear thinking for the chance to bathe in their glow.

He knew at once that I was special, but what he doubted was that we could share a stage together. Would I bend to his will or would I betray his hidden secrets? He looked at me and I could swear he saw past the wood and strings, right into my very soul. Niccolò recalled William's tale. He had heard of such things; the great Tatini's dream of 1713, in which he made a pact with the devil for his soul. It mattered little whether the story was true. Such tales created legends and my bewitching Paganini sought to craft his own infamy ... perhaps with my help.

We took to the stage and there was an immediate hush. His eyes, greedy for adulation, scanned the crowd. His mere presence had caused a young woman at the front of the stage to faint. As he played the opening notes of 'Le Streghe' – 'The Witches' – I made an unbecoming, scratching sound. He immediately stopped and looked down at me as though he might break me in two. He had no fear of a beautiful young woman – would eat two for breakfast, he joked – and he proceeded to bring me to heel with a forceful playing of 'The Witches'.

A battle of wills ensued as each fought for dominance over the other, and it was this fury and passion that intensified his performance. As he played with ever increasing complexity, pushing me to a point where I thought my bones would buckle and the strings would break, I came to understand his *raison d'être*. He played not merely for money and notoriety, although he craved both. He played with such skill for skill's sake. The performer in me understood. He wanted to push himself, as well as me, to the boundaries of his ability and beyond if he could. He wasn't satisfied with being merely another gifted violinist. He was a revolutionary. He wanted to take all of the rules and break them into pieces, which he would then pick up and create an entirely new repertoire. This was what his audience was responding to. His daring to explore the unknown and to take them with him.

Finally, I acquiesced and as he felt me slacken into his embrace, he held me with all the tenderness of an adoring lover. We soared that night; we fought, fell in love, became something not entirely human and not entirely divine. We were somewhere in between, and the music we created together captivated audiences for years to come.

Berlioz compared him to a blazing comet, while Goethe fell back exhausted following one of our performances in Paris and said it hit him like a meteor. My Niccolò was certainly closer to the heavens than anyone, but still people feared his devilish reputation. *'You draw a deep breath after he has departed and ask yourself if what you have just seen and heard be not a dream,'* one critic wrote. Even Mendelssohn and Schumann exalted his virtuosity, the former breathlessly enthusing, *'Paganini's faultless execution is beyond imagination. His style utterly unique…'*

We achieved greatness together. And so it was that when he fell ill, I began to think of my return to William.

Perceiving my longing to be reunited with William, he began to compose his last will and testament. He showed it to his son, Achille, who could hardly make out his hand.

'Take the violin to Signor Rathbone,' he said, breathlessly. 'He will know what to do.'

In his final hours, Paganini waved away the priest who had come to read his last rites. Not for one moment did he believe that he was at death's door. And so, when he had breathed his last, no one would bury him. His corpse was grotesquely moved from one part of Europe to the next, fuelling ever more rumours and earning him the title 'The Devil's Violinist'. Only I knew different. But who could I tell?

1841

Achille, following his father's wishes, travelled to London. The violin was to be returned to a William Rathbone. He was said to have opened a workshop in the heart of Soho. My soul soared at the thought of being reunited with him. Although I hated the darkness, I hardly felt the crossing on the boat or the carriage ride to central London. The area was a bustling centre for harp, violin and pianoforte makers. There was an uninterrupted avenue of shops two miles long from west to east, taking in the High Street, St Giles. Yet, when he arrived at the shop on Prince's Street, it was boarded up. On further enquiry, it appeared the luthier in question had perished six months before.

A coldness crept over me. Was it true? My William,

dead? How could he leave this world without me? I felt brittle and exposed. I needed to escape the confines of my wooden box. Forced to live eternally without him, how could I carry on? Achille, a sensitive man, went to visit William's grave. It was a small paupers' churchyard in St Anne's. I wanted him to leave me there, stretched on his final resting place. How could my story continue when his was at an end? I heard Achille speaking to the vicar and before I knew it, we were inside the church. He signed his name in the book of records. There was nothing more to be done. His respects had been paid. We were leaving London again, moving further and further away from where my soulmate lay frozen in the ground. I had no inkling of where we were going to next and at that point, I no longer cared.

Chapter Nineteen

♪

Gabrielle woke with two uncomfortable sensations, a pinching crick in her neck and drool running down the side of her mouth. No, three uncomfortable sensations: Satie was sitting on her head.

'Oof,' came the involuntary groan as she tried to straighten herself. She'd forgotten to draw the curtains and the sunlight was almost blinding her. That's when she saw the message on the dressing table mirror.

WE KNOW YOU HAVE IT

Written in her red lipstick. She mustn't have noticed it before. She buried her face in the crook of her arm. Who was V anyway? An idiot, if she thought Gabrielle was going to be so easily threatened. Thanks to her father, she'd had plenty of experience dealing with shady types. She grabbed her phone off the nightstand and tapped in her pin before clicking on the email again.

Miss Wilding,

You are in possession of an item that rightfully belongs to me. You are aware by now that I know everything about you, so there's no point in running to the police. Besides, I can see that you are a businesswoman at heart, so let us not waste any further time. $20,000 will be transferred into your account next week, a generous commission, you'll agree. I prefer not to use force, but my associates possess no such qualms. One week.

V

Anyone could have gotten her email, and it was hardly impressive detective work to locate her flat over the shop. But why were they bribing her rather than Devlin? Yes, she was the expert in antique instruments, but the violin didn't belong to her. Still, anyone could see that Walter and Devlin were in way over their heads. Such a valuable instrument deserved to be appreciated by people who understood its value.

The trouble was that this V person was most likely a private collector, so it would probably spend the next hundred years in a vault gathering dust if she handed it over to them. But more importantly – she would never discover the violin's provenance if V got their hands on it. Did they also believe that it was a Stradivarius? All of his violins had been accounted for in the fifties, but valuers were always happy to go along with the idea that there were more missing Strads out there, hidden in attics or buried in basements. The story alone would increase its value and Gabrielle could be the one to uncover the mystery. This would make her career. It would remove the stain of her father's making that still threatened to tarnish the Wilding name. It would prove to everyone who had ever underestimated her that she had what it took. That she could spot something special. This industry was all about reputation, and discovering the true identity of this luthier would make hers. Everyone else was out for themselves, why shouldn't she be, too? This violin could erase the past and make her brand new again. She continued to persuade herself with these arguments, knowing all the while that it was the money she really needed. Wilding's would soon go under; there was no denying that fact when she looked at her bank account. And then she would lose her home as well as her livelihood. If she could just figure out a way to play both sides – let V think that she was cooperating with them, while letting Walter and Devlin believe she was working for them.

Satie, who had been fastidiously cleaning his right paw at the end of the bed, cast a cold eye in her direction.

'What? It's only a matter of time before the thieves catch up with them. I'm doing Walter a favour.' She wasn't sure when she had begun having these conversations with her cat, or when Satie had cultivated such an annoyingly adroit moral compass, but it had become second nature when thinking through her problems.

'Look, they got lucky with the break-ins and managed to stay one step ahead, but they'll catch up with them eventually,' Gabrielle assured Satie, who twitched his ear.

V seemed very definite in their email that they were the rightful owner and who was Gabrielle to argue? Violins were always being stolen – in fact she had only recently read of the theft of a cello! The more she thought about it, the more she became convinced that if she could identify the luthier, she could keep everyone happy. And once she revealed her findings, the authorities could decide who it belonged to. It was a dangerous game, but all she had to do was keep one step ahead.

Chapter Twenty

♪

As Gabrielle rushed along the rain-soaked pavement, a black cab sped through a puddle and splashed her legs.

'Oh, for f—' she shrieked, knowing that she would have to spend the next hour sitting in damp tights.

'Sorry, I've had a bit of a … situation,' she said, shaking out her umbrella and sitting tensely on the edge of the chair. The second-floor room was away from the noise of the street and glowed with the orangey light of a Himalayan salt lamp. Her therapist, Trudy, was German and although not Gabrielle's first choice (too holistic) she was highly intelligent and scarily intuitive. Gabrielle had taken the wrong door by mistake over six months ago when her GP suggested counselling, and as Trudy had been available at the time, she'd kept coming ever since. Trudy called it serendipity.

'Just take a moment to breathe,' Trudy said from the chair opposite.

'I don't really have time to breathe.' Gabrielle realised what she'd just said and rolled her eyes. 'You know what I mean.'

'Let's pretend I don't,' Trudy said with a hint of a smile.

'I've been burgled.'

'Oh no, are you okay?'

'It's fine, nothing was taken.'

And in that moment, Gabrielle had a flashback to her first session with Trudy. They were talking about *him*. Max. She had not used the exact words but the sentiment was the same – *it's fine, nothing was taken*. But something was taken – something she still found hard to quantify was taken from her. No; she had given it, hadn't she? She agreed to it all – let it happen. He could always say that he had her consent. But it wasn't given freely – that's what Trudy had crystallised for her. He used his power, his position. She was coerced.

'What is it?' Trudy asked.

Gabrielle had almost forgotten where she was. It felt like it was happening again. The dissociating. Her posture had slumped. She straightened herself again, but only half-heartedly.

'I'm just so tired,' she admitted in a small voice. 'It's exhausting.'

'What is?'

'All of it. Life.'

Gabrielle stared at the Kandinsky print on the wall. It seemed to represent chaos and momentum. A strange choice for a therapist's room. She wondered if it was the abstract nature of the painting that allowed the viewer to interpret it in any way they wanted. But what if there was nothing to interpret? What if it was just a jumble of shapes and colours, utterly devoid of meaning? She couldn't tell Trudy that. It sounded too fucking bleak.

'You're not wearing your bandage?'

Gabrielle looked down at her wrist.

'Oh' was all she could say. How had she forgotten to put it on?

'Is it something you'd like to discuss?'

Gabrielle shrugged. It definitely sounded like something Trudy wanted her to want to discuss.

'Oh, I don't know, maybe it's nothing. But I am noticing some changes...' She wasn't sure how to put it. That even despite being burgled, over the last few days, she'd begun to feel slightly less crippled by existential dread. No, best to keep these little glimmers to herself. She'd probably just imagined them, and in any case they wouldn't last. They never did.

Over the years, Gabrielle had grown suspicious of her emotions and blocked their entry accordingly. Sadness was a gateway drug to self-pity, and she wouldn't have that. Anger meant a loss of control; again, out of the question. But the emotion she treated with the greatest suspicion of all was happiness. Happiness was worse than all of the others because it came cloaked in promise and light. Like love, it tricked your brain chemicals into believing some fantasy story, but unlike love, it swooped without warning. In an unguarded instant, it could tempt you into a smile or a carefree laugh. But the momentary high was inevitably drained of all its reality. Gabrielle couldn't afford the cost of lifting her heart only to have it slammed to the floor. Better to remain earthbound and leave the heavens for angels.

Equilibrium, that was the path of the intelligent woman, and Gabrielle trod that path with the discipline of a tightrope walker. No missteps. Ever. Until now.

'I have a client, well, clients actually.'

'Oh?'

'They brought in a violin.' That same smile that snuck up on her when talking to Walter wiggled its way onto her mouth again. 'There's something about it… I played it.'

Trudy betrayed nothing of her inner thoughts, which was difficult for Gabrielle to adjust to. Her validation had always come from the outside and so when she could ascertain no hint of how she was being perceived, she wasn't sure if something was good or bad. She took a chance.

'I think I liked it. It didn't hurt, strangely,' she said, looking at her wrist as though expecting some kind of explanation from it. It had become the villain in her story and the target for all of her blame. At some point, she had dissociated from it. 'I'm not sure what it means…'

Somehow, the hour was already up. She felt the way she used to when the bell rang at school. She escaped the treatment room as though she'd been detained against her will, rather than actually paying money to be there. She wasn't even sure if it was working.

Chapter Twenty-One

♪

Later that evening, Gabrielle got a call from Devlin, arranging to meet at the pub on the corner. He wanted to 'talk tactics', as though he were preparing for a Cup Final rather than dodging the police and hiding from a criminal gang. Gabrielle spent a ridiculous amount of time debating whether she should change into a different outfit. It did technically qualify as an 'outing' and people generally chose alternative clothing when 'going out'. But then that would make her feel as though she'd made an 'effort', as though some kind of outcome would now be skulking around in brackets – it's not a date (but if something were to happen…). In the end, she didn't change out of her long black dress, but put on a pair of earrings. It seemed like the best compromise.

'I want to apologise again,' Devlin said, as soon as she walked in and found him already at the bar.

He was wearing a corduroy jacket and jeans, which sort of made him look like a cowboy from Montana. It wasn't displeasing. Gabrielle wondered if he'd changed his outfit or not.

'It's been a crazy couple of days,' he continued. 'What can I get you?'

Devlin was gushing with all of the kindness and empathy he cursed himself for not showing sooner. Gabrielle was a difficult person to console. Something about that cold stare or her body language made it very clear she did not wish to be on familiar terms with him. But after spending an entire day walking aimlessly around the city, thinking about everything, he decided it was time to stop feeling so intimidated by her. They had to be equals now. Perhaps she could even become his friend. A friend who made his heart beat faster every time she walked into the room.

'I'll have a tequila.'

'What?'

Gabrielle arched an eyebrow.

'Right. Tequila. Actually, make that two tequilas and a pint.'

'Two pints and two tequilas,' Gabrielle corrected him, with a mischievous smile. That's what she used to drink back in college, and she suddenly felt like winding back the clock. Just for a little while.

As soon as the drinks were poured, Gabrielle licked her wrist and sprinkled some salt on it, before offering the cellar to Devlin. He was completely bemused. Whatever he had expected this evening, he hadn't expected shots. They knocked them back like synchronised swimmers and retired to a small table in the corner with their pints.

'God, I needed that,' Gabrielle said, unwinding a silk scarf from around her neck. 'How's Walter?'

The truth was that Devlin didn't know. He hadn't called him since the break-in at Gabrielle's. He'd needed time to get his head straight and decide what he wanted to do with the violin. But now he was starting to feel a bit guilty. Which filled him with resentment because he didn't want to feel responsible for Walter. Not in that way. Not like his life depended on it. He couldn't cope with that. This violin had turned his life upside-down. His very uneventful, predictable, suffocating life.

'I'm sure he's fine. I'll give him a call tomorrow.'

Gabrielle drank another mouthful of beer. She hadn't had beer in years and had forgotten how thirst-quenching those little bubbles were.

'Actually, I've been thinking about the violin,' she said, putting her glass down. 'Do you really want to keep it, considering the person you bought it for…' Gabrielle let the unsaid words speak for themselves.

'This might seem strange, I mean I know I can't play it or anything, but yes, I do want to keep it.'

'Hmm.' Gabrielle bit the inside of her lip. How could she convince him that keeping it was a bad idea?

'It doesn't really matter to me, if it's a Stradivarius or some kind of copy. I don't have many possessions, but I like to keep things that have a story to them, you know?'

Gabrielle was surprised by this. She hadn't realised that he was such a sentimentalist at heart.

'I understand. Some possessions end up possessing us.'

He looked at her then, in a way that made her palms clammy and the tips of her ears tingle. Like a spotlight had been turned on her and she wasn't sure how she felt about it. She coughed and carried on.

'Like I said, my friend is the best in the business. If he says it's not a Stradivarius – I believe him.'

'Great. So, we just tell the gang that then,' Devlin said, clutching at whatever straws she was giving him.

'Well, that may not be enough. Inconclusive results don't really prove anything. I'll have to go to the source.'

'What does that mean?'

Gabrielle bit her lip again.

'Same again?' she offered.

'Sorry?'

'Another round?' she asked, getting up to go to the bar.

Devlin nodded, looking at his pint, which he had barely touched. He did his best to catch up before the next round of tequilas arrived. They went through the same routine and then Gabrielle spoke in hushed tones.

'Look, Devlin, I'm going to be straight with you. Anyone who holds that violin or plays a note on it knows that it's special.'

Could she feel it, too? Devlin wondered to himself.

'It's obviously very old – even if we can't date it accurately – and it's clearly made by someone who learned his trade from the best. And the best tend to have been in Italy.'

'So?'

'So, if we can match your violin to that of another, we can find out who the luthier was and then we can officially claim that this is not the violin they're after.'

Devlin nodded. He seemed to be on board with her

plan. Did she feel guilty for prioritising the money V had offered? Yes. But guilt wouldn't pay the bills.

'Just one question,' he said, leaning a little closer, 'what's a luther?'

Gabrielle burst out laughing – a joyous sound that made Devlin smile foolishly, even if the joke was at his expense.

'A *luthier* – it's what we call a violin maker,' she said. She realised he was actually quite sweet, once you got to know him. She caught herself just as she was tucking her hair behind her ear – that tell-tale sign. She was officially flirting, albeit unintentionally. It had to stop. Getting close was only going to complicate things. Still, she argued with herself, it was hard work being so defensive all the time and being around Walter and (God help her) Devlin gave her that rare feeling she'd been missing for so long – connection.

She excused herself and visited the ladies' room.

'Right,' she told her reflection, 'thank him for a lovely evening and then leave.' Her reflection giggled back at her. The drinks were going to her head. When she arrived back at their table, Devlin had lined up another two shots of tequila. Picking up on her hesitation, he immediately apologised.

'Oh, sorry, I'm not trying to get you drunk or anything.'

Gabrielle frowned.

'Right. Well, that definitely sounded weird,' he said, flustered. 'I'll drink them. Get myself drunk.'

'Okayyy.'

'It's been a long day,' he said, rubbing his forehead with his hand.

Quite spontaneously, Gabrielle took one of the glasses and knocked it back. He raised his and did likewise, while a spotty-faced kid with a guitar set himself up on a high stool in the corner.

'Oh God. If he starts playing Oasis, we're out of here.'

'Agreed,' she said.

The youngster began strumming his guitar and nervously sang the opening lyrics of Hozier's 'Too Sweet'.

Devlin tapped his foot. They wouldn't have to leave after all.

'That's who you remind me of actually,' Gabrielle said.

'Hozier?'

She nodded. 'I mean, if your hair was longer. And your face shape was more angular.'

'So, nothing like him at all, then,' he said and they both laughed. 'It's the Irish charm,' he said, rubbing his jawline between index finger and thumb.

Gabrielle blushed slightly. 'You're Irish?'

'I am indeed, but we moved here when I was a kid, so I kind of lost the accent.'

Gabrielle found herself wanting to know more about him, completely ignoring her own decision to leave. She realised that her first impressions of him were flawed, or perhaps she hadn't allowed herself to see him properly.

'So, tell me, what were you doing before you decided to specialise in finding lost violins?' she asked, leaning forward, her elbows on the table.

Devlin inhaled swiftly. Had this been Instagram, he would have dug out some old photos – curating a social life full of travel, meals with friends and concerts. Why wasn't his life more interesting? He hadn't completed any triathlons or taken a year out to build houses for the poor in Africa. He wasn't a TikTok sensation, he didn't even have a

TikTok account. It was pretty clear he was an awful liar, too, so he decided to just be himself, for lack of any better options.

'Well, let's see, I work in the very exciting, cut-throat business of ... um, handling other people's baggage.'

Gabrielle almost choked on her drink.

'You're a psychotherapist?'

'What? No!' he said, emitting a high-pitched laugh that she hadn't expected from a man like him. 'I'm a baggage handler.'

'Oh, thank God for that,' she said, taking a large gulp of her pint.

'Not the usual reaction, but okay,' he said. 'Every day is different – I mean, you just never know what kind of bags you're going to get. Lots of hard cases.' That joke always got a laugh. 'And what about you? What do you do when you're not being a violin hunter?'

Gabrielle dreaded that question. She didn't do anything else. Her life would look utterly boring and empty to anyone on the outside. But that was how she liked it. She was a lone wolf.

'I'm a lone wolf,' she said, grabbing onto the first thought in her head.

'Yeah, that makes sense.'

'Does it?'

'Well, yes. I mean, that's how you come across. Independent.'

'Oh. Okay.'

The silence that followed was an eleven on the awkward scale. He wasn't sure how, but he'd definitely offended her in some way.

'I mean, in a good way. Like Wolverine.'

Gabrielle could see he was trying to make her feel better, but the truth was that she was embarrassed. Not about being alone. But about her inability to form any kind of relationship. It hadn't taken long for Devlin to stumble across the borderline between the carefree girl she was before and the defensive, suspicious woman she had become. Perhaps her true self lay somewhere in between. She decided (with help from the tequila) to go a little off script.

'Okay, look, the truth is, the business is my life. I don't have lots of friends or go to parties or … I don't know, go hiking at weekends. I just work and then I go home. Which is pretty much the same place.'

'Why is it that everyone is hiking now?'

'I don't know,' she laughed. All of a sudden, they were on the same page again.

'Or are they just photoshopping themselves onto some mountaintop to make the rest of us feel crap?'

'You know, I saw a woman doing that on Instagram. She'd just splashed a load of water on her face and said she'd done a marathon.'

'"I was ashamed of myself when I realised life was a costume party and I attended with my real face."' Devlin spoke the words as though reciting a line of poetry.

'That's beautiful,' Gabrielle said, as she allowed her gaze to drink in every detail of his face. The expressive eyebrows, thick and dark, that framed his deep blue eyes. The stubble that was the same dirty blonde tone as his hair. His soft lips.

'It's Kafka,' he said, nodding, suddenly self-conscious. 'Anyway—'

'A Kafka-quoting baggage handler,' she said, smiling at him. She cleared her throat and her mind of any silly notions about where this could lead. 'It's getting late, I'd best be getting home to my cat.' Why had she said it like that? As though the night had been boring when it had been anything but.

'And I'd best be getting home to Helga,' Devlin said, as though she were a sentient being, too.

'Helga?' Gabrielle asked, wriggling into her coat.

'My campervan. It's a long story. For another time,' he said, handing her her scarf.

♪

Devlin swayed slightly and realised that the tequila had gone straight to his head. At least he would sleep tonight, he thought. Van life had been much easier in his twenties. On the way out they passed by the spotty kid whose unenthusiastic rendition of 'Take Me to Church' hadn't exactly set the crowd alight. He was unplugging the amp and wrapping things up for the night. Devlin gave him a friendly head bob. He'd been that soldier, nervously massacring songs in front of an audience who'd rather he'd stayed at home. But that was the business, that was how you cut your teeth. By the time he started busking around Europe, his performances had changed utterly, in that he was actually performing, rather than just playing the song.

As he passed by the stage, he felt that old familiar pull. It was too easy; he could just pick up the guitar and strum the strings. It would be just like holding the violin – natural and easy. Maybe the time had come to get back on the horse. The alcohol in his bloodstream was like liquid bravery. He reached out to take the neck of the guitar, but that was when all the memories came flooding back. The screech of the brakes, the scream and then the deathly silence. The world turned upside-down. The heartbeat of his life, flatlining.

'Devlin. Devlin!'

'Sorry, what?'

Gabrielle had a hold of his arm. Suddenly he was back in the pub, standing by the stage, a few of the punters looking at him with undisguised alarm. He looked down and saw his hand was gripped tightly around the neck of the guitar, almost white.

'Are you okay? You look like you saw a ghost.'

He let go of the guitar and stumbled towards the door on his own steam.

'Too much to drink, I think. Are you all right getting back?'

'Of course,' Gabrielle said, declining his weak attempt at offering to walk her home. 'I should be walking you home. Are you sure you're okay? I can call you a taxi from the shop, it's just across the road.'

He walked out into the night, saying the night air would do him good. She'd seen that look before, or at least, she'd experienced it before. When she was due to give her final recital at university, she just choked. And then the pain hit. Strange; she always thought that the pain had hit first, then she'd choked? Maybe she was remembering it wrong… She couldn't let her thoughts go back there and so she slammed the door on them.

Chapter Twenty-Two

♪

Devlin couldn't sleep. There were many thoughts swirling around his head, but two felt as though they were physically gnawing at him. He checked the time on his phone – five a.m. Something had to be done and perhaps now was the perfect time to do it, under the cover of darkness. He dressed quickly and took the violin with him. The streets were quiet at this time of the morning, but he kept looking over his shoulder, regardless. Taking a roundabout route to the Tube station, he got on the Jubilee Line and switched at Baker Street, before alighting at Paddington. On platform 12, he found the luggage storage facility. He'd downloaded the app and prepaid for a locker. It was all so simple, he wondered why he hadn't thought of it before. It wasn't like he could walk into a bank and ask them to store the violin for him, so this was the next best thing. It was hard to let her go, but it just wasn't safe keeping her in the van. Devlin wasn't a hundred per cent sure how safe this option was, but for a fleeting moment he thought – maybe it would be better for everyone if it did get stolen. Again. None of them were safe while this criminal gang was after them. And so he got back on the train to sort out problem number two.

♪

Walter ignored the doorbell. At this hour of night, it was probably some drunken revellers on the way home from the pub. He had hardly slept. It was almost six a.m. There would be no more sleep now anyway. He hopped out of bed and stood in front of the toilet for what felt like ten minutes before he was finally able to relieve himself. Not a particularly good sign.

He felt ghastly about the break-in at Wilding's. What had he been thinking? It was his decision to keep the burglaries a secret from Gabrielle – never thinking that she might be next on their list. He didn't think this gang, whoever they were, would take it this far. If your stolen property ends up in Lost Property, surely you'd just let it go? Cut your losses. But that assumption had been a rookie mistake. He was the elder statesman of the group, after all – they were relying on him, and he had let them both down. The truth was, he had been naive. He saw it all as a bit of a game – something to keep him occupied for a while until those dark feelings had passed. Looking in the mirror, he was forced to confront his reflection: the dry skin and pale pallor – tell-tale signs of ill health. But perhaps the violin adventure wasn't the panacea he had hoped. He now realised that this was far more serious. Someone could get hurt.

And then there was the violin. Ever since Devlin had brought the violin into his small, uneventful life, it was as though the walls had been pushed down and now a vast world with an endless horizon stretched out before him. She was a restless spirit, who had left a trail of fascination and despair in her wake. Her song travelled on the wind, igniting passions, inciting madness and sparking forbidden desires. The thrill of belonging to a story greater than his own, that might outlive him and offer him a small footnote in the history books…

Then his phone lit up. Devlin.

> Let me in. Please.

♪

'Why are we at an archery club?' Walter asked, in a good-natured but slightly baffled tone.

Devlin had taken Walter out for a fry-up at the local greasy spoon and then informed him that he'd book a 'Have-a-go' class with the local Hampstead Bowmen club. At nine a.m.

'Why not?' Devlin replied, putting away his phone once he'd confirmed the address. 'Hobbies are an important part of a well-balanced lifestyle,' he said, sounding oddly like a health brochure from the local GP.

Walter nodded, but watched Devlin as though he were an egg-timer. He'd ping eventually and Walter would finally uncover what all of this was about.

'Besides, it might come in handy,' Devlin said, jotting down their names on a consent form, presumably absolving the club of any responsibility, should an arrow end up in someone's head.

'How's that?' Walter asked, taking up a spot several feet from a target painted onto a board.

'You know, the criminal gang,' Devlin said, before the instructor began the class and Walter was saved from making any kind of a sensible reply.

An hour and a half later, Walter had to admit that the archery had been great fun. He'd met people of all ages, and even shot a bullseye.

'I've booked us into a pottery class next week,' Devlin told him, once they'd reached the front of Walter's apartment building.

'I see. Pottery. Fancy that.'

'And there's something else—'

'Tai chi? Choir practice?'

'No, but I'll definitely look those up, see if there are any classes locally—'

'Devlin, listen—'

'I thought I could move in with you for a while.'

Walter sighed.

'Come upstairs. I'll put the kettle on.'

♪

Once the tea was poured and an obligatory biscuit dunked in his tea, Walter broached the inevitable conversation.

'You are not responsible for me, Devlin.'

'I didn't think—'

Walter raised his hand for him to stop talking.

'Please. We can't keep ignoring the elephant in the room.

You've been very ... courteous, not mentioning my predicament.'

'The pills?'

Walter nodded.

'It was a moment of desperation and, for whatever reason, fate or happenstance, you knocked on my door and I didn't go through with it.'

'I'm glad you didn't,' Devlin said, wrapping his hands around his mug for warmth.

'As am I. But like I said, you're not responsible for fixing whatever was broken in my life. That's my job.'

'I just wanted you to know you're not alone. People care about you.'

Walter's eyes were watering, but he had to keep it together. This young man had enough on his plate without taking on more problems.

'And I am very grateful for that. But you don't have to book archery lessons or move in with me. I'm not a charity case.'

'I never meant it that way. Okay, maybe the archery lessons were a bit random—'

Walter laughed and shook his head.

'But my offer to move in, that was more out of self-interest. I've been living in my campervan since splitting up with Mel, and honestly, it would be nice to live in the same building as a toilet for a while. Plus, after the break-in, maybe it's wise to stick together.'

'Safety in numbers?' Walter added.

'Look, I'm sorry I've been so cack-handed with all of this—'

'It's very nice that you care. I just don't want you to

worry. But perhaps you could stay here until you find somewhere else, with a toilet.'

They clinked mugs and Walter even broke out the fig rolls.

Chapter Twenty-Three

♪

THE VIOLIN

Moscow, 1875

I have come to view fate and chance as two sides of the same coin. In Paganini's possession, I had some modicum of certitude. I knew my journey would bring me back to William. Somehow. In the dark shadows of the violin case, my wooden sides creaked like the timbers of a ship at sea. I heard voices: the frivolous laugh of a young woman, speaking a language I had never heard before and yet somehow understood. Suddenly, the case opened and light streamed in. I found myself in a very grand apartment. Artworks hung everywhere and canvases were stacked against the walls.

'Maria, you must tell the maid what you wish to pack,' said an older woman – her mother, I assumed.

'Yes, yes,' she replied, dismissively. She took out my bow and caressed the long, soft hairs with her finger. 'This will make a fine gift for Cousin Pavel,' she said to herself.

And then she whispered to me, 'We won't tell Mama that I paid twenty thousand roubles for you.' She winked. 'But how many people can say that they purchased a violin from Achille Paganini?'

'How many people can say they sold a violin to Maria Bashkirtseff?' her maid whispered from behind her, giving her a fright.

'You are quite right, Nina. I must say he was very impressed by my paintings in the salon this year.'

Maria was not modest about her talents and, I have to say, it was a breath of fresh air to be in such high-spirited feminine company for a change. She certainly had no reserve using her voice and I spied a diary on the bed entitled, *I Am the Most Interesting Book of All*.

So, my new life was to be with an outspoken, witty and multi-talented young artist. I breathed a sigh of relief. However, it was short-lived. On the Nord Express train, travelling from Paris to St Petersburg, I felt my case tumble. I was tugged and roughly handled, spending days in the darkness. I was headed for Russia, that much was certain, but not with Miss Bashkirtseff. There were unseen forces at play. Universal laws of attraction, drawing me into the lives of strangers. But to what end? I decided then and there that I could either continue to fear the unknown or embrace it wholeheartedly. There was no going back now. If this was to be my legacy, I wanted it to be a good one.

♪

Anton Pushkin began playing the violin at the age of eleven. His father pawned his suit to buy him a three-quarter size violin and promised to send him to lessons when he could earn enough money. But Anton preferred to learn on his own, in the streets, watching how other violinists played, and began making his own money by busking there. When his father could afford it, he enrolled Anton in the St Petersburg Conservatory in 1871, under the tutelage of Nikolai Rimsky-Korsakov. There he blossomed and, by the age of twenty-one, joined The Mariinsky Orchestra, one of the oldest in Russia. But now he needed a violin befitting his position. He was given the name of a man with questionable connections, who had recently arrived from Paris with a violin of exceptional craftsmanship. As soon as Anton saw me, he agreed to the price – and so my new life began.

Natalya Petrova spent her poverty-stricken childhood in the small town of Uglich, north of Moscow. An orphan, she grew up on a poor diet, sometimes going days without proper food, and as a result, she had a very fine, elfin figure. She made a beautiful dancer and her parents could see her earning potential. She was first sent to the Bolshoi Ballet school, which was more like a military camp turning out soldiers. It was strict and it was tough, but for a girl who had known nothing but hunger in her short life, Natalya found it a place of nourishment for her soul. The music, the art, the passion – they fed her in ways she didn't know she needed. She clung to her ambition like it was the last flight from hell. Through years of dedication and practice, she was granted a place with the Mariinsky Ballet in the winter palace of St Petersburg.

The Imperial Mariinsky Theatre was a magical place, where the entire company turned fantasy into reality for the adoring audiences. Yet behind the scenes, there were countless hours of hard work and endless rehearsals. It was during these months of preparation that Anton first spotted Natalya. She stood out from all of the other dancers; not because she was so petite and elfin-like, but because she worked the hardest – and yet, when she danced, her graceful movements seemed effortless. But how could such a special individual ever notice a violinist in the sea of orchestral musicians? There was a constellation of moments where she might have glanced in his direction, brushed past him to the stage, offered a brief smile; meaningless to the untrained eye, but it was these pinpoints that Anton clung to until he could figure out how to impress her. He was besotted with her. I could tell because he played as if she were the only person in the room. Everything else in the theatre receded into shadow, but for her white silhouette, rising and gently landing, a heavenly body not meant for this world. Anton began to feel as though he had no existence, except in her presence.

It was late one night and they were rehearsing Tchaikovsky's *Sleeping Beauty*. The violin soloist, caught in a blizzard outside of the city, had failed to show up and Anton took his opportunity. He stood at the front of the orchestra and, with a deep breath, he began to play the notes. Softly at first, delicate, just as she. He glanced towards the stage and watched as she began to sway to the music, then twirled in delight. I sang notes that resonated throughout the theatre, and everyone fell under our spell. But he wasn't playing for them. In fact, he played just for her.

Natalya's heartstrings were plucked, that was

undeniably true. A woman can tell these things. But she wasn't sure what to do with this unfamiliar feeling. She had always been alone, fighting for her survival. She had grown into a diva – had to – in order to get the parts and stare down any competition. You had to own your place – go beyond yourself and become a character with invincible powers. So, when Anton finally worked up the courage to approach her at the end of the evening and offered to take her to dinner, she hesitated.

'What do you want from me?' she asked.

'Nothing,' came his simple reply.

Perhaps she would give him a chance, this young man who seemed both self-assured and terribly nervous. At the restaurant where the more well-off patrons dined after the show, she listened and watched his deep brown eyes gaze at her over the candlelight. She grew charmed by his story. Like her, he had begun with very little, only a love of playing. She told him how she used to invent her own little dances, but now her favourite was the waltz. From that evening on, they dined together and waltzed to the music of an old accordion player, when she was not too tired after rehearsal. On the night they first kissed, Anton could have sworn his feet left the ground.

The ballet was a resounding success and the theatre manager insisted on more shows. Matinees and weekends, with no time for rest. He did not care about the performers' welfare. Natalya was exhausted and her muscles were strained. Then, the inevitable happened: an accident. Her dance partner failed to catch her and when she landed on the wooden boards, everyone heard the horrific sound of shattering bones. She broke her leg in two places. Anton jumped up and rushed to her side as the curtain fell down around them.

'My love!'

This is the end, she thought, *I might as well be dead.*

The doctor took her to the hospital and declared her unfit to walk. She lay in her hospital bed in black despair. Anton spent every waking hour at her bedside, but she refused to speak. One day, he brought me with him and began to play some old tunes that might remind her of better days. But our plaintive melodies only wounded her further. Finally, she cried with such awful angst, he could hardly bear to witness it.

'I will never set foot on the stage again,' she said. 'Without my dancing, what am I good for?'

It bruised his heart to hear her speak in such a way, and yet he understood. The ballet was her life and dancing her means of self-expression. If he couldn't play…

Her fighting spirit had finally relented, and it was without a word of protest that she agreed to stay with him in his home until she healed. He had very little to offer, but he made his bedroom a sanctuary of healing for her while he slept on the chair. He made soup, as she had little appetite. In the afternoons he would read to her, secretly choosing books that offered stories of hope overcoming adversity. In the evenings, he would take out his violin and play. Anton could not be sure, but he thought he could hear soft cries coming from her room. He resolved to practise elsewhere.

In sleep, she dreamed that she was dancing and would wake in tears. He held her closely and absorbed all of her anger. She had become his entire world and yet still she lamented that her life was useless. I felt such an affinity with poor Natalya. Singing was my first love, my true passion, my very essence. William had somehow given me the power to use my voice now in a way that I never could, but I would have traded it all in a heartbeat to feel his arms around me again. Perhaps it was my own desires that seeped out through Anton's playing, or mere coincidence, but as the weeks went by, I sensed a change in the air.

One evening, as they finished supper, Natalya waited for Anton to leave for rehearsal.

'Why do you not go to the theatre?' she asked, after some time had passed.

He placed a tiny box on her lap and knelt down before her.

'You are my music now,' he said, before opening the box and taking out a golden ring. 'Will you marry me, my love?'

Natalya's eyes shone with emotion.

'But how could you afford this?'

'I sold my violin.'

'You sold your violin?' she repeated. 'For me?'

'I have found something more rare in this world than my beautiful violin. I hope that you will grow, in time, to love me as much as your dancing.'

It did not take long, merely the time it took for her lips to find his.

Chapter Twenty-Four

♪

Through the open window, Gabrielle heard the trill of a blackbird and the beat of a basketball bouncing off the pavement. She began to tap her foot and became aware of another sound, the syncopation of rustling leaves. The movement was cyclical, unrepeatable and yet there was a pattern to it. Blending and composing a symphony of its own. Obviously, any of these sounds could occur naturally at any time, but here and now there was a rhythm and a harmony that could not be denied. At least, not by Gabrielle. It was nature's music.

She could never really remember a time when she didn't hear it and had assumed it was the same for everyone. As a child, she would hum the melody and grown-ups would ask her where she had heard it. *In my head*, she would answer. Except that her imagination could transform this music into marks on paper: crotchets and quavers on a stave, with their little black heads and stems reminding her of flowers growing on a trellis. This seemed to convince everyone that she was some kind of prodigy.

That was when everything changed. Suddenly, she was no longer a little girl, she was *gifted*. And now people expected things, speaking of her future as though it were a destination they were all sailing towards in a boat she herself must build. But the grown-ups forgot to ask her if she wanted to go to that place. *It's what your mother would have wanted*, her father used to say. And no one can disobey a dying woman's wish. You just can't.

'Oh, I've spoken to the neighbours about this,' Trudy said, getting up and closing the window with a thump. 'Now, where were we? Last time you mentioned the compulsions. Would you like to talk about that?'

'Oh yes, they're much better,' she lied.

How to fill this hour by not giving too much away, but just enough so Trudy would feel like she was getting somewhere. That was Gabrielle's tightrope walk.

'Perhaps you would like to talk about Max.'

Even hearing his name made her bristle. The great Maximillian Daunt. Just to be 'spotted' by him was cause for great excitement. 'He wants to work with you,' her old tutor had said. 'He sees something in you.' And wasn't that every young girl's dream? For someone to see them as special. To be chosen. It felt like a fairy tale coming true.

'He was tough on his students, but fair. Everybody knew that. That's why he was the best.'

Trudy tilted her head sideways before asking, 'Can you explain what "tough" means to you, in this context?'

'Okay, he could be a bit … controlling. Critical. But that's normal. You have to expect that if you want to succeed. You have to put your emotions aside.' She began rubbing her wrist. It was becoming painful again.

'I see. It sounds like a lot of pressure for a young girl.'

She didn't trust herself to respond. If she said she was fine, it would sound like she was too detached, or in denial. She didn't want to talk about it or 'hold space' for her feelings as Trudy had so often said. Why was she even coming here? It was like a form of torture.

'I'm sorry, Trudy, I just don't think I can do this right now.'

With that, she got up and left, heading for the nearest wine bar before changing her mind and waving down a black cab.

'Where to, love?'

'North,' she said, before dialling Walter's number.

♪

'Where is the violin?' Gabrielle asked, declining Walter's offer of tea and a plate of biscuits. Fig rolls. *Did people really eat those?* she wondered, completely off topic. It was almost lunchtime and her stomach rumbled, but even hunger couldn't coax her to eat a biscuit stuffed with figs. She was already slightly discombobulated to find Devlin there.

'I left it in a locker in Paddington Station,' Devlin said.

They hadn't spoken in days, not since the other night at the pub, when he'd had that strange turn. He looked tired. For a wild moment she considered asking him how he was feeling, but then she remembered herself. This was about the violin and the violin only.

'Sorry.' Gabrielle pinched the bridge of her nose,

'I could've sworn you said that you left it in a locker in Paddington.'

'Well, I couldn't bring it home again, could I? None of us could. It's not safe with that gang after us.'

'So you've left a priceless violin … in a train station. To be safe.'

'Yup.'

Gabrielle sighed with her entire being. She turned to look at Walter who was still standing by the kettle, teapot in hand.

'Do you have any coffee?' she asked, before taking off her coat and sitting at the dining table.

'Right,' Walter said, spooning out some ghastly instant coffee powder into a mug. 'What's the plan?'

Devlin sank most of his face into the mug and inhaled.

'Well, ideally, I would hand the violin over to Beare's,' she said. 'They are the specialists, but things being as they are, I think the fewer people who know about this, the better.'

Walter nodded and she felt only a small pang of guilt for making sure her name would be the only one associated with the discovery.

'Roger, my friend in Bristol, suggested we travel to Milan. I didn't mention it before because, well, I wasn't sure if you wanted the extra expense. But I think we can safely say we are dealing with a high-value item at this point.'

'Why Milan?' asked Devlin, visibly uncomfortable at the thought.

'I need – *we* need – to get to the Museum of Musical Instruments in Sforza Castle. It's full of rare and ancient instruments – one of the most important collections in the world. If we can find another example from your luthier, which I'm confident we can...'

'Excellent!' Walter said, seeing an opportunity to regale them both with the number of times he had intended to visit Italy, but never did. This was followed by a roll call of destinations – Lake Garda, Tuscany, Verona – ah, fair Verona! Which then descended into some Shakespearian monologue that fell on decidedly deaf ears.

'Okay, so I can book us some flights – if we're lucky we could be there by nightfall.' Gabrielle began tapping her phone, a sense of calm running through her neural pathways. This was exactly what she needed right now, an assignment that would whisk her away from London, from Trudy, from herself.

Walter beamed and got up to search the drawers in the sideboard for his passport. Devlin, however, kept his eyes fixed on his cup of tea, as though his future would appear in it. While they discussed airlines and hotels, Devlin mumbled something incoherent.

'What is it?' asked Walter.

'I can't go.'

'Whyever not?'

'I – I can't just leave my job and swan off to Italy, can I? I've got commitments.'

'Come, don't come. It's all the same to me. All I need is the violin,' Gabrielle said flatly and got up to put the cups in the dishwasher.

♪

'What was all that about?' Walter asked Devlin after Gabrielle had left. 'We're helping *you*, remember? You're the one who came to me. You're the one who picked up that violin in the first place.'

'I know, I know, look ... I just couldn't say it in front of her.'

'Say what?' Walter was trying very hard not to sound like a teacher scolding a student, but he wasn't having much success.

'I have a fear of flying.'

There was a pause, in which Devlin felt much smaller than his actual height.

'Don't be ridiculous, man. You work in an airport.'

'That doesn't mean I fly the planes!' he whisper-shouted.

'Hmm, fair point. Well, not to worry, I'm sure we can work something out.'

'There is nothing to be worked out. I just can't go.'

♪

The sky was streaked with red and pink by the time they reached Paddington Station. Walter scratched at his receding hairline as he watched Devlin fiddling with the key in the lock. If someone had told him a week ago that he would have the chance to visit a museum in Italy on the hunt for an unknown luthier, he would have laughed in their face. His life had become a predictable conveyor belt between the supermarket, his flat and the odd lunch at the local pub. Why this adventure had come his way at the exact time when he needed it most, he would never know, but the thought of having it all cut short now was too dispiriting to contemplate. Perhaps he could still go to Milan without Devlin, but he hardly knew Gabrielle and she would probably rather make the trip without some stuffy old, retired teacher slowing her down.

'Couldn't you take some type of pill? For the plane, I mean. The trip could do you good, you know. Get out of London, change your perspective on things.'

Devlin opened the locker and took out the violin. Once it was again in his arms, he realised that handing it over to Gabrielle would be impossible. It was one thing leaving it at her shop, but letting her carry it overseas?

'Fine! I'll get my passport,' he said, 'but I'm not promising anything.'

Devlin had no intention of getting on that plane. He was going to bring Walter and Gabrielle to the airport, then make up some excuse when he got there. But by the time they arrived at check-in, he still hadn't come up with one.

'Here,' Gabrielle said, handing him a small brown bottle that rattled with pills inside.

'What's this?'

'Just a mild sedative,' she said calmly.

Devlin blinked.

'Xanax. Should take the edge off.'

He wanted to ask why she happened to just have these on her person, but instead he twisted off the lid, shook two pills out into his hand and smacked them into his mouth before swallowing hard.

'You're meant to take them when you're on the plane,' said Walter.

'I will. Now let's get going before I change my mind.'

Chapter Twenty-Five

♪

At 30,000 feet, somewhere over the English Channel, Devlin began to feel the full effects of four Xanax.

'Did I tell you why my mother called me Luke?' he bellowed, as one of the flight attendants passed by, questioning her life choices.

'Yes,' Gabrielle said, 'three times already.'

'For God's sake,' Walter hissed, sitting in the middle, 'use your inside voice. Or better still, take a nap!'

'If I had four of those I'd be out for the count,' Gabrielle stage-whispered. And as though her words had cast some curious spell, Devlin's head lolled onto Walter's shoulder and he was mercifully asleep.

'He's taken the break-up pretty hard,' Walter said.

'It would appear so.'

'Although why, I can't fathom. They sounded like a complete mismatch. Not that I'm an expert in the field.'

'That makes two of us.'

They shared a smile. Two lonely hearts recognising each

other. Walter always believed it was a numbers game – you were bound to end up with somebody. It was pure maths. Just his luck though – he seemed to be an odd number.

Holding the violin on his lap (he had been nominated primary caregiver for the flight after a tense debate between Gabrielle and Devlin), he wasn't so sure anymore. That strange voice was speaking to him again, but not in words, exactly. It felt more like curling smoke, wrapping around his heart. From an old cottage chimney, perhaps. Where the image had come from, he could not say, but it made him feel warm. Hopeful. He looked down at the case.

'There's something that's been bothering me about this,' he said, looking up to find that Gabrielle was also staring at the violin. 'What's the motive?'

'For the theft?'

'Yes, I mean, if it's true what you said and no one in their right mind would try to sell a Strad—'

'*If* it is a Strad,' she corrected him.

'Yes, but whatever it is, it's clearly valuable. Only, you can't sell this violin, you can't take it to an auction house, or to a dealer. It must be like stealing a Rembrandt. Who would touch it?'

It was true, she agreed, but that didn't stop unscrupulous collectors from wanting to own a masterpiece, at any cost.

'There are countless stories of priceless violins that are still missing, despite rewards being offered and years of investigations. They simply vanished without trace, probably languishing in attics, closets and under beds, and perhaps under the chins of unsuspecting violinists.'

Devlin snored with abandon and Gabrielle pinched the

bridge of her nose before releasing a long sigh and turning back to Walter.

'Have you ever heard of the 1732 Duke of Alcantara Stradivari?'

'Remind me,' Walter said, a hint of humour in his voice.

'It was on loan to David Margetts, a violinist in UCLA's Roth String Quartet. It vanished after an evening rehearsal in Los Angeles when it was stolen from his car.'

'Good grief. So, an opportunistic theft? Or do you think they were watching him?' Walter thought of the state of his apartment after it had been broken into and gave an involuntary shiver.

'Well, according to a police report, they said it was possible the violin was left on the top of the car and fell off!'

'Never!'

Gabrielle nodded enthusiastically, glad to have someone who seemed to be interested in her specialist subject of violin trivia.

'A Spanish teacher said she found it on the side of a Los Angeles freeway. She took the violin home and kept it under her bed, and that's where it remained until her death. She bequeathed it to her nephew and he gave it to his ex-wife, whose teacher took it to a violin shop a few years later to have it valued. From the stolen property register, it was found that it had been listed as stolen twenty-seven years earlier. UCLA naturally wanted it returned, and spent a year in court fighting an ownership battle.'

Walter marvelled at how priceless items could just slip through the cracks. No big heist, just a simple case of forgetfulness. Imagine your entire destiny being buffeted about by the careless hands of others? He held the violin a little closer.

'What a fascinating world you inhabit.'

'I suppose it is, to an outsider. It's all I ever knew, really. Before Dad—'

'He must have been a terrible loss to you,' Walter said, patting her hand before she pulled it swiftly away.

She looked out of the window at the miles of air below. She read somewhere once that it was the air pressure that kept the plane in the sky, as if the atmosphere was a bowl of jelly and you didn't have to worry about falling through. Lies were a bit like that. They were keeping her aloft, but they were also keeping her stuck.

'Then there's the 1727 Davidoff–Morini Strad. That's still one of the FBI's top ten unsolved art crimes.'

Walter gave her a look that seemed to say, *I see what you're doing and I understand.*

'I'd love to hear about it,' he said, as the flight attendant offered them coffee.

'Erica Morini. She was one of the greatest violinists who ever lived. A *New York Times* critic called the greatest *woman* violinist,' Gabrielle said, stirring the sugar into her coffee and trying to ignore the pool of drool that Devlin's open mouth was dropping onto Walter's jacket. 'But that didn't impress Erica one bit. "*A violinist is a violinist,*" she said, "*and I am to be judged as one – not as a female musician.*" She was an outstanding concert violinist but of course she's largely forgotten about today. They say that paper will take any ink, but I've never found that to be true of history books and the achievements of women.'

Walter was taken aback. In all of his years as a history

teacher, he had not so much omitted to question the lack of female perspectives and subject matter as accepted the status quo. He hadn't sought out other, lesser-known texts that might offer his students (and himself) an alternative view of the world. A world where women had an equal voice. Because that world didn't exist, at least not outside some dystopian work of fiction. As he felt his entire career in teaching crumble beneath him, he felt buoyed up by another, even less likely thought. He wished he had a daughter like Gabrielle. She was fierce, erudite and wore her capabilities lightly. As Devlin snored sonorously against his shoulder, he asked what happened to Miss Morini.

'She was a great success, that's what happened. But now, she's just a footnote to the mystery of yet another missing Strad. It was stolen in nineteen-ninety-five from a locked bedroom closet in Morini's Manhattan apartment and replaced by an empty case. The door to the apartment was locked and there was no sign of forced entry. She was ninety-one and in hospital at the time, and died shortly thereafter, not knowing that the Stradivari had been stolen.'

Walter shook his head.

'I imagine these stories only add to the allure.'

Gabrielle gave him a tight smile before buckling her seatbelt as the captain announced their descent. She would have to watch herself around Walter; he made it too easy to let her guard down, with his kind, interested manner. She couldn't let on that it was the provenance of this violin that kept her invested in this wild goose chase. V, whoever they were, was going to get this violin back one way or another and all she could do was delay that inevitability until she had the violin's full story and knew every change of hands. She had to keep things professional.

'The stories themselves are worthless if they can't be proven.' There, that would put him off the scent. 'Certification is most important to violin collectors. It appeals to their vanity to say so-and-so once played this violin. The truth is, they might never play it at all. It's an asset. Bragging rights.'

'Gosh, that seems like a waste. It's a bit like those billionaires who buy art and keep it stored in some freeport in Geneva! I mean, what is the point of it?'

'Prestige. Being the person who owns the only one. Their value is maintained by their scarcity and that's worth a lot to people like that.'

'I haven't even heard this one yet,' he said, patting the case affectionately.

Gabrielle's story was interrupted by a moaning sound coming from the aisle. Devlin was attempting to stand up.

'Where the hell am I?'

A flight attendant promptly shoved him back into his seat and buckled his seat belt, just as the plane was flying over the Alps.

'Isn't it marvellous?' Walter said to them both, at which point Devlin was promptly sick into a paper bag.

Chapter Twenty-Six

♪

Milan

Arriving at the airport in Milan was a bit of a blur for Devlin. He wore his dark Ray-Bans as the glare of the city loomed before him. His mind was foggy from the Xanax and so he simply allowed himself to be led by Walter and Gabrielle, who seemed to navigate their sudden arrival in a foreign city with ease. He, on the other hand, wondered yet again what he was doing. This whole violin caper felt like trying to keep hold of a puppy's leash, yanked from one incongruous place to another. A part of him wanted to give up and leave them to it, but there was something about the violin. Even now, he insisted on carrying it. He couldn't explain its allure, nor did he want to. It wouldn't make any sense. And yet it compelled him to follow this path to who knew where.

A taxi took them to their hotel, where they dropped off

their bags at reception and promptly turned back out into the street.

'Can you hear that?' Gabrielle said, as they jostled uncomfortably on the train towards the city centre. She was tapping the laptop case on her lap like a drummer.

'Hear what?' Devlin asked.

'The music of the city,' she said, an unaccustomed smile on her face.

All Devlin could hear was roadworks, a crying baby and a cacophony of people talking on their phones, albeit in Italian, which made it slightly more bearable than the Jubilee Line. They made their way to Sforza Castle, which was more of a fortification than a fairy-tale castle. Essentially, a large square with thick walls and inner courtyards, it was surrounded by beautiful gardens that Walter looked at longingly before Gabrielle shuffled them indoors so they could get down to business. Devlin found her laser-like focus on the task at hand both impressive and annoying. It was his first time in Milan; he wanted to eat pasta, have a gelato, throw a coin in a fountain! It took all of his willpower to get on that plane, and he felt due a reward of some kind. A bit of fun. It was a concept Gabrielle seemed unfamiliar with and Devlin couldn't help but wonder why.

They entered the building and descended a flight of stairs to the Monzino Collection.

'And who is Monzino?' Walter asked, brandishing a notebook and pen as though they were a sword and shield.

'The Monzino family are Milanese royalty when it comes to producing musical instruments. Their legacy dates back seven generations,' Gabrielle explained as Walter scribbled happily.

The walls were lined with display cases of what at first looked like broken violins but were actually all of the pieces that made up the instrument laid out like a jigsaw puzzle. On the wall opposite were a series of giant posters featuring a pair of disembodied hands crafting a violin through various stages, under the heading 'Collezione Monzino'. Beside that was a black and white image, dated 1910, of a man with a fantastic moustache. He was sitting in a workshop, chiselling the scroll of a violin and surrounded by instruments hanging from the walls at various stages of completion, waiting to be turned into masterpieces. The workbench held an impressive array of cutting tools, calipers and moulds.

'It's basically like carpentry, isn't it?' Devlin remarked, looking at the chisels and sketches with f-holes marked out. 'In a way,' he added, not wanting to appear plebeian.

'You're not wrong,' Gabrielle replied. 'Carpentry is a part of the craft, along with artistic sensibility and exceptional technical ability. It is said that making a violin is the marriage of mathematics and nature.'

The trio looked at the image with a newfound appreciation.

'There's such a sense of calm,' Walter remarked, looking at the man in the photo. 'Not like nowadays when everything is rush, rush, rush. You get the sense that the instrument is dictating the pace, not the maker.'

Gabrielle regarded him thoughtfully and suddenly felt quite glad that she had not come on this trip alone. Whether he knew it or not, Walter was such a calming presence.

Steady. Dependable. Everything her father wasn't. But before she had a chance to grow too maudlin, Devlin interrupted.

'I'm not sure what was in those pills you gave me, but surely there's something wrong with this violin over here,' he said, lifting up his sunglasses and squinting at an unusual instrument in a glass case.

'It's a harp guitar,' Gabrielle said, permitting herself the briefest of smiles. She felt a bit bad for him, really. This wasn't his kind of world at all and yet here he was, gripping tightly to the violin case and facing his fears.

'I wonder what it sounds like?'

Gabrielle bent her head and began explaining the technicalities of playing such an instrument. Walter couldn't help but feel his heart soften. It was good to see them getting along. Age didn't bring many benefits; it played havoc with your eyesight and his knees felt like they belonged to a hundred-year-old man. But one thing it did bring was clarity. Love was all that mattered, in the end. And yet self-preservation, ego and sheer bloody-mindedness all stood in the way of seeing that. If he had his time over, he would do things so differently. He wouldn't listen to that scared voice inside his head that had some kind of mortal dread of being embarrassed. As though making a fool of himself was the worst thing that could happen. What stupidity!

'So, do you think one of these Monzinos could have made the violin?' Devlin asked, breaking Walter's reverie.

'Probably not, no.'

'Oh. So why have you brought us here?' he asked matter-of-factly.

'I didn't *bring* you.'

Gabrielle stiffened and Walter could see the moment of proximity between them was broken. He merely shook his head. *Young fools.*

'This collection represents several makers, including those who built for the Monzino label or whose instruments were sold through the Monzino shop, and also older, unrelated instruments from Antonio's personal collection. It will take meticulous research to find a match, so I need to concentrate.' She fixed them both with an admonishing look. Walter, unwilling to watch the two of them bumble their way through another fraught exchange, suggested Devlin should go back to the hotel and get some rest.

'Well, if you're sure,' he said, already turning back towards the exit.

'The violin?' Gabrielle called after him.

'What?'

'I need it, for comparison.'

'Oh, right, of course.' Why was it always so hard to hand it over? Devlin wondered, but he was too tired to argue.

♪

Devlin had somehow managed to sleep right through to the following morning, when he met Walter and Gabrielle at the reception desk.

'Oh, good, you're up. Let's get breakfast, I'm starving.'

'It'll have to be on the train,' Gabrielle informed him, without looking up from her phone. 'I've just booked tickets to Cremona and we've only got twenty minutes to catch it.'

Devlin looked at Walter, who simply shrugged his shoulders.

♪

Half an hour later, they were whizzing past the verdant Italian countryside.

'So, why Cremona?' Walter asked, having polished off a cornetto, which was basically the same thing as a croissant, but more Italian.

'Cremona is the birthplace of the modern violin,' Gabrielle explained, again turning the handle of her coffee cup to align at a right angle with her spoon. 'The Amati dynasty began making the Cremonese-style violins in the fifteenth century. Antoni Stradivari studied under Nicolò Amati and the museum will have more examples that we can examine. And of course, the great Giuseppe Guarneri del Gesù.'

'I've never heard of him,' Devlin said, although to be fair, he wasn't familiar with the majority of violin-related trivia that Gabrielle seemed to unreel from the top of her head.

'Oh my, well, he is said to be the most important successor to Stradivari. Del Gesù violins are in fact preferred by soloists – they have a very robust tone—' Gabrielle broke off. She wasn't sure if he was interested or not and she didn't want to appear condescending. 'Paganini famously played a Guarneri.'

Silence.

'And Daniel Hope?' she continued. 'He's a contemporary violinist, so perhaps you've heard of him?'

No one said anything for a moment, then Devlin piped up, 'Do you know, I can only name one violinist. Nigel Kennedy.'

Gabrielle wasn't sure what to make of this – was it a confession? A challenge?

'I just mean, it's always felt like a world apart, you know? As though they don't want the plebs to have access or something. I mean, no offence,' he added, aware that he and Gabrielle came from very different backgrounds.

'Oh no, none taken, I know exactly what you mean. It's a bit like opera – in Italy it's something that everyone does because the ticket prices are so reasonable. Art is a democratic act, not elitist at all.'

'Exactly! If it weren't for Banksy bringing art to the streets—'

'And did you see the art auction at Sotheby's? Where the painting self-destructed with the shredder!'

'Priceless,' Devlin said, shaking his head.

'It sold for, like, eighteen million pounds after that,' she said.

'That's insane,' he replied, leaning across the table as the two of them began discussing the traditional art world's commercialisation and exclusivity.

Walter sat back bemused. When these two found common ground, the air sparked with electricity. Lord knows, he had very little experience of such things, but even a blind man could see they were made for each other. He wondered if there was something he could do to aid things along... However, as he held the violin case in his lap, his body swaying to the gentle rocking of the train, he realised that there were greater forces at play than he could ever conjure. A thought floated into his mind like a leaf tumbling from a branch; was it still possible for him to meet his special someone? A woman he could talk to about music and art? Travel on a train and visit European cities with? And it was these thoughts that cradled him into a very satisfying nap.

♪

Just over an hour later they arrived at the Museo del Violino, in the heart of Cremona. Much as in the museum in Milan, they walked solemnly around a room of glass cases in which some of the world's most priceless violins were suspended. It was called the treasure chest, as it contained Amati, Stradivari and Guarneri.

Gabrielle couldn't help thinking that it was almost like a mausoleum. The violins seemed to be trapped, frozen forever in space, when they were made to sing!

'Ah yes, seeing them displayed all together, I'm starting to see the difference now,' Walter remarked. Up to that point, all violins looked largely the same to him, perhaps differing in colour. But now he could see the proportions of the Strads were longer than the Amati, which to his untrained eye were 'curvier'. 'I prefer the Amati,' he pronounced, 'although I suppose the real proof is in the sound.'

'We take each violin out to be played regularly, to keep the sound quality good,' said a guide who happened to be passing through the display room. 'In fact, we invite soloists to perform concerts in our auditorium,' he added and Walter looked at Gabrielle, whose face lit up briefly before her features rearranged themselves. He nodded. She wouldn't be playing today.

'Another time, perhaps,' she said, with that professional veneer that Walter hoped was cracking, like varnish on an old masterpiece.

'Shut. The. Front. Door.' Devlin's voice came from the next exhibition room.

'What is it?' Gabrielle asked breathlessly, as she rushed in to see what he'd found.

'You never told me Stradivari made guitars,' he said, eyes wide like a child on Christmas morning. 'This is amazing!'

There, behind a display case, was a classical guitar beautifully designed and stamped with the Stradivari name.

'It's a classical guitar, possibly made for the Spanish court of Philip the Second,' she said.

For once, Devlin felt like he was on solid ground. Violins were not his forte, but he knew where he was with a guitar, albeit a classical one that looked far smaller and more intricate than any he'd ever seen.

'I'll leave you to your side quest,' she said, pleased to see him enjoying himself, and followed Walter into the next room.

He was marking something down in his notebook.

'Do you see? This one has a similar inlay design to ours,' he said, pointing at a violin that was displayed without a name.

The shape and colour were different, but there was something in the curve of the scroll that caught her eye. Apparently, the violin maker was thought to have been a student of the Stradivari style, but it was unknown who he was. She eased the violin case from under Walter's arm and sat on the floor in front of the glass case, cross-legged, with the stolen violin on her lap. She opened the case, then waited a moment before doing anything.

'What are we waiting for?' he asked, switching his glance from the glass case to Gabrielle.

'We're waiting for them to speak to each other.'

Walter couldn't tell if this was some kind of technical term. Gabrielle didn't seem the type to be prone to whimsy, but her expression as she sat there, cradling the violin in the crook of her arm, told another story altogether. There was a perceptible charge in the air, a strange vibration, now that the two violins were in touching distance of each other. It was as though, when the case opened, a presence had entered the museum room and Walter looked around him, half-expecting to see someone.

'How can they know who he was without knowing his name?' Walter asked in a whisper.

'Not everything was written down in those days. People may have heard talk of this luthier, but perhaps he wasn't famous enough to be remembered.' Even Gabrielle had a hard time believing that someone with such skill had been lost to time. 'Perhaps he wished to stay anonymous?' she suggested, looking up at Walter and hoping for some kind of academic explanation.

'It's possible. After all, not everyone desires fame. Creative types especially can shun the limelight. Perhaps his reward was in the craft itself, rather than the ego's desire to make a name for himself.'

Gabrielle paused and wondered about what she'd agreed to with V. She justified taking the money to save the

Wilding family name. But who was she saving it for? Did it matter? As Shakespeare famously wrote, *'What's in a name? That which we call a rose by any other name would smell as sweet.'* She couldn't think about it here, in front of Walter and Devlin. She needed to get back home and think about it properly.

Gabrielle took several pictures on her phone and told Walter that she couldn't be certain if both violins were made by the same hand.

'I'll have to get back home and do some more research,' she said, getting up and making her way towards the exit, the violin neatly tucked under her arm.

Walter watched as she left the room and thought to himself, *Wasn't that why we came here?*

Chapter Twenty-Seven

♪

Cremona

The evening light cast an amber glow on the old buildings of Cremona. After freshening up at the hotel, they settled on a little trattoria for dinner, nestled in the small piazza across the street. The setting was like a picture postcard: tables with parasols, and a crowd of relaxed diners, enjoying the old city. However, there was still a slight awkwardness between Gabrielle, Devlin and Walter as they sat down for a meal together. Up to that point they had been just three strangers, thrown together by fate and circumstance, sharing only a brief coffee or a sandwich wrapped in plastic. Sharing a meal? Well, in Italy, that practically made them family.

Gabrielle ordered aperitifs and, as they sipped their Aperol spritzes, they perused the menu. The evening was balmy but not too hot – just how Devlin remembered his last trip to Italy in Helga. He'd lost count of how many years ago it had been. Tonight, he felt very far away from home and yet closer to the beating heart of what it meant to be alive. He watched as people strolled along the cobbled streets: tourists searching for some place to eat, a child with an ice cream in one hand and his father holding the other, lovers with arms draped loosely around each other's bodies. The cathedral bells rang in the distance and, at the tables close by, people spoke Italian with such melodic accents that Devlin felt a timeless quality to the evening that he wanted to capture forever.

'I'm afraid I'm a bit lost here,' Walter said, looking at the menu.

'*Prendo linguine alla vongole, per favore,*' Gabrielle ordered in perfect Italian as the waiter approached.

'*Lo stesso,*' Walter piped up, having just googled 'linguine with clams' on his phone and how to say 'the same' in Italian. He winked at Devlin, as much as to say, 'Take that!'

'Pizza,' Devlin said, making life easy on himself. '*Quattro formaggi, per favore.*' He smiled, before handing back the menu.

As the trio ate their meals, washed down with a crisp prosecco, all of the stress and worry over the violin seemed to melt away. It began to feel more like a holiday than a research trip, and as the night sky turned to midnight blue and a full moon shone above the rooftops, they began to get to know each other on a new level. As friends.

'So, what kind of a student was he?' Gabrielle asked Walter, as she handed him the bread basket, filled with slices of sourdough, to mop up the delicious sauce.

'The ideal kind, wasn't that what you were saying before?' Devlin joked.

'Ah yes, well, where to begin?' Walter said, dabbing his chin with his napkin. 'A bit scattered at times. Always jotting down lyrics when he should have been learning the wives of Henry the Eighth.'

'In my defence,' Devlin said, 'I'm not even sure Henry the Eighth remembered their names.'

'No, I have to say, Devlin did stand out in a very important way.' The memory had stayed with Walter all of these years and while he didn't want to embarrass the lad, she had asked the question and perhaps it might restore to Devlin the spark of who he was. His essence. 'I was quite fortunate in that I had the boys' respect. I'm not sure how or why, but I was established at the school and earned my dues, I suppose. But there was that month when I took leave, do you remember? My mother had passed, and the school hired a supply teacher.'

Gabrielle filled their glasses and found herself leaning forward to hear the story better. Walter noticed her cutlery askew on her plate, the glass and napkin no longer aligned with imaginary angles. Perhaps she was finally beginning to feel at ease. It warmed his heart to see it.

'She told me afterwards,' he continued, 'how she'd struggled to keep the students disciplined, until one day she overheard a boy speaking before she entered the classroom. Apparently, he told everyone to give her a fair chance, but of course that didn't work. So he told them that she was his older cousin and if anyone gave her trouble, they'd have him to deal with.'

Devlin smiled to himself. 'I can't believe she overheard that,' he said.

'We teachers have bionic hearing,' Walter pointed out astutely.

When Devlin looked across at Gabrielle, she was smiling, too, and watching him in a way that made him feel a bit embarrassed. As though his mother had just shown her a cute childhood photo.

'Anyway, on another note, how about a drinking game?' he said, catching the waiter's eye and ordering another bottle of wine.

'Oh boy,' Gabrielle groaned.

'I might be a bit too old for games, Devlin,' Walter insisted.

'No, listen, you'll like this one. Are you a good whistler?'

'What?'

'Okay, so you have to whistle a song, and we have to guess what it is. If we guess correctly, you have to drink and, well, you get the picture.'

And so they began, whistling and drinking, whistling and drinking, much to the chagrin of their fellow diners. Gabrielle whistled classical tunes that Devlin didn't know and Walter couldn't decipher and so it was that by the time they finished off their meal with a glass of limoncello, the two men were ready for their beds.

'I'll stay here for a while,' Gabrielle said, taking care of the bill. They were too drunk to argue and she assured them that she would be fine seeing herself back to the hotel, which was just paces across the piazza. As she watched them stagger slightly across the square, she ordered an espresso and took out her phone from her handbag.

Scrolling through the images of the two violins, she felt an excited rush spiral in her belly. It was still just a hunch, but something told her that it was the same luthier who had built their violin. She wondered again about the fact that so little was known about him. Was he born in Cremona? The violin in the museum was dated to the mid-1800s. She'd have to talk to Roger again once she returned home.

When the old town clock struck midnight and the air grew chilly, Gabrielle walked across the square to the hotel and wished a *'Buona notte'* to the night manager on duty before getting into the lift. Reflected in the mirrored interior, she looked tired but happy. The best combination. They had adjoining rooms on the third floor and before the elevator doors even opened, she was imagining the click of her room door behind her, slipping off her shoes and having a nice, soothing shower before bed. But when she walked down the hallway, her eyes caught something jarring. Something that shouldn't have been there. Someone.

Chapter Twenty-Eight

♪

Devlin was having a strange dream. It was one of those dreams where you know you're in a dream but you're too tired to wake up. Someone was in his apartment, knocking things over and making lots of noise. But then the noises started coming from outside his subconscious, and within seconds his eyes were opening. Someone was hammering on his door. Then he heard her calling his name. It was Gabrielle.

'Jesus Christ!'

Devlin found Gabrielle leaning against the doorjamb with a knife in one hand and a bloodied towel in the other. 'What the fuck?' he added, when no answer was coming.

'I-I...' she shook her head, as though trying to dislodge the explanation from somewhere deep inside her mind. Should she tell him the truth? No, not now. How could she explain that she'd already been in contact with the head of the gang, allowed herself to be bribed for $20,000? If he knew that she was seriously contemplating handing the violin back to them. Especially after Walter's story about how he stuck up for the supply teacher. Devlin was a man of integrity and she...

'I lost the key card to my room,' she said, her voice trembling. 'I grabbed a knife from a tray outside,' she said, pointing to a trolley left by room service for one of the other rooms.

Devlin blinked so hard he felt sure it must have made a sound.

'Okay, so you've just had a bit of an accident,' he said, piecing the rest of the story together himself. He walked out into the hall and stretched out his arms towards her, like a lion-tamer trying to approach a wild cat. 'Just put the knife down and we'll get you sorted.'

Gabrielle looked at the knife in her hand, as though someone else must have put it there. Half of her story was true; she did grab the knife from the room-service trolley.

The man standing outside Devlin's room had been twice her size. She should have run back down to reception or called the police. But her instincts had taken over.

'Who are you?' she'd shouted at him, pointing the knife at him.

The man had turned around and almost laughed when he saw her.

'I'm here for the violin,' he'd said. 'Just give it to me and no one gets hurt.'

He sounded American, but with a French roll to his 'r's.

'We had a deal.'

'The deal did not involve taking the violin on an Italian holiday,' he'd said.

'Tell your boss I will hand the violin over, okay?

I guarantee it. I just need more time to prove its provenance.' She'd hoped the men couldn't hear her.

He'd taken several steps closer, until she could smell the staleness of his breath.

'This is not a negotiation, princess.'

Gabrielle had squeezed the knife tighter in her hand. She shouldn't have approached him. What was she thinking?

'I think you'll find it is. Your boss has agreed a payment of twenty thousand dollars. Tell them I will hand the violin over as soon as I get back to the UK.'

'Give me one good reason why I shouldn't break down this door and take the violin now.'

'Because it's not here. It's in a storage locker. At Paddington Station.' She'd remembered watching a film once, a spy thriller maybe, where they said that if you have to lie, stick as close to the truth as possible. Technically, the violin had been at Paddington at one point and she felt a sense of conviction in her voice when she told him.

'Why should I believe you?'

She had taken out her phone and showed him the app that Devlin had used.

'Here's the security code.'

Just then, the man's phone had rung. He'd stared at her for a long time before answering. She'd started to think that perhaps she was getting away with this. Her heart was pounding and the blood thrummed through her ears. The man had spoken in French and after two or three sentences he hung up.

'Boss says you have twenty-four hours to deliver the violin.'

'Okay. Thank you.' Gabrielle had almost collapsed with relief.

'The deal is now ten thousand dollars.'

Gabrielle nodded. She had no intention of going along with this anymore, so what did it matter? She just wanted him to leave. And he was leaving. He'd walked past her, slowly, looking her up and down in a way that made her skin crawl. It was almost over.

'Just one more thing,' he'd said, turning around and reaching from behind her. 'Boss said to give you a message.' With that, he'd taken her hand that was still holding the knife and thrust it into her upper thigh. The white-hot pain was so intense that she didn't even scream.

'That's it, lean on me,' Devlin said, guiding her into his room. She wobbled slightly and landed heavily in the leather tub chair by the window, the lights of the city beyond.

'Gabs, if you don't mind my saying, you don't look so good.'

She was pressing a towel tightly against her leg. Gritting her teeth with grim determination, she heaved herself upward again.

'Devlin. We've not known each other for very long. I'm not prone to hysterics, but I think I may have accidentally severed an artery.'

'Wha—' She pulled up the hemline of her skirt and briefly lifted the towel to reveal a gash in her inner thigh – pumping blood.

'I can't look,' she said timidly. 'Is it bad?'

'Um… No. Not that bad. It'll be fine.' Thankfully she didn't seem to notice the high pitch of his voice as he scrambled into a T-shirt and jeans. 'But just to be on the safe side, we might as well take a quick trip to A&E, yeah?'

Her bottom lip began to tremble and her eyes filled with tears before she flopped back onto the chair.

'Everything's spinning,' she said in a detached way.

Devlin sprang into action, narrowly avoiding tripping over his suitcase, and with one arm held her upright while dialling for reception on the phone with the other.

'Don't go to sleep on me, Gabs, okay? And keep pressure on the wound.'

She acquiesced, a novelty in their rocky relationship so far, and Devlin silently thanked the health and safety course he'd taken at Heathrow. Phone call made, he knelt down in front of her and explained that he would have to carry her downstairs. Every minute counted when it came to a wound like this. It was a strange feeling, taking charge. She always seemed so … together. Or, if he was being unkind, rather bossy. But now she just nodded lethargically and whispered a solemn 'thank you'. He pulled on his shoes, then swooped her up expertly into his arms and made a little joke about baggage that brought a faint smile to her lips.

'You're going to be fine,' he said, holding her a little closer as she rested her head on his shoulder.

♪

Speeding through the streets of Cremona in the back of the ambulance, Gabrielle held Devlin's hand tightly. The paramedics had managed to stem the bleeding, but it was clear that she had lost a lot of blood.

'The violin,' she said.

'What about it?'

'It's with Walter. It's safe.'

Even now, she knew he'd want to know, and in the midst of everything, it played a chord in his heart that felt familiar and brand new, all at once. He looked deeply into her eyes and smiled at her, as though that smile could contain everything he felt about her in that moment. To his surprise, she held his gaze and smiled, too.

'Am I going to die?'

'Hah!' His silly laugh had broken the spell. 'I hate to be *that guy*, but yes. We all will, someday.'

'You are infuriating, do you know that?'

'It has been said. But you're still holding my hand, so...'

'I don't want you to be the last person I speak to before I die,' she remarked, pulling her hand away, but he could tell it was an act.

'Well, talk to this guy then.' Devlin pointed to the handsome paramedic.

A ripple of amusement crept across Gabrielle's pale face, but just as quickly, her eyelids began to flutter and her head lolled to the side.

'No, no, no, you have to stay awake, Gabs,' he said, taking her hand again. Devlin knew he had to keep her talking, keep her mind off the pain.

'Tell me about your cat, what's his name again?'

'Satie,' she replied, wincing as the tyres bumped over a manhole cover.

'Why d'you call him that?'

'Because it's his name.'

Devlin turned to the paramedic and assured him all would be well, her sarcasm was perfectly intact.

'I named him after Erik Satie. The composer.'

'Of course.' Devlin nodded.

'What's that supposed to mean?'

'Nothing. I didn't say anything.'

'There was a tone. That sarcastic one you always use.'

Devlin gave her a quizzical look before adding, 'We used to have a dog called Snowy.'

'Why did you call him that?'

'Because he was slightly cold to the touch.'

Gabrielle turned away to hide her smile.

'You're an idiot.'

'I do my best,' he said.

It felt surreal, having this ridiculous conversation in the back of an ambulance in Italy, and yet it was exactly what she needed to keep hold of some sense of okayness. *She'd be okay, wouldn't she?* She released a long and shuddering sigh.

'This is all so unlike me,' she said, her features strained with self-admonition.

'Hey, it's okay,' he soothed.

'I let my guard down and I shouldn't have done that,' she continued.

Devlin wondered if this was actually the real Gabrielle or the infallible, not-a-hair-out-of-place professional she always portrayed. He felt like he was listening in on her internal dialogue and it wasn't pretty. He wanted to shield her from it, but how do you shield someone from themselves?

'You forgot your room key. We've all been there. It's hardly a crime.'

'No, you don't understand—' Gabrielle wanted to tell him about the thug, about the fact that she'd just been stabbed – but she couldn't do any of this without revealing the bribe she'd agreed to. Even if it was only a temporary case of bad judgement. She couldn't tell him. That's when the tears came.

The paramedic intervened and broke her stream of consciousness, saying '*calmo*', gesturing with both hands that they should bring the emotion down a peg or two. It worked and she didn't speak again, just stared unseeing at the ceiling until they arrived at the hospital.

Chapter Twenty-Nine

♪

'She nicked her femoral artery,' Devlin explained to Walter later on the phone, feeling bizarrely as though he was in an episode of *Casualty*.

'Good Lord, shall I come down? I was just getting dressed.'

'No, no, it's fine. She'll be fine. She was lucky, according to the consultant. It wasn't too deep. Lost quite a bit of blood, though, so she'll need a transfusion.'

'Have you been there all night?'

Devlin yawned what sounded like 'Yeah.'

'Right. Text me the address and I'll bring you some breakfast.'

Devlin looked up and down the hallway. It was almost seven a.m., and the place was bustling with staff and patients. He made his way to the bathroom and rubbed some cold water onto his face, before staring at his reflection in the mirror. Not exactly what he had expected coming to Italy. In fact, he couldn't help thinking how peculiar it was that these two relative strangers had suddenly become two of the most important people in his life. How had that happened? He splashed some more water in his hands and ran it through his hair before going back to the room.

'Oh, you're awake,' he said, as he watched a nurse plump up the pillows behind Gabrielle's head.

'Thanks to you, it would seem.'

He couldn't quite read her expression, but her words gave him a warm feeling in his chest. A young man came in with a trolley and left a tray of breakfast beside her.

'Oh, maybe I should go and leave you to it,' he began, but she shook her head. The nurse nodded at a chair beside the bed and he sat down.

'My consultant said you didn't leave my side,' she said, taking the lid off of a yoghurt pot. 'He spoke English, by the way. My Italian doesn't stretch to medical jargon.' An ironic smile that showed she was definitely on the mend.

'I know, we spoke last night. Don't you remember?'

'Oh, right. Yes. Maybe.' She struggled to open a packet of plastic cutlery and Devlin promptly intervened, taking the knife and handing her the spoon.

'Very funny,' she said.

'How are you feeling?'

'A bit groggy, but not too bad.'

'Any pain?'

It felt pleasantly strange, his concern for her well-being.

'Just feels like someone gouged out my thigh with a knife, but the painkillers are helping.'

Devlin nodded, then rested his elbows on his knees, looking at the floor for some unknown inspiration.

'You okay?' she asked.

'It's none of my business, but—'

'People only say that when they're about to make it their business.'

'Last night, when he asked you if you were on any kind of medication that might interact…'

Gabrielle continued spooning her yoghurt into her mouth, as if the conversation were not happening at all.

'I know what Citalopram is. And Clonazepam.'

'Well, bully for you!'

'No, I mean, I'm not being—'

'What? Judgemental? Nosey?'

The last thing he wanted was to upset her. He thought a wall had come down between them, but he'd managed to build it back up in thirty seconds.

'I was here with you, I couldn't *not* hear what you were saying.'

'Devlin, with respect, this is none of your business and just because you helped me out last night does not entitle you to intrude on my private life.'

He nodded again, then stood up to leave. She refused to look at him and for a moment, he tried to put himself in her shoes. That fierce pride was covering up something he knew all too well.

'I know what they are because I used to take them.'

Gabrielle put down the spoon and the half-empty pot of yoghurt. When she looked up her eyes were shining with unshed tears. She said nothing. In that moment he could see that she would never ask why. She would never ask for anything, not even for help when she so clearly needed it. And that could only mean one thing. She had asked for help in the past and not been given it. How he knew all of this, he couldn't say. Melissa had often accused him of being clueless about her feelings. But with Gabrielle, this fortress of a woman who had, quite frankly, intimidated the shit out of him when they first met – he could just intuit. But he would have to offer something of himself first. He would have to tell her the story he hadn't told anyone.

'Ever since I was a kid, all I wanted to be was a musician. I had these grandiose dreams of playing Wembley Stadium, just me and my guitar.' His voice felt rusty and it reminded him of the violin, quiet and cold in its case, seizing up through lack of use. He would have to run through some scales first and warm up to this honesty thing.

'Every bit of pocket money I had went on buying new strings for that battered old guitar I'd bought second-hand. I worked on my songwriting, listened over and over to performers I wanted to emulate: Tom Petty, Clapton, Joni Mitchell. I just—' He paused for a moment, smiling at the memory. 'It sounds ridiculous now, but I just believed I could be someone special. That I'd be able to create something new, but timeless all the same. I loved music and I couldn't see myself doing anything else.'

Gabrielle leaned back against her pillow. She wasn't sure what he was trying to tell her or why, but despite everything, she didn't want to be left alone. She wanted him to stay and there was something about the sound of his voice that made her feel safe. As he sat there in his creased T-shirt and faded jeans, it was as though she were seeing him for the first time. The night's scenes flashed through her mind: how he'd carried her to the elevator and held her protectively until they reached the reception; the way he pulled himself up into the ambulance to sit beside her – no hesitation or question that he would leave her; the way he'd looked at her, the dimples in his cheeks when he smiled, how he'd kept her spirits up and held her hand as though he'd always be there. The sudden realisation of her feelings – feelings that she had no problem in suppressing in normal times – almost took her breath away.

'What happened?' she said, her voice breaking from the thick emotion in her throat. 'At the bar that night, you walked away.'

'I used to busk a lot, and started making some decent money. So I decided to travel, get more experience. I moved back to Ireland and started busking on Grafton Street. It was amazing, I mean, I had to play a lot of covers but I really grew as a performer.'

Gabrielle couldn't help but notice the muscles in his arms rippling as he got up and sat on the edge of her bed. She shook the inappropriate thought from her mind.

'Then everything changed. Valentine's Day 2015. At two thirty-five in the afternoon, to be precise.'

Gabrielle's body tensed. She wasn't sure she wanted to hear this story now.

'We'd only been dating for five months, but to be honest, I knew after five minutes that she was the one. Summer, that was her name.' He closed his eyes for a moment, as though trying to conjure her up in the parts of his mind where time had stood still and she looked exactly as she had then. Blonde hair, wild and flowing, dressed in some loose-fitting dress and sandals, squinting in the sunshine.

'Summer, the perfect name. It was her whole nature. She filled me with a warmth and optimism I didn't realise it was possible to feel without copious amounts of booze. Only with Summer, there was no hangover. She was Australian. An exchange student studying design. Have you ever met someone who just *gets* you?'

Gabrielle smiled weakly. No, she hadn't. At least, not yet.

'Just, everything I was about, everything I wanted to achieve, she just completely got me. The way her eyes shone when I sang one of my original songs instead of the covers that persuaded passers-by to part with their change. She believed in me – no hesitation – and that made me believe in myself. She was a part of my future. My music and Summer, that was all I lived for.'

Was this it? Gabrielle wondered. A break-up story? That was his big life trauma and the reason he ended up on anxiety meds?

'Look, I know you're trying to make me feel better about the medication, but you don't understand—'

Devlin looked at her, his eyes growing red and the muscles in his jaw twitching under the skin. He seemed far away in the past, as though he had left the hospital room altogether.

'I was playing a song I'd written for her. I had it all planned. Valentine's Day, St Stephen's Green. The day was bright and I had the ring in my pocket. She always took the Luas, the tram. I couldn't have known…'

'Known what?' she asked, pushing down the covers and gingerly moving closer to him, letting her legs hang over the side of the bed so they were side by side.

'That's what everyone kept telling me. I couldn't have

known that she'd take the bus instead; that it would drop her off on the other side of the street.'

Oh, Jesus. Gabrielle had a horrible realisation that this wasn't just a break-up story anymore.

'She looked across at me – I could see her blue eyes shining the way they always did. Then she saw the handwritten cardboard sign I had propped against my guitar case. *Will you marry me?* She didn't look when she stepped off the kerb…'

Devlin held his hands out, as though he were still carrying her, or wondering what to do with them now she was no longer here.

'The funeral was just—' He shook his head. No words would come.

Gabrielle didn't think or hesitate but took him into her arms. He let his head lean against hers and she could feel his whole body just let go. She couldn't imagine his loss. She had never loved anyone the way he had just described. She'd never been loved by anyone like that. So how could you miss what you never had? It amazed her that he had opened himself up to another relationship after such heartache. He was braver than her, that was for sure. But now here he was, heartbroken again.

'I'm so sorry,' she said eventually.

'I'm sorry for her family. I felt so responsible. For all of it.'

She pulled back from him but kept her hands on his shoulders.

'You know that wasn't your fault, right?'

'So they tell me,' he said, with the saddest, most world-weary smile she'd ever seen. Before she knew what she was doing, she reached out and put her hand on his cheek.

'You can't spend your life blaming yourself. And if you think that not playing the guitar is some kind of penance, you're wrong. You're just punishing yourself.' She meant every word, even if it made her a hypocrite. Wasn't that exactly what she had done to herself? *But that's different*, a voice whispered inside. *You deserve it.*

He turned to face her and touched her hand that was still on his cheek.

'You know, you're actually quite likeable when you're not bossing me around.'

She was glad to see his smile had returned, and even though one short conversation was hardly going to change how he felt about the past, at least it was a start. All of those sessions with Trudy had stood for something.

'Shame the same can't be said for you. You're still the most annoying person I've ever had the misfortune to meet,' she replied, beaming up at him innocently. And next thing she knew, her hand had quite naturally slipped down and around his neck and then he was closer and smiling and her head tilted and her lips just met his. It all happened in a fraction of a second – no time to consciously decide anything, but then there they were, lips touching, and it suddenly felt so good that neither of them wanted it to end. Before she knew it, Devlin's arm had reached ever-so-lightly around her waist, and it felt so right on a molecular level that she kissed him harder and then he parted his lips and she could feel the wetness of his tongue.

'Oh, *perdonami*,' said Walter. He had almost walked in on them, but turned to leave just in time to collide with the nurse. Gabrielle and Devlin parted suddenly, as though they'd just committed some awful crime, when all they'd done was be young and fall in love. The nurse, oblivious to the romantic scene she'd walked in on, told them all to leave so she could take Gabrielle's blood pressure.

'We'll come back later,' Devlin offered.

'No, it's fine, I'll probably be discharged tomorrow anyway,' Gabrielle said, before the nurse pulled the privacy curtain.

The two men walked slowly down the corridor.

'Perhaps it's for the best,' Walter assured a very downcast-looking Devlin. 'Hospitals give me the collywobbles,' he added. He'd seen the inside of enough hospitals to last him a lifetime.

Chapter Thirty

♪

'Listen, about yesterday,' Devlin said, as Gabrielle was ordering them some coffees at the airport bar. He glanced back at Walter, who was surreptitiously watching him over the top of his broadsheet. Devlin had hardly slept the previous night, turning everything over in his head. But it all came down to this one realisation. For so long, he'd felt as though he were running away. From his feelings, from life, from love. But now, it finally felt like he was running towards something, and the lightness in his heart made him sure of what he was about to say next.

'I must apologise.' Gabrielle decided to cut him short. The last thing she could stomach right now was his remorse. When Walter had walked into her hospital room, Devlin had practically jumped off the bed as though he'd been electrocuted, and she'd hardly seen him since. She'd said she was tired and needed to rest and so Walter had rebooked their flights.

'God, no, it was my fault,' he persisted. 'You were on all

those painkillers…' Devlin began to fear that the feelings were all one-sided. Maybe she wouldn't have looked at him twice had it not been for the traumatic nature of events. She needed someone to cling to and he was just happy to have been that person for her. But when they kissed, something melted inside him. Something he had thought was frozen, or perhaps missing altogether. He'd left the hospital room unsure if he could risk the pain, or, worse, a life of unrequited love. But now here he was, trying to be vulnerable and it was all going wrong.

'It is a bit blurry, to be honest,' Gabrielle agreed, pouring milk into her coffee and refusing to make eye contact. She wished with every fibre that he would simply let it go. It was mortifying, baring your soul like that and having it rejected. No need to rub salt in the wound.

'Of course, I just didn't want you to think—'

'Already forgotten.'

Devlin frowned. He didn't want her to think it didn't mean anything to him, because it did.

'It was just a silly mistake,' she continued, hardly able to bear the fact that he might pity her – a sad, needy weirdo whose life was clearly going off the rails. 'It doesn't have to be awkward between us,' she added, trying to win back an iota of her professionalism.

It could not have been more awkward. Walter sat physically and metaphorically in the middle seat on the plane, once again acting as a human barrier between two people who obviously had feelings for each other but had decided (as humans do) to over-complicate the entire endeavour with thoughts. Thoughts about the past, the future, themselves and why they were profoundly unlovable.

The trip itself had been valuable, in terms of the violin, but on a personal level? A complete shitshow. Who knew what awaited her when she got back? She felt wretched and exhausted but she kept her phone in her hand, waiting for a reply from Roger. She had sent him the images of the violin. She was hopeful they were a match, but she wanted to be proved right in her findings. Everything had gotten so sidetracked. She'd let herself get carried away with Walter and Devlin. Their friendship felt like a breath of fresh air in her stagnant life, but no sooner had she finally let go than the universe came back to remind her in the form of that thug in the hotel lobby. The best way forward was to keep the focus on her career. That was something she could control. If the violin was as special as she believed it to be, she would prove her credentials and finally win the respect of her peers. Then, she promised herself, she would be happy.

Chapter Thirty-One

♪

THE VIOLIN

Budapest, 1910

On a dark, cold evening in October, Zita Karman and her sister, Alara, lit candles and settled themselves on the bare floorboards. Before them, a board marked with letters. They each asked the board questions. Alara wondered when she would meet her husband and if he would be good-looking. Zita, however, asked the same question she always did: 'Will I become a world-famous virtuoso?'

Alara rolled her eyes. I lay on the floorboards beside them, adjusting to my new home. I wondered if William could sense my location through the Ouija board? It wasn't good to dwell on such thoughts. I simply had to put my faith in the belief that one day, I would see him again. For now, my fate had led me to these two likeable sisters. Unlike my own sibling, who was utterly unknowable to me and in the end, unpredictable, Zita and Alara wore their hearts on their sleeves. They were both accomplished musicians and had fought good-naturedly yet fiercely over who would inherit their uncle's favourite violin. It was the one he carried with him at all times, and even the sisters noticed his mood darken if it ever left his side. He said he'd bought it from a Russian who played with the orchestra but gave up his entire career for love. *The fool*, he'd said. But the sisters thought it was hopelessly romantic. Yet when Zita heard the sound it produced, like a softly lamenting angel singing to the gods, she was determined to possess it. She knew her talents were average, but with that violin ... who knew what heights she could reach?

In the end the argument was settled by her uncle's will. The sisters should share the instrument. It was a fair outcome. They were used to sharing.

'Knowing you two, you'll end up sharing a husband!' their older brother had jeered once.

They placed their fingers lightly on the pointer and watched in fascination as it slid along the wooden board. Y – E – S. The candles flickered and Zita knew in her heart that her dream would come true. But when?

Alara's wish was granted sooner than either of them had anticipated. The European figure-skating competition was to be held in Budapest in the winter of 1909, and the sisters were invited along to provide a musical accompaniment to the athletes. Zita felt sure that this was her chance to step onto the world stage, but playing outdoors during an Austro-Hungarian winter did not lend itself to her uncle's rather temperamental violin. Alara, however, was moved neither by the cold nor by the strained notes of the violin. Her heart was captured by, it had to be said, an extremely attractive figure skater from Sweden. Lucas Olsson was tall, blue-eyed and unhesitating when he set his sights on a goal. He claimed a silver medal and Alara's hand in marriage. We all know the saying, 'marry in haste, repent at leisure', and while Alara soon began to regret her choice, her marriage had opened an unexpected door for the sisters.

Lucas moved to London, where he became the star skater at the Prince's Grand Skating Hall. Zita took the opportunity to travel with them and they found lodgings close by. Mixing with the great and good of London, Zita soon found herself booked out playing at salons and various concerts. There she met Maurice Ravel, whom she inspired to write his rhapsody 'Tzigane', enthralled by the Hungarian folk style of her playing.

Zita was a woman who was so self-possessed and sure of her voice as she played that piece for the first time, it was she who was breathing life into me. The freedom with which she played unlocked the tight, dark corners of my wooden frame. It was like opening my ribcage as wide as it could go and taking my first full breath. She had much to teach me, and I found myself wishing that my journey could pause there, with Zita. However, the lesson I was about to learn was not from Zita herself, but from a man so jealous that he would try to silence us both.

On a midsummer's evening, Zita played a small concert as first violinist with a string quartet. The cellist, a young American from Philadelphia, was besotted with her. Her long dark tresses and mysterious steel-grey eyes mesmerised him, and as they played together, she challenged him with every note. Before the audience had even stood to applause, Peter Broderick knew he would make her his wife. No one was more surprised than Zita herself when she said yes to his proposal of marriage six weeks later.

After a whirlwind wedding and the romance of setting up a new home together, the slowness of marriage began to change them both. As young people do, they assumed that a baby would come next, but no baby came. Peter grew resentful and bitter, accusing Zita of pouring all of her vitality into playing instead of becoming a mother. Finally, he insisted that there could be only one composer in the family.

'The role of musician falls to me, yours is that of a loving companion,' he announced.

Zita cocked her head. He had always admired her playing and yet, in her heart of hearts, she had sensed a certain amount of jealousy in his.

'I'm asking a very great deal – but it is important for my reputation, you understand. And as we are dependent on my reputation for the food on our plates and the splendour of our home, you will agree that this is how it must be.'

Zita nodded. She had been well-schooled in what was expected from her as a wife. She just hadn't realised that the sacrifice would be called for quite so soon, or quite so definitively.

Her resentment grew like a thorny rosebush, choking her voice. Every day she served her husband, he was the sun around which she revolved, her own talent eclipsed by the great Peter Broderick. In the privacy of their home, she sometimes played a piece, but her eyes could no longer make sense of the musical notation. 'I have been firmly taken by the arm and led away from myself,' she wrote in a letter to Alara. 'I long to return to where I was.'

And so it was that every time she drew the bow across my strings, I filled the air with the haunting sound of a woman stolen from herself. That her greatest achievement should be to sacrifice herself at the altar of her husband's dreams was the myth that bound so many women into slavery. *Why be an artist when you can be my muse?* Every woman wants to be adored until she realises the price she has had to pay. Despite my efforts, she refused to see the error of her ways. She had given her heart to a jealous man.

One evening, Lucas and Alara invited her to attend a party with a Swedish diplomat. It was a dull enough affair and Zita drank until she was tipsy, smoked cigars and played poker with the men. In the small hours of the morning, reluctant to return home to her controlling husband, she had an idea.

'Alara, let us summon a spirit with a Ouija board!'

Her eyes were aflame and while Lucas hesitated, Alara assured him it was nothing more than a childhood game. But as the group gathered around the dining table, the room lit by candlelight, Zita called on the otherworld.

'Is there someone present?' she asked, an edge of desperation to her voice.

'What shall we ask them?' Lucas whispered.

'I used to ask who I would marry,' Alara giggled. 'But not Zita.'

'Oh no? What did you ask, Zita?'

Zita's eyes closed. Her mouth tasted metallic with wine and cigar smoke. All of her life she had dreamed of being a virtuoso and yet she had let go of her passion, like a sleepwalker calmly stepping off a cliff. Yes, she had wanted a family, a happy ever after, but now she had neither. Then a strange urge took hold of her. It was foolish in the extreme, but when you have nothing to lose, looking foolish matters little.

'I call on the great composer Robert Schumann,' she said, her voice shaking.

Some of the others laughed out loud, but that only made her more determined. Clearing her throat, she said the words again, but louder this time.

The candles flickered and suddenly blew out. Alara gasped and the men attempted to conceal their agitation by pushing back their chairs and searching for the light switch. When the lights came on, Zita's face was white as a sheet.

'Zita, are you well? You look so pale,' her sister said, brushing her hair from her face which felt clammy.

'Alara, he spoke to me.'

'Who?'

'Schumann.'

Of course no one believed her, but Zita followed the instructions she had received. She packed her bag, told Peter that she was visiting a sick relative back home, but travelled instead to the Prussian State Library in Berlin. There, just as she had been instructed, she found a long-lost work – the manuscript of Schumann's Violin Concerto. It was written on the cusp of his descent into madness and was the last orchestral piece he wrote. It had not been seen in over eighty years; his wife Clara had kept it secret.

'He has instructed me to play his piece, Alara!' she told her sister when she returned to London. With their connections, all of high society and the press were invited to a concert. Zita played me with the passion of a prisoner set free. The crowds were fascinated and charmed by the melody and the once-in-a-lifetime experience of being the first to hear this lost work. Peter, on the other hand, saw it as an act of war. When she came home that night and fell into a blissful sleep, he packed up everything he owned and, at last, took my case with him. I was terrified as to what he would do. He took a carriage as far as Tower Bridge, got out and stood at the railings. I could smell the briny water below. All of my senses recoiled. *No. Not again. Not the water.* He threw me with a ferocity that at first sent me skyward. Then I tumbled down, down, down, down…

Chapter Thirty-Two

♪

Verity pulled up the collar of her coat against the swirling breeze that blew through Crawford Place. Keeping one eye on the entrance to Wilding's, she found herself distracted by a shop window further up the street. The display featured antique dolls and teddy bears having a tea party. One of her earliest memories as a child was putting her teddies to bed every night and telling them all about the life she would have when she was older.

'And we'll live in a nice house, with a pretty garden, full of flowers. I will marry a handsome man who is kind and brave and we will have two children. No, three children,' she'd corrected herself, since two didn't seem like enough. 'And we will all love each other very, very much—'

'Go to sleep and stop your infernal chatter!' her father had spat at her.

Verity had jumped under the covers and turned the light out, holding her breath until he would leave. Through the darkness, the words carried like an evil spell.

'Who'd marry you anyway?' he'd said, tossing out the line with such casual cruelty that Verity wasn't sure which was worse: the prospect of never being loved or the knowledge that even her own father didn't love her.

Her dark reverie was broken by the sight of a customer leaving Wilding's shop. She walked with purpose and pushed open the door, the bell overhead clanging.

'I'll be with you in a moment,' came a voice from behind the counter.

'How is your leg? Healing nicely, I hope.'

Gabrielle froze. She didn't recognise the voice and only two people knew about her wound.

'I hear Italy is lovely this time of year,' the voice continued.

Somehow, Gabrielle found her composure and turned to find a woman with long grey hair draped over her shoulder like mink fur, and a long dark coat, completely at odds with the season.

'Who are you?'

'You know who I am,' she answered plainly.

'I should report your thug for GBH—'

'But you won't.'

Gabrielle dug her fingernails into her palm.

'Let's talk money.'

'I don't want your money. I never should've agreed—'

'Perhaps your father might see things differently?'

Gabrielle thought she would vomit right on the counter. The woman opposite her was disturbingly calm. *In fact*, Gabrielle thought to herself, *she's enjoying this*.

'My father is dead.'

The woman laughed scornfully and casually walked

around the shop, eyeing up the various instruments on display.

'Come now, we both know that isn't true.'

The pain in Gabrielle's leg became amplified. She didn't have the strength for this anymore. How long had she been holding everything together by herself? And now this violin business – why was she the one protecting everyone else again?

The woman came back to the counter and spread her hands on the surface.

'We checked the locker at the train station and what do you think we found?'

Gabrielle curled her lip.

'You know, contrary to what you might think, I quite like you. You remind me of myself.'

Gabrielle tsked.

'It's true. You're a lone wolf. I can tell. But you cannot protect your father any longer—'

'I'm not protecting him!' Gabrielle spat. 'I'm protecting the family name. Our legacy.'

'Well, in that case, may I suggest you hand over the violin, or your legacy—' at this the woman cast a disparaging glance around the shop '—what there is of it, will be ruined.'

'How many times, I don't have the violin. It doesn't belong to me, I was merely asked to appraise it.'

'And what did you uncover?'

Gabrielle saw her chance.

'You don't know who made it, do you?'

A slight twitch in her temple. Gabrielle spotted it.

'Look, just give me a few more days. I'm so close to

finding out its provenance. Then I'll give it to you and we'll both have what we want.'

'Why should I?'

'Because you know as well as I do – half of the value of owning something is knowing where it came from, right?'

The woman let out a long sigh.

'I don't trust you, but I'll admit I'm intrigued. Complete your research,' she said, turning for the door. 'Do not double-cross me, Gabrielle. Next time, that knife will be aimed at your heart.'

Chapter Thirty-Three

♪

Devlin found immense satisfaction in hearing the efficient noise of his screw gun. The same could not be said for Walter.

'Not that I don't appreciate your efforts,' he shouted, index fingers blocking his ears, 'but I actually have an appointment to get to.'

Devlin had picked up new bolt locks at the hardware shop and was making sure the apartment was burglar-proof for the violin. And themselves, of course.

'Sorry about that,' he said, stepping back to let Walter out. 'You'd tell me if I was outstaying my welcome, right?'

'You're always welcome here,' he assured him, the skin around his eyes crinkling in such a way that Devlin knew he meant it.

'I'll cook us something nice for dinner,' Devlin called out to him. He suddenly had an unwelcome vision of growing old in this place, two bachelors with nothing else to do except the crossword. He shook it quickly from his head, only to find it replaced with an even less appealing thought. Gabrielle. He'd completely opened up to her and even though he didn't regret it exactly, he wasn't sure where things stood between them now. They'd grown so close to each other, only to take a giant leap backwards. He wasn't even sure if they were friends anymore. Maybe it was all happening too soon after Melissa. Was he even in the right headspace for this? All of these questions were pointless when the answer remained annoyingly the same. He was falling for her. Walter knew it and now Gabrielle probably knew it, too. He picked up another screw and drilled it into the doorframe, trying to forget the whole damn thing.

♪

Walter found he was able to drop into a zone of blissful nothingness as he lay on the table for yet another scan. He'd stopped asking what they were scanning for. At this point, it made little difference. And no matter how often he visited this place, he still hadn't perfected the art of tying the paper robe in such a way as to not leave his arse hanging out at the back. It made him smile now. Dignity was something he'd had to forgo a long time ago.

'So, I don't think there's any need to change your meds at the moment,' the resident doctor assured him in a light-hearted tone that belied the inevitable fact that Walter was dying. Death was an everyday business within these walls, and before long Walter found himself talking in that same practical manner. He hadn't reached the point of gallows humour yet, but it wasn't far off. Once he heard the word 'terminal', he had wanted to take control back. Choose when he would toddle off this mortal coil, rather than have the illness choose for him. The prognosis had been delivered at his previous appointment, just two months ago. The weight of it had almost crushed him. Clearly, he hadn't been in his right mind since. But now that the violin had entered his life, everything had changed. He wanted to live every day until his last – however soon that would be. The man who was about to swallow all of the pills before young Devlin rang his doorbell felt like a stranger to him now.

He hardly recognised the person he was just a few short weeks ago. It was almost like a portal through which he had to pass in order to get to the other side of really living. Death had come, and now he could see the real meaning of life. It wasn't about making a good name for yourself or earning a decent salary. It was about fun, silliness, touching other people's lives in some way, and letting them touch yours. Letting yourself be blown about and shaped by experience. Being curious rather than scared all of the time. Living in dread of the future – that seemed to be the common thread that kept everyone tied in knots, weighted down with painful memories of the past. Yet Walter found the more his thoughts stayed in the present, the simpler everything became.

♪

Gabrielle was stuck in traffic and staring out of the window when she spotted Walter. He was walking out of the main entrance to the hospital. In fact, the signs pointing to that building were *Maternity* and *Oncology* and she knew he wasn't pregnant. The lights turned green and as she eased on the accelerator, it began to dawn on her that perhaps she wasn't the only one keeping secrets.

Chapter Thirty-Four

♪

As Gabrielle steered the old Volvo through the Buckinghamshire countryside, it was hard to believe that she was visiting a prison. Known as a category D, it was a low security prison and possibly the least bad place to serve a custodial sentence. There were employment courses and horticulture. She'd read the brochure but never visited once. It was too hard. Besides, he'd asked her not to.

As she drove up the drive, the ornate Victorian building came into view, with bay windows and high chimneys. It looked less like a prison than a country manor, which in fact it had been before the war. Then it was used as a base for MI6. Everything about it was surreal. She had booked her visit online, which seemed terribly modern, and now it was as though she'd stepped back in time. As soon as she'd pulled up the handbrake, she slipped off her seatbelt, opened the door and got out. She knew that if she didn't leave the car immediately, she'd turn back. The only way to get through this was to focus on the violin – that was why she was here.

After Milan, she had begun the painstaking process of comparing the pictures of the violin she had found in the museum to her own database. She sent them to Roger, but despite several promising leads, they all turned out to be dead ends. She couldn't ask any of her usual contacts, given the situation, and so she was desperate. The only way to truly figure out who this mysterious luthier was, was to find out who he studied under. And there was only one person in the world who held that kind of esoteric knowledge. The man she swore she'd never ask for help again.

She handed her driver's licence to a prison officer who also searched her bag and pockets. Another man showed her into the visiting room and told her where to sit. Another five minutes passed and then the prisoners came in through a different door. They wore their own clothes. She was grateful for that. She couldn't bear seeing him in a tracksuit. That would have been even weirder than being in jail. It was all very efficient and normal. People embraced, got up and bought tea and bars of chocolate from a vending machine. Then he appeared. Her heart almost broke at the sight of him. Yet he held his head high, smiled, nodded hello to people as he walked towards her, as though they were in a restaurant meeting for lunch.

'Hello, Dad,' she said.

'Haven't heard that for a while,' he said, stopping short in front of her. 'You look tired.' He gave her a light kiss on her cheek before sitting down opposite.

'You're positively glowing,' she said, not sure whether

she felt relief or resentment. Had he any idea what he had done to her life? 'Prison life agreeing with you then?'

He gave her a look that she couldn't decipher. Annoyance, perhaps.

'Shall I get us some tea?' he said, getting up and searching his pockets for change.

'I have money,' she said.

'I can afford to buy us a cup of tea, Gabrielle.'

She sank back in her chair. Why had she come? This was excruciating. Three years she had been pretending to the world that her father was dead. His great plan, not hers.

'Reputation is everything in this business,' he had said, that frantic evening before the police came to arrest him. He had been dealing in fake copies of Gaglianos and selling them as genuine. They were good violins, there was no argument there. But forging Italian makers' labels inside their instruments was the ultimate betrayal. Instruments that are faked are, as a rule, meant to be purchased by the eye and not by the ear. Gregory Wilding was wise enough to sell these violins to collectors who knew practically nothing about what they were buying. They were looking for investment pieces, somewhere to hide their money, as was often the case. The problem occurred years later when one of them decided to sell it on and of course the paperwork led back to Gabrielle's father.

'It was all for you,' he'd added desperately, as the policeman clicked the handcuffs on his wrists. She had stood in the doorway of the shop, Satie in her arms and the weight of her father's expectations on her shoulders. Now the sole proprietor of Wilding's, a business she had never intended to pursue, she finally had access to the accounts.

Ten years ago, her father had indeed sold three violins for between fifteen and 20,000 pounds each. And the beneficiary? Maximillian Daunt. Her old violin tutor. She remembered her father saying that the fact Max was investing so much in her meant that she had real talent. Stupidly, she had believed him. The truth was that her father was paying him a small fortune. If only he hadn't bothered, neither of them would be paying for it now.

She watched as he carefully placed two plastic cups on the table between them. He'd put too much milk in. He always put too much milk in. She couldn't even be honest with him about that. All of her anger was mixed up with so much guilt. What if he blamed her for what happened with Max? Told her it was her fault? It was bad enough that she felt the pressure to make him proud of her, to be a great virtuoso and prove that his belief had been well placed, but the resentment that he never saw what was really going on filled her with bitterness and left her isolated. Even now, she felt responsible. He wouldn't be in here if it weren't for her. But wasn't she in a type of prison, too? Her therapist had told her once that everyone is responsible for their own choices, but Gabrielle had a hard time separating out her role in other people's decisions.

'Still telling people I'm dead?'

'It was your idea, remember?'

He nodded in a self-pitying way.

'Yes, but you do seem to be a little too enthusiastic about it.'

She shrugged and picked up her cup of tea before putting it back down. It looked pale and gross and had some weird scum on the surface.

'I'm hardly Dietmar Machold,' he said, referring to the Austrian dealer who swindled upwards of forty million euros from banks and investors with fake violins. The press called him the Bernie Madoff of violin dealers.

'I'm simply doing what you asked – protecting the family name,' she replied, refusing to be drawn into his vortex of self-pity.

'Well then, to what do I owe the pleasure of this visit?'

'I have something I want you to look at.'

His eyebrows arched upwards in surprise.

'You're still the most knowledgeable appraiser in the business,' she pointed out, with some reluctance.

'No need for flattery. I'm bored senseless in this place. I'd welcome the distraction.'

'It's not flattery. Trust me, if there was anyone else I could ask, I would.'

There, that would set him straight, she thought. She handed him photocopies of the pictures she took in Milan and of her violin. She had to stop calling it that.

He took out a pair of tiny glasses and perched them on the end of his nose. Gabrielle felt a sudden chill, like someone walking over her grave, and she rubbed her arms briskly before giving in and taking a mouthful of milky tea. *Gross.*

'So, you're assuming he's Italian?'

'You're assuming it's a man.' She said that just to annoy him. She was certain that there must have been female luthiers, but their names and their legacy never lived beyond their own lifetimes. There were historical accounts suggesting Catarina Guarneri, the wife of Giuseppe

Guarneri, was involved in making violins, with some instruments bearing her name on the label.

He pursed his lips and returned his gaze to the images.

'It's certainly in the Amati style,' he said, confirming her suspicions. 'Many workshops in Europe crafted such copies of the great maestros. Back then it wasn't viewed as forgery,' he added, a tone of vindication in his voice. 'It was simply a matter of supply and demand. There weren't enough genuine articles to go around and so they made these copies to order, which often sounded far superior to the originals.'

'Thank you for the history lesson, Father, but can you tell me something I don't already know?'

'Impatient as ever,' he said. 'Spruce front, wide grained on the bass side and super fine on the treble side. A deliberate choice. The ribs and back are a sugar maple, if I'm not mistaken. But the bridge, it's startling. Is it … bone?'

Gabrielle said nothing, but drank more of the disgusting tea, trying to warm up her insides. She knew this was no ordinary violin, but having her father confirm it was unsettling.

'Where did you get this?' he asked, taking off his glasses.

'I … a client. Found it. You know the way, emptying an old relative's attic,' she lied.

He nodded but his eyes narrowed in a way that showed he did not believe her.

'So, what do you suggest? How can I find out who made it?'

He returned his gaze to the pictures and tapped the arm of his glasses against his chin.

'You've checked the underside of the belly?'

'Please, give me some credit.'

'You came here for my help, didn't you?'

Gabrielle bit her tongue, a familiar sensation.

'It's difficult to tell at what point in the luthier's career this violin was made. They hone their skills over time, learn ways to uniquely express their own artistry, but what they never lose are the guiding principles of their masters.'

'Meaning?'

'Meaning, if you can find out who his tutor was, you'll be one step closer to solving your mystery. And I think you should be looking a little closer to home.'

'What do you mean? You don't think he's Italian? But what about the violin in Milan? It's undoubtedly by the same hand?'

'People did travel in the old days, you know.'

British violin-making in the eighteenth century was hardly lauded in the history books, Gabrielle knew that. The social conditions at the time didn't exactly inspire creativity and art in that area and besides, the lute was far more popular at the time. If her father was right, she had a lot more digging to do.

'There's something about the scroll,' he said, breaking into her thoughts. 'How it's carved. It's so elongated and refined.'

'It is very elegant,' she agreed. In fact, now that he had drawn her attention to it, there was a strange human quality to it. Like a woman's head arching backwards, as though all of her cares were thrown onto the wind. Even the pegs now had a familiar look to them; something she hadn't perceived before, despite studying every inch of the violin when it was in her possession. They almost looked like delicate finger bones. She blinked her eyes shut and when she looked up she noticed her father staring at her.

'I must go,' she said, rather abruptly.

'Might I keep these?' he asked, pointing to the pictures.

'Of course, they're copies.' She slung her bag over her shoulder and suddenly realised she hadn't a clue how to bring this meeting to a close. *See you soon* hardly seemed appropriate.

Folding the pages, Gregory Wilding noticed some musical notation scribbled on the back.

'What is this?'

'Oh, it's nothing,' she said, taking the sheet back from him. It was something she'd been playing around with since Milan, a piece of music that kept coming to her, as if on the wind. It was different to anything she used to write. In fact, she wasn't sure she could compose anymore, but this little air was persistent.

'Such a shame,' he said, getting up to leave. 'You had wonderful talent, Gabrielle. You could have been every bit as successful as Nicola Benedetti.'

She rolled her eyes. He was always comparing them.

'I'll never understand why you threw it all away.'

Gabrielle's stomach twisted. He'd never believed her about the pain in her wrist. The shame and anger fighting it out inside of her but never permitted to be released. She had to hold it all in. But something was different about today. She couldn't swallow it anymore. She hardly had time to make the decision, her voice sprang forth like shot from a canon.

'Fuck you!' she shouted, and everyone in the room

swung their heads to look at her. 'How could you not see what was going on?'

Her father's lips trembled, and she could see the guards striding towards them.

'W-what are you talking about?'

'Max. He … he…' Her throat was suddenly thick with unshed tears.

'Look, Miss, we don't want any trouble,' said the officer, taking her by the arm. It was as though she had been sleepwalking and now she was awake. She shook her head. God, she'd almost told him the truth. A truth she could barely admit to herself. Almost brought their whole world crumbling down. But that was just it; her world had already crumbled. All of the lies, they were what she had to do to keep everyone else's world safe.

She sat outside the prison in her car and waited until her hands stopped shaking before slowly turning the key in the ignition and letting off the handbrake. She would not go back there. It was over now. The search for the violin's true provenance was the only thing stopping her from falling off the edge completely. She headed straight for South Kensington and the Royal College of Music.

♪

Gregory Wilding was perturbed for two reasons. He had done everything to ensure that Gabrielle had the best shot at becoming one of Britain's brightest classical stars. He had risked his livelihood by selling those fake violins and ended up paying the ultimate price. He had lost everything. And yet all these years later, when she finally came to visit him, she had lashed out so viciously, as if everything was his fault. He would never understand what went on in her head. At a certain age, he wasn't exactly sure when, it was as though his little girl walked off into the woods and disappeared, only to be replaced by this sullen, unknowable young woman. Well, he wasn't going to take the blame. He'd sacrificed his career and his freedom for her, only to watch her abandon it all. Perhaps this violin was the key to their redemption?

He looked at the photographs once more. There was something about it that lit up his temporal lobe – a memory that he couldn't quite place. So many violins had passed through his doors over the years, but his mind stored each one, like a Filofax. Further and further back he rummaged until, finally, it came to him. The last time he saw a violin like that was during his time studying in Montréal. A shy young girl had come to him, asking for a lesson. Her name was on the tip of his tongue – something beginning with the letter V.

Chapter Thirty-Five

♪

THE VIOLIN

Paris, 1935

It still caught Caroline's breath, the sight of the Eiffel Tower from the steps at Trocadero. Doctor Raynal had his treatment rooms on a street close by. As she walked, she attempted to focus on the everyday things. A woman carrying a basket of groceries; a discarded piece of paper swirling playfully in the breeze. It was a fine summer's day, the kind of day where nothing should go wrong.

'We are having some success with a new treatment.' The doctor spoke optimistically in fluent English, only letting slip a rolled 'r' here and there. 'Radiation therapy. Oh, don't look so frightened, Mademoiselle, it is based on the X-ray. Many physicians are reporting the control and indeed regression of cancers due to radiation exposure.'

The office was sparse, the only decoration anatomical. A skeletal frame here, an unnerving diagram of flesh pinned from bones there. It called to mind a dead zoo. She hated the place and always felt a chill there, no matter the season.

'Yes, but if inappropriately applied, is it not true that radiation can also be harmful?' she asked, wrong-footing him once again with her increasing knowledge on the subject.

'Well, I mean, of course, there is always a risk, Mademoiselle... Life itself is a risk, *non*?'

That made her smile and he felt encouraged in his argument.

'So, I shall make the arrangements, yes?'

'No, doctor. That won't be necessary. I would like to thank you for all you have done, but the only arrangements I intend to make do not involve you or your radiation therapy.'

He swallowed hard and Caroline watched his Adam's apple bob up and down like a life buoy. She did not need anyone to save her anymore. It was the most liberating sensation she had ever felt in her life.

♪

'You cannot be serious, Caroline!' Sybil shrieked, dropping the parasol that shaded them from the hot Parisian sunshine. Caroline broke the news on their daily walk around the Tuileries Gardens, just opposite their hotel, The Regina Louvre.

'You're not in your right mind, it must be the illness,' Sybil continued, and Caroline bore the monologue with good humour. She had anticipated this reaction and felt it was best to treat it like a small fire and let it burn itself out.

'And what will your parents say? No doubt they'll blame me. And what of my position?' Sybil covered her mouth with her large hands – 'unladylike' as her mother called them. 'I'm sorry, Caroline, I didn't mean—'

Caroline waved away her apology. Sybil had been Caroline's chaperone for the last decade. Having missed her own chance of a good marriage, Sybil was now a spinster and all she could hope for in life was a good position as a companion for the daughters of wealthy families. Although she had never said as much, it was clear to Caroline that Sybil envied her life – the money, the clothes, the jewellery, the fine things. But the funny thing was, Caroline envied Sybil's freedom, such as it was. Spinsterhood seemed like an emancipation of sorts.

'I should apologise,' Caroline said as they settled on a wooden bench by the pond. 'It was too much, blurting it out like that.'

'Let's not waste time with apologies, we know each other too well for that. And I know you too well to delude myself with thoughts that you'll change your mind. But going to Istanbul alone, are you sure?'

Caroline nodded, a look of determination in her eyes. Sybil looked out across the manicured gardens, as if hearing a distant call. 'Your mother always said you were stubborn,' she said, smiling.

'But for all my stubbornness, where did it get me?' Caroline had wanted to be a performer, a musician. Or as her father put it, *a goddamn showgirl*. They were embarrassed by her passion, her desire to be somebody. *Couldn't she just play the violin for her husband?* Have cultured soirées where the other wives could come and listen to her play doleful tunes? She couldn't breathe in their world. And in a strange way, as her lungs deteriorated, Caroline's appetite for life only increased and became more desperate.

♪

Istanbul, one month later…

Caroline sat on her own private balcony in the Pera Palace, overlooking the vibrant city of Istanbul. The Golden Horn lay in the distance, offering a sheltered harbour to ships laden with goods, just as it had done since the Byzantine Empire. A muezzin's call drifted on the breeze from one of the towering minarets, calling the Muslims to prayer. She could hardly believe she was here. The journey on the Orient Express had been beyond her wildest dreams. It was such a thrill to see the world from her carriage window – wonders just waiting for her. Had she chosen to spend what remained of her life at home, her mother would have sequestered her to bed rest and she would have died looking at those same four walls. Her father would greet the news as he did all bad news, with an arrogant refusal. Such things as misfortune and illness should never visit the doorstep of the Bradshaw dynasty. His vast wealth was always there to protect him from whatever knocks life had in store, and he would not endure adversity like ordinary folk. It was beneath him; beneath the family name. Here, she felt enlivened by the bustling streets that surrounded the Pera Palace, where she could hear every language being spoken, by travellers who had come to this crossroads to experience a doorway to the east.

In the early morning, when the sun began to rise, she took to walking slowly down an old cobbled street, Galip Dede Caddesi. It was far more peaceful than the Grand Bazaar, Kapalı Çarşı, which was always busy with tourists, and the effort to walk the vast maze of covered streets would have taken too much of a toll on her lungs. On this quiet street there were cafés and shops selling trinkets and beautiful rugs, but the real reason she went was to look in the windows of the countless music shops, selling instruments of every kind. One particular morning, a man sat outside his shop playing an instrument she had never seen before. It was like something between a guitar and a lute, with about a dozen strings and a pear-shaped body. The sound was mesmerising and as she stood in the shadows of the old buildings watching him, she hardly noticed the woman who had settled at her side.

'Magnificent, isn't he?' she said, taking a notebook out of her satchel and scribbling down some notes with a pencil.

Caroline turned to see a middle-aged woman with greying hair, matronly but with an air of adventure about her.

'Don't I know you?'

'From the hotel, we're staying at the Pera Palace,' she said, in a schooled English accent.

'Of course,' Caroline said, introducing herself. 'You're the writer, Ms Christie, aren't you?'

'Oh dear, well, I suppose if one must be known as something, that's as good as anything. You can call me Agatha.'

They decided to enter the shop together – Agatha taking notes for research, Caroline simply delighting in the surroundings. They had to walk single file through the shop, as it was crowded with instruments. Drums covered in animal skin stood like toadstools on the floorspace whilst stringed instruments hung from the walls and the ceilings.

'It's like an overgrown garden of musical instruments!' Agatha joked.

Caroline brushed past several bouzoukis to the back of the shop, where she spotted an old violin case, closed.

'Excuse me?' she called out to a young man who was almost hidden by a large cello. 'May I see what's inside this?' she asked.

'Of all the instruments in the shop, you plump for the one that is hidden? Very interesting,' Ms Christie said, jotting down some notes.

Caroline wasn't really sure why, but she felt drawn to it. Curious why it was not on display as the others were.

'Of course, Madam,' the young man said. 'This violin is quite old. An antique, in fact. It has travelled a long distance…'

♪

I felt the case move and shift, then the loss of gravity. I was being carried away again. Time had become liquid, my senses blunt. The last thing I remembered was the water coming in. That sloshing sound. My greatest fear. I cried out but no one heard. Or so I thought. Perhaps some hours had passed. Then I was pulled from the murky Thames water and into a barge. An old man with a deeply lined face, weathered by time and softened by a kind nature that grew despite the hardships of his station. He opened the case and, delighted by what he saw, he cradled me in his arms like a babe and took care to remove any moisture with a dry cloth.

'Water and wood, they don't mix at all, my girl, do they?' he said, his voice soothing. 'Not to worry, old Tim'll see you right.'

And so he did. He took me to a place in the East End of London. He knew people there who spoke with different accents and played instruments in a manner I had never heard. I let the sounds drift over me. I had no will to care what happened. I could no more set my course than a sailboat on a windless sea. Before long, I was travelling again. I could feel the air growing warmer, languages transforming from clipped consonants to soft, rolling vowels. When the case opened I found myself in a small workshop. I could see violins in various stages of repair. My breath steadied. I was in a safe place again.

The luthier inspected me carefully and though I could sense his dismay at seeing the damage the water had caused, I felt reassured by his determination to fix it. He replaced one of my pegs that had swelled, and scraped away some of the glue that had dissolved at my seams. In no time at all, I felt whole again. He ran through some scales, gave me a quick tuning and with that, I was placed at the back of the music shop on Galip Dede Caddesi.

♪

'You should buy it,' Ms Christie told Caroline, on hearing her play 'Clair de Lune', albeit inexpertly.

'Do you think?'

'My dear, you've been mooning over it for a quarter of an hour!'

It was true. Caroline couldn't remember the last time she had truly wanted something. Yet it seemed something of a waste. How much time remained to her? Months? Weeks?

'I don't know. I'm not very skilled.'

'Tosh! Besides, why must one be skilled to enjoy an instrument? This violin is clearly calling you and if you want my advice, you'll buy it. Still, as I always say, good advice is certain to be ignored, but that's no reason not to give it!'

With that, she was gone, and Caroline was alone with her decision. The shape of the instrument, the feel of it in her hands, brought back memories of taking flight on notes, out of her childhood bedroom and into the air. It felt like freedom. She clutched it to her breast and shut her eyes, as if to make the memories feel more real.

The violin was of a light russet colour – like an autumn leaf on the verge of turning crimson. The neck seemed unusually long, which gave the instrument elegance, and the scroll was remarkably bold and free. It had an inexplicable allure and she longed to play it again. Just when she needed to find her voice, a voice she recognised from long ago, this beauty came her way. She would have never thought of playing again, but this was fate. She would not go home without it, she told the young man as she paid him.

Back at the Pera Palace, she felt full of life and energy – she almost began to wonder if perhaps the doctor hadn't made a mistake. She took me out of my case and placed me gently in the crook of her neck. As soon as the bow touched my strings, the sound that filled the air almost broke her heart and mended it in the same note. She was a little rusty – it would take time for us to acquaint one another with our edges and hollows, the boundary where both of us could meet. But I was nothing if not a forgiving instrument, bending and yielding until Caroline became a little more sure of her fingering and found the old familiar routes on the fingerboard.

Her bowing technique had never been perfect, but now, taking a deep breath, she relaxed her muscles and let her hand hang loose. Raising the bow again, she began to play the 'Minuet No. 1' by J. S. Bach, a piece she had always enjoyed playing, as it was light and merry. Lost in the moment, she could feel her spirit drifting on the notes over Istanbul, sharing herself and her voice with anyone who cared to listen. And there was someone listening, very close by. Just downstairs, in fact.

♪

In the room below, Edward Faulkner cursed his inability to resist a good story, but this time he was driven by money. The Bradshaw family were willing to pay handsomely for any information on their runaway heiress. He despised these wealthy families, who were immune to the changing circumstances of life, unlike everyone else. The Great Depression had driven Edward's father to an early grave, his mother not long after him with a broken heart. The skinny kid who used to write unoriginal travel features to entertain the suburban housewives had disappeared and he had transformed into a hard and twisted man, living on scraps. As he stood there, listening to the music coming from above (which was anything but heavenly), he took his frustrations out with a broom handle and thumped the ceiling with it. The scratching stopped momentarily, before resuming with even more gusto.

♪

Despite the knocking that came from downstairs that first evening (which Caroline had put down to an overactive imagination and a creaky old building) it quickly became a ritual; every afternoon and often late into the evening, she would play me on the balcony. In rain or in sunshine, her heart soared on the notes. She bought sheet music of various compositions she had always wanted to try – Vivaldi, Saint-Saëns. She slept, ate and played. That was all she needed. All thoughts of the illness were banished to the dark corners of her mind, while the music shone its bright light. Our friendship grew, and in a way, we began to heal the darkness inside each other. But whereas my scars healed, Caroline's could not.

One evening, as Edward returned dejected from another day of walking the streets and frequenting hangouts of American expats, he opened the windows as wide as he could and listened to the 'music' that was coming from above. There was something about the hopeful notes, the eager repetition, that made him angry. Leaning out as far as he dared, he found it impossible to see the musician, so he went back inside and began to thump the ceiling again to make it stop.

Caroline froze. She wasn't imagining it this time; there

was definitely someone banging on her floor. When she began to play again, it knocked in time with the music.

'Well!' she said, her eyes lighting up with defiance. Her temper had always been quick, but she had been taught to bite her tongue, for no one liked a passionate woman (according to her melodramatic mother!). Well, she was no longer a lady of any standing, so she was damned if she was going to act like one. She dropped her violin onto her bed and pounded down the stairs, finding the door to the apartment directly below her.

'*Merhaba*? Is there someone there?' she called out, letting her closed fist have its revenge on the wooden door. She heard footsteps moving purposefully on the other side and the door swung open to reveal a young man with auburn hair and bright hazel eyes, carrying the offending broom. Never have a person's facial features transformed so quickly from anger to surprise.

'Oh, you're—' He stumbled, taken aback by the Renaissance beauty that stood before him.

'Sir,' Caroline began, 'I assume that my playing has disturbed your peace, but a gentleman might have come to my door and told me so, face to face, rather than thumping on the ceiling!' There, she'd let him have it.

Edward knew immediately from the picture in the papers that it was her. Caroline Bradshaw. He had found her without even looking! Luck was finally on his side. It was clear from her photograph that she was a beauty, but in person, he hadn't expected her to be so ... mesmerising. He immediately turned on what little charm he possessed.

'Madam, I beg your forgiveness, but what you heard

was not a request for you to stop playing, but encouragement to continue!'

'You're American?'

'Yes.'

'From the Midwest?'

'You have an impeccable ear. Indiana. Grew up on the shores of Lake Michigan. You see, where I come from, we do this to compliment a musician,' he continued, thumping the ceiling as though she needed a re-enactment to understand.

Caroline's features melted into a puzzled smile.

'Well, now I know you're lying.'

There was nothing for it but to throw himself on her mercy.

'Permit me to introduce myself. I am Edward Faulkner and clearly have no concept of when I am standing in the presence of a musical genius.' He bowed slightly and put out his hand for her to shake. 'Please, continue playing and ignore my rudeness.'

'Are you saying I need the practice?' she said, the smile still on her face. There was no point in making him feel any worse than he already did. 'Maybe my playing is a little … rusty.'

'On the contrary. I found it to be—' he searched the air around them for the right word '—spirited!'

'Have you always found it this easy to lie or is it a skill you've mastered over time?'

Edward couldn't deny it, she was the most charming woman he'd ever met. Smart, funny and not at all what he expected her to be. Still, he had a job to do. He had to stay focused on the money. He asked her how long she'd been in the city and if she'd gotten to know the area. From the sound of it, she rarely left the apartment. She didn't strike him as the reclusive type, but perhaps she was aware that her parents were searching for her. For all he knew, they could have hired more than one private investigator.

'Let me take you to lunch.'

Caroline hesitated. She wouldn't normally entertain the idea, but wasn't she living on her own terms now? Had she not promised herself to grasp every opportunity that came her way? To be brave, until the end? Still, even when death sat on your shoulder, it went against every fibre of her being to appear to a man to be too keen.

'I'll think about it.'

'Well, don't take too long!' he shouted after her.

If only he knew. Time was a luxury she no longer possessed.

♪

Edward telegrammed Mr Bradshaw informing him that he had found his daughter. Of course he wanted her home immediately, but Edward explained that it would be better, especially given the long journey, if he could convince Caroline to come willingly. Mr Bradshaw was impatient but acquiesced. What could he do from across the Atlantic? More money was wired. It was partly true – Edward could hardly drag her home by her hair. But the delay was also because he was falling in love with her. Now that he no longer had to scour the city, he spent his days in his hotel room at the Pera Palace, listening to Caroline play her violin. Although she was no virtuoso, the violin was just like her voice: playful, inviting and charmingly fallible. For someone like her to be perfect at everything would have been boring, predictable even. But she wore her heart on her sleeve when she played.

Caroline was wearing a white, gauzy dress that fastened easily with a wide sash and not too many buttons. She was not used to dressing herself and found the whole thing quite fiddly. She chose to wear her hair simply in one long braid to the side, and just a pair of pearl earrings. When they met at a little café, she told him that she had no appetite today and ordered a glass of pomegranate juice, known for its healing properties.

Edward joked that it must have been fate, two Americans staying at the same hotel, on different floors.

'Just imagine if I had played Vivaldi's music as he had meant it, perhaps we would never have met at all!' But her laughter turned to wheezing, then coughing. 'I ... need ... air'.

He saw the droplets of blood on the handkerchief she held to her mouth.

'Do you need to see a doctor?'

She shook her head and struggled to catch her breath.

'Take me home.'

'But you're ill,' he protested, to no avail.

He did not see her for days. No sound came from her room, and she would not answer the door. Edward started to panic. Mr Bradshaw was pressing him for news. He was running out of money. Yet all he cared about was her. For some reason, life was giving him a second chance. When he was with her, he could erase the unhappiness of the past and believe in a future he never thought possible. What if she'd run off? Caught on to his real reason for being in Istanbul?

He banged on her door for over half an hour. The concierge complained and was eventually persuaded to open the door. He found her on the floor, pale, breathless and weak as a kitten.

'What in God's name...' He swooped her up into his arms and carried her to the bed.

'Fetch some water,' he said to the housemaid, who had halted at the door in shock. 'And call a doctor!'

Caroline shook her head weakly and mumbled something incoherent. It was only when he held her that he could feel how thin she was.

'Caroline, I think I need to take you to the hospital.' Just saying the words filled him with dread.

She shook her head again.

'Too late.'

♪

In the golden light of the evening as the sounds of restaurants setting up their tables drifted up to the open window, Edward sat on the edge of Caroline's bed. He hadn't left her side, only to answer the door to the maid, who had brought up some broth. He held a bowl in his hands and wondered whether he should wake her. She looked so peaceful and yet it was only now that he noticed how truly thin she was, without her fine clothes and her hair done up. Her eyes fluttered lightly.

'Hello,' he said.

She flinched a little.

'Wh-what are you doing here?'

'Watching you sleep.' He blushed when the words were out. He wasn't used to being so transparent.

'Oh God,' she moaned, 'I must look terrible.'

'You look beautiful, except for the drool, that is.'

She wiped her mouth hurriedly, then saw the beginnings of a smile on his face.

'Idiot!' she said, poking him on the arm and almost spilling the soup.

'How long have you known?' he asked when she had finished after only a few spoonfuls.

'Known what?'

'That you're dying.'

His directness disarmed her.

'My uncle, back home. I watched him go the same way.'

Caroline stared at him. In some silly way, it felt like her prognosis was not real because she hadn't told anyone. She could almost pretend it wasn't happening. That her body would somehow recover of its own volition and everything would return to normal. Now, with this handsome, clever, funny man looking into her eyes and piercing her soul, she could no longer deny the truth and the tears came like a flood. Her life was being ripped away from her and there was nothing she could do to stop it. And all the money in the world couldn't buy her the only thing she'd ever wanted in her life: love. At that moment, he took her into his arms and held her fiercely until her sobbing subsided. Her face buried in his chest, he kissed her head over and over.

'How much time?' Edward asked.

'Not long now. Maybe weeks.'

He nodded, as though he could absorb this information rationally, then made a decision. He held her at arm's length and looked her directly in the eyes.

'I'm working for your father.'

She shook her head and gave him a confused look.

'He sent me here to find you and bring you home.'

At first, anger blazed on her face and her skin grew blotchy with temper, but just as quickly it transformed into a mirthless laughter.

'And are you going to take me home, Edward? So Daddy can try to marry off his dying daughter?' More unnerving laughter. 'I'm no use to them now, don't you see? I never was.' She reached to the other side of the bed and there I lay quietly observing. She brushed her fingertips lightly on my strings for courage and found a deeper source of strength. 'And so I'm of no use to you now, either. You won't get your reward from bringing home a corpse, so you might as well leave.'

Edward sat back stunned by her words. How could she not know?

'Caroline,' he implored, trying to take her hand, but she snapped it back from him. 'It's true, I came here to find the Bradshaw heiress. It's also true that I needed the money and I had no moral qualms about taking it from people who never earned it in the first place. Your daddy isn't down in those mines, risking his life for profit. He sits in his fine mansion living off of the backs of people like my father. So I saw an opportunity to even up the scales and I took it.'

'If you expect me to feel sorry for you, I don't.'

'Well, I don't feel sorry for you either.'

She fixed him with a cross look.

'But ... I'm dying,' she said, somewhat petulantly.

'I wasn't aware it was a competition!'

The tension between them suddenly snapped and improbably, their harsh words broke into genuine laughter. Caroline laughed so hard that her breath wheezed and eventually she had to stop and take a few sips of water.

'I'm sorry. You win, obviously.'

'For once,' she said, catching her breath with difficulty, 'I don't want to win this game.'

He reached for her hand again and this time she let him take it.

'The truth is ... the most important truth is—' he paused to look up at her and reached out to tuck a strand of hair behind her ear '—the truth is, I've fallen in love with you, Caroline.'

Those words... Had she truly heard him speak them, or was it her imagination? It was too good to be true.

'I-I'm not sure I heard you properly.'

He smiled and then leaned forward, stopping just as his lips hovered above hers. Softly, he said, 'Caroline, I'm in love with you,' before kissing her, lightly at first then more deeply. She still had her hand resting on my strings that almost pulsated with emotion. Finally, she let go and wrapped her arms around his neck. *I love you, too,* came the silent response with every touch and caress. Love, she realised, can never come too late.

♪

Within a fortnight Caroline was buried in a small cemetery overlooking the Bosphorus. As per her instructions, Edward sent a letter to her parents explaining everything; and, as per her instructions, he returned me to the shop where she had found me all those months before.

As I lay there, gleaming under the soft golden glow of the shop's vintage chandelier, I felt a strange melancholy. What a fleeting thing love was. And yet we would each of us sacrifice an eternity to spend just one moment longer in the arms of the one person who possessed the key to our heart. I was comforted by the knowledge that I had played a part in connecting Edward and Caroline, even if only for a short time. But now here I was again, on the precipice of a new adventure, a new heart with secret desires and hidden longings. For the first time, I saw the world with the eyes of a grown woman, emancipated and willing to abandon herself to its treasures and tribulations. Caroline taught me that and I would always be in her debt.

Chapter Thirty-Six

♪

Directly opposite the Royal Albert Hall, the impressive red-brick building had always seemed like a fairy-tale castle to Gabrielle, with its rectangular towers at each end, topped with pyramidal spires. Making her way directly to the library, she signed in and began to search the shelves containing books on the subject of English luthiers. Her phone vibrated in her pocket and when she took it out to look at the screen, she saw a reminder on her calendar for an appointment with Trudy in half an hour. It would take her that long to get there on the Tube. She considered cancelling, but Gabrielle could not bear the unprofessionalism. A martyr to other people's perception, that's what Roger once said.

'Why do you care what people think?' he'd asked, in the blithely unaware way that men sometimes do. As if her entire worth as a person wasn't tied up in what people thought of her. As if her whole childhood had not been built on the four words, *be a good girl*. She shuddered. There must have been an entire army marching over her grave today. She fished a hairband out of her pocket and scraped her hair back into a low bun, before applying a small amount of lip balm and straightening up her coat. If she left now, she would only be a couple of minutes late, at worst. Just as she was about to leave, she noticed a trolley of books that were yet to be reshelved and, on the top, a book by Reverend W. Meredith Morris entitled *British Violin Makers*. It seemed as good a start as any, so she checked it out and caught the 452 bus to Portobello Road.

Gabrielle ran the last few hundred metres and by the time she got to the office, she felt like a racehorse that had seen better days. Her leg was still aching since her incident in Milan, and she knocked back some painkillers while Trudy lit a candle in a Himalayan salt lamp.

They sat there, staring at each other for what felt like interminable minutes. Gabrielle got up and paced the small room, hoping the movement would quell the buzzing feeling she had inside. She shook out her hands, rolled her shoulders, but that reminded her too much of the violin. She would always prepare her body by loosening it up. Max said that the music would flow better if her muscles were soft and it was important to release the tension. She could feel his hands on her shoulders and remembered how embarrassed she'd been when his fingertips moved across her bra strap. She was only sixteen. She wasn't sure what exact age he was, but he was a man in his thirties. They'd been spending more and more time rehearsing together. Her big performance was coming up, the one that would launch her solo career. She could remember how grateful she always was that he had chosen her as his star pupil, and he did nothing to dissuade her from thinking that her success was in large part due to him. He had become more important in her life than her friends, even her father. She hardly had time for anything but practice and Max. She trusted him. He was looking after her. An adult who wanted her to reach her greatest potential. That was why she never spoke against him.

'The secrets began with him,' she said, her head nodding. It was time. Time to tell her story. '"Best not to tell your father." It was quite innocent at first. Little gifts. A bar of chocolate. Maybe a can of Coke. At the time, I wasn't sure why he was asking me not to tell my father, he wouldn't have minded in the slightest. But then the gifts became more substantial. Tickets to the cinema. On my birthday he bought me a charm bracelet. That was when the secrets took on another meaning.' Gabrielle wasn't sure how she knew this, but she just did.

Trudy poured her a glass of water and she drank it down in one go before continuing.

'It was better Father didn't know. Only for whom? That was the question I hadn't known the answer to then.'

'But you know it now,' Trudy said.

'I know it now. I remember thinking it was so cool that he didn't behave like other grown-ups. He treated me almost like an equal and made it clear that we were working together. There was no hierarchy. And I fell for it. The more he praised my ability to take criticism, to mask my feelings, to ignore my own instincts, the more I did what he asked of me. Stupid.'

'Why do you say that? Do you think you were stupid?'

'It's obvious now, isn't it? I should have known all along what was happening.'

'How could you have known? You were barely seventeen.'

Gabrielle's breath was shallow and her hands jittery. Why was Trudy making her relive all of this? What good would it do? She couldn't change the past or how she felt about it. He had taken every bit of joy and left her with nothing but regret and self-loathing. How had she ever let him touch her that way?

'Take your time, Gabrielle. This is difficult work.'

She stared unseeing out of the window, tears blurring the view. A memory flickered like an old film. It was her birthday and she told him she had to leave early for a party. He was angry. No, he was furious with her. He kept her for an extra hour, running over the same piece she had played a thousand times already. And then, when he finally said she could leave (which was already too late to get to her party with what few friends she had left), he grabbed her wrist as she reached for the door handle. He looked her dead in the eye and squeezed it harder. She would not cry, though she wanted to. She had heard him call the other students 'cry babies' and she wanted to prove to him that she was tougher. She thought he would respect her more for it. It felt like her bones would crack in his tight grasp. Eventually, he loosened his grip but did not let go.

'Forget those friends. Nothing is more important than this,' he'd said. 'Do you want to be the greatest?'

She nodded, yes. She wanted to be the greatest for him, for her father. For herself? Well, she'd never even thought to ask. Was it really what she wanted? And if not, what else?

He pulled her closer and kissed her full on the mouth. Then smiled and let her hand go.

'Happy birthday,' he'd said and once free, she'd run down the stairs of the building, unsure what had happened. Did it mean he had forgiven her? Perhaps that was what grown-ups did. And he was treating her like a grown-up. Gabrielle recoiled at the memories.

'My God' she whispered, clutching her sore wrist to her chest.

'What was that?' asked Trudy.

'He should have known.'

'Who should have known?'

'My father. I went to see him yesterday.'

Trudy's face was full of compassion.

'You've never spoken about visiting his grave. How was that?'

Gabrielle shook her head and fidgeted with her hands.

'He's not dead. That's just what we tell everyone.'

Trudy's features momentarily lost their normal inscrutability. She was clearly shocked at these new developments in her client's case history.

Gabrielle gave her an apologetic look for concealing the truth about her not-quite-deceased father. But the pressure of keeping all the lies inside was getting too much. Besides, maybe there was, like, attorney-client privilege? What was she saying? Trudy wasn't going to tell anyone. No one in the business, at any rate.

'He should've known, you know? He should've seen what was happening.'

Trudy gave an almost imperceptible nod.

'When my mother died, he said we'd have to look out

for each other more. But he didn't look out for me. He became so fixated on my future that he stopped seeing what was happening right in front of him. All of the hours spent with … that man. A grown man. Wasn't he even in the least bit suspicious?'

Trudy handed her a tissue. She hadn't even noticed that she was crying. Suddenly, and for reasons that had no logic, she needed to sit on the floor. To feel solid ground beneath her. She got up and sat on the rug, cross-legged. Inexplicably, she felt a bit better. Like she could cope with it all a bit better from down there.

'All of these years, I've carried around all of the shame, the guilt, the responsibility. But I was the kid, you know? At sixteen, you think you're an adult, but you're not.'

'No, you're not,' Trudy agreed, getting up from her chair and sitting on the floor beside her, their backs supported by the wall.

'There's something else: the pain in my wrist, I remembered it all wrong. It came after…' She took a deep breath and steadied her focus on a loose thread in the rug. 'Max told me that once I'd performed my solo, I'd be a real woman. He'd make sure of it.' She shuddered with the fear that had been buried deep for so long. 'I knew what he meant, and I just smiled at him. I felt like I had no way to protect myself from him. He had all of the power.'

'And that was when the pain hit,' Trudy said.

'Exactly! And then my story became all about this mysterious injury and how I'd lost my career because of it. But now I'm wondering if I saw it as my only way out of the situation.'

She turned to look at Trudy, who seemed to be deep in thought.

'Have you ever heard the term "disavowal"?'

Gabrielle shook her head.

'It's when you know something, but you can't let yourself fully know it. A split occurs in the mind, when a truth threatens our safety. It severs the link between thought and feeling and represses our memory of events.'

'So, we disconnect to protect ourselves?'

'Yes. But the truth does not stay buried. It sometimes expresses itself as a symptom. And sometimes this story is our only means of avoiding the difficult truth.'

'Maybe that's why my wrist is no longer as painful as it used to be? Perhaps I'm finally ready to face the truth?' Gabrielle felt hopeful, but in the way that a baby deer hopes to take its next step.

'I think you've been very brave, Gabrielle. But you're only human. You've been carrying so much, alone. You have support here, you know this?'

Gabrielle nodded slowly. For so long, coming here had felt like a waste of time. Or more like another chore she had to complete, without really knowing why or who she was doing it for. Yet today it all seemed to click into place. The routine of it – Trudy was showing her what it was like to have someone reliable in your life. A steady presence, week in, week out. She never had to do anything or show up in a certain way for Trudy to give her support. Up to that point, all of her relationships had felt like jobs she had to work at, to earn approval or love. But not here. It felt liberating.

'I just feel so alone in all of this.' She spread her arms out to include the whole world, then fished a tissue out of her pocket. Sprawled on the floor like this, so unlike her normal well-presented self, was a kind of a surrender. She was waving her white flag and wondering if trying so hard to keep everything together was even working. It certainly wasn't making her happy.

'Disconnection can be very isolating, but also understandable, given what you've been through. There's safety in being alone, not trusting anyone. But it might not be the most sustainable option. You can connect with the world again, with new tools. With your boundaries that you choose. When we grow up without boundaries, we never learn how to protect ourselves, or that we even have permission to do so.'

'That's it exactly,' Gabrielle said, turning to face this wonderful woman who had gently yet persistently sat through countless sessions, patiently waiting for her to find her true voice.

'You'll come back again next week?' Trudy asked and with that, Gabrielle realised their hour was up.

'Of course,' she said, wiping her eyes. She detected a flutter of fear in her belly. What if this breakthrough didn't last until next week? What if all of her walls built themselves up again while she wasn't looking? And what had knocked them down in the first place? Perhaps it was some kind of coincidence, but she could pinpoint exactly when this transformation began. In her mind's eye, she could hear the bell ring over the shop door and see Walter and Devlin standing by the counter with the violin.

Chapter Thirty-Seven

♪

Devlin found himself whistling a tune as he hung his uniform in the locker at the end of his shift. The realisation made him smile. He was doing more of that lately, too. Oddly, he was starting to enjoy living with Walter. It was only ever meant to be temporary, but they had slotted into a nice little routine together. They went to the pub for dinner in the evenings and Walter insisted on making a full fry-up every morning. Both men had had to loosen their belts to the next notch. But it was their evening routine that gave them both the most satisfaction. They had begun to teach themselves how to play the violin. Devlin found some lessons online and while he couldn't exactly say they were improving, or even showing any talent for it whatsoever, there was something addictive about it. They would sit at the kitchen table, open the case and take a moment just to appreciate the beauty of the instrument. The patches where the varnish was worn to a lighter colour, where it had rested on countless people's shoulders and tucked under their necks, were almost like invitations to a forgotten world. They felt like members of an elite club, and while the bow scratched at the strings, carrying the vibration through the cracks in the wood, it was as though Walter's apartment was imbued with a richness neither one of them could fully describe or contemplate relinquishing. They had allowed themselves to wallow in a false sense of security that the gang were no longer pursuing them, and life was becoming infinitely better with every passing day.

He'd promised to pick Walter up a book on the history of the violin and decided to take a swing by one of the bookshops in Departures when he spotted her, her long dark hair uncharacteristically loose and wild as she bent over her suitcase, fighting with the zip.

'Tell me you're not going to attack it with a knife again,' he said, jokingly.

'Jeez, you gave me a fright,' Gabrielle said, somehow managing to look both annoyed and relieved. She said nothing else but returned to the struggle with her zip.

'How've you been?' he asked.

'Um, good, yeah. Good. You?'

'Brilliant.' What? Why had he said that? When the only thought really running through his mind was how he still felt there might be something between them because he hadn't stopped thinking about that kiss?

'Right, well, I have a flight to catch so…'

'Maybe I could drop by some day this week and settle up our account…' It was the only thing he could think of saying.

'I haven't finished working on it yet. Don't you want to know who made the violin?'

'I mean, of course, but it's not like I'm ever going to sell it. I'm actually teaching myself to play—'

'That violin is a priceless work of art. Don't you understand? You don't *own* something like that, any more than you own a lake or a forest. You're the custodian. It needs care and respect and—'

Just then the tannoy announced a call for an Aer Lingus flight to Dublin.

'Look, I have to go,' she said. 'You might be able to delude yourself that a priceless stolen violin has gone completely unnoticed, but believe me, the person who broke into your apartment is not giving up. Sooner or later, you're going to have to give it back.'

All this time, Devlin and Walter had believed they were the ones holding all of the cards, deciding how much Gabrielle needed to know. It suddenly occurred to him that they had had it the wrong way around. Perhaps she was the one keeping secrets and knew more about the thief than she'd let on.

'Wait, where are you going?' he called out, as she walked away.

'Ireland.'

'What? Is that where you think the violin…'

'I don't have time to explain,' she said, in such a mysterious way that Devlin heard himself say words he never thought he would hear.

'I'm coming with you.'

'You can't. You don't have a ticket for starters—'

'There have to be some perks to working here. Look,' he said, placing his hands gently on her shoulders, 'I'm the one who brought this violin into our lives. I should be there.'

'But you hate flying, and besides, this might just be another dead end.'

Devlin stepped away and spoke some unintelligible words into his walkie-talkie. Seconds later, a static-sounding voice replied and he took Gabrielle by the arm.

'Right. All sorted. Please tell me you've got some Xanax in your bag.'

A mischievous grin played on her lips.

'Always.'

♪

The wild exhilaration of spontaneity wore off far too quickly for Devlin's liking and the Xanax did not take effect at all. Everything was still very real. Where was that nice floaty feeling he had last time? His mouth was unbelievably dry and he began rolling his tongue around, trying to create some saliva. His eyes felt the size of two dinner plates as he stared down at the violin case between his ankles on the floor.

'At what point did you think bringing the violin to work with you was a good idea?' Gabrielle asked.

'Eh, somewhere between the break-ins and you making it very clear that Paddington was a stupid idea,' Devlin snapped. *These pills weren't working at all*.

'I mean, it's kind of genius when you think about it; it's the last place anyone would think to look, right?'

Gabrielle slowly nodded and kept her reservations to

herself. It wasn't the time to start splitting hairs, and besides, she felt better knowing that they had the violin with them. And she realised that it wasn't merely for security reasons, she just felt more optimistic when that little case was around. She assumed it was a throwback to her youth. Her violin was her constant companion, her best friend.

As the engines roared into action and the jet began hurtling down the runway, Devlin could feel himself shivering and sweating at the same time. Was that normal? He gripped the armrest and, as the wheels lost touch with the earth, a wonderful thing happened. Gabrielle placed her hand on top of his. He closed his eyes and tried to focus all of his attention there, to where their skin met. Reducing his entire awareness to this one point of contact. Everything else disappeared and it wasn't until the 'ping' of the seatbelt sign broke his consciousness that he reopened his eyes.

'You okay?' she asked, her brow furrowed.

'I'm ... coping.'

She smiled and ordered some teas from the flight attendant without moving her hand from his. It felt strangely comforting, as though they were an old couple travelling together. Familiar with each other's idiosyncrasies.

'Don't worry, the flight won't be as long this time. You'll hardly feel it.'

Devlin wanted to believe her, but his hand was shaking so much that he could hardly pick up the cup. Reluctantly, he slid his other hand out from underneath hers and lifted the cup with both hands. The warm liquid revived his senses a little, but he was still 30,000 feet above ground in a tin can.

'Why Ireland? Tell me all about it in as much detail as possible for as long as you can.'

Gabrielle tried not to laugh. He was clearly very nervous, and it was really quite sweet that he'd insisted on coming. She'd never been to Dublin before, and it would be good to have the company. His company. Perhaps he really did like her. Would he really want to spend more time with her if he wasn't interested? *Oh God, Gabrielle, shut up!* she shouted internally. It was actually embarrassing how much she thought about him and wondered what, if anything, might happen. Only someone as deep in denial about her feelings as she was could outwardly pretend that these thoughts weren't there. And why was falling in love so bloody complicated anyway? Other people seemed to do it with little or no effort. It was called 'falling', after all; an idiot could do it. But not her. She was seemingly doomed to overthink things until they expired while waiting for her to figure out what to do. Like now.

'Gabs, seriously, just talk about anything or I'm going to lose my shit.'

'Of course, yeah, sorry. Okay, so let's see, oh yes! I found this amazing book in the library.' She fished around in her handbag and felt the hard corners with her fingertips.

'Okay,' she said, flicking through the pages. 'Let's begin.'

'Hang on,' Devlin unbuckled his seatbelt and turned towards her. 'If we're gonna die—'

'We're not going to die.'

'Yeah, but if we did, there's something I have to say to you.'

Gabrielle felt her insides clench. She wasn't sure she could deal with this kind of deathbed confession. Why couldn't everybody hide behind a mask of politeness, like she did?

'I don't regret kissing you.'

Oh.

'Well, that's ... generous.'

'No, hang on. That didn't come out right. I'm glad we kissed.'

Somewhere behind them a baby began to wail. It wasn't at all how Devlin had imagined it going, when he'd planned it, three seconds before he opened his mouth.

'Um, I don't know what to say, really,' Gabrielle said, looking down at her book.

'You don't have to say anything. I just wanted you to know that. I'm sorry if the timing was weird.'

The timing isn't great now, she thought, as another flight attendant asked if they'd like to buy some duty-free. She watched Devlin as he politely looked through the list of items and made some amusing remarks, making the woman smile. Even though he was dying inside, his priority was always to make people smile. He was one of those rare species facing extinction – a good person. You could hardly see his eyes when he laughed; they creased at the sides and almost closed. His short, trimmed beard hid them, but he had dimples, too. It seemed slightly incongruous to Gabrielle, because he had such a manly physique, like what a farmer would look like, in her limited experience of farmers. When he rolled up his shirt sleeves, he had strong forearms, which probably suited his job, and broad shoulders. Yet he was such a soft person and the most alluring thing about him was that he didn't try to hide it. He saw kindness as a strength. Most of the disastrous relationships that Gabrielle had had were with men who she could see, with hindsight, were painfully insecure. So they had to act tough to overcompensate. Devlin wasn't like that. He was what would be described as 'steady'. A steady presence. Even despite what he had told her about his heartbreak in Dublin and the accident, she couldn't imagine him ever having Googled 'Will I be okay?' She'd done that just last month. Surprisingly and rather comfortingly, all of the results said that she would, in fact, be okay.

Devlin turned back to her, and she realised he'd seen her staring at him.

'Well, thank you, for your candour,' she said haltingly, before pointing back at the book. 'We're not going to die, Devlin, I promise. But shall I tell you what I've found out?'

'Please, for the love of God, yes,' he said, sitting on his hands and actually thinking it wouldn't be the worst thing if there was a mid-air emergency. Nothing could be more excruciating than that conversation he'd just royally ballsed up.

Gabrielle wasn't sure if you were supposed to take library books out of the country. Probably not. Satie had already fallen asleep on top of it. Surely that was frowned upon. It had turned out that her father's hunch was right about finding the luthier's tutor. According to Rev. W. Meredith Morris's book on British violin makers, a man called Thomas Perry was one of the most notable luthiers of the eighteenth century. While precious little was known about his origins (even his birthplace was not known for certain) his violins stood the test of time and even now commanded great prices at auction.

'They call him the Irish Stradivarius,' Gabrielle added, after explaining her findings to Devlin.

'Wow. This is brilliant! And you think he made our violin?'

'Our violin,' she repeated with a slight smile. 'I don't think so, but there are enough similarities to make me believe he might have taught our mystery violin maker. He had a shop in Dublin on Anglesea Street and it was common for luthiers to take on apprentices. I'm going to head to the National Museum first. They have a small collection of his work and that way we can do some comparisons.'

She pulled out her phone and left a note for herself to call Roger as soon as she got a chance. If her father's hunch turned out to be true, it might explain the mystery surrounding the type of wood used.

'Ladies and gentlemen, we would now ask you to fasten your seatbelts as we begin our descent into Dublin Airport,' the steward announced.

'Crikey, you weren't kidding, that was quick.' For some idiotic reason he'd thought it would be similar to the ferry he'd taken all those years ago. Why the hell had he agreed to come along? He hadn't been back to Ireland since Summer… Talking about what happened was one thing, but was he really ready to face his past?

'Just tell me something else. Anything,' he said in a tight voice while he fumbled with the seatbelt buckle.

'Umm…' Gabrielle wasn't good at this kind of stuff. Something personal? God, no. She tried to think about what calmed her when she felt overwhelmed. She would think of her mother's voice singing lullabies to her when she was home from school and poorly. She'd set Gabrielle up on the couch with a hot-water bottle, some tea and toast, and put her favourite cartoons on the telly. The memory caught her unawares and she almost forgot where she was.

'Gabs? Final descent happening!'

She looked over at Devlin, his face clammy, his knee bobbing up and down as though working a snare drum. Well, she wasn't about to sing to him. The only thing that soothed her as a grown-up was research. As though finding the answers to inexplicable things might make up for the fact that she had no answers in her own life. Well, it would have to do.

'Did you know that the violin was modelled on the human voice?'

Devlin gave her a look that might have said, 'Seriously?'

She persisted.

'They did a study at the University of Taiwan and, using sonic analysis, they found that Andrea Amati's violins were built to mimic the vowel sounds of the human voice. They were literally crafted to sing like us. Isn't that amazing?'

Devlin was hardly listening. He was pressing himself so hard into the seat he wasn't sure he'd ever be able to unglue himself from it again. That's when Gabrielle shoved one of her earbuds in his left ear and filled his head with the most beautiful music he'd ever heard. He wanted to ask her what it was, but that could wait. He closed his eyes. He was no longer on a plane. He was walking down a midnight street in Bohemia with only the light of a waxing harvest moon glistening wet on the cobbles. For nine, glorious minutes they were both lost to this world and existing entirely on the stave lines of Mahler's 'Adagietto'. They were Marc and Bella Chagall, floating across a timeless cityscape. Devlin reached for Gabrielle's hand, eyes still closed, feeling her fingers curl around his in a slow, deliberate way. And then the tyres hit the tarmac, the music ended and the real world stole them back.

Chapter Thirty-Eight

♪

Walter washed down his medication with a large glass of green juice. He'd got chatting to a man at the clinic the other day whose wife had done lots of research into the power of greens to slow cancer's growth. He wasn't entirely convinced, but the man seemed so enthusiastic about it that Walter found himself in the middle aisle of a supermarket with a juicer under his arm and a basket full of spinach, cabbage, broccoli and asparagus. He'd also gone to the health shop for chlorophyll supplements. His consultant would have pooh-poohed the idea, he was certain of that. Whatever the case, he definitely felt healthier, drinking something that tasted like grass. More than that, he felt his mood had improved. He just felt more positive about everything and whereas only a few weeks ago he had contemplated shortening his life, now he wanted it to last as long as possible.

With Devlin in Ireland – *he really had a thing for that young woman if he was willing to get on a plane again* – Walter found himself at a bit of a loss. Despite his own reluctance, he'd grown quite accustomed to Devlin dragging him to some new hobby or other. Last week was a poetry evening at the library. He sighed deeply. It unnerved him that, once he was on his own again, the motivation to find meaning – or at least a little enjoyment – in life seemed to fade. He was old enough to know that he had responsibility for his own reality, no one else. But there was something else; something none of them had spoken about but had surely felt. There was neither rhyme nor reason to it, but that violin was … changing them. Somehow. Walter was not given to flights of fancy, but facing down your own mortality did tend to narrow the gap between the supernatural world and this one. Standing in his North London flat, he felt foolish for even having these thoughts.

'Ridiculous,' he murmured to himself.

With the long day stretching out ahead of him and all of the hours and minutes waiting to be filled or endured, Walter opened the drawer in the sideboard where Devlin had stashed all of the flyers for local events. He shuffled them in his hands like a deck of cards. There was a life-drawing class that he'd been interested in, but that wasn't until the following week. The next flyer was for a line-dancing class.

'Well, I draw the line at line dancing,' he chuckled to himself, imagining a group of septuagenarians in cowboy hats and spurs.

A flyer slipped from his hand and floated to the floor. It was brightly coloured in corals and greens, advertising a salsa class in the local community centre. He bent down to pick it up, his knees complaining. He was not a dancer.

Maybe a waltz, at a push. There was a cartoon couple dancing with palm trees in the background. A dapper-looking man with an open shirt and a woman wearing a red dress. There was something appealing about the idea, but also the very real risk of making a complete fool of himself.

'Beginners welcome!' a speech bubble assured him.

It seemed as though every inch of his body was fighting him to not go. Walter checked his watch: 10:45 a.m. The class began at eleven. If he left now he might just make it. But what if he was late? He hated walking in late. All eyes would be on him then. And everyone would already be partnered up. On and on his thoughts went around. But his feet still took him out the door, down the stairs and onto the street.

♪

'*Ola!*' a woman welcomed him as he stumbled through the swinging door.

Walter raised his hand hesitantly and mouthed an apologetic hello. He was late, and just as he'd feared, everyone was already partnered up and stomping around the floor to the beat of Latin music. While they weren't exactly professionals, they seemed to know what they were doing. Walter was suddenly seized with the desire to be anywhere except where he was. Why had he assumed that an afternoon at home, listening to his records and reading a nice book, would be boring? He was already taking a backward step. Just a few more steps and he would be back in his comfort zone. Which was where exactly? Just outside. Always just outside. A witness to life, but not a participant.

'Are you coming in or going out?'

A voice came from behind him. He turned to see a woman standing in the doorway. The first thing he noticed was her eyes. They were kind and bright. Her face had lines, much like his own, but they gave her a look of wisdom and mischief. Her greying hair was cut short and framed her face – like a film star from the sixties. She wore a yellow raincoat. And Walter's heart found itself beating to a rhythm that felt unfamiliar.

'Oh,' was all he managed to say.

'*Excelente!*' the teacher called over the music. 'We have another couple!'

The woman smiled at him.

'I suppose we should go inside,' she said.

Walter hadn't realised they were still in the doorway.

'Of course, yes, please do come in,' he said, as though it were his house.

'Now I want you to stand side by side. We're going to learn the basic salsa steps,' the teacher said, stopping the music.

'Just a moment,' the woman said and began to unbutton her raincoat. To Walter's surprise, underneath she was wearing a red dress, just like on the flyer.

'Ready?' she asked, taking her place beside him at the back of the hall.

'I have never been less ready for anything in my life,' Walter said. The woman let out a full-throated laugh, which also made Walter laugh. He hadn't intended to be funny, but he was glad that he had been. By stealth.

'Okay, so the rhythm is quick, quick, slow. Left foot steps

forward, right foot steps, then left foot back together, AGAIN!'

Walter took to the steps as though he were in a marching band, pounding the floor with more force than flair. His partner was lighter of foot, but equally lacking in rhythm. The only difference was that she didn't seem to care. Whilst Walter felt like a prize lemon taking a salsa class at his age, this woman was swaying her arms with abandon. Simply enjoying the movement through her body. She looked across at him and smiled and he found himself smiling back.

'Good job, everyone! Now take your partner's hands and try the steps together,' the teacher said, switching the music back on.

'Crikey,' Walter said.

With his head down, he spent the next quarter of an hour staring at his feet moving forward and then back, praying that he wouldn't stand on this lovely woman's feet. When the teacher came around and asked him to lift his head, straighten his back and actually look at the person he was dancing with, he felt himself blushing with embarrassment.

'You're very good at this,' he told her, slightly out of breath.

'You are kind. But I don't think so.'

She had a foreign accent. German perhaps?

'No, really. You're getting all of the steps right.'

'It is not the steps that matter to me.'

'Oh?'

'Dance,' she said. 'To me, it's a primal language. The movement keeps me grounded in my body.'

Crikey.

Just then she let go of one of Walter's hands and turned in time with the music. When she faced him again, they were closer. He could feel the rhythm of the music moving through her body, down her arms and into his arms.

'We spend so much time in our heads,' she continued, before turning again. 'Cerebral!'

She was slightly out of breath and her face flushed with perspiration. She was so, what was the word... Alive! Uninhibited. Interested and interesting. Everything Walter assumed he wasn't. And yet here he was, dancing with her. Maybe life still had some surprises in store.

The hour passed in a blur and at the end he fought a mental battle over whether he should ask her out. Surely, she already had a partner. There was no ring, but that didn't mean anything nowadays. He watched as she fetched her yellow raincoat and stood motionless, still arguing with himself. *You're dying, man! What have you got to lose?*

'Maybe see you next time,' she said, waving goodbye. And with that she was gone. Along with Walter's chance to be brave.

Chapter Thirty-Nine

♪

Devlin could see Gabrielle's shoulders visibly relax as soon as they entered the Irish National Museum. This was her natural environment. The ease with which she spoke about rare and antique musical instruments was impressive. Weirdly, he found himself feeling a sense of pride, which was ridiculous. She wasn't *his*. And she'd made it clear she didn't want to be. Yet somehow that hadn't altered his feelings for her, and he was doing his best to convince himself they could just be friends.

'I'll take you to the collection,' said a middle-aged man with the nametag 'Mr Sherlock'. Devlin just had time to say the game was afoot, before the elevator arrived and a rather weary-looking Sherlock led them into the heart of the building. Collins Barracks, which was conveniently located across the road from Heuston Station, was a former army barracks built around a quadrangular courtyard. It was an impressive building, but you couldn't escape the regimented air that permeated the place.

'So, tell me again, what makes you think this Perry guy was our guy's tutor?' Devlin asked, as their guide walked on ahead.

'I got a tip from someone who's an expert in this area,' Gabrielle said, forcing herself not to think about her prison visit. 'It's a long shot, but an Italian luthier, Vincenzo Panormo, was also one of his students and the style is really quite similar, so it stands to reason that *our guy* might also have been an Italian who came to learn his craft in Dublin. Assuming the violin we found in Milan is one of his. Either way, let's keep an open mind, shall we?'

Devlin wasn't certain if she really wanted him there. He wasn't even sure why he'd come. He didn't know anything about this sort of stuff. Yet he felt a bit protective of Gabrielle. Not that she seemed to need it most of the time, but at the hospital in Italy he'd seen a vulnerable side to her that was so briefly glimpsed, he wasn't sure that he hadn't imagined it. There was no doubting her incredible fortitude and courage, but there was something about the extreme independence she displayed – pushing people away – that struck a chord with him. So he wanted to be there, just in case she needed him.

He began humming a song by Paul Simon about standing guard like a postcard of a golden retriever. He loved that song. Simon had written it about watching over his daughter as she slept. The thought suddenly popped into his head that he really missed songwriting. It came from out of nowhere, but the longing pierced him in the gut. He wished he had a notebook and pen, then and there. Performing just didn't hold the same allure for him anymore. Maybe it never would. But telling stories, that was the part he really missed. Gabrielle glared at him, but he kept humming anyway.

'Can I hold it?' Gabrielle asked, as they stood in front of the glass case displaying the Thomas Perry collection.

'You can play it, if you like,' Mr Sherlock said.

'Seriously?'

'No,' he sniggered, amused at his own joke. 'But I'll get us some gloves and you can have a closer look.'

They sat at a desk where the violin rested on a thick piece of velvet material. Gabrielle began pointing out all of the features that were unique to Thomas Perry.

'How do they know he made it?' Devlin asked.

'Because it's branded under the button on the back,' Gabrielle said, showing him the engraving. It was kind of exciting seeing the name *Thomas Perry* chiselled neatly into the wood.

'The two-piece back and sides are flamed maple, and of course, spruce pine for the front. You can see the f-holes here have a slightly wider aperture at the bottom?'

Devlin looked at what he always thought were decorative 'S's. They did look more attractive than the standard violin, and it was the same with his violin. Perhaps Gabrielle's expert was onto something.

'This one was made in 1814, four years before his death. There's some damage to the scroll but it does look a lot like ours. A light golden varnish, inlaid purfling.'

She glanced around her to see if anyone was close by. It seemed they were quite alone.

'It's said that Perry violins have a warm, velvety timbre.' She gave the bow a longing look.

'Go on. Be a rebel.' Devlin moved the bow closer to her with his gloved index finger.

Looking around again, she quickly took up the bow and briefly swept it across the strings. It sounded awful.

'It needs tuning,' she said. Before Devlin had time to persuade her to tune it, the curator returned and asked if there was anything more they would like to know. Gabrielle's face felt like a hotplate; surely he'd heard. She decided to pander to his ego and asked him for more details on the life of the great Irish Stradivarius. He hardly needed prompting and gave the speech he had been gearing up to for his entire career.

'Well, you see, late eighteenth-century Dublin was the second city of the British Empire, home to a society of well-educated, affluent people who were discerning in their tastes and demanded genteel and sophisticated entertainment. Concerts and theatrical performances were a prominent feature of life in the city.'

Devlin found himself unexpectedly interested in the history of the place. He'd always felt that Dublin had its soul steeped in music, but all he knew about were singers like Phil Lynott and maybe some traditional Irish ballads. That's as far as it went. The city that this man was describing sounded profoundly different, yet still the music flowed through its arteries.

'Of course, you had Christ Church and St Patrick's Cathedral, so choristers performed choral music from the early 1700s. In fact, the first performance of Handel's Messiah took place in the Music Hall at Fishamble Street in 1742.'

'Handel was here?' Devlin asked, to Gabrielle's surprise. She assumed he wasn't listening.

'Oh yes, he stayed here for almost a year. For various reasons, his career had stalled in London and he was invited to Ireland by the lord lieutenant, Lord Devonshire, and packed in his luggage the score of a piece of music he had written the previous summer. Handel adored Dublin. He liked the easy openness of the people. In any case, he decided that he would premiere his new work here, using the choristers from the two cathedrals. Can you imagine, when the morning of 13th April 1742 dawned, the seven hundred or so who had fought to get tickets couldn't have known that they were about to witness history being made.'

'This is fascinating,' Gabrielle whispered under her breath, not wanting to break his flow.

'It is said that, in order to create more space, the women had been asked to come without hoops for their skirts, the men without swords. Such was the success of the concert that it led to a second a few weeks later. Handel finally returned to London in August of that year, but the Messiah proved less popular with the fickle English audiences, whereas in Dublin they loved it from the off. Anyway, I digress. The point is that Thomas Perry would have lived in the kind of Dublin where demand for instruments of quality, particularly for chamber music, was very high indeed. To say he was prolific is an understatement.'

'Might I take some photos of the violin before we go?' Gabrielle asked, already taking photos on her phone. 'Also, would you have any information on the apprentices who might have worked with Perry?'

'Any name in particular? They were numerous.'

'I'm not sure. I'm researching a violin that has a very particular scroll carving, not like this one.'

He took a look at the pictures on her phone, then fished a pair of tiny glasses out of his jacket pocket and looked again.

'Remarkable!'

Gabrielle looked at Devlin with a covert grin.

'Where did you get this?' he asked, reappraising them both in a new light.

'I'm working on behalf of a client,' she said, offering him her card. Once he knew her credentials, she knew he'd be more forthcoming.

'In the records office, we keep the archives of the Museum Bulletin. It's full of articles written when the original Museum of Science and Art was established. I'm afraid there's a dearth of information on Thomas Perry in general, much of our knowledge is conjecture, so the chances of finding anything are slim. Still, we do have a café downstairs and I'm sure that if you get a bit of fuel into you, you stand a good chance of finding something.'

They thanked him and took his advice. Gabrielle ordered them both coffee and bagels, while Devlin booked them a place to stay for the night and tried to call Walter.

'That's weird,' he said, when she returned to the table. 'Walter's not picking up his calls.'

Gabrielle smiled while pouring some milk into her cup.

'What?' Devlin asked.

'You two. You're like an old married couple already.'

'He could do a lot worse,' Devlin retorted, quick as lightning.

He tore into his bagel. Gabrielle sat back for a moment and let the scent of coffee fill her nostrils. Despite the awkwardness that sometimes hung between them, he was still easy company.

'Do you mind being here? You know, in Dublin.' She waited for his answer until he'd finished chewing.

'I'm trying not to think about it too much.'

'Denial. It's highly underrated.'

He watched as she bit into her bagel. She was always so neat, not a hair out of place. Her cup turned at the right angle, napkin folded just so. He felt like an untamed gorilla around her. But while it had intimidated him at the start, now he found her efforts to keep everything perfect kind of endearing, but also the tell-tale signs of someone who needed to do this to feel safe. She looked up and caught him staring.

'What?'

'I just … I don't think I've had a chance to say this but – thank you. I don't know why you've bothered to help me, and Walter, of course. But I'm really glad you did. Whatever happens, I'm glad we've been on this journey together.'

Gabrielle bit the flesh on the inside of her mouth. She found herself wanting to open up to him about everything. About the attack, the woman who came to her shop, her father, even Max. All of it. But where could she even begin? If he knew that she'd been planning on handing over his priceless possession to a thief, for a price, what would he think of her then? And why had she done it, anyway? Just so she could claim the glory and redeem her family's reputation? How naive she'd been. She would never be able to reveal her part in this without also revealing that she'd played both sides. That would mean the end of her friendship with Walter and Devlin. Which reputation mattered most? The professional one her father had left in tatters – or her personal integrity?

Chapter Forty

♪

THE VIOLIN

Berlin, 1939

Mikhail stumbled into the apartment, just as the morning light betrayed the moth-eaten curtains. He tripped over his own shoes as he made a clumsy and ineffectual attempt not to wake his wife. But Sofia had not yet slept. How could she? Wondering where her husband had been, and how much, of the little money they had, he had wasted on whisky. She was not yet thirty, but she felt weary and worn out like her threadbare clothes; spread too thin like the tasteless food she prepared every day. She had gone against her parents' wishes and married a man with no prospects.

Mikhail was a good storyteller. He made her believe that he was going to be the finest virtuoso in the Berlin Philharmonic. He had studied at a good school and showed promise early on. But he seemed to spend more time talking about performances than actually performing. He failed to get a place with any orchestra. When it came to playing serious classical music, he would choke. Sofia pitied him – she knew how hard his mother had pushed him in those early years to become great – to become *someone*; as if he were not already someone, or enough of a someone. In a rare moment of candour, he told her how his mother had once broken a violin over his head when he failed to impress a visiting tutor.

But her pity had run out. They were now living in his mother's cramped apartment with two small children and no future. Mikhail could drown his worries and fears in a bottle, earning pennies playing in bars and outside restaurants, entertaining the well-to-do of Berlin with ditties like 'Lilli Marlene'. But how could Sofia escape the life her parents had predicted and warned her against?

The bed rocked violently as he fell into it. A pungent smell filled the air and she could feel his stale breath on the back of her neck. His rough hand grabbed her breast.

'Hello, *meine schöne*,' he slurred.

'I am not beautiful, and you are drunk. Get your hands off me,' she hissed, praying he would not wake their children, who were sleeping behind a curtain that divided the room.

'I want to make love to my wife,' he said, the sense of entitlement rising in his voice.

Sofia turned her face to him.

'That's what you call it? Forcing yourself on me when you're so drunk you cannot stand?'

A long moment passed while Mikhail stared at this woman who had a terrible way of seeing him for who he really was. A fraud. He wanted to slap her, or fuck her, but the baby began crying and she got up to tend to her. He would not become his father. He would not.

Sofia held her daughter close and thanked God. She wasn't always this lucky; some nights she just had to give in.

♪

'I mean it this time,' Mikhail assured his wife, his eyes moist with contrition. 'No more drinking.'

They sat at the kitchen table. Sofia was breastfeeding little Ari, staring unseeing out of their fifth-floor window.

'I have an audition tonight with a quartet.'

This made Sofia look up. She didn't dare hope, but she was prone to the same delusions as Mikhail's mother: that if he just got a bit of luck, his fortunes could change. She sighed – a great long exhalation – then eased the sleeping child's lips away from her breast.

'You'll be needing your good suit then. I shall give it an airing.'

'Thank you, *meine schöne*,' he said, throwing himself on his knees before her, kissing her hands, the baby's head and lastly, tenderly, her cheek.

'I will make you proud. I'll make you all proud.'

'Mikhail, make yourself proud. That is all I want for you. The rest will follow.'

♪

He was lying. There was no audition, but there was a concert he wished to see. A woman, no less: Eva Mudocci.

An English 'violinist', passing herself off as some kind of prodigy. The press had begun calling her 'The Nightingale', such was the sweetness of her playing. It was said she had a very special violin, sourced on her travels to the Orient, the sound of which could bring the hardest of men to tears. Mikhail was intrigued, although he doubted if this spoiled brat had any actual talent. She was known as Edvard Munch's muse, a reputation far more fitting for a woman in his eyes.

He arrived at the concert hall just as the orchestra was warming up. He charmed his way past the doorman and stole back to the dressing rooms. He could see Ms Mudocci speaking with her accompanist, Bella Edwards, about some arrangement and ducked into the nearest room, waiting for her to be alone. To his surprise, he found himself in her dressing room. It was filled with flowers and champagne and there on a chaise longue was the violin, waiting like a rose to be plucked. He couldn't resist – the case lay open, like the shell of Venus, inviting him in. The bow called to his fingers, and he was as helpless as Eve in the garden of Eden. He lifted me ever so carefully and played one long, solitary note. He was overcome. It was the sound he had always imagined in his soul, the perfect pitch. This violin, he thought, with its wonderful soprano, would make his career.

There was no time for questioning whatever was left of his conscience. His family was barely existing on watery stew and handouts from his mother. Eva Mudocci had already made her name. She would not go hungry. It was Mikhail Abramovich's time now. Quickly, he replaced me in my case and disappeared with me under his coat through the back door.

He took me back to his tiny apartment. The paint was peeling off the walls and the cold made my wood contract. While his family slept, he opened my case on the little kitchen table. He searched for markings, a name or a stamp. But of course, there were none. Still, I could tell he had heard the rumours. When Eva Mudocci purchased me on her trip to Istanbul, I was charmed at the idea of entering great music halls once again and performing for the crowds. A born storyteller herself, she embellished the story of a mysterious provenance, which the salesman had told with great conviction. *This violin has a hidden power*, he told her, *and the voice of a nightingale.*

Mikhail knew there would be a search for such an exquisite instrument. He had to disguise me and so he retrieved a pot of boot polish from the little cupboard under the stairs and, with an old cloth, began to obscure my rich amber varnish. He was pleased with his work; he had made me appear much older and less valuable, but the sound – that was what would earn him his fortune.

The very next week, just as he was on his way to the concert hall to audition for the orchestra, Mikhail was attacked by a group of thieves.

'Give us your money!' they shouted.

'I have nothing to give, I promise you.'

'What about that?' one of them said, pointing at the violin.

'Oh this? No, I cannot give you this.'

The smaller one took out a knife.

'Is that so?'

'It's merely a violin. It's of no use to you if you can't play!' he pleaded. But the thieves would not be satisfied. The smaller man thrust the knife at Mikhail who, instinctively protecting himself, put his other hand up to stop him. The pain seared through him like a scorching firebrand, but the man did not stop. He struck again and again Mikhail raised his hand. The knife went right through this time. Just then, a policeman blew his whistle and the thieves fled. Mikhail fell to the ground, his hand bleeding profusely. He did not need a surgeon to tell him. He knew he would never play again. The nerves were severed.

'The damn thing is cursed,' he told his wife and instructed her to get rid of me. But Sofia could not do it. She did not believe in curses and thought she might keep me for one of the children. Perhaps they would inherit their father's talent, but not his rage. And so she took me to the old janitor's room in the basement, when no one was around, and with a cloth dipped in oil she began to clean my wooden frame. To her surprise, the cloth quickly turned black with the layers of dirt. Underneath, she could see a glowing amber colour, like a hidden treasure. She carried on cleaning until she realised that I was no ordinary violin. She had learned a thing or two about the instrument in her years married to Mikhail, and two things now became clear. One: it was a very expensive violin – one that Mikhail certainly couldn't afford. And two: she had seen it before. It belonged to the English lady violinist: 'The Nightingale'. The papers had been full of it over the last few weeks and the unlikely theft. She knew what she had to do.

♪

'Where on earth did you find it?' Eva Mudocci had taken quite some time to regain her power of speech. Even now, her voice was thick with emotion and caught in her throat.

Sofia stood in the lobby of a very expensive hotel, embarrassed at her old clothes and her fingernails, dirty from peeling potatoes. Her hair was greasy and she knew she looked far older than her years. Yet this shame, she could bear. It was honest. But her husband's crime? That was a shame that made it hard to meet this young violinist's eyes.

'I…' she began.

'Do you know what? It no longer matters a jot to me! She is back in my arms and that is all I care about.'

Sofia breathed a sigh of relief. As did I. This young woman may have been born privileged, but she possessed a pragmatism that Sofia admired.

'Well, then,' Sofia said, almost bowing her head as though the girl were royalty, 'all is as it should be.'

Eva watched the woman walking slowly away from her and towards the revolving door of the hotel. It was clear from her appearance that she was quite poor and the dark circles under her eyes betrayed many sleepless nights. But it was the star sewn onto her coat that called Eva to act.

'Where do you think you're going?' Eva called out and Sofia froze. It had been too easy. The girl was going to call the police. Or, worse, the Gestapo.

'Miss, I'm so sorry—' Sofia began.

'It is I who am at fault, my dear. In my elation I almost forgot to give you your reward,' she said, tucking my case under her arm and opening her purse.

'Oh no, Miss, I did not come for a reward.'

With a deft hand, Eva pressed quite a few notes into Sofia's hand.

'Things are getting worse here by the day. For whatever reason, fate has brought us together. Have you ever had occasion in your life to do one small, kind act for your fellow man, something which may mean the world to them but costs you hardly a thought?'

'I'm not sure I understand...'

'That is what you did for me, returning my violin. You will never know what you have done for me, but it cost you nothing. Now, my dear, allow me to do the same for you,' she said, with a knowing smile.

'Thank you, Miss, this is very kind. But I could never leave, I do not have the papers.'

'My violin and I are travelling back to the UK and then it's on to Canada. And we'll be needing a reliable assistant. What do you say?' Eva said.

Sofia was dumbstruck. Then she stammered, 'But my husband, his mother, the children.'

'Why, bring them all!' she said, as if it were a day trip to the sea and not an escape from the only home Sofia had ever known.

She went straight home to Mikhail and told him of what had happened. When he heard that she had returned the violin, he beat her so badly that he almost broke her nose. The following morning, before the sun came up, she dressed little Ari and Sacha, took a small suitcase of their clothes and fled with them from the apartment before Mikhail or his mother woke. She met Eva outside her hotel and as the taxi drove them to the train station, Sofia closed her eyes and never looked back.

Chapter Forty-One

♪

The archives room at Collins Barracks was stuffy with decades of guarded secrets and a maze of confusion, but once they were seated with the correct folders, it was simply a matter of sifting through the newsletters and bulletins for anything about Thomas Perry. Gabrielle was in her natural element: a hushed room and an historical mystery to be solved. Devlin, on the other hand, thrived on noise and activity. Sitting at this desk felt like being back at school, and he found himself fidgeting like a distracted teenager.

'Oh, here's something,' Gabrielle said, after twenty minutes had passed in a mindless blur for Devlin.

'Museum Bulletin – July 1911

    Mr A. McGoogan

    Even the country of Perry's origin is unknown for certain. Guesswork has assigned his birth to the year 1767 and it is said that he is related to Claude Pierray – a Parisian violin maker. Wilson's Dublin Directory of 1787 has a musical instrument maker at No. 6 Anglesea Street, but this locality has long since been altered beyond recognition. It has been proposed by some historians that Perry may have studied under the great Molineux, although the style of their instruments is quite different; the signature under the back button has become the Irish style. The firm produced almost 5,000 instruments...'

Gabrielle set the bulletin aside and opened the next one.

'Keep an eye out for this A. McGoogan, he seems to have an interest in Irish violin makers,' she said, without lifting her eyes from the page.

'Right, boss,' Devlin replied, happy to take a back seat. He reached into his backpack and took out a pair of glasses, black-framed and, Gabrielle had to admit, quite fetching. He ran his hands through his hair and rested his chin on the inside of his palm. She couldn't seem to pull her eyes away, as the little muscle in his jaw twitched.

'Something the matter?' he asked, suddenly aware of being watched.

She shook her head and returned to her research, but the words were black ants marching across the page now. All she could think about was pulling off his glasses and running her hands through his hair. *What the hell?* Where was this coming from? It was embarrassing, fancying someone who'd kissed you out of pity and decided against anything further. She let out a big sigh, shifted in her seat and tried to settle back down.

'Hey, I've found something!' he said, after ten long

minutes in which Gabrielle read the same paragraph over and over.

He began to read from an old scrap of paper that was slightly torn at the end.

During his long working life, he trained a number of younger men in his craft, who went on to become important makers in their own right.

There was a list of six names, but one stood out to Gabrielle immediately. *William Rathbone*. It was the only name on the list she had never heard before and for the most unscientific of reasons, she just *felt* that this was the name she should investigate.

'What does it say about him?'

There was a short paragraph on each maker, but Rathbone's was the shortest of all.

'*Dr Graham suggests that he served his apprenticeship with the firm around 1815,*' Devlin read aloud.

'That tallies with Roger's dating of the wood. This is a really good sign!'

'*Born in Waterford, his formative years were steeped in carpentry. In cutting a scroll, Rathbone was unequalled. He varnished his violins in the Cremonese style, limpid fire of amber and golden glow. Looking at the surface through the varnish, Rathbone's beautiful lines led to his violins being described as "lilies dipped in wine".*'

Devlin looked up at Gabrielle.

'That might be the most poetic phrase I've ever read,' he said.

'You've got the bug,' she smiled. 'Research seduces all of us in the end.'

Devlin rolled his eyes, but she knew she was triumphant.

> *'Violin historians say that he kept a shop in Soho, and I have searched old directories and records in vain for any evidence of this. If he had a shop at all, it was evidently of such modest pretensions, as to altogether escape the attention of directory compilers.'*

'This is incredible,' Gabrielle said, her hand on Devlin's shoulder as she leaned across to look at the page. She could feel her blood whooshing in her veins. Desire was threatening to take control.

Devlin turned to look at her and for a moment he paused. He wanted to capture the moment. They were the only two people in the world who held the key to the violin's past. They were the only two people in the world...

'What else does it say?' she asked impatiently.

Devlin tore his eyes away from hers and tried to find his place on the page.

> *'Authentic Rathbone labels are extremely rare. He sold many of his violins to dealers who frequently relabelled them, attributing them to Cremonese masters, as he worked in the Stradivari style. Many other of his violins have no label at all. Consequently, he never received the credit due to him. As a luthier, he is described as a genius.'*

'That explains why there was no label,' she said, returning to the close-up images on her phone. She bit the inside of her cheek again. It felt swollen and sore. She had no idea how she knew this, but in her bones she knew that the violin in Cremona was a Rathbone, just as she knew that their violin was a Rathbone also. The varnish, the scroll, the f-holes, the wood itself, all fit.

'What do you think?' Devlin asked, removing his glasses and biting on the end of the arm, which threatened to derail Gabrielle's focus entirely.

'Um ... can I just check something in the footnotes?' she said, sliding the book across. 'Here, it mentions a letter printed in the *Galpin Society Journal* from 1963.'

Devlin clicked the search engine on her phone and within a few clicks he was looking at a scan of the original letter, written in 1834 and addressed to a Mr Bartholomew Murphy, an instrument maker in Cork. The young woman writing to him was his granddaughter, Imogen.

'Oh, this is cool, he's talking about a new luthier making violins and violas at his workshop in Cork. A man by the name of Rathbone.'

'So, he must have moved between Ireland and the UK,' said Gabrielle.

'He and Vincenzo swap many amusing tales,' he said.

'Panormo once said that he made a violin from the wood of an old billiards table. When Rathbone remarked that this would impress his friend Paganini no end, Panormo was stunned into silence, which is not a common occurrence, I can assure you! But then, I must confess I am still unsure as to whether it was said in jest. Rathbone told a tale of a piece of music, written in Paganini's

own hand and given to the young man himself. Of course, Panormo asked him to produce it, if indeed it was true. Misty-eyed, he said that he could not, for he had secreted the scroll at the foot of an angel in Starling Manor. I know you are particularly fond of such romantic gestures and will thus appreciate the anecdote. He referred to it as "Bellezza Nascosta".'

Gabrielle's eyebrows shot upwards.
'Say that again!'
He repeated himself.
'What is it?'
Gabrielle had almost lost the power of speech.
'I … you … this…'
'Does it mean something?'
'I-I don't know, but I've been searching for this missing piece for a very long time.'
She looked into his eyes and let the double meaning hang between them. 'It's so strange to find it mentioned here, now.'
'In this random letter,' Devlin added.
'Yes,' she agreed, 'in the letter.'
Devlin looked at all of the research material and notes spread out in front of them.
'So, I guess this means it's definitely not a Strad, then.'
'You seem disappointed,' she replied. 'This is a good thing. Now we can get V off our backs!'
'Who?'
'Um, the thief. Person. Gang.'
Devlin nodded, unconvinced.
'I dunno, I just … I thought we'd found something really priceless.'

Gabrielle reached out and took a hold of both of his wrists.

'Devlin, you have the most priceless thing in the world, don't you see? There are over six-hundred Strads in the world today. Do you know how many genuine Rathbones there are? That I know of?'

He shrugged.

'Two. It doesn't get more special than this.'

He'd never seen her so excited.

'Actually, it's not even two, because your violin has such a rich quality of sound, a resonance, that surpasses any instrument I've ever heard – and I've had the occasion to hear many great instruments played by gifted musicians. I'm not certain where Rathbone sourced this wood, or the techniques he used, but I can guarantee there is no other violin in the world like it.'

He wanted to kiss her, but he wasn't going to make that mistake again. Instead, they sort of shook hands and allowed it to turn into an awkward hug.

'I'll verify things with Roger, but I'm confident in my appraisal,' she said.

'Even without a label?'

'I know it seems like something of a black art. There are many intangibles that are much easier to visualise in one's mind than express in words. To be honest, the label on a violin is the last thing we look at during an evaluation. The presence of a label does help to confirm my opinion, certainly, but there are so many false labels out there—'

'Ah, how are ye getting on?' asked Mr Sherlock, appearing behind them and peering over their shoulders.

'Excellent, Mr Sherlock. We got what we came for.'

'That's very good to hear. You certainly look happier,' he said, then winked at Devlin for some reason. 'So ye'll be off home, then?'

They looked at each other, uncertain.

'Only, if ye were planning on staying, there's a concert tomorrow evening that you might be interested in,' he said, handing Gabrielle a flyer with pictures of a beautiful manor house set in extensive grounds, promising a candlelit evening of violin solos.

'I'm afraid we won't have time. We're heading back to London in the morning,' she said.

'Where is it?' Devlin asked.

'Just outside Waterford.'

'Waterford?' Gabrielle repeated. It was too much of a coincidence that their luthier was born there. Had she not just spoken of black arts and intuition? Perhaps she should go...

'I'm in no rush to get back on a plane, if I'm honest,' Devlin said, slinging his backpack over his shoulder.

All of a sudden, Gabrielle felt reluctant to return home, too. When they got back to London, she would have to face up to the truth; she would have to tell Devlin that the criminal gang still wanted the violin back and she'd fought them off for as long as she could. The adventure was over. And he'd probably hate her for it.

She looked again at the flyer. 'Starling Manor estate,' she whispered, looking up at Devlin. 'Can this be possible?'

He shrugged slightly, then smiled.

'I suppose one more night wouldn't hurt.'

'Now it's black tie, so you might have to spruce

yourselves up a bit.' Mr Sherlock winked again. Devlin wondered if he was some sort of matchmaker on the side, but he wasn't about to complain. Music, posh surroundings, fancy clothes... In any other language, it was a date.

Chapter Forty-Two

♪

There hadn't been time to pack an evening gown and Devlin certainly didn't bring a suit, so Gabrielle suggested they go shopping, once the train arrived at Plunkett Station. Waterford city had a completely different atmosphere to the capital. Set on the water, it had the feel of a holiday town, and Gabrielle had the sudden realisation that she and Devlin were effectively on a mini-break together. It had been different in Cremona – Walter was there. But now, here they were, alone together.

They walked along the street, side by side; him with the violin case slung over his shoulder and her with her executive-style suitcase wheeling along behind her. They were such opposites in every way and yet, underneath the surface, perhaps they were more alike than she realised. When he'd opened up to her in the hospital about his past, her whole body had melted into him, as though it was finally okay to feel her feelings in front of another human being that wasn't Trudy. She looked across at him, as he stepped back to let a woman with a buggy have more room on the pavement. He was nothing like her usual type. He caught her looking and smiled. Mortified, she returned her gaze to the horizon line and quickened her step. Her tendency to over-analyse things was rearing its head and without noticing, she'd completely ignored Devlin's question.

'I'm sorry, what was that?'

'How about this place?' he repeated, slowing down and pointing to a shopfront.

It was a shop, that much was obvious, but the clothes on the mannequins in the window had no relation to each other. Everything was a jumble of styles and colours. She looked above and saw the name.

Second Time's The Charm

'A charity shop?'

Devlin had already pushed the door open.

'Oh no, I just couldn't,' she said, grabbing his arm.

'Why not? It's just for one night,' he said, pushing the door open once again.

She laid her hand on his arm again and he let the door close.

'It's just ... the thought of other people's clothes.' Her face wore the expression of someone sucking a sour sweet.

'They do wash them, Gabrielle,' he said, mock-seriously. 'Fine, well you can go to a regular shop, I'm going to support the circular economy.' There was a challenge in his tone. Good-natured, but still a challenge.

He opened the door again and, at the last minute, she

decided to go in with him. In case he picked out something outrageous like a velvet three-piece. The shop was bigger than the front window suggested, and the clothes rails went all the way back to the rear, punctuated by an occasional display of jewellery and knick-knacks.

'How about this?' Devlin asked, holding up a white tuxedo jacket.

'See, now this is exactly what I was afraid of,' Gabrielle replied, pretending to clear something from her eye.

'That's it,' Devlin said, pointing at her. 'Exactly what I'm looking for – a reaction. I'm going to try it on.'

He disappeared behind a curtain and the young shop assistant asked if she needed anything.

'We're attending a recital this evening,' Gabrielle explained, 'so my friend here is looking for something that says understated elegance.'

'Have you got those trousers with, like, a tape running up the side?' Devlin asked, sticking his head out of the curtain. 'And a black shirt,' he called out, disappearing once again.

♪

Gabrielle walked to the back of the shop with her arms folded. She'd never shopped in a place like this, which probably came across as a bit snobby. But how would you even know what you were looking for? Or if they had your size? It was like emptying out a load of lost suitcases and wading through people's wardrobes. She suddenly thought about Devlin finding the violin at the airport Lost and Found. Weren't violins second-hand? Her entire career, she had dealt in second-hand goods! Why had this only occurred to her now? And that was when she spotted it. A long, flowing, emerald-green dress with spaghetti straps. It was perfect. She looked around and saw that no one was watching. Quietly, she reached up and lifted the hanger from the rail. The material was soft and slinky with a low-cut back. It reminded her of that infamous dress Keira Knightley wore in the film *Atonement*. She checked the tag, which said Roselli. She'd never heard of the designer, but it didn't matter. She was already imagining herself wearing it. Regardless of the size, she would make it fit. It was a 10, which would be a tight squeeze. She decided she wouldn't even bother trying it on. It was priced at fifty euros – a total bargain.

♪

Devlin pulled back the curtain of the changing room and emerged in a white jacket, black shirt and black trousers. The only person she had ever seen pull off a look like that was 007. Yet somehow it looked tailor-made for him, and he looked so handsome she gulped.

'What do you think?' he asked, strutting around the shop floor.

'I think that maybe understated elegance is highly overrated.'

♪

They arrived late at Starling Manor just as the sun was setting for the evening. Devlin had insisted on 'finding a hotel' rather than letting Gabrielle book one on her phone like a normal person.

'But how will we know which one to pick without checking out the reviews first?' she'd asked on the train journey from Dublin, blinking at him.

'Why do you rely on other people's opinions?' he'd countered.

And when she thought about it, he had a point. Perhaps it might be fun to stumble across something, rather than plan it down to the very last detail. It turned out that they found a boutique hotel overlooking the marina, a funky modern hotel that she normally wouldn't have looked twice at online. Being in Devlin's company was almost like the universe inviting her to try on a new personality, and, despite her reservations, she actually found herself liking it. Liking how it felt to be Gabrielle minus all of the rules and walls she'd built up. It felt like fun, something she assumed she'd lost forever.

Later that evening, as their taxi swept up the drive, a palatial mansion came into view, with its smooth white façade glowing almost gold in the sunset. The wheels turned on the gravel and as soon as the car stopped, Devlin got out, paid the driver and opened Gabrielle's door. She stepped out into the evening air wearing her new-to-her green cocktail dress and she felt, quite simply, happy. She was glad she'd followed her instincts and agreed to come. Devlin looked undeniably handsome in his suit, and he offered her his arm in such a nonchalant way, it seemed almost as if he did this kind of thing all the time. As always, he held the violin under the other arm. For a fleeting moment, she wondered if the violin knew it was at home. If, indeed, it had been made in Ireland.

'You look beautiful,' he said, his eyes glinting in the sunlight.

If nothing else was going to happen between them, he was glad they would have this night together. He wanted to show her that life could be fun, people could be trusted and, most importantly, that he had her back, no matter what. The downside to being a lone wolf was loneliness. He could see it with Walter, too. Sometimes people just needed to feel a bit of kindness. And now that the pressure of the violin was no longer putting them at odds with each other, he knew he could be that person. Now that they knew it wasn't a Strad, he could get the criminal gang off his back and maybe life would begin to return to normal. Better than normal.

They took a glass of prosecco from the tray at reception and slipped in through the double doors to the ballroom, which was lit up by candlelight. They were the last to arrive and the staff closed the doors behind them. They were about to take their seats when she saw him. Black hair curling away from his forehead, a little greyer now at his temples. His dark eyes still alight with a desire for what he did not yet possess, and that enigmatic smile, charming everyone who mattered. Max Daunt. How was it possible? Why was he here? Her eyes scanned the room, halting at the stage set up in the bay window. Tuning her violin was a female soloist, a young girl of barely eighteen. It wasn't her first recital, but the early nerves were still there. Max walked over to her, bent his head and whispered something cajoling in her ear. Then Gabrielle saw his hand slip around the young girl's waist. Her whole world began to tilt on its axis. She could see her past playing out before her. Not only had she failed to speak up for herself, now it was happening to someone else. The hand on the waist, the closeness, the imbalance of power and the young girl's unshakeable trust in his good intentions for her and her career. She saw her visibly tighten at his touch, but her facial expression betrayed nothing. Gabrielle wanted to be sick.

The room became unbearably stuffy and, as the audience gathered, she started to feel trapped. Devlin was looking at her, asking if anything was the matter, but his voice seemed fuzzy and far away. She turned back to watch the girl, to make sure she was okay, only to find Max staring straight at her. The bottom of her world fell out and she was spinning, spinning, without anything to hold onto.

'I need the bathroom.'

Somehow, she had found coherent words. Devlin looked up and nodded, though his eyes showed some concern. It didn't matter. She had to get out. Just as the steward was closing the door, she gave him a pleading look and he let her squeeze past. Once outside the ballroom, she wasn't sure where to go or what to do. Starling Manor was in the middle of nowhere and she'd left her phone in her bag, which she must have left on her seat inside the ballroom, so she couldn't call a taxi back to the hotel. She heard the door open and close again. She should have known he'd follow her.

'Gabrielle.'

Just hearing him say her name brought everything back. The helplessness, the shame.

'What are you doing here?'

'I don't want to talk to you, Max.'

Of all the things she'd fantasised about saying to him, this was a somewhat watery response. Where was the strength she should have built up over the intervening years? She didn't need to be afraid of him anymore.

He took out a box of cigarettes and slowly lit one, as though he owned the room. He always had that sense of entitlement and he always seemed to get what he wanted.

'That could have been you in there, you know. If it hadn't been for your *phantom* injury.'

Gabrielle wrapped her arms tightly around her body, shivering now with cold and fear. She grasped her wrist instinctively. The pain stabbed, just as it had in the early days, but Trudy had shown it for what it really was: protection. From him. She looked at the double doors to the garden, which stood wide open. *Escape.* But why was it always her that had to run away? Why did he get to stay and be the big successful maestro?

'My days of being groomed by an ageing has-been are well and truly over,' she replied in a voice dripping with venom. She was trembling and hoped he couldn't tell. She was doing this for her younger self. Even if everyone else was in denial about what happened, she was going to call it what it was. What was there to lose? He'd already taken everything that mattered.

She braced herself for his response, his anger or rage, but yet again, he was one step ahead. Always prepared to target her weakness.

'Is that what you've been telling yourself?' he said, with a quizzical look, as though she were some sort of simpleton.

'I suppose you had to find a way to rationalise the *real* truth.'

'What are you talking about?'

He took several steps closer to her and although she wanted to move away, her legs wouldn't move.

'That you simply ... weren't ... good enough.' He punctuated each word by tapping his index and middle finger on her bare chest.

She crumpled inside, like a fragile piece of paper inked with all of his poisonous words. And yet she couldn't let him see how much power he still held over her. When she was younger, she used to dig her nails into her palm to stop herself from crying and she found herself resorting to the same thing now. His critical voice was still the one she tried to drown out at night when the ghosts of what could have been came to haunt her. And now here he was, opening all the old wounds again, undermining her efforts to heal the hurt he'd caused. Maybe Trudy was wrong. You could never escape the past. Or confront it.

'I tried to help you, I really did,' he continued. 'In the end I felt sorry for you. But I couldn't turn down all that money your father was paying me,' he said, taking a long drag of his cigarette and looking around the beautifully furnished orangery. 'I do enjoy the finer things in life and if that means indulging a little girl's fantasies about being a soloist, then so be it.'

A fury like she'd never known erupted from the pit of her stomach and before she had time to think, she smacked him hard across the face. He held his cheek and flashed her an angry look before that wolfish smile returned and he smacked her in return, twice as hard.

'Get out of here, Gabrielle,' he said, breathless with the thrill of what he'd done. 'You don't belong here. Girls like you think you're special, but without me, you're nothing.' He looked her up and down with distaste curling his lips. 'Look at the state of you,' he shook his head, 'in your drab old dress. Although I suppose it suits you – you're both damaged goods,' he said, before he flung his cigarette to the ground in front of her and let himself back into the ballroom.

She stood there, swaying with the shock of it all. Her cheek was stinging, but that wasn't the fatal wound. She thought of the children's rhyme, 'sticks and stones may break my bones but words will never hurt me'. It wasn't true. Words hurt the deepest. She looked down at her dress and no longer saw the beautiful material, she just saw a cheap imitation, someone trying to be something they're not. She turned and stepped out into the garden where the evening sky had turned a dark navy blue. It was cold and so she began walking, anywhere. Down the shadowy wooded pathways, half-unseeing, the autumn leaves crunching underfoot. A tiny animal scurried underneath the bushes and she wished she could do the same. Hide away in the earthy blackness until all of this went away. But how could it ever go away when she was carrying it around with her? All of this time, she thought she was putting years between her and what happened.

She carried on, through russet-red wooden gates and into a walled garden. Wisteria tumbled down the stone boundary walls, and she followed a gravel path leading to an oval pond that reflected the moon in its still waters. She sat on a bench, staring into the mirrored surface, and saw her haunted face looking back at her. Just seeing him unhinged every door she had locked between her and the past. She was fooling herself if she thought she could move on from him and what he did to her. All he had to do was look at her in that scornful way of his and she was right back there, trapped between her compulsion to please him and her fear of him. With a few careless words, he'd made her feel like a total fraud. A fake. Just like the violins her father sold. The life she built was on shifting sands – it was not the life she wanted, but she thought it guaranteed her some kind of safety. And yet it was all an illusion. How could she ever feel safe again?

'Gabrielle!'

Devlin's voice carried on the evening mist that had set in. She tried to call out to him but found she didn't have the breath. He called again and soon she heard his footsteps crunching the gravel.

'I'm here,' she said, getting up from the bench.

Devlin followed the path lit with solar lights until he found her, standing alone and shivering at the pond. He immediately took off his jacket and pulled it around her shoulders, gathering her into his chest, before leaving the violin case on the bench.

'What are you doing out here?' he asked, rubbing his hands along her arms to try and warm her up.

'I had to leave,' she said, her voice thick with unshed tears.

'Shhh,' he said. 'It's okay, you're safe now.'

Devlin wasn't sure what was going on. All he knew was

that he would give anything in that moment to make it go away for her.

'Is there anything I can do?'

He could feel her shake her head where it lay against his chest. All was still in the garden around them. Devlin looked up at the silhouette of the trees against the darkening sky and the harvest moon keeping watch over them. Then, out of nowhere, a whooshing sound made them both look up. Hundreds of starlings began to swoop and swirl over the River Suir, shapeshifting every second into something new.

'A murmuration!' Devlin gasped. 'I've never seen one before.'

The birds moved like an amorphous cloud in the late evening sky, creating a magical display, just for them. The air was filled with the sound of their beating wings in unison, but to Gabrielle there was more than that. There was music.

'It's beautiful,' he said, still holding her in his embrace.

'It's protection,' she said, a wistful tone in her voice. 'See?' She pointed to a lone, dark shadow in the sky, apart from the flock. 'It's a hawk. Murmuration is the starlings' way of scaring away predators.'

'I never knew that.'

'Most people don't, they just assume it's a pretty display, but those starlings are protecting each other.'

Devlin gave her a light squeeze with his arms. Maybe that's what he, Walter and Gabrielle were trying to do. Protect each other.

'You know, whatever pain you're carrying, you're not

alone,' he said softly. 'Come on, let's get out of here. You're shivering.'

Gabrielle stayed tucked under his arm as they walked back towards the small lodge by the gate that led to the main road. It was getting darker and the only sound was their shoes on the gravel paths. The way was lined by a box hedge, but as they meandered away from the river, Gabrielle noticed a figure in the shadows. A statue of some kind; with wings. Her curiosity got the better of her and she let go of Devlin, ducking under an arch of willow into a small garden.

'What is it?' he asked, following behind.

'I don't believe it!'

Devlin looked at the stone statue. It was an angel, with giant wings and Grecian style dress. Her gaze was cast downwards. He took out his phone and switched on the torch.

'It's a gravestone,' he said, bending down to clear away the overgrowth of ivy. He read the words aloud:

> 'There shall be
> no darkness nor dazzling, but one equal light;
> no noise nor silence, but one equal music.'

'That's John Donne, I think.'

'It's beautiful,' Devlin said.

'Wait, there's a name,' she said, bending down beside him. 'Clara Dillon.'

The leaves on the trees overhead fluttered suddenly, as though surprised to hear the name uttered aloud in this place, after all of these years.

'Do you think it's possible that this is the statue Bartholomew Murphy mentioned in his letter? Where Rathbone said he hid the sheet music at an angel's feet?' she said.

Devlin gave her an encouraging look and said, 'Only one way to find out.'

Kneeling on the dewy wet grass, they searched the base of the statue with their fingertips for some kind of cleft, or anything that might be concealing a secret hiding place. To anyone else, it might have seemed a ludicrous idea, but to Gabrielle, it felt like the culmination of all those years spent searching. She was led here, by her gut and (if she was being honest) by the violin. At every turn in the road, she felt as though she were being led by its voice.

'I can't feel anything, can you?' Devlin asked, pulling away at moss and lichen whilst shining his torch on the stone base.

'Hang on, what's this?'

Where the angel's gaze fell, there was a fallen bird at her feet. Gabrielle touched it lightly, then realised it wasn't made of stone, but of cast iron.

'That's strange,' she said.

Devlin tried to move it and when he did, a mechanism clicked and the head of the bird opened.

'Okay,' he said. 'Wasn't expecting that to happen.'

Gabrielle stood up and grabbed Devlin's phone, shining the light inside.

'There's something in here,' she said. 'Oh dammit! I can't bear to look. What if it's nothing?'

'Do you want me to look?'

'No! No, I'll do it,' she said, hoping against hope. Delicately, she slid her index finger inside and pulled out a piece of paper rolled up like a cigar. Her heart was hammering against her ribcage. The paper *felt* old. It made a satisfying crinkle as she unfurled it. At first, her eyes couldn't make any sense of what was written on it. The markings were wild and rushed and all over the place. Devlin got up and held the phone for her. After seconds that passed like hours, she finally saw the writing at the top of the page. 'Bellezza Nascosta.' Her eyes darted to the bottom. The final words: *dedicato al liutaio irlandese, de Niccolò Paganini*.

'Devlin?'

'Yes?'

'Can you pinch me?'

'Um, what?'

'Or get ready to catch me because I might faint,' she said, almost wheezing with delight.

'Is it really Paganini's music?'

'I'll have to study it properly, of course, but honestly my gut is telling me yes! It has to be. Why else would it be here?'

She was practically dancing on the spot.

'This is amazing!' Devlin said, taking her in his arms and swinging her around.

'I'm so glad you're here with me,' she said. She kissed his cheek and he stopped spinning. He pulled back to look at her face and gently let her feet touch the ground again.

'Gabrielle Wilding?'

'Yes? Devlin … Devlin…'

'We'll get into that later, but right now, I really want to kiss—'

She didn't wait for him to finish. His lips on hers felt like breathing clear air for the first time in years. Everything was clear to her in that moment. Under the watchful gaze of the stone angel, Gabrielle and Devlin finally let go of the past and embraced the possibility of everything that had always been there, waiting for them.

When Gabrielle finally opened her eyes, all she could see were the stars in his.

'I've been wanting to do that for a very long time,' Devlin said, his voice deep and throaty. He kept his hands clasped behind her, feeling how her body fit so snugly into his.

Gabrielle felt light-headed. Without Devlin's phone torch, she could hardly see, save for the moonlight.

'We better get out of here,' she said, reluctantly, before abandoning the thought and kissing him again.

Several minutes later, Devlin agreed and went to pick up the violin.

'Would you like to play it?' he asked.

She hesitated. Could her wrist manage it? Regardless of what had caused the pain, it was stiff as hell after all these years in a bandage.

'I'm beginning to wonder, what's the point in having this priceless, two-of-a-kind violin, risking our lives and never even getting to hear her?'

A few moments passed and Gabrielle felt the wind pick up, as dark clouds began to cover the face of the moon. She clutched the sheet music in her hand and was struck by a wild thought.

'You know what, you're absolutely right!' she said, before grabbing the violin case and setting off up the path, towards the manor house.

'Where are you going?' he called, picking up his jacket that had slid off her retreating shoulders.

'To play, of course.'

Chapter Forty-Three

♪

Verity searched the face of the man who sat opposite her. His once long golden hair had turned white; his dark blue eyes a watery grey. There was nothing left of the young man she'd fallen in love with all of those years ago in Montréal. She faltered. Perhaps her memory had been embellished over the years. It wasn't like nowadays – she never even had a photo to remember him by.

'I knew you'd come,' he said, a self-satisfied grin on his face. 'The minute Gabrielle showed me the photo of that violin, I recognised it. It's the same one you had all those years ago, isn't it?'

'You look so different,' she said.

'Well, that's what forty years will do to you. You look different, too.'

Verity's heart was beating fast. She had thought of this moment countless times over the years. Wondered how it would feel. Him taking her in his arms, the way he had taken the violin when teaching her the different parts. Suddenly, all of the pain and loss she had felt, the years devoted to searching, the bitterness at her father, the absence of a future she thought was hers, a life filled only with thoughts of revenge, all now seemed pointless. Had she really spent her entire life grieving over *this* man? This stranger sat opposite her. His face betrayed nothing of the young man she had once known. And the vertigo of this realisation threw her entire world off its axis. Gregory reached out an arm to steady her and just then, one of the guards moved to stand closer beside them.

What am I doing here? Verity asked herself.

'So why did you sell it?' he asked.

'I didn't. It was taken.'

Gregory nodded.

'I wasn't born yesterday, Verity. Do you think we don't read the newspapers in here?'

'I don't know what you're talking about.'

'Did you have something to do with the theft from Christie's warehouse?'

She said nothing, but looked down at her hands folded neatly on her lap.

'What do you plan to do now?'

'I plan to get my violin back. I would have thought that was obvious. The only thing standing in my way is your daughter.'

'If you hurt a hair on her head—'

'Oh, hurting her should be the least of your concerns. I've already hurt her. She was in hospital last week, in Italy. Didn't you know?'

Gregory Wilding gritted his teeth and breathed heavily

through his nose. He wasn't sure what made him angrier; the fact that his daughter was in trouble or that she hadn't told him.

'Now I'm sure we can work something out,' Verity said, appraising this man with her gaze and finding him wanting in all the ways that counted. How had she got everything so wrong? And all for the mad obsession with possessing that violin once again. Believing that it would change her fortunes. Having this grubby conversation in this grubby place. How had she been so foolish? A life spent chasing the dream of a seventeen-year-old girl who knew nothing but rejection and neglect. Hungry for love and perceiving any crumb of attention as genuine affection. She shook her head slightly, trying to sort out her thoughts. Reviewing her memories from this new vantage point, she felt like a grown woman walking through the careless playthings of a child and realising that they could never bring her happiness. She stood up.

'I don't know if you've noticed, but I'm already in prison.'

'And?'

'I have nothing to lose by reaching across this table and squeezing your neck with my bare hands.' Gregory meant every word.

'You might have nothing to lose. But your daughter will lose her life, either way. I've instructed my associates. So, here's what you're going to do. You're going to arrange a meeting with your daughter. I know they let you out for special occasions. Tell them it's her birthday, I don't care. But get her to come to you. With the violin.'

Gregory considered his options, which were very limited.

'Understood?'

He nodded slowly.

'Good. I've come too far, for too long. Nothing will stand in my way. Do you hear me?'

Chapter Forty-Four

♪

'Sir, I already told you, once the performance has begun, I cannot let you back in,' the usher said, seeing Devlin approaching the door apace.

'Look, dude, I'm busting down that door either way. It's up to you if you still want to be standing in front of it when I do.'

The young man took barely a second to consider the options and deftly moved aside.

Gabrielle had run on ahead of him, through the maze of garden paths, with only the occasional flash of green from her dress highlighted by the disappearing moon. But once he reached the house, she was nowhere to be seen. Just as he was about to put his shoulder to the door, a bright sound cut through the air. It was like nothing he had ever heard and yet as familiar to him as his own heartbeat.

'The violin,' he whispered to himself. Looking across at the young man, who seemed similarly stunned by the high note that still rang out like a battle-cry, Devlin turned the handle and stepped into the gilded room. On the podium, Gabrielle stood tall, claiming the high ground with the violin nestled deep into the space between her collarbone and her neck. She held the bow aloft like a sword and with a movement that would have rivalled a samurai, she whipped her body into action and began to play. The 'Bellezza Nascosta' sheet music was on a music stand in front of her and she was striking the notes with a powerful ferocity that seemed to emanate from her very core. With a speed Devlin hardly thought possible, her fingers danced along the neck of the violin, her upper body swaying as though in a trance. The audience seemed to rear back, only to find themselves helplessly drawn closer to the performance, in a series of waves.

The opening scherzo, which was light and playful, gave way to an adagietto that shimmered with an aching melody. Gabrielle was stunned by the notes she was reading in front of her – it was the story of the luthier, William, and his great love, Clara. The great maestro hid their names in this piece of music and as she played it, it was as though she was being transported back in time. It began with a tune that frolicked and flirted, representing the start of their courtship. The slower adagietto was full of anguished sighs – despair and longing. A reflection of the years spent apart, living without love, always searching for the road home. It felt like the violin was speaking through her. Coming alive in her hands. All her life, she had known that violinists search for the perfect violin that will amplify their sound and help them to find their own voice. But with this violin it felt like performing a duet.

For the first time since she was a teenager, Gabrielle was

playing, full-throated, in front of an audience and she didn't feel nervous or doubtful or like an imposter. The pain was a distant memory. She felt liberated from the stories she had been told about who she was and who she wasn't. Liberated from the stories she chose to believe were true. Liberated from the limitations that kept her small and scared. To her immense surprise and delight, she wasn't just performing a piece, she was enjoying herself! Expressing her vitality and, for this one long-awaited moment, stepping into her own natural power. And no one could dim her light anymore, because she finally realised she never needed them in the first place. She already had everything she needed inside herself.

As the final movement moved to a joyous fugue, the lively, celebratory notes proclaimed a sense of reunion – of spells broken and love triumphing over all. The virtuosic demands of the final climax, played with full tone and power, concluded with a dynamic and expressive crescendo.

Gabrielle's movements became a blur. The final note rang out across the room and a champagne glass spontaneously shattered.

Several beats passed before the crowd eventually broke into applause. It began slowly, as though they were recovering from some hypnotic state, then grew into a roar as they all stood on their feet. Gabrielle was utterly breathless and for a moment she rested her hands on her knees, gulping deep breaths of air. She had had one clear intention when she stood on that podium. To use her voice. She wasn't thinking about her performance. Something had shifted. When she looked up, her eyes caught two things.

One solitary figure who was not clapping. Max, of course. Still breathing heavily, she let her eyes bore into him – and then, quite unexpectedly, she began to laugh. A mirthful laugh because suddenly he seemed so small, so inconsequential. This was her superpower and he hated her for it. He was the one who had dripped poisonous doubts into her head and turned her passion into something he could manipulate. He wanted her to fail. He was jealous of her talent and had done all he could to ruin it and break her in the process. If only she had known, all this time, that the way to vanquish your enemies was to conquer your doubts and fears and become who you were always meant to be.

Behind Max, she saw him. Devlin. His face open and honest. She didn't need to decode his feelings, and the easiness of it left her feeling weightless. He was happy for her. From one performer to another, who knows what it takes, who understands the courage it takes to let go of your survival instincts and embrace the leap into mid-air, trusting that the notes will catch you. She bowed her head slightly and Devlin clutched his chest, as though she had just shot an arrow through it. A shot he would willingly take, again and again.

Chapter Forty-Five

♪

THE VIOLIN

Unperceived by anyone, I began to feel a strange sensation. Quietly, inside the darkness of my case, there was a loosening of the edges. A flurry of dust and a cracking in the glue. Whatever was binding me together – faith, hope, desperation – was starting to fracture. My connection to Devlin, Walter and Gabrielle had set a change in motion, one that I was powerless to stop. A string snapped and I found myself gripped with trepidation.

Something in the music, the hidden beauty, was working to transform the very fibres of the wood. 'Bellezza Nascosta' held not only the clues to the past, but the key to the future.

Chapter Forty-Six

♪

Walter finally picked up the receiver. The telephone had been ringing for a long time, he knew that much, but how long had he been sitting in his chair, motionless? He was supposed to call someone, wasn't he? His mind was a thick fog since that horrible woman had left him feeling broken and alone.

'Hello?'

'Mr Pickering, I'm calling from Dr Egan's office.'

'Who?'

'Dr Egan in the oncology unit. We have some of your test results back and we'd like you to come in tomorrow morning, if that's convenient?'

Walter wasn't sure if it *was* convenient. He wasn't sure what day it was.

'Mr Pickering, are you there?'

'Yes, yes. I'll come. First thing. Thank you.'

♪

Walter left the hospital in a daze. The tests had come back with some unexpected results. He had gone in fearing the worst – that his time was shorter than he'd hoped. When the doctor explained that he was in remission and, miraculously, the cancer had shrunk, Walter thought the weightlessness in his body would float him out of the building, up through the ceiling and out over the rooftops of London.

'I hesitate to use this word,' Dr Egan said, as he held the door open for him to leave, 'but it's quite miraculous. Sometimes science cannot explain these things.'

Just like that, Walter was given his life back. His future. His hope. Only now did it all make sense to him. Life wasn't about getting ahead, proving yourself, acquiring a nice house, a family, a job, taking the odd holiday. All of those things had you chasing after some kind of future happiness that never really arrived. The happiness everyone sought was here, now. In the golden sunlight of a Tuesday morning, watching the council workers digging yet another hole in the road, the little boy at the bus stop luxuriating over a bar of chocolate as though it were his last meal, a cat slinking into the shadows with all the grace of a ballerina. It finally struck him that it didn't really matter what you did or didn't do in this life. The point was just to experience it, to witness it all through your own unique perspective. He'd read somewhere once that humans were invented so the universe could experience itself. *Who said that?* he wondered to himself as he got off the bus outside his apartment block. *Ah yes, Alan Watts.*

'Through our eyes, the universe is perceiving itself. Through our ears, the universe is listening to its harmonies.

We are the witnesses through which the universe becomes conscious of its glory, of its magnificence.'

An aeroplane crossed the blue sky overhead, a white trail in its wake like the line of an arrow pointing somewhere. It felt like a sign of some kind. That's when it hit him, and he smacked his forehead.

'Good heavens, I never called Devlin!'

♪

'Good morning,' Devlin whispered as her eyes opened.

'Oh, hello,' she replied, squeezing her eyes shut and opening them again. She could hardly believe where she was. Lying in a sun-drenched hotel room in Ireland, wrapped up in a cloud-soft duvet with Devlin.

'How did you get in here?' he asked, his lips placing light kisses on the side of her neck.

'There was a spider in my room, remember?' she said, a playful tone in her voice. It was hard to sound serious when his hands were underneath the sheets, caressing the small of her back.

'Ah yes, the one I would've needed a magnifying glass to see,' he murmured, finding new places to kiss.

'Hey, an arachnoid is an arachnoid. Satie normally takes care of them for me—' She gasped at the touch of his stubble on her breast. 'I mean, I can go back to my room now, if you want...'

'Not a chance,' he said, rolling her on top of him.

Looking down at this man, she wondered if she could trust this feeling. It was almost too good to be true. But maybe it was okay for that doubt to be there. She couldn't erase the past, or pretend it hadn't changed her, but she could decide to move forward.

'You okay?' he asked.

She nodded her head.

'I feel ... safe,' she said, reaching for his other hand and interlacing her fingers with his.

Devlin kissed her palm. He knew that she didn't need rescuing. No woman did; his mother and sisters taught him that well enough. They just needed a safe place to land. He wasn't sure he had it in him to be that person again. After Summer died, he looked for all the world like the same person on the outside, but on the inside, nothing worked the way it was supposed to. But from the moment he met Gabrielle, the rusty old parts started to move again. He sensed her pain from the off; perhaps that was what brought his guard down, seeing someone else so terrified of being vulnerable. But it was what she kept close to her heart that he was falling in love with. That pure, some might say naive, notion that he also shared – that maybe the world could be a happy place, with kind people and good intentions. She was full of hope, despite everything she'd been through, or perhaps because of it. And her hope was infectious.

A tune came on the retro-style radio on the bedside table. Gabrielle recognised it, turned up the volume and mouthed the lyrics.

'*And the only tune that fiddle would play, oh the wind and the rain...* I know this. It's an old ballad,' she said.

Devlin reached over and raised the volume slightly. It was a strange song with a charming melody that immediately stuck in your mind.

'The story's a bit gruesome,' Devlin said, as the singer told of how an older sister pushed a younger one into the stream.

Gabrielle felt the hairs on the back of her neck stand up.

He made a fiddle from her own breastbone, Oh the wind and the rain! Whose sound could melt a heart of stone...

The haunting melody carried on, telling the story of how the man turned the dead woman's body into a violin. But no matter what, she only played one tune. Something stirred inside Gabrielle. She couldn't explain how or why, but she knew this tune had something to do with them. Something to do with their violin. She listened as the chorus repeated over and over.

And the only tune that fiddle would play, was oh the dreadful wind and rain.

Folk ballads were often based on a grain of truth. A myth turned into legend. Had William's story somehow lived on in local Irish lore? And what did it mean, that she only sang one tune? Perhaps it meant that, regardless of what shape people tried to force you into, you would ultimately remain true to yourself.

'I've not been honest,' she said, her voice a whisper at first, then stronger. 'About a lot of things.'

Devlin stretched his hand across and placed it, open palmed, in front of her on the blanket. She took it. Whatever he was offering, she wanted it.

'The people who stole your violin. They contacted me.'

'What?'

'They bribed me to give it back to them. And at first I agreed to go along with it. I'm so sorry. I needed the money, but that's no excuse.'

'Okay. Well, thanks for telling me now. That's all that matters.'

'There's more. In Italy. The knife. It wasn't an accident.'

'Gabrielle,' he said, hugging her close to him. 'What happened?'

'It's fine. I'm fine. But the woman who's behind all of this, she was waiting for me at the shop when we got back from Cremona. She threatened to expose the truth about my father's imprisonment for fraud. I was going to give it back to them to save the reputation of our shop.'

'Wait. I thought you said your father was dead?' he said, turning to her.

'Like I said, I haven't been honest about a lot of things.'

Just then Devlin's phone pinged with a message from Walter.

> Hope all well. Big news to share. When are you due back?

'Hmm, I hope he's okay.'

'You know, I saw him coming out of the hospital a few days ago. The oncology unit. Did you know?' she asked, turning her head to face him.

'No, I … bloody hell.'

'Oh, I'm sorry, I wondered if that's why you moved in with him, to help.'

Devlin wondered if he should tell her or not. But they were being honest now.

'The first time I called round to him, with the violin, he was about to swallow a bottle of pills.'

'Oh, my God, poor Walter.'

'Listen, I think we should get back. I just don't feel right leaving him on his own. All this time I felt like I was being a burden, but I think the violin, it's been giving him—'

'A reason to live?' Gabrielle finished.

'Maybe. Something like that.'

They both stared at the ceiling, gathering their thoughts.

'This is the most intense start to a relationship I've ever had!' she said, suddenly laughing. 'I mean, dodging the police, getting death threats, ambulance rides—'

'Whoa, whoa, lady. Who said anything about a relationship?' Devlin raised his eyebrows.

'Oh, I just, I thought—' Gabrielle began, feeling self-conscious and presumptuous.

His lips met hers, smothering any doubts. She responded with a deeper kiss, letting her desire carry her away from all the darkness and towards his light. Finally, she felt his arms around her waist again and she moaned with the relief of it. He was hers, and at last she could have what she wanted without letting her fear push him away. He placed his hand on her breastbone, feeling her heartbeat, before kissing her neck. The sensation made her gasp.

'Wait, hang on,' she said, slightly breathless. 'As much as I want this, we really need to get back to Walter.'

Devlin slowly rolled over and punched the duvet.

'Dammit, Walter!' he said, before heaving himself off the bed. 'Right, to be continued,' he said with a grin, as he grabbed his clothes from the end of the bed.

Chapter Forty-Seven

♪

Gabrielle unlocked the shutters and turned the key in the door of the shop. The rain was pounding off the pavements, but inside the air was still and timeless. The wooden counter, with its deep and lustrous lacquer always gave the place a solemn feel. She ran her fingertips along the surface, trying to ground herself after the trip to Ireland. It almost didn't seem real. She had gone to the extremes of her very being: from the depths of despair to utter joy, all in the space of forty-eight hours. Leaving Devlin at the airport had been harder than she'd anticipated. He'd kissed her hand like an old-school knight, before heading for Walter's place. Her feelings for him had fallen into place with such ease, with such speed, it was hard to fathom. Here she was, a grown woman with a lovestruck grin on her face, wondering how she would fill in the hours until they saw each other again.

She shook her head, surrendering to the craziness of it all as she climbed the stairs to her apartment. Her thoughts were wrapped up in his eyes, the expression on his face right before he kissed her in the gardens, his voice in her ear, whispering words about how she made him feel… As she opened the door to the apartment, she saw someone walking around her kitchen. Her heart jumped. In that instant, she was sure it must be Verity, waiting for her.

'It's only me,' said Roger. 'You said you'd leave a spare key for the back door under the flowerpot, remember? To feed Satie?'

Her feline friend was in the process of completely ignoring her, as punishment for leaving her alone for all of two days.

'I didn't expect you to come all the way from Bath,' she said, slinging her bag off her shoulder and onto the kitchen chair. She gave him a quick hug and offered to put on the kettle. As she got two mugs down from the cupboard, something occurred to her.

'Hang on, how did you know I was away?'

Roger's knees cracked as he stood up from his squatting position where he had been hand-feeding Satie like a little prince.

'Oof, that's middle age for you,' he said, jokingly, but his face betrayed him. Something was wrong. 'Your father called.'

Gabrielle put down the tin of tea.

'Yes, I was surprised, too. Turns out they don't have phones in the afterlife.'

'Roger, it was his idea—' she began.

'You could have told me.'

'How?' she asked, folding her arms. She didn't want to have this conversation right now. She didn't want to leave her happiness bubble. But real life was always there waiting for you. 'I was too ashamed.'

'I wouldn't have judged.'

'Well, I judged. He should never have done it.'

'We're friends, Gabrielle. You can always reach out to me.'

She thought back to all of the times Roger had dismissed her concerns about Max. She wasn't sure how to explain it then – the power imbalance, the misconduct. But in her body, she had a felt experience that lines were being crossed. 'That's what he has to do to make you a better violinist,' Roger would say. Conversation over. Either it was all in her head or, worse, she couldn't hack the work – didn't have what it took to be a professional.

'But that still doesn't explain why you're here,' she said, folding her arms.

He looked a bit shifty. Roger was never a very good liar.

'Where is the violin?' he asked.

'Oh, my God. I don't believe it. You, too?' Gabrielle felt her heart starting to pound. 'Get out, Roger.'

'Hey,' he said, putting his hands up in front of him. 'I'm not the enemy here. Your father's worried you might be in danger. Apparently, the woman who's looking for this violin came to see him.'

'Dammit,' she hissed under her breath.

'Look, if you let me take it with me, I can keep it safe—'

'Like you'd know anything about keeping things safe!'

The air was taut with the tension of unspoken things between them.

'What are you talking about?'

'I'm talking about Max Daunt. I tried to tell you, but you never believed me.'

Roger shook his head in a way that suggested he knew exactly what she was talking about but, by admitting that, he would somehow implicate himself.

'If you weren't such a coward you'd admit it now. You knew there was something inappropriate going on, but you just turned a blind eye. It was easier to blame me. Well, that's just fine, Roger, but don't come here pretending like you're acting in my best interests now.'

Gabrielle could hardly believe she was saying these things. Yes, they were true, but it was also true that Roger was young then and probably hadn't understood the full extent of it, either. But if she'd learned anything in Ireland, it was that she owed this to her younger self. No longer would she conceal the truth to make other people more comfortable with pretty lies. The truth mattered. Her voice mattered and she was tired of singing someone else's tune.

'I don't even know who you are right now,' he said, stunned.

'And that's the problem, Roger. You never tried to know me. And I think it suited you, that my life went off a cliff.'

'Now hang on a minute—' he said, pointing at her.

'You could have helped me. You could have spoken up. But at the very least, Roger, you could have believed me.' Her voice broke with these words because, for the first time, she realised how much that would have meant. To be believed. Not to be dismissed, minimised.

Roger cast his glance away from her. He didn't want to be the bad guy. He didn't think he deserved to be the bad guy, but there was no excuse.

'If there's nothing else, I think we're done here,' she said, reaching for Satie, who was still pissed off at her absence but knew whose side he was on in a fight. He curled obediently into her arms and then, turning his head, fixed Roger with the most magnificently cold stare.

Roger had his hands on his hips, then threw them in the air.

'Fine,' he said, grabbing his jacket off the back of the chair. 'I was just trying to help.'

'My father. You were trying to help my father. Not me.'

He looked at his old friend and, without anything better to say, opted for, 'This was a mistake,' before heading for the door.

'Keys,' Gabrielle said.

He dug them out of his jeans pocket and smacked them down on the table. When the door finally closed, Gabrielle exhaled a long, weary breath. Satie purred deeply and tipped his nose against her cheek.

'I can't believe I just did that,' Gabrielle said. She had held so much inside and for so long. *Mustn't upset anyone*, she'd always told herself. But why was no one concerned if she was upset? She'd finally come to see that if you didn't speak out about your pain, nobody else was going to do it for you. They either didn't know or didn't want to know. She had to stand up for herself now.

She reached for her phone and began to text.

> Trudy, I'm ready to make that statement to the police. Can I come by tomorrow to discuss it?

She had always bristled at the idea of going to the police

about Max. It was too long ago, she didn't have any real proof and, besides, what good would it do? It wouldn't change anything. But seeing him in Ireland, carrying on with his life completely unscathed while her entire world had imploded made the wound of injustice harder to bear. And watching his behaviour at the recital, how he was with that young girl, she decided that she didn't just owe it to herself, she owed it to every other woman who came in contact with him. They needed to be informed about who they were dealing with.

The following morning, she woke up to an alert on her phone. She slid it off the bedside table and when the screen lit up, she saw two texts. One from Devlin.

> Much prefer waking up with you. Did I tell you Walter snores?!

The second was from a number she didn't recognise. She clicked on it and sat bolt upright. It was from the prison. The words made no sense and almost seemed to dance in front of her eyes.

> Gregory Wilding has escaped and there is a search ongoing as to his whereabouts. Please contact the prison immediately.

Chapter Forty-Eight

♪

THE VIOLIN

Montréal, 1970

The romance of the place was lost on her father from the moment he picked up his first drink. When Verity was a small child, her mother used to tell her that they had a shop full of treasures, just waiting to be found. Now, it was just Verity and her father, who said he felt cursed to rifle through other people's junk for the rest of his life. Overlooking the St Lawrence River, their antique shop in Le Vieux Port was once a thriving business. It was true that the place was filling up with junk, because her father had lost the knack for spotting a diamond in the rough. He bought things he knew he could sell easily: clocks, candelabras and uninspiring pastoral reproductions. But every so often, something would sneak in, something that would make Verity's heart quicken.

Gaston pulled his beaten-up old truck to the back of the store and began unloading his finds. He would disappear for days at a time, with the excuse that he was chasing up a lead – some old woman whose husband had died in Ottawa and who was having a house clearance. Something that should have taken an afternoon turned into a forty-eight-hour drinking session. Anyhow, on this one seemingly ordinary day, he began unloading his latest finds from the truck. Unidentified objects, hiding under dust sheets like ghosts. Except for one. A small, dark violin case.

'I'll take that,' she said, trying not to betray any emotion. If he knew she cared about something, he would break it. That's what happened to her cat and an old cuckoo clock she had grown fond of. And her mother.

She carried me to her room in the crook of her arm, like a baby, and locked the door. Placing the case on her mattress, she slowly clicked the clasps and it opened with a sigh. She was right to keep me from her father.

She lifted me gently from the velvet interior and held me as though I was a living, breathing creature. It was like the sun on my skin, feeling the warmth of another human being after so long. Naively, I had believed my destiny was assured with Eva Mudocci, but life always teaches me that nothing is certain. We all live with uncertainty every day, yet somehow we convince ourselves that our safety is guaranteed. That life is not a fragile thing. That our breath is all that keeps us alive and once that stops… We had boarded a train in Toronto bound for New York, where Eva had a series of concerts to play. I was excited to make my debut at Carnegie Hall. But it was never to be. Bad weather caused a build-up of snow on the tracks. We were travelling too fast. The last thing I heard was the high-pitched squeal of the brakes being pulled too late. At least eight carriages derailed. The Nightingale breathed her last and I was tossed out into the snow. When the locals came to help, someone picked me up and I was kept in an attic for a long time. Silent and alone. Then a man came to clear out the belongings of the entire house and I ended up in Verity's arms.

Instinctively, she tucked me under her neck and plucked at the strings with her free hand. She knew nothing about instruments – a blind man could tell that. Not how to play them or how they worked. The girl felt as though they held special powers that only the most fortunate people could unlock.

Verity adored music. It almost seemed magical to her because even though it was invisible – you couldn't touch it or see it – you could *feel* it. When she would play records, her flesh would prickle with goosebumps, her heart rate would quicken and a doorway would open in her mind. They never had any money for music lessons and she wasn't sure how she would learn how to play it, but already she knew that she was going to keep this violin.

She plucked my strings again. I sounded broken and unloved.

'Kindred spirits,' she whispered to me, gently. That night, she slept with me in her bed.

Just as she had hoped, her father never mentioned the violin. He had probably forgotten all about it. Verity decided to take me uptown to have me cleaned and restrung at the repair shop her father always used, so she would be able to add the cost to his tab. On the way there, she passed by the university and saw a young man busking on the street. But he wasn't just any old busker; he was playing a violin. That was impressive enough, but what really impressed her was that he was playing a song by Fleetwood Mac. 'Rhiannon'. On the violin!

Verity was mesmerised. She stood close by, watching as his body seemed to fuse with the bow and they both swooped lyrically from side to side. Normally she would have been far too shy to approach a boy, let alone one that she found so attractive. Verity never even had any friends. If anyone showed any interest in her, she immediately felt as though she wasn't worthy of their attention and her behaviour would soon push people away. But that day, carrying the violin, she also carried herself a little differently. New things seemed possible. The guarded look she wore had softened and the little voice inside that would have normally spoken cruel, negative words stayed unusually silent. She was free to be spontaneously herself.

'I love that song,' she said, once he'd finished playing.

'You play?' He asked, pushing his blonde fringe from his forehead, slightly damp with exertion.

Verity thought about lying – sounding cool. But she knew her lies would trip her up, and for some reason she wanted to be honest with him. Dating at school was like a game, but she never knew the rules.

'I wish I could,' she said, patting the case like a pet.

He took out a packet of Marlboros and tapped out a cigarette, offering it to her. She took one, thankful for all those hours she had spent practising with her father's cigarettes. He lit both of their cigarettes and as she bent over the flame, their eyes locked. It was one of those timeless moments that, even then, Verity knew she would never forget.

'I could teach you,' he said, in a rather posh English accent.

'Really?'

'I'm studying here, at the conservatory.'

Verity nodded, as though McGill University was a place where she hung out all the time.

'I couldn't afford lessons...' she began.

'Music should be free,' he said, his sun-kissed face becoming animated. Verity could tell that this was a subject in which he was well versed. 'Money destroys art; don't worry about money. It'll be like, my civic duty or whatever,' he laughed. He was so laid-back and comfortable in his skin. Like no one she'd ever met.

'Tell you what, meet me here tomorrow, same time, and we'll start,' he said, slinging a rucksack over his shoulder.

'Okay, thanks!'

As he walked away, Verity was mesmerised by his beautiful blonde hair, his ripped jeans and the way he carried himself – like an artist, so lost in his own world that reality could not touch him.

'Wait! I don't even know your name!' she shouted after him.

'Gregory. You?'

'Verity!' she shouted back across the square.

'See you tomorrow, Verity.'

She had only been in possession of the violin for twenty-four hours and already her life was changing. She wished she had a friend she could talk to about Gregory. But as it was, she had to rely on the old magazines that people dumped in the shop, as though they could pass for antiques (which some of them probably could). She read an article about brushing your hair one hundred times before bed, so she sat on the side of her bed, facing a little looking glass that she balanced on the window ledge, and brushed and brushed and brushed. Her hair was dark and thick and her skin far too pale from hours spent indoors. She regarded herself in the mirror and decided that there wasn't very much she could do to change it. At seventeen years old, she was badly in need of a bra, but she felt too embarrassed to ask for help in the store. Instead, she bought little cotton bralettes that were really for pre-teens, but they worked well enough for her small breasts.

'What am I doing? He's teaching me to play the violin!' she said to her reflection. She'd never had a boyfriend and, try as she might to restrain herself, her feelings ran loose like wild horses.

Verity waited for him the next day. Sitting on the bench, she held her newly strung violin in her lap, stroking the case mindlessly. What if he didn't show up? But she knew he would, although where this certainty came from, she couldn't really say.

'Miss Verity,' came his low and resonant voice from behind her. She turned around to see him in the same ripped jeans and suede jacket, even more attractive than the day before. He was also carrying a violin.

'First things first: this,' he said, tapping her violin case, 'is your instrument. You are one now. She will be your voice.'

Verity liked the way he dived right in; no mindless small talk.

'Don't let anyone else touch it.'

Verity nodded solemnly. She had already made that promise to herself, quite instinctively.

'Okay, well, you need to take it out of the case!' he said, smiling.

'Oh, yeah.' She liked how he didn't make her feel stupid. Unlike her father.

Gregory took out a highly polished, expensive-looking violin, holding it with practised ease.

'Okay, so let's start at the beginning. A violin is shaped a bit like us,' he said, laying it on his lap. 'So here, we call this the scroll, but it's kind of like the head. Then you have the neck,' he said, running a finger down the length of it. There was something sensual about it and Verity had to focus very hard, knitting her brows for good measure. 'And of course, the body – that's what amplifies the sound. Now this is the bridge and these openings here are the heart and the kidneys.'

'Wow, I never knew that, but it makes sense somehow. She feels alive. And what are these two squiggly bits?'

'Good question. They're called the f-holes and they're like the lungs of the violin, breathing sound out into the atmosphere. Playing the violin, holding it so close to your heart, you kind of become one. It's hard to explain, but it's like you are living and breathing together, singing together. The violin lets you express so much of yourself; things you wouldn't dare speak, but somehow, you can play it. Your violin gives you that. Your violin gives you a voice.'

Never had anything felt so right. Verity had never had a voice of her own; it had always been drowned out, repressed, forgotten. Finally, she could sense a way out, an escape from her quiet world. For possibly the first time ever, Verity felt as though she belonged.

Gregory spent the next half-hour showing Verity how to put the right amount of rosin on the bow and how to tighten the horsehair correctly. She was so impatient to play, but that would not happen until their second lesson later that week, after he had bought her a chin rest.

'Now just rest your jaw on it. Yes, I know it's called a chin rest, but this is how you do it.'

She copied everything he did: the way he shook his wrist loose and let it go limp before taking the bow in his right hand; how he tucked the violin close to his neck. For one split second, she wondered what it would feel like to be that violin! But she had to concentrate, otherwise she would blush and spoil the whole thing.

'Ready?' he asked.

'Ready.'

'Now, just glide the bow across the strings and try to play one at a time. Yes, that's it, and now the D string and…'

'Oops,' she said, frowning slightly as I screeched in protest.

'That's okay – nobody likes the sound it makes at the beginning, but it'll improve with practice. Your voices will match, I promise.'

Gregory was so patient and kind; Verity had never met a man who could display such empathy and yet seem all the stronger for it. Her father was such an angry man and saw kindness in any form as a type of weakness.

'Just keep practising at home,' he said, before packing his things away and disappearing back to his own life.

The violin lessons were like a bridge between them, and Verity worried that she might never cross to the other side. Their lives were too different. Gregory was on a year's scholarship from England. As if reading her thoughts, he casually asked her what she was doing the following Friday.

'Not much ... working, I suppose.'

'Tell you what, why don't we meet for a lesson in the afternoon and then you can join me and my friends from university for dinner. There's a little Greek place that has the best souvlaki. You'll enjoy it, I promise. They're mostly well-behaved and they're all as crazy about playing as you are.'

Verity blushed all the way to her toes.

'I'd love to! See you on Friday.'

'Four o'clock, don't be late!'

Verity had no doubt. From the day the violin first came into her possession, it was as though fate had orchestrated their union. Two souls bound by music's ethereal thread.

On Friday morning, Verity opened the antique shop as her father was out on business. She enjoyed the days that he was not there. It was like playing shop, where she was the proprietor. Although she struggled to make friends, she had a way with the customers and instinctively knew how to lure them in with a fascinating story about each object. Even the haggling brought out a playful side in her.

However, as the afternoon drew to a close and it was time to prepare for her date with Gregory, she grew less and less sure of herself. She locked up the shop and went upstairs to get changed. As soon as she entered her bedroom, she reached for me under her bed. I was like a touchstone for her and she always felt calmer and more assured in my presence. Kneeling down on the floor, she stretched her arm under the bed and patted her hand around, but she felt nothing. Lifting up the blanket that obscured her view, she lay flat on the floor and scanned the bare floorboards. Nothing. Within seconds she was pulling the room apart, searching all of her drawers and the old mahogany wardrobe.

'I sold it,' came her father's voice from behind her.

She turned and stared wild-eyed at him. She couldn't comprehend it. He didn't even know she had it.

'You think I don't see what you do, you little thief?' he said, slurring his words. 'I got a good price for it, too.' His smile mocked her. Her innocence, her belief that life could be better. She charged at him. She wanted to push him to the ground so he would never get up again. But she wasn't strong enough. Even in his drunk state, he stood his ground and pushed her back against the bed. He slammed her door and as she heard his footsteps going down the hall, tears stung her eyes. There was no way she could meet Gregory now. Without the violin, she had nothing. She *was* nothing.

And that was the moment she vowed revenge. One day she would be stronger than her father, that imbecile who sold cheap old clocks, watercolours and knick-knacks. She would learn everything she could and take his business from him. See how he liked it. Then she would laugh in his face, at his weakness. And she would get the violin back.

Chapter Forty-Nine

♪

Walter almost collided with Devlin as he opened the door to leave the flat.

'Oh dear, those night shifts are doing nothing for your youthful appearance,' he said, noting Devlin's dishevelled hair and dark-rimmed eyes.

'I'll pass that on to my line manager,' Devlin said with a yawn.

'I put a bit of tinfoil on your fry-up, it's in the oven,' Walter said, enjoying this late-stage glimpse of parenthood. It felt good to care for someone else.

'Walter, I told you, you don't have to go to all this trouble for me.' Devlin's remarks were purely perfunctory. He was already tucking into his scrambled eggs. 'Off somewhere nice?' he asked, buttering some toast.

Walter tapped the side of his nose. Devlin had already done enough for him. It was like friendship CPR. But now his heart was beating on its own steam again.

'Get some sleep and I'll fill you in later,' he said, closing the front door and trotting down the steps in a way that he imagined Fred Astaire might. It was time for his dance class and his heart almost leapt down the street ahead of him at the thought of meeting the lady in red again. He didn't make it very far. The side door of a parked black van slid open and out stepped the most striking woman Walter had ever seen. Long grey hair, almost silver, lay sparkling against her black wool coat. She wore high-heeled black boots and blood-red lipstick. Her grey eyes, rimmed with thick, dark kohl, bore into him with an intensity that could have burned right through his chest. Behind her stood two men in black leather jackets with bald heads, which were not the result of age.

Oh dear.

'I believe you have something belonging to me?' she asked in a smoky voice that reminded Walter of Stevie Nicks.

'I'm sorry?'

She lit a cigarette and blew the smoke in his face. Then with a twist of her palm, she signalled to the two men to enter the apartment building. Walter watched them, helpless to prevent whatever it was that was happening. With a vague hint of a smile, she took out a gun and pointed to the van's interior.

'Get in.'

Walter looked back at his flat window. Devlin was inside, eating his bacon and eggs. How could he protect him?

'Please, surely we can resolve this amicably,' he said.

'I've tried that. It didn't work.'

Something caught Walter's eye. Further up the street,

another van pulled up. Two rather unsavoury characters got out and headed for Walter's building. For a moment, he thought he recognised one of them. But no, *it couldn't be*, he thought to himself. What the hell was going on?

'Who exactly are you?' he asked.

The words were hardly out of his mouth before she hit him on the head with the butt of the gun.

♪

Gabrielle heard her footsteps echoing a little too briskly in the stairwell. The front door to Walter's apartment building was wedged open with a metal trash can and so she didn't bother pressing the buzzer. After the scene with Roger, she was eager to see Devlin, to feel his arms around her, and she knew he'd be back from work by now. But as she got to the third floor, she could hear an awful racket – men shouting and plates smashing. The apartment door was wide open. She walked into a scene that was like something out of a film. Walter's apartment had been trashed: furniture upside down, broken glass everywhere. The air was charged with energy. Something big had happened, but her brain struggled to make sense of it.

'Dad?' It came out as a whisper, as though all of the breath had squeezed out of her lungs.

Gregory Wilding had his knee on a man's back. The man was lying on the carpeted floor, squirming to free himself. It was like an old American cop show and Gabrielle's father was the sheriff.

'Amateurs,' he said, 'you can tell they've never been inside.'

Gabrielle opened her mouth to speak, but nothing would come. It was like finding out your father had a secret life as a WWE wrestler.

'What are you even doing?' she asked eventually. Now the rest of the scene came into focus, she could see two men being restrained: one by her father, the other by a man she'd never seen before. Devlin stood over them, with the violin in one hand and a brass flowerpot in the other. If it wasn't so tense, she would have laughed.

'I should have protected you before. You're right, I should have seen the warning signs.' Gregory Wilding spoke the words like an incantation. Powerful words that held the potential to heal them both.

'I—' Gabrielle struggled to compose herself. The whole thing was so surreal, and now for him to finally say the words she'd always needed to hear…

'I didn't want to see. But when Roger said—'

'You spoke to Roger?' Heat rushed to her face.

'Last night. I asked him to retrieve the violin from you so you wouldn't have to get messed up in any of—' he looked around at the complete disarray in Walter's flat '—this.'

'You mean, he *was* trying to help?' she asked, feeling unsure of everything now.

'Listen, Mr Wilding, Gabs, we kind of have a situation here,' Devlin cut in, still holding the brass pot. 'What do we do with these two?' he said, gesturing at the men, still being restrained.

'Take them down the river,' said the bearded man holding down assailant number two.

'I'm sorry, but who are you?' Gabrielle asked.

'This is Derrick "Three Fingers",' her father replied, as though he were joining them for afternoon tea. 'I met him *inside*. He's my gym buddy.'

'Right, of course,' she said, pinching the bridge of her nose. 'I'm not sure how much more of this story I want to hear.' She looked at Devlin and he shrugged, a slight smile creeping across his lips. It seemed to say, 'Parents, eh?'

'Hang on,' she said, 'where's Walter?'

Hardly a beat had passed when the front door creaked open. There stood a glamorous older woman in a long black coat with grey hair tumbling over one shoulder. One hand was gripping Walter's arms behind his back and the other held a gun.

'Who the hell are you?' Derrick 'Three Fingers' asked, as the others had been struck dumb.

'The owner of the violin,' Gabrielle said.

'You know her?' Walter asked.

'It's a long story,' Devlin assured him.

Gregory leaned into Walter's line of sight on hearing his voice.

'Walter! My dear old friend!' he said.

'Gregory! You're alive!' Walter countered.

'Indeed, reports of my demise have been greatly exaggerated,' he replied good-naturedly. 'And how are you?'

'Yes, yes, very good,' Walter responded politely, with his arms tied behind his back and a gun pointing at his side.

Gabrielle looked at Devlin, mouthing, *'What do we do?'*

'Hand it over and I'll let your friend go. It's as simple as that,' Verity said, getting things back on track.

'Right, can we all just stop pretending that this isn't

completely deranged?' Gabrielle said. 'I'm calling the police right now.' She reached in her pocket but froze when she heard the gun cocking. *It's a real gun, it's a real gun, it's a real gun.*

Everyone in the room seemed to be having the same thought. The atmosphere tightened like a screw and suddenly every word or action was weighted with dire consequences. Gabrielle was the first to break the silence and spoke very slowly.

'V…' she began.

'Verity,' the woman said, her tone emotionless.

'Verity, I have had the violin tested and thoroughly researched the provenance myself. It is not a Stradivarius. This is not your violin.'

Everyone's gaze shifted from Gabrielle to Verity. Surely this would change things.

'Oh, how you are naive. I *know* it's not a Strad! What would I want with a Strad?' Her body jerked and Walter stiffened as the tip of the gun dug into his ribs. 'You've felt it, too, haven't you?' Verity asked, looking at Devlin, who, despite himself, clutched the violin closer to his chest. 'There is a power that transcends mere music. This violin is a key. It unlocks something within.'

Devlin was almost hypnotised by her words. She was describing exactly everything he had felt since he'd first laid hands on the violin. His life had completely changed and something inside him was terrified of losing it, terrified of going back.

Then Walter said something that no one expected.

'Don't give it to her.'

'What?' Devlin and Gabrielle said in unison.

'Devlin, you remember the first night you came here? You remember what I was doing?'

Devlin nodded slowly.

'I was diagnosed with late-stage cancer.'

'Oh, Walter,' Gabrielle said, her voice choking.

'My good man, I'm terribly sorry,' Gregory added.

'So you see,' Walter continued, turning to look at Verity, 'it doesn't matter if you kill me now. I've already cheated death for long enough to see that life always has a new song for the heart to sing. I am dying a happy man and there's not many who can say that.'

Verity shifted her weight and the two henchmen grunted irritably, shaking off their assailants and wondering when this debacle would reach its conclusion. No one knew what to do now, except Devlin. He strode towards Verity without hesitation.

'You're right. This violin is a key. But the door is open now,' he said, looking around at Gabrielle, her father and his now best friend, Walter. 'We don't need it anymore.' He thrust it into her arms and she immediately dropped the gun, which fired a shot that rang out with a clear, shocking sound. Devlin swung around to see Gabrielle's hands covered in blood. His mind felt like it was ripping apart. He ran to her and almost tripped over the body on the floor.

'Dad!' she screamed.

Gregory had shielded her from the bullet and now lay bleeding on Walter's parquet floor. The henchmen saw their opportunity, easily overpowered Derrick 'Two Fingers' and pushed past their erstwhile employer, Verity. Walter, too, shrugged her off and bent down to help his friend.

Grabbing several tea towels from a drawer, he placed them over the stomach wound, just like they do in the movies.

'You're going to be all right,' he said gently, lifting Gregory's head and resting it on Gabrielle's lap. She was holding her father's hand tightly.

'At least I won't die in prison,' he joked, wincing with the pain.

'No one's dying anywhere,' Gabrielle said, finding her voice again.

He looked up at her, as though seeing her anew.

'At least I was able to protect you this time.'

'Oh, Dad,' she said, unable to stop the flow of tears.

'Ambulance, please. Fast,' Devlin shouted into his phone. 'Um, gunshot wound,' he added, a surreal edge to his voice.

The room was subdued, until a shriek from the doorway made them all look up.

'What's happening?' Verity pleaded. 'What's happening to my violin?'

She had taken it out of its case, but something was wrong. Before their very eyes, the instrument began to crumble. Tiny clouds of dust arose as it disintegrated and quickly collapsed into itself. The strangest thing, out of all of the strangeness, was that there was no sound. It silently fell away to dust in her hands.

Chapter Fifty

♪

Gabrielle found herself doing something she had thought she would never do again – holding her father's hand. It was early morning. A bright sunrise painted the entire room a pale golden colour and the birdsong that floated through the open window almost drowned out the beeping sound of the machines. She had laid her head down on the side of the bed and watched as wisps of clouds floated by the window. Her fingers tapped lightly on the bones of his hand, as though it were a fretboard on which she could play a tune. Replaying the events of yesterday, of last week, of last year … all of the years lost to them both. The silent blame, the unspoken grief, the report of the pistol ringing in her ears.

'Where am I?' Gregory Wilding's voice was rasping with dryness.

Gabrielle's eyes snapped up to look at his face. Still a shocking colour of white, but awake.

'Oh, thank God,' she said, pressing the back of his hand to her mouth. 'How are you feeling?'

Gregory wheezed and tried to clear his throat before responding.

'Like a man who has just been shot,' he said, a slight smile forming at the corners of his lips.

Gabrielle shook her head and smiled, despite herself.

'They said the surgery went well. You were lucky the bullet didn't…' She swallowed hard, trying not to think about the moment of impact. 'It didn't hit any vital organs,' she said, still nodding and biting back tears.

'Gabby,' he said gently, 'look at me. I'm okay, love.'

He lifted his hand, a little shakily, and cupped her cheek in his palm, just like he used to do when she was a little girl.

'I'm sorry,' he whispered, his eyes welling up with tears.

'Me, too,' she said.

'You've nothing to be sorry for. I am your father, I should have protected you.'

'You were grieving—'

'We were both grieving,' he interrupted her. 'Can you forgive me?'

All of those months in counselling, she'd tried to forgive him, herself, Roger, even Max. Anything that might help to unburden her. But in that moment, everything changed because she felt it in her heart. Compassion. For both of them. Slowly, she nodded her head, and the unshed tears began to fall.

Chapter Fifty-One

♪

Verity noticed a stain on her dress. The shape almost looked like an outline of South America. If she kept looking at it, the rest of the world could fall away, along with the last twenty-four hours.

'Anything to drink?' the flight attendant asked.

She did not answer.

'Madam?'

'Belvedere,' she said. 'Make it a double.'

She swallowed it hard, barely registering the burning bitterness of the vodka. The plane was high over the Irish Sea now, taking her back home to Canada. She stared at the red maple-leaf logo of the airline on the napkin. Like the colour of the violin. All of this chasing and scheming, only to end up with nothing. She could still feel the dust underneath her fingernails. How had it happened? *Why* had it happened? These were the questions that had surrounded her in a kind of fog ever since she left Walter's flat. Even Gregory's gunshot wound failed to distract her thoughts from the violin. Her entire life up to that point had been consumed by regret and revenge. Having the violin should have changed all of that. She was so close – only to have it evaporate in her hands.

A neighbour had called the police on hearing the gunshot, but it had taken them half an hour to arrive, plenty of time for Verity to walk out of there scot-free. She was still in shock. Her future was lost.

She had hours to reflect on what it all meant. As other passengers fell asleep or watched movies with their headphones on, Verity played out every scene. But it was only as they flew over St John's, Newfoundland, with the drone of the plane's engines in the background, that everything made sense. All along, she'd wrongly assumed that the violin had brought her to Gregory, her one true love. But now she could see her life beyond that point, everything she had achieved – the success, the wealth, the power. She had become her own knight in shining armour. She had rescued herself from poverty, from her father's cruelty. Yes, the pursuit of the violin had been the catalyst, the driving force to sustain her any time she foundered. But it was she, Verity, who had made this amazing life *for herself*. It wasn't about finding someone to love her, it was about loving herself enough to create a better future.

She let her head drop into her hands. She had been searching so hard, she couldn't see what was right in front of her. How foolish she'd been! How blind. The violin had empowered her. Its job was done. In fact, now that she thought about it, it had been the parent she'd never had. And now it was finally time for Verity to take responsibility and stop acting like a petulant child. Wishing she could change the past and recapture some idealised version of her life. A life that her teenage self thought would make her happy. All these years, she'd been a slave to that fantasy – always assuming that the life she had was some kind of mistake. A clerical error. Something the karma police had got wrong.

Verity looked around the cabin at the faces of her fellow passengers. How many of them felt as though they were in the wrong life, struggling against their reality for a childhood dream that promised a happy ever after? How many of them were blind to the wonderful life they'd created, their gaze permanently caught in the rear-view mirror? Verity pushed the overhead button and ordered a strong coffee. She would need a clear head when they landed. She didn't want to waste a second more on the past. You cannot recapture time and you cannot go back.

Neither, it seemed, could the violin.

Chapter Fifty-Two

♪

Six months later…

The audience was already seated and chatting audibly while the young musicians waited nervously in the wings.

'Sorry I'm late, everyone.' Gabrielle shook off her jacket and pulled a folder out of her bag. 'Hand these out, will you, Imani?' She began pulling her hair back into some kind of updo.

'We already have our sheet music, Miss,' Laura piped up.

'Of course you do,' Gabrielle replied, shaking her head. It wasn't like her to be so disorganised. Or 'laid-back', as Devlin had called it. She was experimenting with being slightly less of a perfectionist, relaxing her over-achiever muscle. The results were inconclusive. She had decided to take up teaching, part-time. After the whole Max incident in Ireland, watching that young woman under his control, she decided that the only real way to make a difference was to become a teacher herself. For now, she was tutoring five young girls who all showed great promise, and tonight was their first performance.

Devlin had stayed over late, playing her his new song. They had spoken about moving in together, but he said he didn't want to leave Walter until he was set up.

'And he's sure he wants to run his business from home?' she'd asked, curled up on the sofa beside him, wine in hand.

'You run your business from home,' he'd pointed out.

'But that's different. He's a private investigator. Any old nutter could show up.'

'Any old nutter did show up,' Devlin had reminded her. 'Ever since he stared down the barrel of a gun and basically cheated death, he's a new man!'

Gabrielle still couldn't believe how things had turned out. Her father had fully recovered and even though he was still a resident in His Majesty's Prison service, he had a day pass and had found himself a job – tracing lost property with his new business partner, Walter Pickering. What a pair! Only the other week a three-hundred-year-old Lorenzo Carcassi violin worth at least half a million pounds was stolen in a pub, and Wilding & Pickering were already on the case.

'He calls it his *ikigai*.' Devlin had bent down to pick up Satie, who had grown to tolerate his presence in their apartment. *Their apartment*. It felt nice calling it that. Officially, he was still staying at Walter's, but it was only a matter of time and the transfer of his toothbrush from one side of London to the other. It all felt so natural. Satie, on the other hand, took some convincing of the benefits. Gabrielle believed there was a lot of tuna involved in the arrangement.

'His what?'

'It's Japanese. It means your purpose in life. When he gave up teaching, I think he lost that.'

'And what's your *ikigai*?'

'Apart from you,' he'd said, wrapping his arm around her waist and pulling her in close to him.

'Obviously,' she'd said, melting into him.

'I've started writing some lyrics again.'

Her eyes had brightened, and she'd bitten her lip.

'Does that mean you're playing?'

Devlin hadn't wanted to say anything in case it might jinx things. But, over time, he had come to realise that everything he feared might happen if he played again had already happened. Seeing Verity crumble while the violin turned to dust in her hands brought Devlin face to face with the kind of strange fables he used to read about as a child. You couldn't change the past. It was confronting but he had to face it, accept it and learn to make peace with it. The first song he wrote was for Summer. Then he wrote a song about Walter, then Melissa. He even wrote about the violin. It became cathartic. The irony made him laugh. The one thing he was avoiding was the very thing to heal the pain.

'Can I hear it?'

'It's not finished yet.'

'I don't care,' she'd said.

'Hang on,' he'd said, getting up and heading down the hallway to the stairs. It was convenient to have a shop full of musical instruments just downstairs. He came back up with a guitar and began tuning it, before playing a few chords.

It was so good to watch him play. Gabrielle knew what it was like not to; almost like a part of you had been amputated. She'd read about phantom limbs and how people still felt an itch on their arm even though it was no longer there. Devlin seemed more fully himself now, with his body curled around the guitar, his hand strumming loosely.

> 'That old Italian moon,
> Shone down its light,
> On my broken pieces,
> And your endless fight –
> By the water's edge,
> We heard birdsong melody,
> Now every song I write,
> Is in the key of G...'

Gabrielle had hardly waited for the song to end before taking his face in her hands and kissing him rapturously.

♪

The round of applause from the audience was so enthusiastic, it almost brought Gabrielle to tears. She felt as proud as if she had been performing herself. As the girls took their bows, Gabrielle spotted Walter and Devlin in the crowd, giving her a big thumbs-up. Once she had spoken to all of the parents, she made her way over to them.

'Bravo!' Walter cheered, giving her a warm embrace. 'They played sublimely.'

'Thank you, I'm so proud of them. However, there were some bowing issues in the second movement, the notes sounded a bit choppy—' She stopped short when she noticed Devlin's expression and took a deep, meditative breath. In a calm, slightly hypnotic voice she continued, 'But that's not what matters tonight. What matters is that they gave their first performance and everyone enjoyed it.'

'Never change,' Devlin said, kissing her cheek.

'Congratulations,' came a familiar voice.

She turned around to see Roger offering her a hesitant hand.

'Roger, I'm so glad you could come,' she said, taking his hand and holding it for a moment. 'I wasn't sure—'

'I want to apologise,' he said, lowering his voice.

Walter and Devlin instinctively gave them some space.

'Well, then, I want to apologise also. I should never have put all of that on you.'

'It's okay, I understand you were angry, but you're right. I knew something was off, but to be honest, I was blinded by jealousy.'

'What do you mean?'

Roger rubbed the back of his neck with his hand before leaning in closer.

'I'm embarrassed to admit it now, but back then, I was jealous that he chose you. You were always a more talented musician than I was, and I suppose the fact that he chose you just rubbed salt in the wound. It seems so absurd now – that's what I was focused on. Not our friendship.'

Gabrielle looked in his eyes and could see his younger

self. They were both too young to understand what was really going on. And that was what Max was counting on. He knew no one would ever speak out against him. He had all of the control.

'I want to testify at the court case,' he said.

'I ... I don't know what to say. Are you sure?'

'More sure than I've ever been about anything. It will give me a second chance to get it right this time. To stick up for my friend. If you want me to,' he added.

Gabrielle put her arms around him and squeezed tightly.

'Thank you, Roger.'

Finally, it seemed that there would be some justice for what she went through.

'Gabrielle, my dear!' A familiar voice came from beside her.

'Trudy! You came!' Gabrielle turned and hugged her warmly. She wasn't sure if inviting your therapist to a recital was the done thing, but it felt right and she was so glad she'd come.

'Trudy, this is Roger, an old friend of mine.' They shook hands and Gabrielle reached for Devlin to introduce them. 'This is my ... Devlin,' she said, feeling unbelievably awkward because of course Trudy knew who he was, even if she hadn't met him. 'And this is my dear friend, Walter.'

'Very pleased to meet you, Walter,' Trudy said.

When Walter's eyes locked with Trudy's, his entire being lit up. It was her; the woman in the red dress from the salsa class. Her face, her aura, the way she took his hand, it was all like some kind of dream. The best dream he had ever had in his life. It had finally happened. Walter Pickering was lovestruck.

'Walter?'

'Sorry?' Walter realised that Devlin had been talking to him.

'I was just saying, shall we all go somewhere for dinner?'

Walter turned to look at Trudy, his expression a question. *Should we tell these two young ones that we've already met?*

'I think that would be lovely,' Trudy said, giving Walter a wink.

Gabrielle gave Devlin a quick look that seemed to say, *Are you seeing what I'm seeing?*

As they made their way out onto the street, the sky was illuminated by a full moon and the night air was warm and inviting.

'I know a nice little Italian restaurant just across the square,' Walter said, taking the lead. 'Shall we walk?'

Everyone nodded in agreement. A night like this deserved to be savoured. Devlin put his arm around Gabrielle's shoulders and she leaned in to kiss him on the cheek. Then Walter made a bold move. He crooked his arm and offered it to Trudy. The stars blinked and the universe held its breath. Trudy, calmly and assuredly, slipped her arm into his. And so, a new melody began.

Finale

THE VIOLIN

Oh, the wind and the rain. The older one pushed the younger one in, crying oh, the dreadful wind and rain.

Perhaps the rhyme is tugging at the back of your mind. It sounds like something you may have heard before but cannot recall when or where. That is how the truth is passed down, in echoes that at once feel both real and imagined. Do you want to know how it ends?

Both of my lives flashed before my eyes. I saw myself as a little girl, clutching my mother's skirts, running along the banks of the stream with my sister. Next, I was with William, watching him in his workshop. The hands who made me into the instrument I came to be. Then the hands that played me – Anton, Zita, Caroline, Mikhail, my beloved Paganini. Custodians of a voice that helped them to find their own. Even Verity had understood my power in the end. But it was Devlin, Walter and Gabrielle who were the ones to finally set me free.

I could see my life running through the centuries like a

river, changing course and smoothing out the hard surfaces. It is not for us to know what change will blow our way from one day to the next. Once Gabrielle played Paganini's secretly coded tune, the notes stirred a destiny within me that had been written from the start. It was time to return to my own true love. When Verity last opened the case and I could feel the final light of day touch my wood, I was freed from this world, this binding of string and varnish. My final breath exhaled, it all turned to dust, and in an instant, I found myself standing on the riverbank once again. It was bright; brighter than any day I'd ever seen. And across the water stood William, young and strong as he was when we first met.

He was not surprised at my presence. It looked as though he had been waiting for me.

'I'm come home!' I called and he smiled broadly.

All I had to do was step across the stones and I would be in his arms.

One, two, three…

Acknowledgments

Firstly, I would like to thank all of the music makers. Musicians, composers, lyricists and singers. I cannot imagine my life without music. It has scored every moment, every memory. I feel lucky to have grown up in a family who are equally as passionate about music as I am, so I've been exposed to everything from country to classical, folk to pop. But no matter the genre, one thing remains the same – music helps us to feel what words cannot say.

Secretly, I always wanted to learn how to play the violin, but as my siblings were already taking piano lessons, I followed suit. My playing career ended when the examiner said my nails were too long and he couldn't hear the music over the clacking on the ivories! I refused to cut them and that was the end of that. Fortunately, I instead took up musicianship at school, where I learned all about the lives and works of the great classical composers. It gave me an early appreciation for the power of this universal language that speaks directly to our hearts.

The Violin Maker's Secret was therefore a welcome return to the world of luthiers, violin lore and classical music for me. This novel became a symphony of intertwining lives and stories progressing through time and place. My ode to music, composed with words.

I would like to thank the Arts Council of Ireland for

their support, giving me the time and resources to research this book. Thank you to my editor, Charlotte Ledger, who was undaunted by the sprawling first draft of this ambitious novel! Writing a book is a long process and I spent many years of my career doing it alone, so getting to work with someone I trust and admire has been a wonderful experience. My continued appreciation goes to the entire team at One More Chapter who work their magic behind the scenes. It's thanks to them that my books have travelled so far and wide and made it into the hands of my readers.

As always, my heartfelt gratitude goes to my family. Through all the ups and downs, their constant love is a precious gift. Last but not least, thank you reader! Every book is an invitation. It is only when the reader accepts it and packs their imagination for the journey that the story can come to life and breathe. Thank you for coming along and I hope we'll go on another adventure very soon…

DON'T MISS THE INTERNATIONAL BESTSELLER

On a quiet street in Dublin, a lost bookshop is waiting to be found…

For too long, Opaline, Martha and Henry have been the side characters in their own lives.

But when a vanishing bookshop casts its spell, these three unsuspecting strangers will discover that their own stories are every bit as extraordinary as the ones found in the pages of their beloved books. And by unlocking the secrets of the shelves, they find themselves transported to a world of wonder … where nothing is as it seems.

AVAILABLE IN PAPERBACK, EBOOK AND AUDIO!

FALL IN LOVE WITH THIS EVOCATIVE AND
CHARMING NOVEL FULL OF SECRETS AND MYSTERY!

In a quiet village in Ireland, a mysterious local myth is about to change everything...

One hundred years ago, Anna, a young farm girl, volunteers to help an intriguing American visitor translate fairy stories from Irish to English. But all is not as it seems and Anna soon finds herself at the heart of a mystery that threatens her very way of life.
In New York in the present day, Sarah Harper boards a plane bound for the West Coast of Ireland. But once there, she finds she has unearthed dark secrets – secrets that tread the line between the everyday and the otherworldly, the seen and the unseen.

AVAILABLE IN PAPERBACK, EBOOK AND AUDIO!

AN ENCHANTING AND ESCAPIST NOVEL

Nestled among the cobblestone streets of Compiègne, there existed a bakery unlike any other.

Rumours were whispered through the town that its pastries offered a taste of magic, chasing away the darkest of sorrows. Just one bite of a croissant might bring luck, unlock a precious memory or reveal hidden longings.
For Edie Lane, a recipe for disaster doesn't require that many ingredients. Take an unhealthy amount of wishful thinking and a sprinkle of desperation and that's how Edie left everything behind in Ireland for her dream job at a bakery in Paris. Except the bakery isn't in Paris – and neither is Edie.
This might not be where Edie intended to be but she soon realizes it's *exactly* where she needs to be…

AVAILABLE IN PAPERBACK, EBOOK AND AUDIO!

The author and One More Chapter would like to thank everyone who contributed to the publication of this story...

Analytics
Imogen Wolstencroft

Audio
Fionnuala Barrett
Ciara Briggs

Contracts
Laura Amos
Inigo Vyvyan

Design
Lucy Bennett
Fiona Greenway
Liane Payne
Dean Russell

Digital Sales
Laura Daley
Lydia Grainge
Hannah Lismore

eCommerce
Laura Carpenter
Madeline ODonovan
Charlotte Stevens
Christina Storey
Jo Surman
Rachel Ward

Editorial
Janet Marie Adkins
Rosie Best
Kara Daniel
Charlotte Ledger
Laura McCallen
Jennie Rothwell
Tony Russell
Sofia Salazar Studer
Emily Thomas
Helen Williams

Harper360
Emily Gerbner
Ariana Juarez
Jean Marie Kelly
emma sullivan
Sophia Wilhelm

International Sales
Peter Borcsok
Ruth Burrow
Bethan Moore
Colleen Simpson

Inventory
Sarah Callaghan
Kirsty Norman

Marketing & Publicity
Chloe Cummings
Grace Edwards
Katie Sadler

Operations
Melissa Okusanya
Hannah Stamp

Production
Denis Manson
Simon Moore
Francesca Tuzzeo

Rights
Ashton Mucha
Alisah Saghir
Zoe Shine
Aisling Smyth
Lucy Vanderbilt

Trade Marketing
Ben Hurd
Eleanor Slater

The HarperCollins Distribution Team

The HarperCollins Finance & Royalties Team

The HarperCollins Legal Team

The HarperCollins Technology Team

UK Sales
Isabel Coburn
Jay Cochrane
Sabina Lewis
Holly Martin
Harriet Williams
Leah Woods

And every other essential link in the chain from delivery drivers to booksellers to librarians and beyond!

One More Chapter is an award-winning global division of HarperCollins.

Subscribe to our newsletter to get our latest eBook deals and stay up to date with all our new releases!

signup.harpercollins.co.uk/
join/signup-omc

Meet the team at
www.onemorechapter.com

Follow us!

@onemorechapterhc

Do you write unputdownable fiction?
We love to hear from new voices.
Find out how to submit your novel at
www.onemorechapter.com/submissions